Threepeat

Book 3 Rule of Three

Ann Grech

Edited by: Hot Tree Editing
Cover design: CT Cover Creations

Blurb

The star recruit at her real estate agency. A plan to dominate the real estate business. Cassie is aiming for the top.

None of her plans involve her competition, Jacob Denyer—sexy, suave, insufferable. The man steals her clients and makes her see red.

There are a million reasons why they shouldn't be together.

But somehow, they work. He understands how Cassie loves big. Big enough to want to add another man to their fledgling relationship.

When Jacob finds Phoenix, Cassie knows he's their perfect match.

Disaster strikes, and they're torn apart.

Can they heal and move on from Phoenix? Or will he be the one who got away?

The third MMF romance in the Rule of Three series, *Threepeat* crosses over into Ann Grech's Pearce Station universe. It features star-crossed lovers, a one-night stand gone awry, two men who find themselves through the love of their partners, and a woman who gets it all.

For the real Jake and Phoenix.
I'll always love you
xx

ACKNOWLEDGEMENTS

I knew I wanted to write Phoenix's story when I met him as Pete's flatmate in Outback Treasure I. There was something behind his shiny veneer that called out to me. He came back in Three of Us and started murmuring to me, asking me to tell his story. The thing was, I had no idea who he was supposed to be matched up with—he wasn't yet able to talk about it. Funny how a conversation with someone who was only just figuring things out for themselves gave me a clue. Then Triple Beat came along and all the pieces fell into place. These three deserve their happily ever after so hard, and I love that they chose me to tell their story.

Thank you to Kariss Stone for our telephone chats and your incredible suggestions and advice. It was very much appreciated.

My beautiful friends who make up the MM DreaMMers authors (Viva Gold, LJ Harris, JJ Harper, Angelique Jurd, Tracy McKay and Megs Pritchard), thank you for your advice, inspiration, daily pics, motivation and most of all, your friendship. I'm grateful every day for you being in my life.

To the team at Hot Tree Editing, thank you. Becky, my gorgeous editor and all-around story advisor, I couldn't do this without you. You and your team's advice polished this story into something I absolutely adore.

Clarise Tan from CT Cover Creations, your artwork has once again helped bring these three to life, and I adore it.

Linda Russell and the team from Foreword PR, thank you for being a fabulous cheerleader and always being there to bounce ideas off. I love working with you. Thanks for all the work you do behind the scenes to help my stories reach the world. It's truly appreciated.

To my hubby and kiddos, I couldn't do this without your support either. I love you all to the moon and back.

Last and most certainly not least, thank you to you, the readers and bloggers, for your unending love and support. Sharing, reviews, general shout outs and, importantly, reading our words means the world to every author. I never dreamed it would be possible to make writing my career, but you've made it a reality for me. For that – the realization of a childhood dream – I'll forever be grateful.

Ann xx

GLOSSARY

This story is set in Queensland, Australia. It uses Australian English. There are some terms that you might not have heard before, so I have set out a few for you. If you come across more, please let me know and I'll try to explain our slang. You might also want to take a peek at my website too—I'll add more there as they come up.

Billabong – a pond or small lake filled from the offshoot of a river. It is often filled seasonally.
Bloke – man.
Byron's gold – a fictional character who was alleged to have found a quartz reef in outback Australia laden with gold. He was the subject of Pete's fascination (see Outback Treasure I and Outback Treasure II).
Coppers – the police.
Footy – rugby league, a full contact sport played between two teams for two forty-minute halves where the objective is to score more than the other team by carrying the ball over the 'try line' and, after making a try, kicking the ball between the posts to add an extra two points to the score (called a conversion).
Goldie – Gold Coast, Queensland.
Jam – jelly.
Jumper – sweater.

Kilometres - a metric unit of measurement. One mile is the equivalent of 1.6 kilometres.

Kitchen bench – kitchen countertop.

Knocked for six – reference to a cricket term where one hits a ball so hard it crosses the perimeter line of the pitch without bouncing. In popular vernacular, depending on the context, it can mean hit very hard, knocked sideways or knocked over with a feather.

Mardi Gras – the Sydney Gay and Lesbian Mardi Gras.

Perentie – a lizard native to Australia that can grow to 2.5 m (8 ft 2 in) in length.

Rubbish – trash.

Scone – a sweet biscuit (i.e. American-style biscuit, not a cookie) that you traditionally eat with jam (i.e. jelly) and whipped cream.

State of Origin – footy match between the mighty Queensland Maroons (the Cane Toads) and the meh at best New South Wales Blues (the Cockroaches). Usually, the Blues have the blues because even though the stubborn bastards will never admit it, Queensland is by far the better team. Go Queenslander!

Station – equivalent to a ranch.

Trackie bottoms – sweats.

Tourist park – an RV park.

Uni – university.

Ute – equivalent to a pickup truck.

ONE

Cassidy

Cassidy ran her fingertips along the sandstone wall, the once roughened surface worn smooth from the thousands of students who'd meandered along this path over the university's long history. The country's best and brightest studied there. It was almost hallowed ground for those with a love of learning. Cassidy wanted her name to be remembered among the greats. Both the university and the bastions of capitalism—the blue-chip companies that called Sydney home—would one day count her as worthy of her place among them. She was working on it. Steps one and two in her grand plan—secure a business degree from the country's leading university and land a job in one of Sydney's best real estate agencies—were ticked off. The next step—make a name for herself in that agency—was well on its way to being achieved.

A year post-graduation and Cassidy had found her niche—commercial property. The C in CIR, the agency she worked for. Industrial and retail were the engine room of the city, but Cassie loved everything about the corporate world she operated in.

Dressed in a knee-length slim-fit black dress and stilettos, she looked like she was heading out to party. But disconnecting from her laptop and putting down the research was purely strategic. The industry was as much about who you knew as what you knew. Connections were everything, and Cassidy was at the mixer to network. Her targets were the three executives from one of the world's largest co-working platforms in town for business meetings.

They just so happened to be the very same people her boss had arranged a ten-minute pitch to the next day. Michael had heard the rumour only days earlier. Accord Hub was seeking to expand into Sydney. It was no coincidence that the executives flew into the city overnight. Cassidy's instructions were simple—pull together the results of their key marketplace research, business start-up statistics, and any government grants available for new businesses, and synthesize it into a single-page flyer that he could discuss over a coffee. Instead, she'd dashed out of the office at 6:30 p.m. to race home, change, and head to the university for the exclusive alumni event.

The executives were in town, and Cassidy was determined to get more than ten minutes with them.

If she managed to pull it off and win the contract to find them their first location on Australian soil, she would be up for a quick promotion. Details stayed with her, the market research she'd buried herself in nightly was burned into her brain, but she wouldn't be giving the presentation, which didn't fly for Cassidy. Connections were hard to come by, and seniority always took priority when they had none. She might have done all the work, but her boss would get the credit for landing the client. So, when she'd made the connection between the event speakers and the company, Cassidy jumped on the chance to muscle her way into that presentation. Michael would have done exactly the same thing, so she'd kept the information close to her chest.

CIR only hired people who were greedy for success, so it was as cutthroat as it came. She didn't trust any of her colleagues. They would take advantage of her hard work and claim the success as their own in a heartbeat. It had happened before. She wouldn't let it happen again. Especially when Michael, through Cassidy's hard work, had just signed on the most up-market, about-to-be-completed office building in the city. The untenanted space stretched over fifteen floors. It would give a tenant such as Accord Hub, with an international reputation to match the exclusivity of the building, the flexibility to create the perfect space for their Sydney debut. The timing couldn't be anything but serendipitous.

Cassidy smiled to herself, picturing the neat red bow that tied her plan together. She was going to pull it off.

Rounding the corner, the glass addition to the sandstone building, nicknamed the fishbowl, came into view. It was ultra-modern, a contrast that some traditionalists had criticized when its design was unveiled, but Cassidy loved it. The new mixing with the old, seamlessly integrating to modernize an outdated building, dragging it from the last century into this one. It was an apt comparison to her generation entering the workforce and revolutionizing the way business was conducted and by whom.

Light spilled out into the courtyard, a warm yellow in the cool of the evening. Men in designer suits and women in elegant dresses and pantsuits gathered around sipping wine and chatting, the odd business card being exchanged.

Cassidy signed the register and clipped her name tag to her dress while she scanned the attendee list. She had her targets, but it never hurt to get to know a few others too.

One name stood out. His. Fury, hot and heavy like a burning oil slick, descended on Cassidy. She ground her teeth and glared at the name before her, wanting to erase its very existence. Even the letters written on the page offended her.

Jacob. Fucking. Denyer.

That man, that thief, he'd stolen her listing, reviewed her confidential report, then shit on it. It had taken weeks of fact gathering, statistical research, and identifying potential listing strategies to get the property in front of the right tenants for such a blue-chip investment, not to mention writing the report before it was perfect. She knew it back to front. Cassidy's presentation answering every question thrown at her should have won her the clients. It had.

Until Jacob Fucking Denyer called. He'd interrupted their meeting, and Cassidy, trying to be accommodating, encouraged the director to take the call. The next three minutes had derailed all her hard work, much to her disgust. He'd criticized the report, then stole the listing from her.

After all that, he had the audacity to use her marketing approach to sign up the very company Cassidy had identified as an audacious target to upgrade the quality of the tenants in the building.

All she'd needed was fifteen more minutes with them. But no, the thieving bastard had cost her far more than the hundreds of thousands of dollars in commission her agency would have been entitled to. It was the listing itself Cassidy really wanted. The feather in her cap that would skyrocket her career.

Where was the son of a bitch? She needed to give him a piece of her mind.

Cassidy spun, her gaze laser focussed. She searched for a face she didn't know among a crowd of dark suits. She would have to work the room to find him, but damn it, it'd be worth it just to see him taken down a notch.

Stalking forward into the crowd, Cassidy ignored the waiter with the tray of champagne and the two others who tried to feed her. She didn't know what Denyer looked like, but she sure as hell could pick his type. Slimy and in a cheap suit—the car salesman lookalike—he'd no doubt smell like he dumped a bottle of bargain bin aftershave on himself too. Urgh, Cassidy despised even the thought of him.

Her gaze roamed the crowd, and she picked out the three best-dressed people in the room. She liked fashion, enjoyed the feel of silky material sliding on her skin, and loved seeing her strategically bought pieces hanging in her room, but she was a simple girl at heart. Nevertheless, in her industry, it paid to be able to identify at a glance who had money and who was posing. The Dior and Armani suits, Louboutin and Gucci shoes told her the four men were a whole echelon on the business ladder above her. She could place three of them—the executives of Accord Hub—but she had no idea who the fourth was. He was gorgeous. Two decades their junior, fit and tanned with his blond hair pulled back in a bun and his perfectly fitted charcoal suit a contrast to the blacks and navy blues everyone else in the room wore. The pop of colour from his shirt—a pale pink— stood out too.

Cassidy sucked in a breath, her pulse pounding in her veins for an entirely different reason than anger now. She held it before exhaling slowly, refocussing. She was dying to know who the man before her was, but she had to focus. Dickhead Denyer and the Calvin Klein model lookalike would only derail her plans if she let them. And Cassidy had far more important fish to fry.

Cassidy plastered on a professional smile, straightened the sleeves of her dress, smoothed the front down, popped a mint, and made her way over to the group of men. "Gentlemen, hello," she purred, holding her hand out to shake when there was a lull in the conversation.

"Evening," the oldest man, who was probably midsixties, said politely. His smile tipped up the corners of his lips, but it was like every other smile she'd seen on men that age in her industry—patient and placating. "Marcello Ortiz, Accord Hub. Pleasure to meet you."

"Cassidy Phillips, CIR Real Estate, and the pleasure is all mine." Introductions were made, and she shook hands with

Daan Janssen, the thirty-nine-year-old investment whiz, and Dieter Meyer, the company's international business strategist. Cassidy bit back a giddy grin at having zeroed in and met her targets and listened intently as they answered her question about whether their trip over was a good one.

"Jacob Denyer, City Space," the blond man interjected with his hand outstretched. She stilled, the name sinking in. From the corner of her eye, she saw him flash her a lopsided smirk. A ha!-I've-gotten-the-upper-hand smile. An irrational desire to maim the man consumed her. How dare he!

All pretence at professionalism fled. Her head on a swivel, she glared at him, her nostrils flaring and her nails leaving crescent moons in her palms. He shouldn't be there. Not when she was talking to the three men who would mean the difference to her career. Not when she was on the edge of success. Not when he would try to steal her hard work again.

"You!" she growled, far louder than was appropriate in the gathering, and with smug satisfaction, she watched him drop his hand.

"Do you two know each other?" Daan asked, surprise colouring his tone.

"No," Cassidy spat at the same time as Denyer said with a smile, "Yes."

Dieter raised one eyebrow and flicked his gaze to his colleagues. Cassidy could practically hear him call her unhinged. She needed to explain just what kind of man they'd been speaking to and quickly. She had to strike while the iron was hot. Hard and fast. She had to give Denyer a taste of his own medicine. Cassidy explained, "Through a prior deal. He stole a listing from me."

"I won the client fair and square," Denyer said quietly, his eyes downcast and hands in the pockets of his dress pants. Cassidy could see the shame oozing from him like the stench of the cheap aftershave she thought he'd wear. A cold smile formed on her lips, a win in her war against him buoying her.

But then his words registered, and Cassidy narrowed her eyes, her smile turning into a sneer. "You took my research—"

"They wanted something different to what you were offering."

Cassidy laughed, the haughty sound filled with derision. "Oh yes? What did they want?"

"Someone a little less ruthlessly efficient." Denyer lifted his gaze and gave her a sympathetic smile, his lips pressing together and one side of his mouth twisted up, before he turned to the men watching on with interest. None of them met her gaze, and Cassidy's gut sank, a knot forming deep inside. Denyer held out his hand, shaking each of theirs firmly. "Gentlemen, it was great seeing you again. If you'll excuse me."

"Ms Phillips." Denyer nodded and walked away slowly. She watched silently as he picked up two glasses of wine and slipped out the door.

What had just happened? Cassidy stared at his retreating form, speechless. His words had struck her with the force of a nuclear bomb, slamming into her and leaving only

charred ashes in their wake. She blinked. Sucked in a stuttered breath. Blinked again. "Ah..." She hesitated, totally
lost for words. How could she rescue the conversation?
He'd done it again—completely derailed any chance of success that she had, leaving her to stitch back the tattered
remnants he left in his wake. The man was a menace. With
the ethics of a jackal, he'd waltz in, destroy everything in his
path and then pick at the scraps until he'd had his fill, leaving everyone wanting. "I apologize about Mr Denyer. He's
somewhat unsavoury."

"If you'll excuse us, we need to get ready for our presentation," Marcello replied. Cassidy forced her lips into some
semblance of a smile. She guessed it looked more like a grimace with the heat crawling up her throat to her face until
it flamed, and shook each of their hands.

"I hope that we get a moment to speak later in the evening." What else could she say? Dickhead Denyer had struck
again, blowing any chance she had. Now her only hope to
avoid losing the account altogether was to do what her boss
had instructed, leaving the presentation to him. What an
arsehole Denyer was. Of all the places he had to be, and of
all the times he had to be there, he'd chosen that one. At
least the executives knew what he was like. They knew the
truth. Not that they seemed to appreciate the inside
knowledge.

"It's not a bad trait, you know. Being ruthlessly efficient." Marcello's words jolted her out of her spiralling
thoughts, and Cassidy nodded mutely. He tilted his head to
the small stage set up in the corner and led the men over to

it. A projector screen was mounted to the side, the Accord Hub logo dancing across the screen.

The evening passed in a blur, none of the presentation sinking in. Denyer's words played on the loop inside her head. There was no doubting it—she was ruthless. She was efficient, but she wasn't a bitch. She had personality. Drive. That was good. It was a trait she admired. She was popular too, wasn't she? She had friends. Some, at least. Cassidy reached for a glass on a passing tray and downed half of the rich red in a single gulp, but it could have been vinegar for all she tasted. Or was that just the bad taste that Denyer left in her mouth?

The hum of conversation rose as the drinks flowed, and the evening slipped into a more relaxed vibe after the executives stepped off the stage. Ties were loosened and jackets slung over arms. Laughter became louder and the flirting more brazen. Even though Cassidy was right there in the middle of it, it was as if she were in a glass box, separating her from the people around her. Sound distorted as her mind turned over Denyer's words. She had goals, damn it, and a career path that would lead her to the top. She wanted to be the best of the best and was going to get there in the shortest possible timeframe. If it meant people thought she was a shark, so be it. The apex predator of the ocean had a nice ring to it.

But that glass box she was stuck in was suffocating. Cassidy needed air. She needed to escape. She looked longingly at the three executives who'd been surrounded by people since they spoke on stage. Cassidy knew when to admit defeat. They would have to be tomorrow's problem.

The quiet of the courtyard outside beckoned, and Cassidy wound through the mass of suits gathered in the intimate space before pushing through the doors. The chill of the evening hit her first, a surprise after such a mild spring day. She couldn't decide whether to stick around and just take a breather or head home early. Her feet ached in her stilettos, and she was starving, not having eaten anything since breakfast. Trackie bottoms, a greasy pizza, and her TV keeping her company while she caught up on her work sounded perfect.

Cassidy scanned the shadow-filled space, noticing for the first time two men wrapped in each other, their lips locked as they kissed in the shadows. The click of her heels on the slate pathway as she wandered along it must have alerted them to her approach. They turned to her in unison with lips swollen and pink and kiss-drunk eyes. She recognized Mal, a business banker she'd worked with on a deal a few months earlier, and she forced a smile she didn't feel as she made the snap decision to head for home.

Straight ahead, standing in the shadows, was another man. Denyer. Leaning against the sandstone wall, ankles crossed as he twirled the stem of his empty wine glass between his fingers, he looked lost in thought. His bun was loose, locks of hair having fallen and now framing his face. He stared at the ground, and Cassidy watched him silently. His chest rose on a long inhale, and she heard the soft rumble of a groan as he rested his head back. His eyes slipped closed, and he shook his head, the subtlest of movements.

Damn, he was beautiful. How could a man with such an ugly personality, the worst possible traits in business, be so incredibly sexy? She wasn't sure whether she wanted to slap him or get lost in those vivid blue eyes, but Cassidy found herself closing the distance between them. She shook off the unreasonable desire coursing through her—he was not a man to get involved with—in favour of embracing her justified anger. She needed to finish the discussion they'd started earlier. Put him in his place once and for all. If he was out to thwart every move she made to level up her career, he was in for a painful trip. Like the couple she'd just passed, the click of her heels drew his attention, but he looked away quickly. Good, he should be intimidated. She wanted to shake him, grasp his pale pink shirt, and make him understand just how pissed she was.

Her hands trembled with pent-up rage, and her voice cracked as she spat, "Look, I don't care what you think of me, but it was completely unprofessional—"

Denyer peeled open one eye and huffed, shaking his head. "What was completely unprofessional was you accusing me of theft—"

Cassidy threw her hands up in the air, taking a step closer to Denyer. Her voice was a harsh whisper, the words grating between her clenched teeth, "They were about to sign on the dotted line. That listing was important to me. You. Stole. It." She punctuated each of her words with a poke to his chest, her pale pink nail polish almost an exact match to the hue of his shirt.

Denyer grasped her hand, his warm palms and long fingers curling around hers, stopping her from continuing her assault. Cassidy froze, and heat pooled in her belly. He bought her knuckles to his lips and pressed a kiss to them, the scrape of his five o'clock shadow above his top lip only adding to the sensory overload. "Let me make it up to you," he rumbled. "Let me take you to dinner."

Shock electrified her. Or was it the instant flash in her mind's eye of naked bodies writhing together that she experienced when those sinfully sensual lips touched her bare skin? Confusion reigned supreme. An equal desire to ride him like a bucking stallion and simultaneously maim him fought for dominance. Cassie snatched her hand back, balling it back into a fist, needing to put some space between them, stat. "You can't be serious. Are you serious? There's no chance in hell."

"I am, and you should say yes. I dare you to." This time his smile, that seductive tilt of his pouty lips and secretive heavy-lidded bedroom-eyes stare, held more of a challenge, and Cassidy couldn't help but narrow her eyes. He was dreaming.

"Yeah, no."

"It'll give you a chance to apologize to me." He quirked an eyebrow, gave her that same lopsided grin, cheeky and teasing, and slipped out from against the wall, placing the wine glass down. He took a few steps before he tossed over his shoulder, "Come on, I know a good place."

"I have nothing to apologize for," Cassidy called, chasing after him. She had to make him understand that he was in the wrong here, not her. Why didn't he get that?

He slowed down, waiting until she caught up, and smirked. She wanted to wipe it clean off his face. "Yet you're still coming."

"No." She shook her head and glared. "I'm not coming with you. That'd be idiotic. I'm making sure you understand what you've done wrong."

"Mhmm."

"Oh my God! I'm not joking." She resisted the temptation to shove him until he landed on his arse. Where she could climb on and kiss him. *What am I thinking? Stupid. Stupid. Stupid.* Relationships weren't worth the trouble. Not when it'd mean she'd have to compromise her goals. Make time for others when she needed to have a singular focus. "You owe me an apology. I'm not going to let you sabotage me." He was really something. Un-freaking-believable.

A gust of wind howled between the historic buildings, blowing her hair around her face and stripping Cassidy of the little warmth her dress afforded. She shivered, rubbing the fine material on the sleeves. Denyer didn't hesitate, taking his jacket off and draping it over her shoulders. He pressed the lapels together, wrapping Cassidy in its warmth.

And the scent of him.

Her brain short-circuited, her belly flip-flopping as desire coiled inside her. She inhaled deeply, breathing him in until her lungs were filled with his very essence. Holy hot

damn, he smelled good. Something crisp and fresh that reminded her of the ocean and long summer nights. And sex.
Over and over, round after round.

"I'm sorry, I should have done that sooner. I didn't realize how chilly it was." He pressed his lips together and
added, "Are you warm enough?" She nodded dumbly, and
he smiled gloriously, a dazzling happiness lighting up his
face. He slipped his arm around her waist, guiding her with
a few fingertips at the small of her back. He pointed to the
rideshare pickup spot and called up the app on his phone.

"There's an Italian place on the water that I know. It's
not much more than a hole in the wall, but they make the
best pizza around. You up for it?"

Cassidy stopped walking and gazed at him, puzzled at
the confounding man beside her. He was intriguing, absolutely infuriating, and a complete arse. She didn't want to
be anywhere near him, yet she couldn't bring herself to give
back his jacket just yet. Pizza sounded great too. She
shrugged, her pride and better judgement at war with her
lips, which just wanted a taste. Cassidy wasn't ready to admit whether it was a taste of him or the pizza she wanted
more. "I could go for a couple of slices."

* * * * *

The trip to the pizzeria was quick at 8:30 on a Tuesday
evening. That wasn't a bad thing. It was awkward being in
the back seat of the rideshare with Denyer. Cassidy had

nothing nice to say to him and was questioning her sanity for even entertaining the idea of spending more time with him, never mind actually eating a meal with the guy.

But she did have to admit he was being a gentleman, opening her door and helping her out, his hand always either holding hers or guiding her along with a soft touch to the small of her back. Cassidy wanted to be annoyed, she wanted to tell him he had no right to be chivalrous with her, but something held her back. Maybe it was the way his hair fell about his face tempting Cassidy to run her fingers through his blond waves. Or maybe it was the way he turned to gaze at her, giving Cassidy all his attention despite the vibes worthy of a frost giant that she was putting out. She couldn't fathom why he was even bothering. She certainly wasn't trying to play nice. If Cassidy had it her way, she wouldn't even see him again.

The driver pulled up along the Esplanade, and Denyer scooted out before holding his hand for her to grasp. As reluctant as she was to accept his help, Cassidy needed it. Getting out of the low car in stilettos without wobbling like a baby giraffe taking its first steps was a challenge. It was made even more difficult with a slimline dress and aching feet.

The pizza place was exactly as Denyer described it. Seeing it was little more than a serving window facing the street, she was surprised at the queue of people waiting to pick up their orders. Cassidy hadn't been in this area of town before, but there was no doubting it was affluent. The houses built along the steep hills facing the water were classic architecture personified. Victorian-era and regency mansions lined the street, mixed in with modern pavilion-style triple-storey buildings. A walking track intersected the waterfront park before them, joining the boardwalk running the length of the quiet cove further along. The park was pristine, its bushes trimmed and grass mowed until not even a single blade was out of place.

It may have been midweek, but the boardwalk was oddly busy, filled with joggers and people taking their dogs for an evening stroll. She could imagine just how popular the park would be during the day and when events were held on the foreshore. The view of the city skyline alone would guarantee the park being filled to capacity for every fireworks spectacular that lit up the harbour.

Denyer led her to the counter and greeted the older man serving customers by name with a smile. "Can I get a large please and two drinks?"

"A large what?" Cassidy questioned. "Where's the menu?"

"They make traditional Italian margherita here. One option only."

"And they're still in business?" she asked, bewildered at how the restaurant had survived longer than a few weeks with a single item on the menu.

"Forty-five years," the server replied with a patient smile. "I've watched young Jake here, and many of our regulars grow up and grow old from this very spot."

"Oh," Cassie whispered, shame suffusing her. Why didn't she ever use her filter? Keep those thoughts that tended to tear people down to herself? They were clearly doing well if the queue was any indication to go by. Maybe she did need to improve her people skills. Brush up on Conversation 101. Cassidy blinked and turned away, hating the sting in her eyes. "I, ah…"

"Let's wait out of the way." Denyer wrapped his arm around her again and guided her across the road to the park, stopping when it intersected the timber boardwalk. He may be an arse, but she'd give him points for avoiding the timber walkway. She'd ruined far too many pairs of stilettos getting the heel stuck in awkward places. Denyer hadn't even attempted to lead them there. Cassidy was low-key impressed at his consideration.

She looked out over the water, at the reflected lights shimmering in the ebb and flow of the current. Wash from a boat that had long since passed lapped at the pylons, the only noise breaking the quiet of the night now that they were away from the shopfront. Peace surrounded her, the tension she carried in her shoulders loosening. Cassidy sighed happily.

"It's peaceful down here," she murmured. "I'd love to live where I can hear the waves one day."

"Me too. When I was a kid, Mum and I would always stay with my aunt near Batemans Bay. They had this little cottage close to the water, and I remember waking up every morning hearing the waves. I loved it there."

"Was it just you and your mum?"

Tension, as sudden as the flick of a switch, vibrated through Denyer. She'd hit a raw nerve, but before Cassidy could tell him to ignore the question, he answered, "Nah, but my father didn't spend much time with us. He was always busy." His voice went flat, devoid of the fondness he'd spoken with only a moment earlier. Acting on instinct, Cassidy leaned into Denyer's touch, wrapping her arm around him and trying to comfort him without words.

She couldn't explain why, but the need to see him smile again, to be the one who brought it out in him, burrowed under her skin and wouldn't let up until he'd shaken off the shroud that had descended. The warmth radiating from him when he spoke about those happy memories set off the flutters in her belly, and she was already lining up for a second serving.

TWO

Jacob

The captivating woman in his arms had unknowingly hit a nerve. One that was far too sensitive. The less his thoughts lingered on his family, the better. He relegated anything to do with them out of bounds, even for himself. Especially so. That dumpster fire always made his thoughts spiral, dragging him down into a quagmire of self-recrimination and misery that he struggled to break free of.

He stilled when Cassidy nuzzled closer to him, silently comforting him. He hadn't expected her to even tolerate his touch—not that the suspicion helped him resist repeatedly reaching out for Cassidy. But when she'd reciprocated, she could have knocked him over with a feather. It was the best kind of surprise.

He'd seen her striding into the function room with purpose, her head held high and her eyes assessing the room, zeroing in on her targets. He'd been transfixed, soaking up the confidence she exuded. Cassidy's magnetism drew him in and held him there, and he'd been spinning around her since, the pace dizzying. Like the planets orbiting the sun, he was ensnared in her gravitational pull. For all the shade she'd thrown at him at the networking event, she'd noticed him now. She'd picked up on the dip in his mood and reacted. She'd reached for him, comforting him. He could have shouted out, victorious, excitement pulsing through him. But he reined it in and went for mature instead, shoving down his inner giddy teenager crushing on the most beautiful girl he'd ever laid eyes on. He cleared his throat, and his tone lightened when he asked, "What about you? Did you grow up in Sydney?"

Cassidy's lips turned up in the tiniest of smiles. He wasn't sure whether it was because of him or because she was thinking about her family, but he'd take it either way. She'd been frosty to him from the moment they'd met, and he didn't blame her one bit. He could understand how his involvement in the deal she'd been trying to strike had been perceived, but he'd told her the truth. The company she was courting had no intention of signing her agency, opting for the more back-slapping boys club Charles, his boss, nurtured with them. They'd confided a desire to compare the terms of CIR's retainer with City Space's to make sure they weren't paying too much, and Charles had encouraged them.

He pulled himself back into the present when she answered, "Dad works for the government and Mum's a teacher. I grew up in the western suburbs, but I don't remember spending a single summer there. Dad used to save up his leave and we'd road trip it up to the Gold Coast for a few weeks. Mum and Dad still have their holiday home at Land's End."

That sounded nice. Much like his own early childhood memories—minus his father—but even that had ended pretty soon after he'd turned eight. His father had hired people to look after Jake from then on, delegating as much of Jake's childhood needs to them as possible. He was just like every other mundane obligation to his father, no more worthy of the man's time than paying bills or folding socks were. His family life from that point onward had been cold and lonely. He had great memories of the au pairs his father hired playing games with him and riding bikes together, then later on staying at friends' houses and experiencing their families, but his own had been less than stellar.

When Jake saw the names on the invitation to the university alumni event, he'd immediately accepted. His motivation for being there wasn't for work, like everyone else was. He was there to say thank you. There was a long story behind how he'd gotten to know the three executives, but it focussed too heavily on his father, so Jake preferred not to think about it. The night they'd met, Marcello had been kind to him, and over time, he'd become like a pseudo father figure to Jake. Daan and Dieter had encouraged him to follow his dreams, and like cool older cousins, had asked him to sneak them out of the party so they could get away from all the stuffiness.

Jake hadn't ever expected to meet Cassidy, never mind be standing next to her as she introduced herself to his friends.

She'd floored him. Rendered him utterly speechless, not just because of their fiery encounter, but because of the sultry purr of her voice and her sublime beauty. Long blonde wavy hair and green eyes the colour of emeralds had narrowed at him, and her lips, all shimmery with just a touch of colour, had pursed. His dick had thickened, desire pulsing through him as his eyes had slid over the lines of her body. A slim waist with a perfect butt and legs that he wanted more than anything to be wrapped around his hips. Delicate fingers with perfectly manicured nails topped with pink polish that was understated but bold at the same time, clenched into fists. He could imagine the crescent indentations in her palms as she white-knuckled her restraint. The look she'd given him was all fire and passion. His cock had gone from interested to hard enough to hammer nails with. Her snark was a hell of a turn on. Jacob wanted to tease more of that acerbic tongue out of her just to see the flash in her eyes and the fiery passion bubbling in her. He loved the banter, the quick-witted comebacks, and even though he knew better than to poke a bear, she was unexpectedly fun to bait.

Jake collected the pizza and a couple of the old-fashioned glass bottles of 7Up, and they walked back over to the park. He hadn't expected Cassidy to accept his dare, but there she was. He just hoped she enjoyed their time well enough and could look past their history to give him a second date, because Jake already knew that one wouldn't be enough.

He opened the box and offered the first piece to Cassidy, who took it and moaned when flavours hit her tongue. The sound was heady. Intoxicating. Jake was already addicted. "Come on another date with me. A proper one."

Cassidy shook her head, a smirk tilting her glossy lips upward. "I don't date."

His eyebrows ratcheted upward, and his mouth popped open. "Not at all?"

She shook her head, looking out toward the bay. "Relationships complicate things. I'm focused on my career, and I'm not prepared to compromise that for a hook-up."

"What if it wasn't just a hook-up?" He was treading on dangerous ground, trying to poke the bear again. He was lucky she was giving him the time of day, never mind discussing a relationship with him. Her reaction, though, was exactly as he'd hoped. She turned to him wide-eyed and stared him down for a moment before she belly laughed. Her hand covered her mouth as she snorted out a giggle, tears forming on her long eyelashes.

"That's the funniest thing I've ever heard," she gasped between laughs. "There's no chance."

Jake raised an eyebrow at her, challenging her words. "You said the same thing about coming to dinner with me, and look where we are. I can be persuasive when it's called for." One of the many traits he'd inherited from his father, but unlike the other man, Jake didn't use his powers of persuasion to make the world bow down at his feet.

"I was hungry, and pizza sounded good. I would have been just as happy to be sitting on my couch eating it with my TV for company. In fact, think I prefer its company to yours." He had to give her props; she had no qualms about being blunt. He admired it and still couldn't understand why those idiots had chosen his agency over having a gun like Cassidy working for them. Where his boss was brilliant at talking the talk, he relied on the people in his team to try and match his promises, more often than not struggling to meet them. Jake had no doubt that Cassidy would call it as she saw it and over-deliver every time.

"Eh, TV doesn't converse with you."

"No, it's completely passive, and there's a mute button, so when I've had enough of the banal conversation, it stops. I can even turn it off altogether when I don't want it there anymore." It was Cassidy's turn to raise her eyebrow at him, and Jake couldn't help his grin.

"Passive and quiet? You'd get bored. You secretly love listening to my voice."

Cassidy huffed out a laugh and patted him on the arm. "You keep telling yourself that, Denyer. While you're living in a fairy tale, I'll be here kicking your arse in the real world."

"That's perfect." He smiled. As employees of the two leading commercial agencies in Sydney, they were each other's main competition and bound to cross paths again soon. Jake was prepared to wait. He was patient and knew a good thing when it was in front of him. "Next time you better me at work, I'll let you buy me dinner. Oh, wait…" Cassidy rolled her eyes but didn't answer him, and Jake took it as a win. He grinned happily.

"I still maintain that you stole my clients."

Jake bit his lip, stifling his laugh. "Of course you do." She whirled on him, eyes flashing, and brows furrowed, and Jake lost the battle, snorting out a laugh and trying not to spit food all over her.

"You're an arsehole," she said with a pout.

"Agreed." He chuckled harder and nudged her shoulder with his. "But you don't hate me, right?"

"Oh, I totally do, but the pizza makes up for the shitty company, so I'll stick around." Jake grinned harder, barely containing the fist pump.

* * * * *

His mind wandered, questioning why he'd chosen commercial leasing as a career. Oh, right. His dad had chosen it. Jake had been sitting at the developer's offices for half an hour already—a complete waste of his time. He was supposed to be closing a deal that day, but thanks to a last-minute hiccup, the details were still being nutted out. He'd used his commitment to an existing deal as an excuse to sit to the side and work, but it was really just because he was so far behind. He needed the extra time to catch up. A certain woman hadn't left his thoughts in the two weeks since he'd met her. He found himself daydreaming, fantasizing about running his fingers through her hair and bringing those pouty lips to his and kissing her. Unzipping that black dress and letting it pool at her feet as he kissed every inch of her. Repeatedly.

He glanced up, grateful that none of the eyes in the room were on him. He adjusted his semi, trying to resituate it in his suit pants. It had been a constant problem since he'd met Cassidy, and his palm was getting raw from over-use, never mind his dick.

His boss was doing a lot of back-slapping in the room. Charles was in his element schmoozing the client with stories of golfing in Scotland. Apparently, the courses were spectacular, but Jake had heard all the anecdotes before. He rolled his eyes, mouthing the punchline to Charles's favourite joke about his playing skills finally finding their match.

Jake shook his head and went back to his phone, pulling up the email that had just come through. Thankfully, his client and their tenants were getting closer to an agreement and wouldn't need his input for the moment. The door opened behind him, but Jake didn't look up, too busy typing out a response.

"Good morning, gentlemen," the newcomer said, followed by a round of responses. He added, "This is my offsider, Cassidy Phillips." Jake's breath caught, and he snapped his head up, excitement fizzing in his veins. He knew there would be three agencies present at the meeting, but he had no idea Cassidy was one of those involved.

"Hello, pleasure to meet you," she greeted them, and Jake watched her, taking in every inch of the beautiful woman. She was even more gorgeous than he remembered. In a crowd of middle-aged men with beer guts, flushed faces, and bald patches on their heads, she stood out like a graceful swan. Cassidy spotted him, their gazes snagging. The blood in his veins turned to fire as desire burned through him. Jake sucked in a breath as heat travelled up his throat to his face, and Cassidy smirked, not giving any other hint of acknowledgement. But it was enough.

She turned back to the man before her and smiled. The professional, polite tilt of her ruby-red lips captured Charles's attention as easily as they'd ensnared Jake's. "We were just talking golf courses. Do you play, Cassie?"

"No, I haven't had the pleasure," she answered politely with steel in her tone. Was it the condescension in Charles's tone or the fact he'd called her Cassie that pissed her off? "What part do you enjoy most?"

"Getting out of the office. I don't spend as much time outdoors for recreation as I'd like," the developer answered.

There was a chuckle. "Polite way of putting it, John." Jake watched his boss clap their potential client on the shoulder, and he rolled his eyes again. "It's a man's game." The leer Charles gave Cassidy was revolting, and Jake ground his teeth together, wanting to do violent things to the man. Jake placed his phone gently on the table. Stood up. "Out there among the wilds. Leaving my wife and PA at home or in the office. These women, they nag me to death."

Jake closed his eyes and breathed out slowly so he wouldn't lay out his boss in front of a room full of people. He moved over to the group but waited until Cassidy responded. She was more than capable of grinding Charles into the dirt, and it would be fun to watch him being taken down a notch. Her put-on smile didn't slip, but there was fire in her eyes. "To-mah-toe, to-may-toe."

Huh? Jake furrowed his brows at her cryptic response. *What was that supposed to mean?* He'd soon find out. "Ms Phillips, good to see you again," Jake greeted with a hand outstretched, inserting himself into the conversation.

She flashed him a smile that was far more genuine than the one she'd had in place for the other men. "Mr Denyer." She extended her hand until their palms met. Her grasp was firm and warm, a spark of awareness passing straight through him with her touch.

Captivated, he watched as she crossed the circle of people to stand by him. She was dressed to kill in a red pantsuit with a shimmery black blouse and black stilettos. It would have been too much on anyone else, but on her, it was an aggressive mix of hot as hell and professional kick your arse.

"Care for a coffee?" he squeaked, clearing his throat and mentally rolling his eyes at himself. Suddenly he was in the middle of puberty again, his voice cracking as nervous energy pulsed through him.

She nodded, then added under her breath so only he could hear, "Anything to get away from those condescending arseholes."

Jake laughed quietly. "And you thought you hated me."

"Between you and them… it's a tough choice."

He passed her a mug before grabbing one for himself and motioning to the coffee machine. While Cassidy made her coffee, he searched the pods until he found an espresso. While his was dripping into the cup, he asked, "To-mah-toe, to-may-toe?"

"He calls it nagging. I'd call it sheer frustration in begging the man to perform." She quirked up her eyebrows and batted her lids innocently, and Jake lost it, cringing and laughing at the same time at the picture she painted of his boss.

"That's an image not even brain bleach will scrub away."

Cassidy laughed, a light melodic sound that he wanted to hear more of. "You'll be right."

"Come to dinner with me."

"Why?" She leaned against the buffet and sipped her coffee, challenging him to give her a good reason.

"Because you want to."

"Or maybe I need to collect. Did you hear the news?" She smiled again, looking like the cat that got the cream, her eyes bright. Jake wanted to fall into that gaze and never leave.

"What news is that?"

"Accord Hub signed on the dotted line a couple of days ago. They specifically requested that I be their lead agent." Jake smiled, genuine happiness suffusing him, and moved to wrap his arm around her waist, giving her a congratulatory hug. She cocked her head to the side.

He froze. Stopped in his tracks. Let his arm drop to his side. *What am I doing?* He didn't have a right to hug her, especially not where they were. Jake's eyes widened at how sideways things could have gone. He swallowed hard, flushing in mortification. "Ah, sorry—"

"Ladies and gentlemen, perhaps we can get started."

She nodded, and they went their own ways, sitting on opposite sides of the long boardroom table. Jake couldn't take his eyes off her, but she didn't meet his gaze once. He struggled to concentrate, completely zoning out.

Charles elbowed him in the ribs and pointed to his untouched digital notepad. Heat crawled up his throat and to his cheeks, embarrassment at being called out. It was enough of a distraction to get his head back in the game and start recording the meeting. At least that way he wouldn't miss anything else, and it left him time to daydream about the woman before him.

After an eternity, the meeting wrapped, and Jake sat back. "We're going to nudge the other agents out. I want this building as an exclusive listing," Charles murmured under his breath.

"Hmm?" Jake had already moved on from the meeting, watching Cassidy like a hawk. All he needed was a moment alone. But she was packing up, unclipping the keyboard from her tablet, and sliding everything into the compact messenger bag she carried. She stood, and the man she was with nodded in acknowledgement before she shook the developer's hand and strode out the boardroom.

Jake shoved his notepad into its leather case and dashed after her, paying no attention to the swivelling heads as he passed in a blur. "Cassidy, wait," he called, jogging along the corridor to catch her at the elevator.

She looked over her shoulder as the doors opened, and she stepped in, holding the doors open as he took his last few steps. He shot a small smile at the other passengers. "I have another meeting."

"I won't keep you long. Let me buy you dinner. Please."

Cassidy sighed and stepped closer, lowering her voice.

"Jacob, listen, you seem... nice. But like I told you before, I'm not looking for a relationship." The elevator stopped at a floor, and he shifted to the side, letting people on and off. There were even more people in it than before. "Even if I was..." She shook her head.

"It's just dinner."

"It's never just dinner. You'll want to start seeing each other more and more, and my work will suffer."

"Cassidy—"

She held up her hand as the lift opened on the ground floor, and he followed her out, stopping when they were out of the stream of people. "Look, work isn't even the main reason. Like I said, you seem nice. That means you'll want to be exclusive one day, and I'm—"

"You just want casual? Because I don't expect a commitment on the first date. I'd be happy just to go out as friends."

Cassidy shook her head. "I'm risk averse when it comes to relationships. It's a lot to negotiate." She looked at the small silver wristwatch she wore.

"You have a meeting to get to, so I don't want to keep you, but I'm open-minded. I'm also not an arsehole. If you tell me something, I'll keep it between us. I'd never say anything to hurt your job or your reputation." He handed her a card. "That's my number. Call or text if you want to tell me what we'd have to negotiate. The ball's in your court."

"I'm polyamorous," she blurted. "I want relationships with more than one man at the same time. I wouldn't ask you to be exclusive, though—I'd expect that you might do the same with other women."

He opened his mouth, but no words came. He wanted to jump for joy—her opening up, her trust meant the world. A slow smile spread across his lips. "And if I decided I wanted to date another man? How would you feel about that?"

"Turned on," she whispered, her skin flushing and pupils blown. She bit her bottom lip, her teeth sinking into the flesh there. Good God, he wanted to be the one doing that. It took all his strength—everything in him—to hold himself back from pinning her against the wall and taking her lips.

"There you are." Charles's voice boomed over the lobby. Cassidy blinked, and her eyes widened.

"Go, you're probably already late."

"Shit," she muttered, already striding away. She looked over her shoulder, her lips pursed, and shook her head. Jake wanted her to stop, but he knew she couldn't even if she wanted to. Looked like he'd been right; the ball was indeed in her court.

THREE

Cassidy

She sucked the last of her Pepsi through the paper straw, frustrated that she'd ended up the designated driver for her girlfriends. Again. They were supposed to be cheering her up. How had she been roped into staying sober? She watched as they tore it up on the dance floor of the club while she sat and minded their seats. They were wasted, and Cassidy knew she'd end up with puke all over her car. Another thing to add to the topics currently pissing her off—one, her friends, two, losing the leasing contract to the sanctimonious arsehole at City Space, three, being unable to get the cute arsehole from City Space out of her head, and four, not being able to wear underwear with this damn dress. Chalk it up to another stupid idea from her friends.

Cassidy toyed with her phone, tempted to call Denyer and give him a piece of her mind. It was the second time in only a few weeks that his agency had screwed hers over. It was no coincidence that it happened right under her nose when he'd distracted her. The developer had an agreement with them; not locked in writing, sure, but an agreement, nevertheless. Each of the agencies was supposed to represent them, leveraging their different strengths to find the right tenants for the building. But she'd been met with silence when the developer failed to return the signed agency appointment. It was only after calling on a favour from a friend of a friend that the truth of why she was being stonewalled was revealed. Apparently, an exclusive appointment had been signed the day of their meeting. With City Scape.

Bastards.

Cassidy swiped her phone screen, her hands shaking. Anger surged through her like a violent thunderstorm, and she clenched her jaw, barely resisting the temptation to throw her empty glass. Bugger this. She opened her message app and bought up Denyer's number, growling at the letters forming his name.

Her fingers flew as she typed out her thoughts in all caps. Yelling by text wasn't nearly as satisfying as doing it face to face, but whatever. She didn't proofread it, didn't adjust anything before she hit Send. If she didn't put it out there, didn't tell him exactly what she thought of him, Cassidy would explode. But there was no release when she'd pressed the button and slammed her phone down, only seething rage that boiled her blood.

Whatever. At least he'd know. She'd teach him.

Within moments, her phone lit up, flashing with an incoming message.

I had no idea he was going to do it
I had no part in it, but I understand you feel betrayed

For what it's worth, I'm sorry

"Bullshit," she muttered. "What a crock."

For what it's worth, I DON'T forgive U. I can't believe that a professional would stoop to the level U did. Your agency is a joke, and U...

Cassidy blew out a breath, shaking her head and staring daggers at the screen, willing him to respond so she could continue that sentence.

Can we talk about this face to face? I have some things I'd like to show you

"Ha!" She laughed, but it held no humour. Oh, if only he was there. She cracked her knuckles, wishing she could actually take out her frustration on him.

Sure, why the hell not. @ Depraved

His response was immediate. *R U drunk?*

She shook her head, disgusted. *What? Coming in on your white stallion to rescue me? You'd be the last person I'd call*

B there in 15

Cassidy glared at her phone, incensed. How dare he? The pompous arse actually thought he'd go there to keep her safe? As if anything he could say would make a difference. She wanted to see him one time. Just once to punch him in his beautiful face and break that perfect nose of his. Then, she wanted him out of her life and away from her career. She was sick of looking over her shoulder and getting kicked in the nuts when she let her guard down, even for a moment.

"So did it hurt?" She looked up to see a cute older man, who reminded her far too much of her dad, sliding onto the seat next to her on the tall bar table.

"What?" It was a mental leap to shift from the POS on her phone to the man in front of her. Who was he?

"When you fell from heaven. Did it hurt?"

Cassidy blinked at him. That was by far the worst pickup line she'd ever heard. Was that what he was trying to do? Pick her up? She giggled, clamping her hand over her mouth to stop it from spilling out and offending the poor guy. His lip twitched, and she couldn't hold her laugh in.

"I'm sorry, but that—"

"Is the worst pick up line ever, I know. But it got you to smile."

"I'm here with friends. I'm not looking to hook up." He nodded and pointed to her phone.

"If they're making you that upset, it's time to trade them in."

She smiled, her mood lifting with every moment. "Thank you, I'm good."

"Sir, I think it's time you leave." Her spine straightened, and her skin prickled. She'd recognize that voice anywhere. It had invaded her dreams and her every waking moment. But while he'd been painting the picture of a future Cassidy had never dared to imagine could come true, his boss had been screwing her over. The first time she'd been tag-teamed, and there'd been no happy ending for her.

Denyer stood in her personal space, sliding his hand into her hair in a show of possession. Cassidy clenched her fists, her nails making half-moon indents into her skin. "Hi, baby," he added, leaning close to nuzzle her face. Denyer didn't kiss her, but he came close to it. Cassidy's rage flared again, and she gripped his chest between her forefinger and thumb and twisted hard. He hissed, and Cassidy registered what she'd grabbed—his nipple. It gave her a grim sense of satisfaction knowing she'd dished out a little of the sweet-tasting revenge she craved.

Cassidy looked away from him, turning to the man who'd made her smile, ready to apologize for their rude interruption. But he was nowhere to be found.

"You need to step back," Cassidy directed.

His breath ghosted along her throat, sending a ripple of awareness through her. Her nipples peaked, hardening from the weight of his stare. His voice was a low rumble, close to her ear. "You need to let go of my nipple." Shock struck her, and Cassidy reared back, immediately releasing him. Her breath hitched, and heat flashed through her body.

"Why are you here? I told you I didn't need rescuing."

Denyer pointed to an empty seat, silently asking her permission to sit. Cassidy sighed. He was a persistent son of a bitch, and she knew he wouldn't back off as easily as the last man. She shook her head dismissively and carelessly motioned to the chair. "I came because I wanted to set the record straight. I want you to read my email exchange with Charles, my boss."

"I don't want to hear it. I don't want to see it." She raised her voice above the thumping bass, needing him to hear every word that passed through her lips. He was vile. A slow-acting poison that had gotten under her skin and was festering. "You've got an excuse for everything, and I'm sick of dealing with you." She jabbed him in the chest. "It's like you've got this hard-on to see my career go down the shit chute." Rage boiled within her like a volcano ready to erupt. Geysers of steam and ash had already exploded, but the lava flowing through her veins would incinerate everyone around her if she detonated. And the dickhead in front of her was standing there with a jackhammer, trying to break through the thin crust of her waning temper.

Cassidy had heard enough. She wasn't sticking around anymore. Leaving him sitting at the table, she stalked onto the dance floor, stomping over to the only friend she could see.

The weight of Denyer's stare was on her the whole time. It lit an awareness that Cassidy wasn't prepared to acknowledge. She hated how gorgeous he was. She hated that she couldn't see any hint in his eyes of the lie she knew he was telling. She despised how that simple touch, the brush of his stubbled cheek against hers and the whisper of his breath along her throat, sent a pulse of desire through her. Mortification slid along her spine when she catalogued the ache low in her belly. Wetness slid along the crease of her thighs between the heat of her legs with every step she took. The rub of the delicate shimmery material of her gold dress against her nipples sent jolts of electricity through her.

It coalesced to shift the tectonic plates she was standing on, grinding the pressure within until she was fit to burst.

She tapped her friend on the shoulder, but Tamara was too wrapped up in the man she was dancing with. Cassidy gripped her gently and shook, getting her friend's attention. "I can't do this. I'm out. Tonight is an absolute shit show. You girls are going to have to find your own way home. I'm done."

"What? You can't leave. You're supposed to be driving." Tamara was indignant. Her brows furrowed, and her lips pursed in an annoyed frown. "That was the deal."

"That was your deal." Cassidy pointed to her. "I called you because I needed my friends, but as soon as we got here, you all ditched me for drinks and dancing. I'm leaving." When had Cassidy's life turned into this? Her friends were using her, her competition was walking all over her, and no matter what she did, it all blew up in her face. She was surrounded by a sea of people, but Cassidy had never been more alone.

A warm body pressed against her back, and one hand went to her waist, the man's thumb caressing her through her dress. He leaned in close and shifted her hair back off her shoulder. Cassidy tensed, terrified she'd completely lose control if she had to manhandle someone away from her. She pulled out of his embrace and stepped away, but the man grasped her wrist. Suddenly too tired to deal with everything, Cassidy looked up to him, ready to beg him to leave her alone. What she saw had her breath catching. Denyer's eyes held so much heat, his lips wet as if he'd licked them. Desire radiated from him, want screaming from the fluttering of his pulse at his throat and the shallow breaths he was taking.

She looked him over for the first time since seeing him that night and swallowed. Dear God, he was handsome. His navy blue suit looked like it had been tailor-made for him, creating perfect lines and highlighting all his best assets. He'd paired it with a crisp white shirt that, even after she'd gripped and twisted it, was almost completely uncreased. But it also hinted at a long day screwing people over. His top button was undone, and the knot of the blue-and-silver check tie he wore hung loose. He probably came straight from the office, speeding across town in... whatever villain-mobile he drove.

Then she noticed the darker circles around his eyes and the pinch lines around his lips. The furrow of his brow. He swallowed, and the motion drew her gaze down to the V in his shirt where a smattering of blond chest hair poked up. It looked soft to the touch, and Cassidy instinctively stepped forward, reaching up to finger the strands. She felt more than heard the groan rumbling through his chest, but her anger spiked again when their gazes clashed.

She gripped the hair and tugged hard, and his eyes flashed, his jaw clenching.

"Have you got what you wanted? Seen me having a shitty night and watched my friends treat me like crap. Anything else you want from me?" Cassidy blinked back tears, her lip trembling as anger, frustration, sadness, and a sense of uselessness overwhelmed her. She fought to maintain her stoic façade.

Denyer wrapped his arm around her and walked her backward until shadows fell across them. They were in the corner of the room, out of the way and in the dark. He pressed her into the hard wall with his hips, and the bulge he sported had her body firing. His heat burned into her, but Cassidy wasn't going to allow herself to be manhandled like that. She pressed her hands against his chest, readying to push him away. But he leaned in close, his lips brushing her ear when he spoke. "I want everything. But I don't want to take anything. I want you, Cassidy, and I want you to want me just as much."

Her chest heaved with the sharp intake of breath. She balled her hand into a fist and beat that perfect rounded pec as hard as she could—which, given she could get no purchase, was barely a tap. He was ridiculous, so damn sexy and gorgeous. Perfect in every way except for the ugliness between them. There was a yawning gap in the spot where her confidence used to be. Where her ability to trust once resided. This world that she'd immersed herself into so willingly seemed to be readying to chew her up and spit her out. Was it all another ruse to trick Cassidy into falling for him so she would give him another leg up? She grimaced and let her fist fall against his chest again. "No. I hate you."

"Tell me to leave then. Tell me to walk away and never get in contact with you again. Tell me you don't want me like I want you." Denyer's words were raw, the anguish in his voice clear even with the pounding music reverberating through her.

"You want to fuck me as well as fuck my career up?" she sneered. "How about I spread my legs and give you the password to my computer at the same time?"

"Cassidy," he breathed, his lips trailing a line of soft kisses along her throat. Instinctively, she tilted her head, giving him more room. Her eyes fluttered closed. So good. He kept his touch light, barely-there caresses sending licks of fire along her spine. Her head screamed to push him away, but her body drew him closer. She pounded her fist against his chest again before he pinned her hands above her head, his fingers entwining with hers and holding her fast.

He rolled his hips, and his hard length pressed against her core, the delicious friction making her see stars. She sucked in a breath, her breasts straining against the silken material of the tiny dress she wore. Denyer reached up and brushed his thumb across her breast, his finger slipping under the low-plunging neck to rub the nub of her nipple. Skin on skin. That one move, the soft caress, was as powerful as a lightning bolt, electrifying her as it coursed through her veins. She arched into his touch and strained to free her hands from his grip.

"Fuck work. Fuck my career. I'll walk away from it if it means I get you," he growled. The possession in his tone was like a drug. The absolute certainty that settled in her gut with his words and the promise that it wasn't a lie in his gaze was a high she could easily get addicted to. She wanted him, but she hated him too. Hated that he had so much power over her.

His hand slid down her side and slipped below the high split in her skirt, reaching around to cup her bare arse. "This, right here, is what I want. You are what I want. What do I have to do to prove it to you?"

"Kiss me," she ordered, her mind short-circuiting as he hitched her leg up, so her stilettoed heel was resting on his calf.

The soft brush of his lips against hers was incendiary, sparking a wildfire within. Cassidy strained to close the hair's breadth of a gap he'd put between them. She growled and forced her hand free, sliding her fingers into his silken locks and pulling him closer. Their lips crashed together in a fierce claiming. She bit down on that plump lip and sucked it into her mouth before thrusting her tongue to parry against his. Jacob's taste exploded in her mouth, something sweet and minty at the same time. She couldn't get enough. Ravenous, Cassidy rubbed herself all over him like a cat and purred when he slid his hand back up to her arse, gripping it in his strong hand.

She tugged her other hand free and traced her fingertips down the front of his body to the thick meaty erection straining his suit pants. His moan rumbled from deep within his chest as she pressed the heel of her palm down his length. He shuddered when she did it again and punched his hips forward as she stroked his balls through the fabric.

She wanted skin on skin. Needed it. She needed him.

Cassidy pulled back a fraction and gasped for breath, her world spinning as Jacob cupped her face and kissed her gently along her jaw. When his lips met hers again, his moves were slow and sensuous, each press and stroke of his tongue communicating what she hadn't believed when he'd spoken the words. But she needed more. That ironclad control she prided herself with was non-existent when confronted with the man in her arms. From the moment she'd heard his name at the alumni event, it had been MIA, being replaced with a wild streak that thoroughly consumed all sense of reason.

Cassidy unzipped his pants and slid her hand into his underwear to cup the heated flesh between his legs. Satin-coated steel met her fingers, and she tugged him free, gliding her fist up his length. Her thumb dipped into his slit, gathering a pearl of clear liquid and sliding it down, circling the cluster of nerves there. The noise and throng of people surrounding them fell away as Cassidy focussed on getting her fill. Jacob's pupils were blown, his gaze lust drunk. She gripped him harder, and his eyes rolled back, a hiss passing through his clenched teeth.

"You make me want to claim you," he growled. "Slide inside you until you're screaming my name and never want another man. Then we'll find our third, and you'll be ruined for everyone except us."

Cassidy whimpered, and Jacob slid his hand lower, around her rear until his fingertips brushed her pussy. Wet with arousal and throbbing with need, she dragged his face closer and claimed his mouth again as he slipped his thick fingers into her. "Fuck," she breathed against his lips as he groaned.

"Mmm, no panties. I love it. So illicit, so dirty. It's like you were waiting for me. Hmm, you want that? You want me to slide inside you and make you mine. You want me to find us another man too."

Any illusion that Cassidy was still in control snapped, and she shuddered in his hold. She wanted everything he was promising. "Need you."

"This isn't just a one and done, Cass. I mean it. You, me and our third."

"Yes," she breathed, a sob hitching in her throat as she came apart at the seams, needing Jacob to stitch her back together.

"Once will never be enough with you." He kissed down her throat, his thumb and forefinger teasing her nipple as he kept up the steady motion with his fingers, sliding in and out of her pussy and hitting her G-spot with every stroke.

"Fuck me, Jacob," she begged.

"Say my name again. I want to hear you shout it." He slid his hand away from her core, and the emptiness that followed left a hollowness in its wake, one that could only be filled by him. He gripped her arse, kneading the flesh there as his other hand found her other cheek. Jacob's muscles bulged in his suit when he lifted her. Cassidy snapped her legs around his hips and her arms around his shoulders, tightening her hold on him. This right here was almost what she needed. Sans clothes it would have been perfect, but right here and now, it was close. Her dress slid up as he adjusted his hold and Cassidy gasped. His hot flesh pressed against her clit, rubbing her deliciously as he ground down.

"Jacob," she pleaded, and he responded, rewarding her with a slow thrust, burying himself balls deep inside her heat. She clenched, wanting to hold him there forever. He was long and thick, and the intrusion sent her spiralling. The coarse pubes at the base of his cock rubbed against her clit, and his fingers pressed the lips of her pussy tighter around his cock. He massaged her there, and it was as if he had a direct line to her clit. He withdrew slowly before slamming her back down onto him. His movements were as controlled as a ballet dancer, and if the measured thrusts were anything to go by, he instinctively knew how to work her body until it was humming.

His stubble brushed against her lips as they kissed, and his bulging pecs abraded her nipples while he impaled her on his cock. Cassidy spun, flying and soaring. It was overwhelming. Taboo and dangerous right there in the club—albeit in a shadowed corner—but Cassidy was beyond reason. Her thoughts had been stolen, replaced with a need as old and primal as the human race itself. All she could do was hang on while he slaked his lust, careening her toward an orgasm of epic proportions as he pumped inside her.

"Feel that, Cass? How hard you make me. How much I want what you want."

"Tell me," she breathed, licking the sweat dripping down his temple, his salty taste exploding on her tongue. She couldn't wait to suck him down until he painted her tongue with his cum, and she could taste his musky essence.

Tingling began, a rushing in her blood as she neared the precipice.

But her orgasm was just out of reach.

"We'll find him together," he growled, his heated breath in her ear. All attempts at propriety were gone. His hips were slamming into her, his deep thrusts sending her teetering. "He'd be right here with us, you pressed between us."

Cassidy squeezed her eyes closed and shivered as the picture his words conjured—of being taken by both of them, speared at either end—appeared in her mind's eye.

"I'd sink into him as he spread your pretty legs and licked you until you screamed our names." His tongue snaked out and traced the shell of her ear before delving inside.

Those words, the image he painted, and his wicked tongue pushed her over. Her orgasm slammed into her. Cassidy's pussy clamped tight, waves of ecstasy radiating throughout as she moaned his name.

He never stopped, never slowed his carnal assault until he stiffened in her arms and heat flooded her core. Her name on his lips sent aftershocks rocking through her, zapping up her spine and renewing tendrils of the orgasm-induced endorphin rush. Jacob's kisses—sometime throughout the night she'd begun thinking of him as more than her competition-turned-enemy—turned lazy, and he pulled back, resting his forehead against hers. Cassidy blinked her eyes open, and the reality of what they'd just done and where hit her. She shifted, squirming to get loose, but Jacob still had a tight hold on her, his twitching cock still buried deep inside. As delicious as it was, still thick after having screwed her stupid, panic set in. The high faded fast. "Jacob, you need to let me down. What if people saw us? Oh my God."

"Hey, it's okay. I'll let you down. Fix your dress while I'm standing in front of you, and we'll walk straight out of here. You can wear my jacket if you need it."

Cassidy unwound herself, and with the adjustment, he slipped out of her core. Her jelly-like legs hit the floor, and she stood, testing her balance and coordination as if she were a newborn foal. Liquid leaked from her, more than her own essence. Wide-eyed, she looked up at Jacob. "You didn't wear protection. Fuck." Cassidy sucked in a breath and raised a shaking hand to her mouth. Fuck, what had she been thinking? She hadn't. That was the problem. Every rational thought, every lesson that had been drilled into her since she'd learned what her body was capable of and what the risks were with sex, had fled. The prudish instruction to abstain or face hell had bunched up its long skirts and frilly knickerbockers and hightailed it out of there. The more open-minded, practical education of why condoms were so important had laughed in the face of that reaction, stretched out naked on the sundeck, and smoked a joint. And all the while, Cassidy had hopped on for a ride. It was, undeniably, a hell of a rush, but where did her sensible nature go when this man showed up? He was the match to her fuse, able to light her up until she exploded.

"I've never been with anyone without protection, Cass. My last tests all came back negative for everything, and I'll drive you to the doctor myself if you want to get tested or need the morning-after pill."

"No. I'm on the pill." She shook her head, waving off that concern as their mingled essences slid along her thighs. She squeezed her legs together, tightening her pelvic floor and hoping no one would see the evidence. "Bloody hell, I don't have any underwear on."

His grin turned wolfish, possession firing in his eyes. "I told you, Cass, you make me want to claim you." He pressed her against the wall and slid his fingers under the hem of her dress, swiping at the liquid slipping along her thighs. His fingers glistened as he painted her lips and leaned in to lick it away. He growled against her mouth and her pussy clenched. "Feel like a damn caveman beating my chest. Now, you know you're mine. And I'll know that it's my cum running down your legs as you walk out of here."

"Oh, fuck," she gritted her teeth, fighting the wave of desire crashing over her. She was ready to hop on to ride the crazy train again.

"Mine and his, Cass. We'll mark you. Own you, and we'll be your slaves. Greedy for you whenever you want us."

"Tuck yourself in, Jake," she ordered. "We're going." She was crazy. Nuts, in fact, and she'd probably regret it in the morning, but for now, she was leaving her sanity in that dark corner of the club and taking him home. Cassidy needed to get out of her head. She needed to blow off steam.

Hate sex, anyone? Yes, please.

Four

Jacob

A MONTH LATER

Jake was new to that particular part of town, despite it only being a two-minute walk from his office. He'd arrived fifteen minutes early for his appointment to show an office to a potential tenant, and he'd walked a couple of blocks to check out the food and coffee options. Aside from the specifics of the tenancy, where they could get good coffee was always the first question people asked. What the food options were was the second. This bustling street seemed to have it all, especially the good coffee. The aroma wafting from Grounds, the coffee shop two doors down, was heavenly. It was as if perfectly roasted beans had soaked into the very essence of the building, calling to him at a base level and every connoisseur in the area.

The young accountant who'd decided to strike out on her own was off considering the information Jake had provided to her. He was following his nose. Pushing through the door to Grounds, Jake was greeted by the buzz of conversation, the hiss of the coffee machine steaming milk, the click of keyboards, and the scratching of pencil on paper. He looked around, seeing an eclectic mix of patrons, some in school uniforms with textbooks piled around them, working during their free period, others in casual clothes typing away on laptops, businesspeople chatting around small tables, and what looked to be a parents' group with a mix of men and women cradling babies. The furniture was mismatched, the walls painted in rich coral, emerald green, and deep blue, and the interior designed so that each table was tucked into its own space. High-backed chairs, walls of greenery cascading from hanging pots, and strategically placed timber privacy screens gave the large, industrial space a sense of warmth and homeliness. The polished floors were scuffed, and the bookshelves dotted throughout overfilled. Both gave Grounds an unmistakable charm that Jake loved instantly.

The man he'd followed in led the way to the counter and huffed when he had to wait to be served. Jake rolled his eyes and fished his phone out of his pocket, considering whether he had time to sit down or get a takeaway.

Less than a minute later, he heard a throat clear and looked up into the most striking hazel eyes he'd ever seen. Kind but sharp and inquisitive, they pinned him. Unable to move, unable to breathe, Jake took the man in. Scruffy jet-black hair parted on one side and flopped in front of his eyes. He had a perfect jawline with a smattering of dark stubble and bronze skin. Jake swallowed. He opened his mouth. No words formed. He closed it again. His brain had shut down. Blue screened with a fatal error.

"What would you like?" The man's bedroom voice, all deep and husky, rolled over him, and Jake sucked in a breath. His heart pounded in a staccato rhythm. *Fuck me.* Awareness prickled through him, his skin tingling. He shivered. Jake fought his body's reaction, begging his cock to stay down. His reaction was visceral, so powerful it knocked him for six. He hadn't experienced such an immediate and all-consuming attraction before, except with Cassidy. But it was different with her. He loved poking the bear and watching her roar. The night they'd hooked up the first time, she'd all but dragged him out the door, barely giving him a moment to tuck himself in and slip his jacket off to hide the mess he'd made of the front of his pants. They'd tumbled into bed and passed out a few hours and rounds later.

"Buddy? You need some more time?"

Jake blinked, being torn back to reality and the attraction fizzling in his veins for the man before him. He'd gotten completely side-tracked, his imagination going at warp speed to triple X-rated. Best of all, he hadn't said a word, just stared like a creep.

"Ah, sorry. Um, just um, what the guy before me had." What was he saying? Jake ordered one thing and one thing only—espressos.

"You want what the guy before you had? A large almond cappuccino with an extra shot, a second extra shot, a drizzle of vanilla, extra chocolate on top, sweetened with honey, and a shot of caramel flavoured almond milk froth on the side?" Jake didn't register a single word the man said. He watched those perfect lips pronounce every syllable and that sexy-as-sin eyebrow lift, and he was gone. Utterly lost in his eyes. He found himself nodding, just wanting the man to keep talking. But instead, he nodded once, pressed a few buttons on the touchscreen in front of him, then tapped a long finger on the white card reader sitting on the counter-top. Jake absentmindedly paid, unable to break the man's gaze. "What's your name?" When he opened his mouth, nothing came out again, but the Adonis smiled patiently, and Jake could almost see the eye roll in the tilt of his lips, and added, "It's okay. We'll just read out your order."

He nodded and stepped to the side, heat crawling up his throat to his cheeks. Jake pressed his clammy hands to them, trying to will away the embarrassment of becoming so completely tongue-tied. He shifted his jacket in front of his groin and adjusted his hard-as-nails cock in his pants. There was no way anyone would miss the thing sticking out at an awkward angle if they looked. As subtly as possible, Jake eyed the counter, his gaze settling on the other man.

When he wasn't a deer in headlights, ensnared by those eyes, Jake could let his own wander. Taller than Jake by a good few inches, he wore a black T-shirt that clung to broad shoulders all the way down to a slim waist. Was it unrea-sonable to be jealous of the black apron secured around his middle, right where Jake wanted to be? He had a swimmer's body—streamlined rather than being overly buff. Deft hands moved between the computer and takeaway cups where he scrawled names onto them, passing them along the production line. He was efficient but friendly too, taking the time to smile at every customer and thank them for any coins they dropped into the tip jar. Jake's eyes were drawn to the white name tag pinned to the other man's chest. Phoenix. Even his name was exotic. He had a presence, and Jake wanted to bask in it for as long as he could. Immerse himself in the man.

"Almond cappuccino with an extra cup of foam."

Jake swallowed. God, that sounded awful. He looked around, trying to figure out who would order that.

"That's him." Phoenix pointed to Jake, and his belly flip-flopped before swooping. The other man's attention being focused on him, even only for a moment, was enough to give him a high.

Then his words registered. *The coffee was his?*

"Sir? I have your order." A young woman came out from behind the counter and handed him two cups. "Thanks for visiting Grounds."

He nodded absentmindedly, his focus still trained on Phoenix and took a sip.

Milky coffee slid over his tongue, the burst of sweetness that it bought entirely overpowering the taste of the beans. It was a cacophony of flavours that weren't in any way har-monious. Vanilla, honey, chocolate, and the nuttiness of the almond milk clashed, and Jake had to resist the urge to spit it straight back out.

With his eyes watering, he turned and dashed from the coffee shop, racing outside and spitting the contents into the cup of caramel froth. What was the man in front of him thinking? That coffee was an abomination. The worst thing he'd ever tasted. He shuddered and headed straight for the rubbish bin, dumping both cups into it. He hesitated, warring with himself to march straight back in there and order an espresso. His body craved it, almost as much as it craved another glance at the spectacular man who'd served him.

Oh shit. The man who'd served him. There was no way Jake could go back in there and ask for what he wanted now, not when he'd fumbled his last order so badly. There was only one thing left to do. Run. Never, ever go back there. Dying of embarrassment was another option.

The butterflies that had lifted off in his belly the moment he'd laid eyes on Phoenix stopped flapping, falling to the ground in a dramatic heap. The sickening lurch in his stomach at the possibility of never seeing Phoenix again bought him up short. Maybe he should try to order what he wanted.

But he was already pushed for time.

Jake wiped his sweaty palms down his charcoal suit pants and sucked in a breath. It would take a bit of mental cheerleading to pluck up the courage to walk back into that store, but until then, duty called. He had more meetings and more paperwork he needed to get to, and if he didn't get a move on, he would be late. His next client was expecting a package of documents, and if he was lucky, Jake wouldn't have to see him. It also meant he needed to be fast because, in all likelihood, his next client—his father—would be between meetings on the hour. So, if Jake wanted to avoid seeing him, he needed to be in and out within the next fifteen minutes.

Jake popped a mint to get the horrid taste of good coffee ruined by all the extras out of his mouth and made his way back to his building. When the lift opened in front of him, he settled back into the corner of the elevator as its shiny doors slid closed. The sinking in his gut had only grown, but it had nothing to do with going up to his office or the embarrassing encounter in the coffee shop. Rather, it had everything to do with his upcoming appointment. He hated that his father held so much power over him, even now after he'd done almost everything ever asked of him. The only thing he'd failed at—that his father actually knew about—was the lack of a law degree, and he'd never live that down. Even at twenty-two, the only thing Jake wanted to do was make his father proud. He doubted he'd ever achieve it.

Jake collected the papers Charles needed signed and headed out at a jog. For anybody else, they would simply be emailed. If the clients were technologically inept, a courier would deliver printed copies. But Jake's father, the Maxwell Denyer, expected certain standards of operation and even his oldest friend—Jake's boss—knew to comply with those demands.

He strode the two blocks to the law firm's offices, wishing he could drop them at the ground-floor lobby.

The differences between the entrance of the building he'd just come from and this one were stark. Where the lobby to his was stylish, if not a bit dated, the tower housing one of Australia's largest and most prestigious law firms was downright opulent. And locked up as tight as a vault.

White Italian marble lined the floors, contrasting with the black marble on the walls. Thousands of silver lights, each the thickness of a pen, hung on long wires from the double-height ceiling, creating a blanket of stars reflecting off the polished surfaces no matter the time of day or night. Jake was awed, and yet revulsion filled him at the same time. The building itself was gorgeous, and the owners had invested millions in ensuring the most up-to-date security features and top environmental sustainability targets were met. But the building wasn't the problem. None of it changed the fact that his father was sitting in one of the pretentious penthouse offices ruling over his domain, and by entering the building, Jake was voluntarily putting himself in front of his biggest critic. Well, not entirely voluntarily. His father had demanded his presence, and his boss had readily acquiesced.

He swallowed, willing himself not to puke.

Jake signed in at the security desk, scanned his licence and waited for the armed attendant to acknowledge him. "They're expecting you on the thirty-seventh floor, Mr Denyer. This pass will take you directly there."

"Thanks," he muttered, putting on a brave face. The whole way up to the thirty-seventh floor he repeated his mantra. *Happy thoughts. Calm thoughts. Water off a duck's back. Don't let him get to you. Happy thoughts. Cassidy... and Phoenix.* He could imagine the two of them together—him all dark and mysterious and her all light and fire. Jake pressed down on his still half-hard dick and gritted his teeth. Damn, they'd be beautiful together.

The lift opened, and a lavish reception area greeted him. Grey marble and white leather. Clinical and cold, but the interior designer had labelled it sleek, minimalist, and professional. Carol, the receptionist, and her two junior staff had been chosen for their model-like looks, but Carol was one of the most intelligent and warm people he'd ever met. "Good morning, Jacob. Your father is expecting you."

"He's in?" Jacob squeaked, his gut sinking, the hope that he'd miss his father fleeing. It wasn't his day. At least he had a few minutes to brace himself for the teardown. Carol nodded sympathetically and motioned him through to the private elevators that serviced the ten floors the law firm occupied. His father and the other executive partners were on the penthouse level, sipping the finest whiskey from crystal tumblers while their minions worked eighty-hour weeks. He closed his eyes, eminently grateful for flunking out of law school and missing this as his fate.

Tayla, his father's latest assistant, greeted him as he passed through security into the executive suites. He knew the drill. Wait until she'd knocked on the double doors and announced his entry before he crossed the threshold. His father gruffly uttered, "Enter," and Jacob shook his hands out, trying to unclench. His stomach churned, and he was twelve again, trying to hide from the cold man who lorded over him.

But it was too late to escape. His father knew he was there, and leaving would be one more thing to add to an already too long list of failures on Jake's part.

He straightened his spine like he'd been taught, pulled his shoulders back and held his head high, faking the confidence to walk through those doors as he threw himself to the wolves.

The quiet on the executive level, particularly inside the offices, was always jarring. No phones rang—they were all silent buzzes—and everyone spoke in a whisper. The sounds didn't penetrate the dark timber panelling on the walls. The oppressive silence contrasted starkly with the sun-drenched vista that opened before him when he faced the wall of windows. Sydney Harbour in all its glory was spectacular. Jake appreciated the city for a moment before casting his eyes toward his father.

The broad desk, stained in black, was centred along the short wall of the gargantuan room. It was bare, aside from a curved screen monitor, a telephone, and three precisely lined-up pens. Sitting back, reading a stapled set of papers, his father didn't spare him a glance. Invisible as always, unless he was being scolded.

Hidden behind the polished panelling was the door to a private bathroom and walk-in change room. Even excluding those rooms, this office was twice as large as Jake's studio apartment. He moved straight over to the white circular couch and silently placed the envelope on the table. He forced himself to look away from his father and concentrate on the view. Jake knew the other man's expectations—wait for an invitation to sit, don't speak first, anticipate what was needed, and deliver it before being asked. Jake recognized the psychological ploy for what it was. Even with his son— perhaps especially with Jake—he employed the technique, keeping everyone waiting until his father was good and ready. It silently set the expectation that things happened when Maxwell Denyer agreed and not before. But Jake hated it. He hated the power imbalance that his father never failed to remind him of and despised how his father weaponised it against him. He never expected special treat- ment—Jake would be sorely disappointed if he did—but he wished his father didn't make him feel so small.

"You have the papers?" Jake startled, focussing so hard on the view that he hadn't seen his father turn his attention to him.

"Yes." He picked up the envelope. "I checked that the tenant signed the correct version. They're ready for your signature."

"Good. Leave it there. I'll have my associate check it." Jake was used to his word not being enough; his father didn't trust him. He never had. The man stood and swag- gered over to the couch, sitting with his leg crossed and his arm along the back. It was a deceptively casual pose, one Jake had seen many times before when his father was about to attack. But if his father could play the game, so could

Jake. He mirrored the other man's stance, praying that his father couldn't see his hands shaking.

"I can have it collected when you've signed it."

His father barely spared him a nod. The man was in his fifties and just as good-looking as he was when he was thirty, but in Jake's mind, he would always be ugly. His blond hair was streaked with grey now, and apart from the beginnings of a few wrinkles on his face, they were the only signs of his age. He knew what he'd look like as an older man, but Jake hoped that the differences between them would be as significant as the similarities. Where his father's lines were from frowning, Jake hoped his were laugh lines. The grey at his father's temples was from stress—no doubt keeping track of all the favours he was owed by his powerful clients. Jake wanted his grey to be from a full life lived, filled with family and friends rather than broken marriages and a child who'd almost rather be anywhere else than with the man who'd raised him after he'd pushed his third wife out of their lives.

Jake dropped his ankle and made to stand. "Well—"

"You're dating a woman from CIR." His father eyed him up and down as Jake eased himself back onto the couch. *Close to freedom, but no dice.* Jake didn't know what his father wanted to hear, but he didn't flinch at the implication he knew what Jake had been up to. That was nothing new. In fact, with his father's connections, it was pretty typical.

"No, not dating. We met at a function at the university and decided to get some dinner together. Not much more to tell." There was, but... Jake swallowed, hoping his explanation sufficed. The last thing he needed in his tricky relationship with Cassidy was his father's interference.

"And yet you left in the middle of a business meeting to chase after her. Hardly professional." Jake's brows furrowed, trying to recall when he'd been in a meeting with Cassidy... the morning before their hook up. He shook his head, and his father raised an eyebrow, challenging him. Daring Jake to call him a liar.

"The meeting was over. It doesn't matter anyway. We won the sole agency for that building." As soon as he'd said the words, Jake knew he'd misspoken.

"The only reason you have that listing at all is Charles's quick thinking. Your lack of professionalism cost the agency dearly. His partners wanted your head, but Charles acted to save your career, jeopardizing his own relationship with them—" Jake opened his mouth to interrupt, to explain what really happened, but the glare he received in return made him close it again. Gone was the casual pose now. His father pointed at him, disgust in the curl of his lip. "I put you with Charles because he has experience in this game and can teach you a lesson or two. But if you're too busy chasing tail, you'll never learn. You're old enough to know better, and acting out like a spoilt teenager isn't impressing anyone." He shook his head. "You're a disappointment, Jacob. You're too soft, too impulsive like your mother. I've tried to drill it out of you, but I should have known her genetics would ruin you—"

"Father—"

"No, Jacob, it's your turn to listen, not talk." His voice boomed through the room, and Jake flinched. Anger radiated from his father, and the man's ice-blue eyes flashed daggers. "Leaving early and getting in late, walking out of meetings to chase a woman... it's pathetic. I shouldn't have to constantly monitor everything you do so I know when I have to clean up your mess. Your career is on shaky ground. Fail again and Charles certainly won't stand up for you a second time. Neither will I. Grow up, or you'll find yourself cut off. Understood?" The hard set to his jaw brooked no room for dispute. It wasn't even worthwhile pointing out that his allowance had ended the moment he'd flunked out of law school. Jake had been paying his own way for years, but reminding his father of that would only serve to enrage him further.

It also wasn't worthwhile trying to explain that he'd been at a series of breakfast meetings, courting a new client. He hadn't put anything in his calendar because they didn't like Charles. They didn't want his boss involved in the deal. Neither did Jake. He'd wanted to sign these clients to the agency on his own steam, if for no reason than to prove to himself that he could.

The only thing that seemed to set his father off in a rage more than Jake's screw-ups was the mention of his mother. More than anything, Jake wanted to defend her, because even though he hadn't seen her in over a decade, she'd left Jake in no doubt how much she'd loved him. It was solely his father's doing that his mum had been forced out of Jake's life—he'd stacked the system against her, using every contact he had to present a case that she couldn't win in front of a judge his father golfed with weekly.

Jake blinked back the irrational tears that threatened to fall, and he clenched his jaw. He nodded, his movements jerky as he fought the confusing instinct to either curl into himself or lash out. Either one would only prove his father's point, and displaying a hint of weakness to the man was like opening a vein in shark-infested waters.

"Good. I have a meeting. See yourself out."

Jake couldn't get out of there fast enough, practically tripping over himself to leave. He forced his legs to move slower and took a breath before exiting the room. He was careful to shut the door with barely a snick, despite wanting to kick it closed after giving his father a double salute. Anything louder than a click and his father would dress Jake down in front of the entire executive staff. His confidence couldn't take that kind of battering twice in one day.

Jake's hands shook as he pressed the button on the lift. The doors slid open a moment later. But it wasn't his day. His father's lacky—his driver, security, henchman, whatever the man's job description was—walked out, coming face to face with Jake. The man didn't budge, blocking the entrance to the lift with his broad shoulders. He was taller than Jake too, standing at close to seven feet.

Jake didn't engage. He couldn't. He simply stepped aside and waited for the man to pass, but he couldn't help his flinch when the man growled, "Pussy," in his ear. Jake stepped into the lift, his movements slow despite his galloping heart. He pressed the button to close the doors, praying that the man didn't follow him in. Keeping his head down as he exited the building, Jake tried to regulate his breathing and slow his heart rate down. Every step he took away from his caustic father loosened the hold of the claws he'd dug in, but Jake still ached. A heaviness weighed him down. The knowledge he was a disappointment, a failure, and someone his only family could never be proud of, was like an arrow to his heart.

* * * * *

It was late. The sky was long past dark as Jake made his way home. He'd had a hell of a day. Being a metaphorical punching bag for his father and then knowing his boss was watching his every move had Jake on edge. He didn't know what he needed, but if he didn't figure it out soon enough, he'd be seeing the bottom of a bottle of whatever liquor he had on hand and paying homage to the porcelain god soon after.

He thumbed his phone, tossing up who to call. His mates from school all knew his father. They knew what he was like, they knew how deep his words cut, but Jake couldn't face them. He didn't want their pity or their boisterous advice on how to escape his clutches. He needed something more. Something he could get lost in. Someone he could escape into.

Cassidy.

Before he could second-guess his decision, he dialled her number. "Sorry, I need to take this," she uttered before a rustle sounded, a door closed, and there was a hush. "Jacob, hi."

"Hey, sorry, I didn't mean to interrupt you. I can call you later or some other time." His voice sounded hollow even to his own ears. Beaten down.

"Are you okay? You're... quiet." Concern laced her tone, and Jake shook his head before blowing out a breath.

"Yeah. No. Kind of. I just kind of wanted to see you."

"I'm at my parents' place, but I've got a few minutes to talk." The mention of family twisted the arrows his father left buried in him, and Jake sucked in a breath. But the rest of her words sunk in, and Jake smiled. Lending an ear, giving him time was the nicest thing she'd ever said to him. Determination filled him. He knew she was worth the wait. "Rough day?"

"Yeah." He exhaled. Just hearing her voice raised his spirits. She made him lighter, buoyed him, allowing him to fight against the current dragging him down. Thinking about her made him smile. "Some parts were better than others, though. I tried out a new coffee place. Grounds on George Street. Have you been there?"

"No." He could hear the smile in her voice. "Was the coffee good?"

"It was terrible." He huffed out an embarrassed laugh. "I didn't get what I usually drank and ended up with a horrible concoction with far too much sugar and milk."

"So, not a recommendation then?" she asked, hesitating.

"No, you should." Jake nodded, a flush crawling up his throat to his face. "Look for Phoenix at the counter. He, um, might be the reason why I couldn't string together enough words to actually ask for what I wanted."

Cassidy laughed, and a husky "Mmm" followed. "Phoenix, hey? And what should I ask him for?"

"His number." Jake coughed, not actually intending to blurt that out. "And maybe an espresso, or whatever you drink."

"I prefer a latte with a phone number."

Jake groaned and shuddered at the memory of the sweet milky clash of flavours.

"So, what happened?"

"I got... tongue-tied. He was beautiful, Cass. I opened my mouth and nothing came out. Then when I tried speaking again, I ordered what the last bloke had. I don't know what he was on, but he had some sweet drink from hell that was so on the nose the whole shop rolled their eyes at me. I couldn't even swallow it. It was awful." The line was quiet for a moment before Jake heard a snort. "Are you laughing at me?" He tried to feign offence, but it was hard not to laugh at the ridiculousness of it, even though he'd ruined any possibility that he'd ever walk back into the shop.

"I'm sorry," she said, not sounding sorry at all as she giggled.

"I can't go back there! He'll think I'm some psycho who likes their coffee... ruined." Cassidy laughed harder, and he heard rustling on the phone again before a murmur.

"He was that hot that you couldn't even speak?"

"Yes." Jake groaned, looking up to the darkened sky. He couldn't see the stars with all the light surrounding him. He wanted to see them.

"Maybe I'll swing by there," she teased, still giggling.

"Cass, I know we're not together, but I'd like to be. If he makes you happy..." Jake's comment was quiet. Far too serious for the conversation that they'd just had, but he needed to get the words out. He needed her to know what he wanted—that he wanted her to explore what made her happy. If he could be a part of that, he'd jump at the chance. If not, he'd be happy for her.

She didn't respond for a long time, so much so that he checked they were still connected. "Thank you," she whispered. "No one has ever reacted the way you have. They always tell me that they want me to change, but you're serious, aren't you?"

"I am." He nodded and smiled. Jake didn't want to limit her. He didn't want to change who she was. He just wanted to share her passion and her fire.

More voices sounded in the background. "I'm sorry, Jacob. I need to go. Can I see you soon?"

"I'd like that."

FIVE

Cassidy

She still hated him. Sort of. But she'd been worried about Jacob too. She hoped their conversation had made him smile as well. He'd seemed down, overly quiet, and that just didn't sit right with her. If she'd been home, she would have gone straight over to his place, but family night was the one night a month she wasn't permitted to flake out on.

Even for a weeknight, they'd wrapped things up earlier than usual, and Cassidy suspected it had a lot to do with the looks her parents and brother were sharing when she'd walked out of her old bedroom. They'd brushed it off, her brother laughing at her and her parents smiling that knowing smile at each other. Next, they'd be asking when they could meet him. As if. Cassidy had laughed them off, but their conversation had stayed in her head, playing on a loop.

There was no sleep that night, even after Jacob's text assuring her that he was okay. Cassidy sat up thinking, staring at the ceiling as she imagined the possibilities. A couple of hours before dawn, she worked up the courage to ask for advice on her favourite forum. Should she grasp onto what Jacob had tempted her with that night at the club? Did she have the courage to ask Phoenix to join them? Flirting was one thing. Actually propositioning him was something else entirely.

Then there was Jacob. What they were to each other was still so uncertain. Cassidy was wary of him. He had the power to break her—both her career and personally. Even the idea of enemies with benefits terrified her because of it. She'd never had anyone affect her like he did, and she could see herself falling for him, if she could get past her issues. And they were her issues. Jacob had told her over and over that it wasn't him who'd caused her agency to lose the accounts. But she had a mental block in the spot where her trust should be. She kept reasoning that he hadn't proven himself, but in all fairness, he hadn't even known he was being tested.

Then there was their chemistry. One touch, one look, and she was putty in his hands. But she wasn't alone. No one had ever reacted to her like Jacob had. It was... empowering. The night they were together at the club, they'd fallen into bed together, and it was like an electrical storm inside a whirlwind went off. After three rounds of mind-blowingly amazing orgasms, Cassidy had been wrung out and riding a high, her body still buzzing. Jacob had crashed, curled around her. Her body screamed at her to cuddle into him, but her head had told her to run. She'd listened to her head that night but keeping a measure of distance between them was getting harder.

She didn't really know why she was standing outside the coffee shop, except that Jacob had told her to go there, and the gravity of his words had sunk in, despite him laughing at himself.

Pushing through the door would change things for them. It would create a link between her and Jacob, greater than just casual sex. Their shared mission was to find a third; did Cassidy want that with Jacob? Her body did cartwheels along the length of a football field. Her head? Her heart? They were undecided. Perhaps a better question was whether she was simply insane.

"Excuse me," a man uttered as she blocked the doorway.

"Sorry, trying to decide whether to get a coffee," she explained, stepping aside.

He let out a surprised laugh. "Is there ever a question? The answer's always yes."

Cassidy grinned in return. He'd given her the exact push she needed. She was overthinking things. Coffee. It was as simple as that. Jacob found Phoenix attractive. Maybe she wouldn't. Maybe he wasn't working, and this whole trip was a waste of time. Maybe he wouldn't be into guys and girls. Or maybe, just maybe, everything would come together perfectly. Regardless, she was going to get her morning caffeine fix.

With renewed hope and a little less of her inner monologue droning on in the background, Cassidy pushed open the door. The smell of freshly roasted beans filled her lungs as she inhaled, and she instantly loved the eclectic vibe the place had. This would be a place Cassidy could sit for hours reading or working in, and she resolved to go there again when she had more time.

There was a lady behind the counter taking orders, and Cassidy waited to be served. A man who was a whole head taller than her backed through the swinging doors carrying three plates piled high with food. She turned her attention to the server. "Skinny latte to go, please, and do you do deliveries?"

She nodded, keyed in her order, and added, "We have a minimum order for deliveries."

"I just want one coffee delivered, but I'm happy to pay for the minimum order and any delivery charge."

"Ah, okay." The woman hesitated. "Let me just check. One sec." The young woman ducked out from behind the counter and trotted over to the man Cassidy had seen before, talking quietly to him. He was gorgeous. Dark floppy hair and bronze skin with a long, lean body—she could imagine him as a swimmer or a runner. Strong legs and narrow hips with a broad set of shoulders. He wasn't bulky, but not skinny either. He looked up, and their eyes connected, a fission of electricity passing through her. Those full lips tilted up in the corners, and Cassidy licked her own, her imagination running wild.

He swaggered over, their locked gazes never breaking, and he leaned his hip on the counter. "You're after a single coffee to be delivered?"

Cassidy mirrored his pose and breathed him in. His cologne, something spicy and rich, screamed sex. It oozed from him, and she wanted to lick him and get high on his scent. His tight black tee curled over lithe muscle, drawing her eyes to the white name tag pinned to his chest. Phoenix. Her breath caught, and her eyes snapped back to his. Jesus fucking Christ, Jacob wasn't kidding. "I am. Can you pull it off?"

"Oh, I can do a lot of things." He grinned, giving Cassidy the same eye fucking she'd given him. "But it depends."

"On what?" Cassidy bit her lip, stifling her grin. He was cheeky and flirtatious, and the butterflies in her belly took off doing loop the loops. Cassidy flushed, heat crawling up her neck as his stare disarmed her.

"Hmm, well, we have a minimum order amount and a delivery fee."

"I heard. It's fine. I'm happy to pay both. I just want the one coffee delivered."

"And we only travel up to two blocks away."

Cassidy scrawled down the address and smiled an I-want-to-undress-you-with-my-teeth kind of grin. "One espresso delivered there, and my order."

"Sure. And what name can I put the order under?"

"Cassie. Delivery is to Jacob."

"Boyfriend?"

"Yes, please." She laughed and covered her mouth in faux innocence. "Oh, wait, did you mean him?" He raised an eyebrow, and Cassidy laughed again, this time more genuinely. "He wants the job. What do you think?"

"Does he treat you right?" She thought about it for a moment. Cassidy had been struggling with her trust issues. She was wary of Jacob. She'd just been thinking that he had the power to hurt her, but that didn't mean he didn't treat her right. "That hesitation right there tells me no. But I could be wrong."

"You're intuitive. I wanted to give you an honest answer."

"Hmm." He nodded. "But if you couldn't tell me straight up that you're the centre of his world, maybe you need someone else to show you just how well you should be treated. And you still haven't answered me."

The young lady handed her a takeaway cup and Cassidy nodded her thanks. "Well, maybe you should deliver the coffee to Jacob and tell me whether you think he's cute tomorrow when I swing by."

"I don't work Wednesdays."

"Well, see you on Thursday then." She turned on her heel and added a swish to her hips when she left the store, sending him a smirk over her shoulder as the door closed. A few steps later—out of view of the coffee shop—she paused and fanned herself, gathering her wits and pressing a hand to her belly to calm the flutters that had erupted. He was…. No wonder Jacob had been completely tongue-tied.

Now the million-dollar question was whether he was straight or if he liked a bit of variety. Cassidy hoped like hell he did, because Jacob was smitten, and she found herself wishing Phoenix would want both of them. She smiled, a skip in her step as she ordered a rideshare to get to her appointment.

* * * * *

"Why do I do this to myself?" Cassidy had barely put the phone to her ear when she heard Jacob's question as a groan in her ear. She couldn't help her bark of laughter. "I got my coffee, thank you. Then I decided I needed another one, so I went to Grounds."

"And?"

"I'm like a goldfish around him. Completely incapable of anything except opening and closing my mouth. I must have made an impression, though; he remembered my order."

"I gave him your name, so maybe."

"Oh no, not today's order. Yesterday's." Cassidy clamped her hand over her mouth to stop the giggles from erupting. Jacob was funny and sweet and so completely adorable. "I ended up with the same hideous concoction that I couldn't stomach yesterday when I couldn't even get out one simple word. How pathetic is it that I can't even ask for an espresso? No, don't answer that." Tears ran down her cheeks, and Cassidy tried to breathe while laughing silently. It didn't work. One inelegant snort later, and Jacob groaned again. "You think I'm just as ridiculous as he does."

"No, I don't think you're ridiculous. It's adorable how tongue-tied you get."

"Great, I'm adorable." He sighed, sounding pained. "Exactly what I needed to hear."

"Would you rather handsome? Sexy? Fantastic in bed?"

"Keep going. I'm liking this."

Cassidy laughed and rolled her eyes. "He doesn't work tomorrow. But he's back there on Thursday. Maybe work on perfecting how to ask for your order in the meantime."

"Ha ha. Hilarious." He paused for a moment, then asked, "How did you manage to find that out?"

"I flirted with him. You were right, you know. He is gorgeous."

"Did he flirt back?"

"He told me he was working Thursday, didn't he?" Cassidy didn't want to go out on a limb and guess Phoenix's sexuality, so she didn't share the last part of their conversation, but Jacob jumped to the most obvious conclusion with what he'd been given.

"That's more than polite flirting, so chances are he's straight." He hummed. "If I can get my brain to function long enough to do more than stare at him, one day, twenty years from now, I might be able to ask him if I'd ever have a chance."

Cassidy couldn't help her laughter. The more she talked to Jacob, the more the desire to maim him faded. She had to face facts. She liked him.

* * * * *

"Hey, you." Phoenix greeted her with a smile. "You must really like our coffee. A whole week of orders and deliveries."

"Can't go past good coffee." Cassidy shrugged as nonchalantly as possible.

"And does Mr Espresso appreciate it too? He's costing you a fortune." Phoenix tapped at the screen, ringing up Cassidy's usual, but she saw straight through the feigned casualness with which he asked the question.

"He does. He's asked me to say thank you for delivering it personally too. You should stick around until he can get to reception to collect it." She paused. "But anyway, do you get the weekend off, or are you working?"

"I'll be here on Saturday. Will I see you?"

"You just might." Cassidy smiled, excitement at the potential plan starting to form in her head, showing in her grin, and she handed him her card. If she could get Jacob and Phoenix in the same room, she would be able to see for herself whether the love-heart eyes were only one-sided or if Jacob stood a chance. She shot Jacob a text. *Let's do coffee on Saturday.*

How about dinner Friday night and then breakfast on Saturday?

Cassidy dialled his number, and Jacob picked up before the first ring had even finished. "I know what you're about to say, but listen just for a minute. I get that whatever we are is a little weird. I don't know what to call what we have, and it's okay if you'd prefer to just be friends, or maybe just the benefits bit if you don't want the friendship. I'm not really sure if we're friends, but I'd like to think that's where we're headed, or maybe more than that. You know that I want more, but I don't want to push you. I'm not trying to drive you away, so if I'm overstepping…. Could you give me a chance? I could show you what it could be like between us—"

"Jacob, stop talking." He did, gasping in a breath like he'd completely run out of oxygen, and Cassidy closed her eyes, gathering her courage. "Dinner Friday night would be great. And, yeah, friends sounds like a good place to be with you. I like you, but it takes me a while to trust people. Maybe we can work toward that."

"I'd like that, Cassidy."

"My friends call me Cassie. You should do that too."

She'd only just hung up when Phoenix said her name, his deep voice sending shivers through her. He stepped aside, motioning away from the crowd of people waiting for their coffees. "Do you have a minute? I'm due for my break. Maybe we could have a coffee together?"

"I'd like that." She looked around the shop and spotted the comfortable-looking sofa just big enough for the two of them to sit on. "How about there?"

Phoenix nodded and licked his lips. "Yeah." He cleared his throat and nodded again. "Yeah." He handed her the cup and motioned to the coffee machine. "Give me a sec?"

She slipped onto the couch and sipped her latte, humming as the rich flavours hit her tongue. There really was nothing better than a good coffee. The cushion next to her dipped and Cassidy turned to watch Phoenix get comfortable. With his ankle tucked under his knee, he sat sideways on the sofa, facing her. He'd lost the apron and now held a mug of steaming coffee in his hand, but he wasn't looking at her, instead focussing on a piece of imaginary lint on his black pants.

"How long have you worked here?" Cassidy asked, and he looked up, assessing her. It was as if he was searching for something.

"Nearly four years. I got the job just after I moved to the city."

She admired that. He must have been straight out of high school when he'd moved. She didn't know his exact age, but there couldn't have been more than a year or two difference between them. For him to have held down such a demanding job for so long at their age, it was impressive. It showed dedication and drive. She respected that. "Nice. I'm not from around here either, but I didn't come far—I'm only from the western suburbs. Where did you move from?"

"I grew up on a farm up north. Sydney's cool though. I love how busy it is. It's the complete opposite of my parents' place. There was nothing going on there—even the pub closed early. When I was growing up, everyone seemed so much older, so I wanted to move somewhere livelier."

"Where's their farm?" Cassidy took a sip of her coffee and turned to face him more, mirroring his pose.

"Little place about an hour south of Brisbane. It's called Tamborine." She couldn't believe it. She knew it. She'd visited the mountaintop showgrounds often, tagging along while her parents checked out the Sunday craft markets, and Cassidy and her brother ate whatever handmade snacks they could persuade their folks to buy.

"As in Tamborine Mountain, west of the Gold Coast? I spent all my summers as a kid on the Goldie."

"No way!" He laughed, his eyes lighting up with a spark of happiness as he spoke of home. "Small world. Tamborine is on the western side of Tamborine Mountain, but yeah, that one."

"And you've been in Sydney for four years? Did you move as soon as you finished school?"

"Yeah. Got a scholarship that covers my accommodation at the uni, so I moved down here." Phoenix was undoubtedly beautiful, his dark and mysterious vibe handsome in an almost opposite way to Jacob's surfer-boy looks, but in the five minutes they'd spent speaking, Cassidy knew he was so much more than that, and the scholarship reinforced the knowledge. "Mum and Dad don't have a lot, so I've been working since, trying to pay my own way."

With those words, she was no longer lowkey impressed, but in awe of the commitment that it would have taken for him to juggle whatever he was studying as well as working enough that he could pay for the myriad things he needed to live in a city as expensive as Sydney.

"Damn, Phoenix, I'm—"

"Phoenix? Sorry to interrupt, but we need you back at the counter," the same young woman who'd served her that first day said. She was wringing a tea towel in her hands and shifting her weight from foot to foot. She clearly hated breaking into their conversation, but Cassidy needed to get back to it as well. "I should be off too. Maybe we can chat more tomorrow?"

"Yeah, sounds great."

* * * * *

Walking with Jacob's arm around her was comfortable. Warmth tingled through her belly, and Cassidy couldn't help her smile. She looked up at the man who had wined and dined her the night before in the most unexpected of restaurants. It was down by the wharf at Woolloomooloo in the basement of what looked to be a dingy old office building. Getting to it had creeped her out a bit, the dimly lit laneway more shadows than anything else. The sign above the steel door was understated, but the food was something else. A wild Asian fusion that was a riot of colour and flavour. They'd drunk warm sake and stumbled into the rideshare when the restaurant closed around them.

She hadn't expected it, thinking that Jacob would go the more traditional route of an upscale restaurant with a view rather than vinyl tablecloths and plastic chairs. But she was beginning to realize that Jacob wasn't the pretentious kind. He didn't aim to impress with money or by throwing around his father's influence. In fact, Jacob seemed reluctant to talk about that part of him, except to say that he was nothing like his old man.

They'd gone back to Jacob's place after—it was closer to Grounds than hers—and, as promised, were going to brunch. Her muscles ached. Every part of her, especially her most intimate, was well used and sated. Jacob had worshipped every inch of her with his lips, his tongue, his fingers, and his cock. Cassidy had lost count of how many times she came. She'd been a sweaty mess when she'd finally passed out, but she'd felt the warm wipe sliding over her skin before Jacob crawled in and pulled her into his arms. They'd stayed like that most of the night, Cassidy using Jacob's shoulder as a pillow, but with the dawn's rays sliding between the cracks in the blinds, she'd slipped down between his legs and finally got to taste him.

Jacob paused just outside the shop next door to Grounds. He chuckled nervously before wiping his palm down his leg. "It's a dead giveaway, you know?" Cassidy turned to face him, clasping his fingers in hers. "When you're nervous, you wipe your hands on your pants." Bringing his knuckles to her lips, she kissed them softly. "You have nothing to worry about. You're charming and sweet. Gorgeous too. If he doesn't like you, it's not because of you. It's because of him, and that's okay. It means that he's not right for us."

"I want to give this to you, Cassie. That was our deal. You're poly, and I want to show you—no, I need to show you—that we fit together. There's something about him..."

"Jacob." Cassidy raised both her hands to his stubbled cheeks and ran her thumbs along the smooth skin on his cheekbones. "You've already shown me that we fit together. I went from hating you to jumping you in a split-second." He licked his lips at the delicious memory and smiled that knowing sexy grin, and Cassidy went up on tip-toe to brush a kiss against his lips. Before it could get heated, before she could lose herself in him, she forced herself back. "Our texts and conversations have given me a glimpse into the person you really are, and I like you. Last night walking to the restaurant I realized something. I've been keeping you at arm's length, telling myself that I can't trust you, but when you motioned for me to walk into that dark alley, I didn't hesitate. I knew you wouldn't take me somewhere dangerous—my head has finally caught up."

He turned and pushed her gently against the window-pane, holding her in place with his hips. The cool surface against her back kept her grounded when his heat made her want to combust. Cassie splayed her hands on the glass, bracing herself when her legs turned to jelly. Jacob tilted her chin up with one hand and ran the backs of his fingers down her cheek to her throat. His touch was a whisper-soft caress, but the fire in his eyes and the press of his bulge against her stomach let Cassidy know exactly what her words had done to him. With his thumb on her pulse point and the other tucking a lock of hair behind her ear, he kissed her. Slow and languid, he made love to her mouth. It had been like that between them the night before too. Passion and fire burning twice as bright as anything Cassidy had ever experienced.

She slipped her hand up the front of his untucked tee and ran her fingertips over his abs, her nails lightly scratching him. He sucked in a breath and pressed their foreheads together. "I like you too," he whispered, pulling back just enough that Cassidy knew he understood not to overwhelm her.

She wasn't ready to admit it yet, but she was falling for Jacob. He'd already crashed through those walls she'd erected around herself. With every press of his lips, every piece of information he gave her about where he'd come from, and the kind of man he strived to be, Cassidy knew he'd soon unlock the vault she'd placed her heart in. He was showing her with every sweet gesture that she could have it all—the career she dreamed of and the great love story in the way she imagined it.

Right on cue, Jacob's stomach rumbled. "We need to get some food in you." Cassidy patted the firm muscle under her fingertips and grasped his hand. "Let's go see if he's in."

Before she could take a step, he tugged her hand, and with a vulnerability that Cassidy had never seen on him before, he asked, "What if he says no?" He looked down and shrugged his shoulders, but Cassidy could see right through the faux casual gesture. "I mean, that's the most likely scenario. He's probably straight, so maybe we should leave me out of the equation. It'll give you a better chance to date him separately."

"No." Cassidy shook her head. "You like him, Jacob. I don't want to start something with him unless you can be involved too, because your feelings matter just as much as mine. I'm not going to date someone that you're attracted to and leave you out."

He squeezed her hand and gave her a small smile. "Okay, let's get some coffee then." Jacob pulled open the door and motioned for her to go first. His hand on the small of her back made her smile up at him, and she leaned in, giving him a half hug.

Jacob stilled, and Cassidy flicked her gaze to the counter. Phoenix stood there glaring at them, his jaw clenched and his fingers squeezing the marker he was holding. His hazel eyes flashed, and he pursed his lips together, his gaze bouncing between them. Cassidy licked her lips, the nerves fluttering around her belly as she took a deep breath and stepped forward. "Hey, you," she murmured, giving him a tentative smile. "This is Jacob."

"Jacob doesn't drink espressos." Phoenix's voice was cold, totally different to the sexy rasp he normally greeted her with. "Or maybe he does, and the ridiculous drink he's been ordering is just to screw with us. Which one is it?"

"No, it's—" she responded, but Jacob's hand on her arm silenced her.

"It's okay," Jacob murmured. He took a deep breath and rested his hand on his leg. Cassidy had seen the move so many times, but he stopped himself, instead flexing his fingers. "I…" He blew out the rest of his breath and laughed before shaking his head.

Jacob was nervous, but Phoenix's reaction told her he didn't know that. He moved out from behind the counter and stood almost chest to chest with Jacob. Half a head taller, Phoenix forced him to look up when he growled, "You should leave and not come back—"

"Phoenix," an older woman snapped. "What's going on?"

"This couple was just leaving." He stepped behind the counter again and wiped the already clean surface with far too much force.

"Take a ten-minute break." He paused midswipe, clenched his jaw and balled up the cloth, shoving it with too much force back under the counter. He stalked through the swing doors into the kitchen before a loud bang sounded. The woman who was clearly Phoenix's boss turned to Jacob and explained, "I apologize for my employee's behaviour. I hope you don't see it as a reflection on Grounds. Can I offer you a coffee on the house?"

Jacob smiled one of those genuine, eye-crinkling smiles. "It's completely okay, but we might come back another time instead. Your espresso is literally a lifesaver."

She laughed and handed him a gift card for free coffees. "Glad to hear our roast is helping you fight the good fight."

He pulled open the door and motioned Cassidy through. But she was confused. Bewildered that he was prepared to give up so easily. She didn't think he was that kind of person; he certainly hadn't been with her. "This way." He pointed to a laneway in the opposite direction from where they'd come. Dumpsters lined one side, and Cassidy held her breath as she hurried past them. "Grounds backs onto this laneway, and I heard a second door slam when Phoenix walked into the kitchen. I don't want to stalk him or anything, but maybe he'll give me a chance to explain if he's still out here."

They rounded the corner only to see Phoenix pacing, both hands in his hair as he looked up at the grey sky. He groaned and ran his hands over his face before shaking his head. "What an arse," he muttered before turning on his heel and pacing toward them. He froze, glaring at Cassidy and then Jacob. "What part of you need to leave did you not understand?"

Jacob rubbed his mouth, and Cassidy squeezed his hand, trying to impart all the encouragement she could. "I owe you an apology," Jacob said quietly. "I wasn't trying to be an arse, but I know that I came across as one. Cassie will tell you I do that quite a bit."

"I don't care what stupid drink you get us to make— you're paying for the damn thing, but if you think it's funny to screw around with the staff so you can big-note yourself? That's a dick move."

"That's not what I was trying to do." Jacob gave him a small smile, one that Cassidy recognized as feigning confidence, and slipped his hands into his pockets before nodding at the chairs pulled under a small awning. "Can we sit for a minute?" Phoenix huffed and rolled his eyes before motioning to the closest one. The other man stayed standing, using the chair sitting kitty-corner to Jacob as a shield between them. Jacob sat and wiped his hands down his pants. "I'm just going to put it all out there, so you understand, but it's not necessary to throw a punch, okay?"

"Why would I hit you?"

"Because straight boys have a tendency to talk with their fists first." Jacob clasped his hands between his knees and sat quietly for a moment staring at them while Phoenix processed his words. But while Jacob sat as still as a statue, Phoenix reacted in the opposite way, letting his eyes roam over Jacob. Cassidy saw heat there. Want and desire coalesced until Phoenix moved around the barrier he'd placed between them. Jacob flinched as Phoenix slowly lowered himself into the chair, and Cassidy rushed to Jacob's side. That need to step in and make sure he was okay was a strange compulsion. She'd never wanted to do it before, but there was no way she could stop herself now. Cassidy curled her hand around his clasped ones and rubbed his back, letting him know that she was there.

"I wouldn't hit you," Phoenix murmured, mirroring Jacob's pose. "It sucks that we have to hide just to stay safe." He paused and added, "I came out to the wrong people a few years ago. But I learned my lesson."

"What happened?" Cassidy asked, a weight settling in her stomach like an anvil. She hated that he was so obviously hurting.

"The usual. Toxic masculinity at its finest." Phoenix shook his head and Jacob tensed, like he was expecting the worst. His voice was flat when he continued, and the muted version of the usually vivacious man tore at her. "I was in my final year at school and the principal was new. He didn't know one of the kids was non-binary. They wore the boys' uniform, because that's what they identified as most of the time, but they wanted to wear a dress to the formal. The principal lost his shit when he overheard what was happening and said boys had to wear suits and the girls a dress. We protested, you know... a whole group of us arrived in dresses. I thought I was safe with them." He huffed out a derisive laugh and his lips curled in disgust. Clasping his hands together and resting his elbows on his knees, Phoenix curled into himself. Cassidy wanted to reach for him, to protect him from the memory in the same way she'd leaped to Jacob's side, but she didn't know if she had the right to.

"We weren't allowed into the formal, so we went and hung out at the sports fields instead. I'd been crushing on my mate for months, and when he started complaining he wouldn't get laid after the dance anymore, I came out to him as bi. I offered to blow him." Phoenix scrubbed his hands down his face and Jacob reached for his knee, clasping it. Their gazes locked and Jake nodded, a silent conversation passing between them. An understanding perhaps? A connection? Cassidy didn't know, but this moment was between the two men she increasingly wanted to share.

"How bad was it?" Jacob asked, his voice low.

"They only got a couple of punches in before the coppers came looking for homeless people in the park. We all took off, but I ran in the opposite direction to the others. I hid out on the farm until I could move here and haven't seen any of them since. Since then... well, I've been circumspect about who knows."

"I'm not out to many people either," Jacob sympathized. "There's no way I could be at work, or to my father."

Phoenix sighed, the heaviness between them settling into a comfortable silence. "I haven't told anyone else about what happened before. Not even my folks."

Cassidy appreciated what he was saying without speaking the words. He trusted them. He understood why Jacob had been reticent to open up to him sooner. Their shared experiences of bi-and pan-phobic behaviour made Cassidy stabby, but sharing it allowed the trust between them to take root. Their blossoming friendship was beautiful to watch.

Cassidy realized that Jacob hadn't let go of Phoenix's knee when he squeezed it again and Phoenix's gaze dropped. Jacob startled, snatching his hand away, gripping hers instead. She loved that he'd automatically gone to her. There was no drawn-out thought process, no analyzing whether he should. He'd acted on instinct, and that spoke loud and clear to Cassidy—Jacob trusted her too.

Leaning back, Phoenix crossed his arms and looked expectantly at Jacob. "But while we both have reasons why we're not out, it still doesn't explain what you were doing with your orders."

Jacob nodded. "You're right. It doesn't. When I walked into the coffee shop that first time, I was like a goldfish. All I could do was open my mouth and stare." He huffed out a laugh, and his cheeks turned a rosy pink. "You're really handsome." Jacob pulled his T-shirt away from his chest as if he was too hot and shook his head. "I got all tongue-tied and stupid and said that I'd have whatever the other guy was having without even hearing what his order was. When you read it back to me, I don't know, I..." He sighed, and his shoulders slumped. Jacob's words were quiet when he said, "I still hadn't figured out how to speak to you."

The silence stretched out, but it wasn't uncomfortable. Rather it was as if the two men were assessing each other, but when Phoenix's intense gaze shifted to hers, Cassidy swallowed and supplied, "I came in the next day because Jacob told me how good-looking you were. I asked you to deliver the coffee to him to give him a chance to speak to you while there weren't as many people waiting for you."

"So, what, all the talk about him auditioning for the boyfriend role is just bullshit? And our conversation yesterday? You don't owe me anything, but it's pretty shitty to lie like you've been doing. Just say you have a mate who's interested."

"I told you the truth," Cassidy said. "We're still working things out between us."

"Yeah, okay." He motioned with his thumb over his shoulder to the door and said, "I need to get back inside. The boss is already pissed with me."

"Are we invited back in?" Cassidy asked.

Phoenix shook his head slowly and retreated a step. "No, I think it'd be better if you didn't." He hesitated with his hand on the doorknob. "I'm not... It's not..." Running his free hand through his hair and pushing back the floppy strands that had fallen in front of his face, he added, "Look, I'm flattered. I really am. But you should go."

Six

Phoenix

"Come on, man. You need to unwind," his roomie complained. Trav wanted to hook up, because, like a superstitious athlete, he went out to get laid the weekend before every one of his exams. The only time he hadn't picked up, he'd failed an exam. Phoenix didn't have the time, though. He had four exams to study for, and one of them—his theories of law class—was going to be a ball-breaker. It was the first exam he had scheduled, and he hadn't even looked at the other subjects he was taking. Yet he knew he still needed more time. The nuances of each theory, how they applied to modern legal frameworks and coloured interpretations of history, to-gether with the real-world impact on anyone who didn't fit within the boxes created by white, middle-class, middle-aged, cis, het men. It was a subject he had a passion for, one that was a foundation for the sort of professional he wanted to become. But before that, Phoenix needed a few more hours to study. Then he needed a solid fourteen hours the next day. By the time Monday rolled around, he would be set. Maybe. Hopefully.

"Nah, I still have another few chapters to review." Phoenix lit up the screen on his phone. It was 10:00 p.m. He'd been at it for nearly six hours after doing a full day's shift at Grounds. He rubbed his eyes and stifled a yawn.

"Dude."

He shouldn't even be contemplating going out—he needed sleep more than anything else—but a beer or three would go down especially well. If he tried to get any rest, he'd just lie awake reciting principles from Dworkin, Hobbes, Rawls, and Kant and trying to anticipate the exam question. His heart rate sped up, and he had to consciously unclench his fists.

Phoenix groaned. Trav was right—Phoenix did need to unwind before he fried his brain. Or had an anxiety attack. "Yeah, okay. I'll come out, but I'm not staying late. I can't afford tomorrow to be a write-off." He still had a whole module in the class to look at again.

"No worries, mate." His roomie's grin was infectious. But when he looked Phoenix over, his nose crinkled. "Get into something less—" He waved his hand in Phoenix's general direction. "that, and we'll go."

He barked out a laugh. His grey sweats with holes in the knees—the only thing he was wearing—were definitely not appropriate for anything other than studying.

"There's this new club—"

"Nope, no clubs or we'll be there all night." When Trav opened his mouth to protest, Phoenix held up a hand, silencing him. "I can't, mate. I'll go to the pub with you and the guys, we'll shoot some pool and have a beer, but that's it. If you want to move on after I leave, go for it."

Trav rolled his eyes. "One drink at the pub and then we go dancing. You'll be in someone's bed within two hours, tops."

Phoenix laughed. "That's your ritual, not mine, and you have far too much confidence in my abilities."

"No, I really don't. I've seen the way you pull people in. One minute you're dancing, then the next you're zipping up after getting a BJ. The only difference is whether your hook-up is teetering on high heels or wiping his beard." Trav was exaggerating. Kind of. Phoenix enjoyed sex, preferred the no-strings-attached kind, and really wasn't fussy about the gender of his partner. When he was attracted to someone, he went with it. Women were beautiful. Men were too. "So, the question is, will it be a he or she tonight?"

Trav raised an eyebrow when Phoenix didn't answer. The question was a loaded one, and he didn't have an easy answer to it. He'd been obsessing over the flirtatious blonde who'd graced his shop every day for the last couple of weeks, but Jacob had haunted his dreams. Both of them were equally beautiful, all suits and style. But it was more than that too. Cassidy's confidence and the way she teased and tempted him made him weak in the knees, and Jacob's shy, fumbling side brought out the protector in him. He couldn't help but imagine what it would be like to see him without inhibitions and her without clothes.

He chuckled. "I know that look," Trav teased. "Who is it?"

"That's the thing. There's two of them. I didn't know they were a couple until today. They've both been into Grounds, but always separately. Then they show up today and the girl I've been flirting with introduces me to the guy she's dating, but who apparently has the hots for me too."

Trav blinked like he needed a second to process Phoenix's words, then opened his mouth and roared with laughter. "First world problems, mate." He shook his head. "You're not seriously complaining about the possibility of a threesome, are you?" He gripped Phoenix's shoulders and shook him gently. "Phoenix, my man, you need to pull your head outta your arse and jump on that shit while you can. You're gonna be chained to a desk seventy hours a week before you know it and you'll regret not getting a piece of that action if you don't hit it now."

"That's totally not what they were suggesting," Phoenix scoffed. "They probably just have an open relationship, and I don't like getting involved in complications." He had a lot going on, and dealing with anything else was more than he could manage. The last thing he needed was to get involved in something that could be complicated. He was finishing up at Grounds in a few weeks, and he didn't want to leave on a sour note. Cassidy and Jacob had already shown up there to hash things out while he was there.

Trav rolled his eyes. "Keep telling yourself that, mate." He opened Phoenix's cupboard and waved to it. "Get dressed. We're leaving in twenty."

* * * * *

One drink at the pub had turned into five, but Phoenix had passed the point of caring. Going out was exactly what he'd needed. His limbs were loose, and his mind was focussed on something else. He was grateful for Trav's insistence that he go with them—grinding up against a cute twink was a whole lot more fun than his mind going around in circles trying to tie whisps of knowledge together.

The band playing covers of nineties grunge songs was brilliant. Lithium was a standout, their guitars screaming as the crowd shouted the chorus. The pub was packed too; bodies pressed against one another as they danced.

He smiled at his mates, giving them a thumbs up for pushing him to have a last hurrah with them. They were the best. Great blokes and top friends.

Arms up in the air, Phoenix welcomed the music flowing through him, his hips moving with the pretty boy who was draped over him. Straddling the guy's leg, Phoenix rolled his hips and groaned when the other man's thigh rubbed against his nuts.

A shot appeared in front of him, and Phoenix looked up to see Trav's drunken smile. Taking the glass, he raised it in a toast before tipping his head back and downing the fiery tequila. He hissed with the burn and spun his partner around until his butt was flush against Phoenix's groin. With hands on his hips, he rubbed against him, sending his cock from half mast to a fully-fledged iron rod.

But Phoenix wasn't fixated on him. His thoughts were wandering to them.

He couldn't get those long blonde waves out of his mind or the painted lips of the woman who'd shamelessly challenged him to check out her boyfriend. And check him out Phoenix had. The way he'd licked his lips and nervously wiped his hands on his jeans before sucking in a breath and confessing his attraction had riled Phoenix up like nothing else. It was as if Jacob had been saving up the words, then sprung a leak, the admission finally bursting free.

Phoenix let his eyes slip closed, and he tilted his head back, imagining what it would be like to have Cassidy pressed between him and Jacob. Which one of them would take her mouth? And would she let the other kiss her throat while he toyed with her nipples? Or rubbed his dick against her arse? It was probably a ridiculous fantasy, but one he was going to indulge in, nevertheless.

The reality of his immediate future was too nerve-wracking to contemplate at midnight on a Saturday night, and concentrating on something—anything—other than his exams was almost a necessity. All that stood between him and the podium on graduation day was those four exams. After the final one, he only had a week to transition from being a broke student into a still-broke junior solicitor. It was exciting and terrifying at the same time. Not having upcoming assignments or exams hovering over him would, hopefully, mean that he could enjoy life for a bit. Go out for drinks, eat with friends, party on a weekend. But for the first time, he also wouldn't have the security blanket of knowing his place in the world. Up to that point, he'd always been a student. Everything would be different in a couple of weeks—new job, new place, and even his clothes were going to change. Gone were the days he could show up looking like a slob. No, he'd be wearing a suit every day, have to have his hair cut neatly and face cleanshaven. He wasn't even sure he would recognize himself.

Phoenix couldn't tell whether the buzz from the alcohol was wearing off, but he wasn't ready to face the coming week just yet. He needed to block it out, just for a little bit longer. When the song ended, he motioned to the bar, breaking away from the cutie he'd been dancing with, before ordering another round of shots. But when he managed to work his way back to the high-topped tables they'd been dancing near, he couldn't find two out of the three of his mates. He passed a glass to Trav and sucked a shot back himself, shaking off the fire roaring down his throat. Trav picked up a second one and shouted, "Can't let 'em go to waste. Bottoms up," before he tilted his head back. Phoenix did the same, downing the two remaining glasses.

The strobe light went off, giving him an out-of-body experience. The room spun. Tequila was a vicious lover, and she always left him worse for wear the next day, but he appreciated how fast-acting it was. Phoenix swayed on his feet, the dance floor moving like a balance board under them. He recognized the Silverchair song he'd heard a few too many times playing on the speakers at Grounds, but he couldn't find the words to sing along.

It was warm. Really hot, in fact. Stiflingly so. Phoenix yanked off his tee and dropped it on the table. He had to get out of his clothes.

He flicked open his belt buckle, but a hand on his stopped him short. A man's hand. Long fingers and criss-crossing veins with blond hairs and a natural tan. Phoenix licked his lips. He could imagine that hand on other parts of him.

Looking up, he laughed. That was new; hallucinating had never been a side effect of tequila before, but anything was possible, he supposed.

Before him was the couple he'd been obsessing over, the both of them looking drop-dead gorgeous.

"Are you sshtalking me?" he asked, poking his finger at Jacob's chest, the digit bouncing off a firm pec. "Mmm… yummy." He tried to lick his lips, but something went wrong.

His tongue wasn't working. Why wasn't it working?

Oh well, it didn't matter. Phoenix didn't care; he could speak with actions instead. He reached out, pulling Cassidy to him. She was so petite, fitting against him like they were made to be together. The thought, the fantasy, made his dick pulse in approval. He ground on her, pressing against her softness as he kept dancing. But the floor was moving too much to balance properly.

He saw Jacob's mouth move as he spoke. But Phoenix couldn't hear him properly. He leaned closer, but the floor lurched under him, making him stumble. "Fucking floor," he muttered, reaching for Cassidy to balance himself. But he missed. Phoenix sucked in a breath, his arms starting to cartwheel. Jacob shot his arm out, steadying him. He was a good bloke. The kind that didn't let his mates fall on their arses.

Sexy too. Jacob wore skinny black jeans that Phoenix wanted to peel off. He could do the same to the grey tee too. Except he was going to use his teeth to take them off. He'd never seen the man's hair loose around his face either. The man bun he always wore was hot, but like this, Jacob was smoking.

He looked pissed too. Pursed lips and a glint in his eyes that looked a lot like disappointment had Phoenix pushing away from him. "What are you doing here?"

"My mate's band." Jacob motioned to the stage, shouting over the music. "He told me they were playing, so we came in to listen. You?"

"Wanted to get laid." Then Phoenix shrugged. "Got trashed instead."

"How much have you had to drink?"

He wavered, the floor rocking like a rowboat in the ocean. Cassidy slipped under his arm, steadying him, and rested her hand on his belly. He groaned. Those delicate hands so close to where he really wanted them were sending sparks of awareness through him. His mind swirled, unfocused, but his body knew exactly what it wanted.

"You're pretty," he slurred, looking at Jacob but meaning both of them.

Cassidy tilted her face up, watching him, but he couldn't remember why. Phoenix swallowed. His eyes were drawn down by the plunging neckline of her red singlet. It didn't cover much skin, and the curve of her breasts where the V-neck met was too tempting. He wanted to run his tongue along the swell as he buried himself inside her. Her nostrils flared and her eyes darkened, while the other arm around his waist tightened.

"Good to know," Jacob muttered. "But I think you've had enough. How about we take you home?" The heat of his breath washed against Phoenix's throat, and he shuddered. Had he described his thoughts out loud? Phoenix was beyond caring. Truth be told, all he wanted was to be in the middle of these two, exploring every inch of their perfect bodies. "Don't worry, we want exactly the same thing. But not tonight. Not when you're so drunk you might not even remember."

Huh, he must have said that out loud too.

They led him toward the doors, Trav giving him a double thumbs up when they passed him. Phoenix tried to resist. He tried to persuade them to stay, but Jacob insisted. Cassidy never let him go. Those red fingernails splayed on his abs as she helped guide him up the street. Her heels clicked, and her hips swished as she helped Jacob manhandle him into a taxi. Phoenix ran his fingertips down her stomach to the button on her jeans. He wished he could see her from the back, just to feast on how well he knew the blue denim would frame her arse. She slid in next to him while Jacob went around the other side and pulled the door closed.

"Where to?" the taxi driver asked. "And if he spews in my cab, there's a two-hundred-dollar cleaning fee."

"He won't," Jacob assured him, then turned to Phoenix and asked, "Where are we taking you?"

"Fishbowl dorms." Jacob nodded, and Phoenix wasn't sure how he'd understood. He wasn't even sure he understood the direction to his place, and he lived there. Cassidy rattled something off to the driver, but Phoenix didn't hear. He couldn't stop looking at Jacob's blue eyes. The way his lips parted and his pink tongue licked across the plump flesh… it was erotic as hell. Phoenix leaned in, watching as Jacob's eyes began to slowly close. A hand closed around his own, slim fingers sliding between his digits. Cassidy. He froze. Looked down, blinked, and sucked in a breath.

What was he doing? They were a couple, and he'd been just about to pash Jacob. His dick throbbed in his jeans, reminding him that he wanted a whole lot more than that too. Phoenix reached down to resituate himself, pressing the heel of his palm against the base of his cock and trying to pull himself back from the edge of control. He'd gone commando. The zip bit into the soft skin being pressed against it by the hard ridge of his erection, and, for once, he wished he'd worn the last remaining pair of clean boxers in his cupboard. The groan from next to him was rough, all man and filled with desire. Phoenix couldn't help but squeeze his shaft with the sound.

He hadn't even realized that they were moving, never mind having arrived at their destination. He tried to pull out his wallet, but Cassidy stilled his hand. "We've got this. Come on," she directed. "We'll take you to your room." Phoenix grinned and followed her, eager to please the beautiful woman. She'd just granted his wish to see her backside in those sexy-as-sin jeans. He hadn't noticed the red heels, but he was seeing them now, unable to decide whether he wanted to see them propped on his shoulders or wrapped around Jacob's waist. He stumbled, the concrete footpath getting closer. Or was that the wall of the building he'd nearly lurched into? Jacob hoisted his arm around his shoulder and pulled Phoenix close. Shirtless, he could feel Jacob's hand on his waist and knew exactly what position he wanted to be in.

"I like your shoes," he slurred to Cassidy, frustrated that his tongue didn't seem to want to work. "They'd look sexy digging into my shoulders."

"Come on, Casanova. You have all the lines tonight, but you need to sober up." She grabbed his hand while Jacob ducked out from under his arm and slipped behind him, sliding his hands into Phoenix's pockets. Those wandering fingers would be the death of him. Phoenix pressed his arse back against Jacob's heat, and the other man froze, stilling his search. The bulge Jacob was sporting was unmistakable, and Phoenix reached back with his free hand to haul the other man closer. He let his head fall back onto Jacob's shoulder and whimpered when Jacob's fingers tightened on his hips.

"You're making this really hard," Jacob grunted.

"Shift your hands a little more to the middle, and you'll see just how much," he moaned, practically begging Jacob to grope him. But the other man was on a mission to deny him, and they dragged Phoenix into the building before taking him up the lift toward his dorm room in the student housing high-rise.

Trav would still be gone for hours. It was too short a timeframe, but he could get each of them off at least once before he stumbled back in. He loved a woman in charge and didn't resist when Cassidy tugged him toward his bed while Jacob switched on the lamp. "This one yours?" When he nodded, she pushed him down. Phoenix fell back, landing so he was lying diagonally across the single. One foot was still on the floor, the other by his knee. Cassidy lowered herself to her knees, and Phoenix moaned. She was something else. Sensual and playful at the same time. She bit down on her lip and blinked slowly at him, one side of her red lips tilting up in a seductive smile as she pushed his legs open further and tugged off his boots with a flourish. Peeling off his socks got him a peek of her tongue between her teeth and a wink. Phoenix palmed himself, lifting his hips into his fist as he watched her watch him. The next moan he let loose was breathier than he expected, but she was so damn tempting there between his legs. He really wanted to touch her.

"Enough of that," Jacob chided, and Phoenix froze. Cassidy chuckled and shifted away as Phoenix's gaze snapped up to the man hovering over him and licked his lips. His throat suddenly parched as he watched the gorgeous man before him. Fuck, as if it weren't bad enough before, now he had two people he was desperate to reach out and touch.

Phoenix huffed out a laugh, surprised at how fantastic his night had turned out to be. He was drunk and horny, and the two people in front of him would undoubtedly satisfy every one of the fantasies running rampant through his hazy mind. "Drink this," Jacob ordered, snapping Phoenix's attention away from his dick. He took the proffered glass and opened his throat, practically pouring the water down it before handing it back empty. With a smirk, he watched as Jacob swallowed, realizing Phoenix had no gag reflex. When his cheeks flushed pink, Phoenix's hand found his cock again, squeezing it. How far down did that colour spread? Jacob passed him a second glass and wrapped cold fingers around his wrist, tugging his hand away from his shaft. Pressing two tablets onto his palm, he added, "It's paracetamol. Take them and drink up. You'll need both to ward off a hangover tomorrow with the way you were downing shots."

Cassidy slid her hands on either side of his hips and tugged down the covers he'd been lying on, and Jacob lifted his legs onto the bed before popping the button on his jeans. "Lift your hips," Cassidy instructed. Phoenix smiled, meeting her gaze as she unzipped him.

"You're so pretty. I wanna have your babies."

Cassidy laughed. "You don't want me to have yours?"

"Nuh-uh." He shook his head. Jacob reached over, grasping his jeans and tugging them down. Phoenix hummed, and Jacob sputtered.

"Shit," he muttered. "You better remember tomorrow that we didn't take advantage of you. Next time don't go commando when you get drunk. People will see your junk."

"Hmm, was hoping you'd see it anyway," he murmured, fighting back a yawn. "Touch it, even. Fill me up."

"Not tonight, sexy."

When Jacob had his jeans off, leaving Phoenix bared to them, his hard cock lying against his hip, Cassidy lifted the covers up to his chest. She leaned down, kissing his forehead, and Phoenix wrapped a hand around his cock while he lifted his lips to her. She obliged, brushing a soft kiss over them. Phoenix reached out, trying to keep her in place, but she didn't linger, stepping back out of his reach far too quickly.

"Night, Phoenix," Jacob uttered.

Phoenix held out his free hand for Jacob to take, and the other man stepped forward. Phoenix tugged hard, pulling him off balance until Jacob fell forward and braced his hand on the pillow beside Phoenix's face. Surprise lit up those sapphire eyes, and Phoenix lurched up, wrapping his free hand around Jacob's nape and pulling him closer. "You make me wanna be brave," Phoenix whispered. "I wanna kiss you."

"I do too," Jacob replied, his voice a deep rumble that was like a stroke to his already hard cock. "But you're drunk."

"I always kiss men in the dark," Phoenix murmured. Jake tilted his head and studied him, clearly trying to understand Phoenix's topic switch. "But it's light now and I wanna kiss you." Phoenix stroked his cock, the liquor in his veins making him brave. He wasn't closeted, but he never flaunted his sexuality. Not anymore. But Jacob made him want to be brave enough to say "fuck you" to the world and take those pouty lips with his.

He flicked his gaze down, watching Jacob's lips part, before Phoenix raked his eyes lower. Jacob's hand was pressed to his jeans, pushing down on his rigid shaft. He was big, the outline showing just how much of a handful he would be. The sight snapped the fine thread of control Phoenix's liquor-soaked brain was holding onto.

Squeezing his cock so he didn't go off like a bottle rocket, Phoenix crushed their mouths together, taking the kiss he desperately wanted. Jacob froze momentarily, then melted with his touch, his lips parting again as Phoenix's tongue explored his mouth. Jacob tasted like beer and kissed him like a man possessed.

Soft lips and a deft tongue mixed with rough stubble was a sensory overload. Phoenix moaned, arching up to get closer. Jacob bit his lip, gently sucking as he let it slip from his mouth. Phoenix shuddered, falling back to the bed. Need pulsed through him, and he jacked himself slowly, resisting the urge to work himself into a frenzy. The other man had a different idea, though, turning to press his lips to Phoenix's wrist before capturing his lips again for a slow kiss that was all sex.

His legs tensed, his abs dancing as his balls drew up, ready to fire their load. Pre-cum lubed the stroke of his hand along his length as Phoenix fucked his fist.

"I want you," he gasped. "Both of you."

"Not tonight. But soon," Jacob promised. Then he licked his lips, his gaze flicking south. He watched as Phoenix shuttled his fist up and down his length. A strangled groan sounded in the back of Jacob's throat, and he palmed himself, adjusting his erection. That was all the invitation Phoenix needed. He kicked off the covers, planted his feet on the bed, and thrust his hips into his fist. Palming his balls, he rolled them in his hands and snuck his middle finger down, rubbing his hole. Cassidy's breathy moan and Jacob's low growl of approval had Phoenix working himself faster, his shaft harder than it had ever been.

"Fuck," he gasped as sensation raced over the head of his cock down to his balls. The tingle at the base of his spine was the only warning he got before he erupted into his hand, stripes of cum landing on his belly and up his chest. He closed his eyes, breathing hard.

* * * * *

He woke to sunlight streaming in the gap between the half-drawn curtains, his head pounding and his mouth as dry as the Sahara. He cracked his eyes open and winced, the light spearing his brain. He rolled over, and the skin on his happy trail pulled.

He sat up and grasped his head, swallowing back the urge to yak. He was naked as the day he was born, and he had flakes of dried cum all over him. What the hell? The dream he'd had the night before was vivid, but he hadn't come on himself like a teenager... well, since he was a teenager. At least his roomie was still out for the count. One less thing to explain.

SEVEN

Phoenix

P hoenix stepped out of the building to a warm night. He'd done it. He'd survived his exams. Centuries of knowledge packed into thirteen weeks of classes, millions of words that he'd read and absorbed, countless hours of studying on little sleep and a blood caffeine level that should have been fatal. All of it had come down to twelve hours of frantic writing. Now it was over. He was done. Free. Finished. Phoenix knew in his gut he'd passed all the subjects he'd taken, but there was still a shadow of anxiety hovering over him, one that wouldn't lift until he got the official word.

Graduation would be in a few weeks. He started his new job in a week. Before his first day, he had to shift out of the student accommodation. He was moving in with his friends—four of them living in a townhouse. It was worth the sky-high amount they'd be paying for rent. Within walking distance of the ferry terminal, they'd skip the bumper-to-bumper traffic for a forty-minute ferry ride into the city.

Everything else was within walking distance, so none of them needed a car for everyday use.

But moving was tomorrow's problem. Tonight was all about celebrating. They were partying. He was supposed to watch the sun come up the next morning with his friends, tipsy and exhausted after a night of dancing. So why couldn't he get excited about it?

A woman passed them, and Phoenix got a whiff of her perfume. He stopped walking, inhaling deeply. He closed his eyes and smiled. The scent was familiar. She wore the same perfume as Cassidy. He'd missed seeing her at Grounds during the couple of shifts he'd taken this week, but since he wasn't there during his normal times, it wasn't surprising that they hadn't crossed paths.

"You coming?" Rachael called. She was the most focussed of their group. Day one of university, she'd announced she would be a partner of a law firm by the time she was thirty. He had no doubts she would.

"Sorry, yeah," he muttered, jogging to catch up to the others.

Trav clapped him on the back. "Keep up, mate," he teased. Trav was a financial planning major. A whiz with numbers. Stevo was a cyber security engineer. He said his job was to design systems that were impenetrable to hackers. But he'd been voted as the one most likely to be doing the hacking. He wouldn't get caught—he was far too good for that—but he definitely tested how secure others' systems were. They were all completely different, but their friendship had stood the test of time. Trav and Stevo had attended high school together, and Trav was Phoenix's roomie during that first semester together. They'd shared ever since, and with Stevo hanging around, the three of them had become tight. Rachael had joined their group almost from the first day too, becoming one of their closest friends.

They'd survived university.

Now it was time to let loose.

If only he could shake the funk that had enveloped him. He didn't even know what it was, except that it was bringing him down.

They rounded the corner and walked the block to their first stop, the same pub he'd seen Cassidy and Jacob at. He wished he could see them again. He'd obsessed over how intense his drunken dreams were. The first one was still so vivid that he could remember every detail of it like he'd lived it. Replaying it over and over in his mind's eye like a movie had left his hand and his cock raw. He hated that he'd woken up, or something had disturbed his dream—he couldn't remember which—and hadn't kissed Cassidy the way he had Jacob. Now it was crunch time. He only had a few shifts left at Grounds before he started his new job. Unless she showed up at the coffee shop and they exchanged numbers, he'd never find out if either one of them could kiss like he'd imagined.

The pub was hopping, but Phoenix was content to hover around the edges. He just wasn't feeling it. Maybe his friends wouldn't even notice if he bailed. Was it exhaustion hitting him? The high from the constant caffeine-fuelled

adrenaline-laced anxiety he got during exams finally waning? Or was it an insane preoccupation with two people
who'd haunted his dreams stopping him from letting loose?
If that was it, he was being ridiculous—he wasn't out to
hook up. He was there to celebrate with friends. Like a
weight lifting, something clicked into place, and Phoenix
smiled, relief filling him. He was ready to finally enjoy himself after the hardest slog of his life.

He decided not to look too closely at why he was finally
okay with it, though. That would need far more introspec-
tion than he was prepared for on a Saturday night out with
his mates.

"Let's move on," he suggested to Trav, wanting to go to
a club. "Where are Rach and Stevo?" His mate didn't answer, his stare never leaving the dance floor. When he
pointed, Phoenix followed the direction and his eyes widened in surprise. Right there on the dance floor, wrapped in
each other's arms with their lips locked, were the two most
unlikely people to see together. They were polar opposites,
Rachael uptight and driven while Steve was a grab-life-by-
the-balls kind and see what trouble he could get up to. They
clashed all the time, yelling at each other about one thing
or another, and yet there they were. Maybe the fights were
more sexual tension than actual disagreement. "Holy shit,"
Phoenix uttered.

"Didn't see that one coming. Do we ask if they want to
come with us?" Trav asked.

"If we interrupt, they probably won't look at each other again, and then we'll have to deal with both getting pissy at us. Let's just text them."

Trav messaged their friends while Phoenix led the way, pushing through the crowd until they were outside. The queue of people lining up to get into the pub stretched half-way around the block, all of them talking and laughing ani-matedly as they waited. Phoenix was excited to get down and party, and while he enjoyed the pub, he wanted the at-mosphere of a club. Music so loud he couldn't think, and shots. He could have had both at the pub, but he needed to get out of his head, and dancing was the best way to do it. With Rach and Stevo doing their thing, he and Trav could get serious.

"What's up, man? A few minutes ago you were acting like you didn't want to be here. Now you're dragging me to a club," Trav asked when Phoenix had to slow his steps to allow Trav to keep up.

"I dunno." He shrugged. "I was tired—this semester was brutal—but I'm good now."

He eyed him closely, not believing Phoenix for a mo-ment, but he let it go. "Okay," he conceded. Phoenix knew he had questions, and Trav wouldn't hold off asking them forever, but his mate wanted to party too. Priorities and all that.

They continued on, reaching the windows of a swanky restaurant. Inside, the lighting was dim, tables with white linen tablecloths that reached the floor, gleaming silver-ware and crystal glasses. Before his eyes, a woman in a charcoal suit with her blonde hair in a tight bun stepped onto the path. She was surrounded by men in suits—the proverbial rose among thorns. But one of the men stood out. Black suit, his own blond hair pulled back in a bun. Phoenix sucked in a breath, his steps stuttering to a halt as the woman looked around, her gaze locking on his. Her red lips turned up in a sultry smile, and Phoenix flushed, heat zinging through his veins to sizzle his nerve endings. Cassidy. The woman triggered an awareness in him like no other person had ever done. Except for one. The man standing right next to her. Jacob.

"Damn." Trav whistled low. "Even I can appreciate that they're hot."

"Keep your hands to yourself," Phoenix shot back, his hackles rising. He wasn't one of those protective alpha jealous types, but he wanted to be when around them.

Trav chuckled. "I thought I recognized them. They're the same two who took you home before exams." Phoenix opened his mouth to question his friend on what the hell he was talking about when Jacob turned and noticed him too. "I thought for sure I wouldn't see you until late the next day, but there you were, tucked into bed like a good boy when I got home."

"They took me home?" Phoenix whispered to him, his tone filled with horror.

"Yeah, mate. At least I assume they did. We left a couple of hours after you did, and you were already fast asleep when I got there."

"Fuuuuck," he breathed. Cassidy and Jacob were already walking toward them, wide smiles on their faces. "Hey, you guys."

"Are you out partying or commiserating?" Jacob asked, his brow furrowed as he looked at Phoenix.

"Definitely celebrating," Trav explained when Phoenix couldn't tear his gaze away from Jacob's lips. He'd tasted them? For real? He trembled, wanting to reach out and pull the man to him. Or Cassidy. Fuck. He swallowed, remembering how he'd touched himself. Was that real too? Jacob dropped his gaze down Phoenix's body and licked his lips. *Fuuuuck.* It was real. He shot his gaze to Cassidy, an apology on his lips, but she wasn't looking at him. No, she was focussed on her boyfriend, giving him an indulgent smile.

Open relationship. Complications he didn't need.

Phoenix took a step back, trying to put some distance between them. When had they shifted so close? Trav clamped his hand on Phoenix's shoulder, and he turned, finding him grinning. "You should come with us. We're on our way to Ember." Phoenix shot him a look, but Trav's smile only widened, a cheeky twinkle in his eye. The bastard knew exactly what he was doing.

Jacob looked to Cassidy, clearly leaving the decision to her. "I'm not really dressed to go dancing, but if you don't mind me hanging around in my work clothes, we'd love to come."

"Sorry, what was your name?" Trav asked in that professional phone voice he put on, holding his hand out to shake. Cassidy introduced them, both shaking hands with

Trav, and Phoenix ground his teeth, glaring at his so-called friend. Trav laughed. "Well, Cassidy, there's nothing hotter than a woman in a power suit." He wiggled his eyebrows at her, and Phoenix stood taller, a growl of possession sounding in the back of his throat. He knew he was staking his claim—over both of them, not just Cassidy. He knew it was primitive and ridiculous, but he couldn't help it. They were his, and Trav was not going to charm himself into Cassidy's bed.

"Okay, arse kisser. That's enough." He steered Trav to the side and inserted himself between his overly flirtatious friend and his couple. Yes, his. He liked the sound of that.

Cassidy and Jacob both checked their jackets at the club, and when Phoenix got a good look at the couple, he salivated. With her hair pulled back, it left the long line of her neck to the thin straps of the silk camisole open for his lips to caress the creamy skin there. Her breasts, those handfuls of perfection, almost distracted him from the lusciousness of her butt framed by the high waistline and form-fitting skirt. The heels she wore only highlighted how gorgeous her legs were, and they reminded him of the red ones he wished had been propped on his shoulders. Phoenix shivered and blinked, willing his cock to behave. He tore his gaze away from her, only to land on her boyfriend, whose rear end rivalled hers for biteability.

Trav snorted out a laugh and clapped him on the shoulder. "You have it bad. When they want to leave, don't stick around because of me." Phoenix looked at him, about to protest, but Trav shook his head and shoved him forward.

The club was dark except for disco balls reflecting the coloured spotlights turning in random patterns over the dance floor. A bar lined one end, and at the back of the room on a raised platform, red velvet ropes cordoned off the VIP area. Trav headed straight to the bar, but when Phoenix moved to follow, Cassidy grasped his wrist and led both him and Jacob to the dance floor. He didn't know how she did it, but within seconds, she had him wrapped around her back, and Jacob pressed to her front. She rested her head back on his shoulder and lifted her arm around his nape, holding him in place. But she need not have worried. Phoenix didn't want to be anywhere else but pressed against this woman.

Jacob ran his fingertips along the rolled-up sleeves of his button-down shirt, then over his forearms, sending shivers through Phoenix. His semi stirred again, thickening in the tight confines of his ripped jeans until he was hard and pressed against the curvaceous goodness of Cassidy's arse. He felt rather than heard the purr in the back of her throat, but Jacob must have seen something. He drew them in, one hand slipping into Phoenix's jeans pocket and the other moving to Cassidy's hip. He leaned in and pressed a kiss to Cassidy's lips before teasing her mouth open with the tip of his tongue. The view Phoenix had was unparalleled, and he watched as their tongues tangled. He splayed his hands on Cassidy's ribs and ran his nose along the shell of her ear, breathing in the scent he couldn't get enough of. Sucking her lobe into his mouth, he bit down gently and hummed when gooseflesh broke out over her skin. Phoenix licked his way down her throat, kissing and tasting the soft skin there as he inched his hands up. When Jacob's hand landed on his, Phoenix froze, but the other man wasn't having it. He shifted Phoenix's hand until it rested over Cassidy's breast and squeezed the hand he still had pressed in Phoenix's pocket, grabbing his butt and pulling him tighter against Cassidy.

She whimpered, and Jacob growled in approval. "Feel how much we want you?" he asked. "Is he hard, Cass?" Cassidy nodded frantically, and Jacob's eyes locked on his. They wavered closer until their lips were a hair's breadth away.

"Please," she begged. "I want to watch you again." Her words kicked Phoenix into action, and he closed the distance to the man he'd wanted from the moment he'd set eyes on him. Their lips crashed together in a frantic kiss. Teeth clashed, and their tongues parried, licking away the sting. Jacob tasted of chocolate and something rich—Bourbon, maybe—and Phoenix couldn't get enough. He cupped Cassidy's breasts, flicking his thumbs over the hardened peaks of her nipples, and ground against her arse as he kissed her boyfriend. Fuck avoiding complications. He wanted this so bad.

Jacob broke away panting and rested his forehead against Cassidy's.

"It wasn't a dream, was it? Trav said you took me home. You kissed me, didn't you?"

"You kissed him," Cassidy murmured. "We both wanted you, but you were drunk."

Jacob slid his hand up to cup her throat, and Cassidy turned to Phoenix. "I want you too," he uttered as his lips found hers. Where Jacob's kiss was wild passion, hers was a smoulder, slow and deep until she'd explored his mouth and had his toes curling in his white skate shoes. She was half his size but clearly had control.

"You're beautiful together," Jacob murmured, kissing a line up Cassidy's throat before swapping to Phoenix and pushing his collar out of the way. "Want to see you both naked. Watch you bury yourself in our woman."

Phoenix groaned. That word. *Our*. It lit a fire in him. Made him want things that he'd thought were impossible. He'd dreamed night after night that he could have them, but he'd written it off as an impossibility. Now, that word was giving him hope. And a raging boner. Jacob gently bit down on the tendon in his throat, sucking on Phoenix's skin, no doubt leaving a mark. Phoenix revelled in the possession. His breath stuttered and his cock pulsed in his jeans. "Keep talking like that, and I'll come all over myself."

"You have no idea how much we wanted to lick it off you," Cassie murmured. "You were so bold, letting us watch you wrap your hand around your cock and making yourself come."

Phoenix closed his eyes, his psyche fighting the confusion between being blindingly aroused and mortified. Arousal won out, and Phoenix thrust against Cassidy's arse, grinding his aching erection against her curves.

"We walked out of that room and barely got into the stairwell. I wanted Cassidy's legs around my shoulders too, but I settled for bending her over and eating her out until she came on my tongue."

Phoenix groaned, jealousy pulsing through him. But the jealousy wasn't a need to possess. Not between Jacob and Cassidy. No, it was a wish that he could have been there. If only he hadn't been so drunk that he'd passed out as soon as he'd gotten off. He wanted to make her come like that. He wanted to watch Jacob inch himself into Phoenix's throat too.

Jacob smiled, the gleam in his eyes pure satisfaction. He knew what Phoenix was thinking, and it just made him hotter. "Then I buried myself inside her tight little pussy. Do you know what she screamed when she came again?" Phoenix shook his head, biting his lip to stop himself from begging Jacob to say his name. "Phoenix." He blinked. Opened his mouth to speak but had no idea what to say. "She said your name. We've waited for you since then. I've wanted to go down on her so many times. Wanted to sink into her countless others. We both went to Grounds every day, but you weren't there—"

"Exams—"

"We know," Cassidy explained. "But now that we've found you, we want you with us tonight. And tomorrow."

"Are you asking me to come home with you?" Phoenix met Jacob's eyes and twisted to look at Cassidy's. "Because if so, the answer's yes."

"Let's get out of here." Jacob grasped his hand and wrapped his free arm around Cassidy, then paused. "What about Travis?"

"He told me to go with you if you asked. Our other friends might meet us here; otherwise, he'll be right to find his own way home. He won't get trashed if we're not all together."

Jacob smiled, clearly pleased with his answer. "Then let's go. Our lady naked is a sight to behold, and this time I have every intention of tasting you, not just her."

EIGHT

Jacob

Phoenix was on his phone, a smile lighting up his dark features as he texted back and forth while they waited for the rideshare. "Trav's good. He ran into a group of girls from his class. He messaged me to say not to wait up."

When his eyes met Cassidy's, the air between them sparked. Jake rested his hand low on her back, and she reached for the man he wanted desperately to make theirs. She tugged him closer and curled her hands around the shirt at his waist. She smiled, and Phoenix hummed, stepping up until they were touching. Jake watched as Phoenix wrapped his hand around Cassidy's hip—the same place Jake had held when they'd been dancing. Fuck, it was sexy seeing the two of them together. He couldn't wait to see them naked and curled around each other, Phoenix moving inside her as Cassidy kissed him.

The woman before him had turned his world upside down. Apart from the crazy desire she sparked within him, she was poly. He'd never imagined wanting more than one person before. Never even really contemplated the idea of a threesome. It was something other people did. But the moment Cassidy told him she wanted to have more than one relationship, his mind had flipped the switch. He wasn't comfortable with the idea of being open or even having multiple long-term partners—call him traditional, or maybe just not open-minded enough—but adding a third? Oh, hell yeah. He'd made it his mission to find a man they could share, never even realizing how much he wanted it, too, until it had become a possibility. Cassidy had given that to him; allowed him to discover another element of himself, and he adored her for it.

The thing was, even if they'd never found someone to complete them, Jake could be happy with Cassidy. He could easily fall in love with her—hell, he was already halfway there. But the man before him fit them perfectly. Hell, the last time they'd seen him he'd been drunk off his face and yet, they'd come together almost seamlessly.

He wanted this, but he also wanted more.

The hint of vulnerability Phoenix had shared in the alley behind the coffee shop, and then when he'd said he only kissed men in the dark... Jake's kryptonite was that confident competence borne from years of hard work and dedication, but Phoenix's vulnerability, his trust in them, and the way he'd completely lost his filter when he was drunk, had gotten under his skin. There was no denying he'd lusted after Phoenix from the moment he'd seen him, but with every little piece of himself that Phoenix revealed, Jake's attraction grew. He was, for tonight at least, their third piece.

Jake just hoped that it would become more, because he had a feeling they'd soon learn exactly how perfect the three of them were together.

Jake hummed as Phoenix cupped Cassidy's cheek, tilting her face up to his and pressing a soft kiss to her lips. He lingered, his mouth resting against hers as he waited for Cassidy to take control. And take control she did. Wrapping her arms around his shoulders and holding him in place, she deepened the kiss, her tongue sneaking out of her mouth and into Phoenix's. Jake's cock bucked happily in his suit pants, and he held his jacket there, hiding the tent pole trying to break free.

A car pulled up ahead. It was their rideshare. He tapped Phoenix's shoulder and motioned to the car. Jake held the back door open for them before he slid into the remaining back seat. Being pressed against Cassidy's curves was heaven, but hell was being unable to touch her the way he wanted. The driver started a conversation, but Jake couldn't concentrate on it. He watched the curve of Cassidy's smile as she charmed the man driving them and met Phoenix's gaze over her head. His features were painted with raw need, his pupils blown and lips pink and glistening. Phoenix reached out, his hand sliding over Cassidy's belly. Jake didn't know whether it was an invitation, but he slipped his fingers into Phoenix's, holding his hand. Cassidy silently linked hers as well, covering them on her lap. This was how it was supposed to be. Call him insane, but their hands linking, the three of them connected, painted a picture in Jake's mind's eye of them together like this, years from now. He knew he was jumping the gun, hoping for something more than he had a right to ask for—they were hardly at the life partner commitment stage—but instinct, or some deep-seeded hope, drove him. It told him, with a far from warranted level of certainty, that they had something much deeper than mere attraction.

An age passed before the car pulled up in front of Jake's building. It was an ordinary-looking five-storey, built in the eighties with four others of similar height. He'd wanted to live there as soon as he'd seen it. Of all the studio apartments he'd seen, his was, by far, the biggest. It hadn't been renovated so it was within his price range too—rent was expensive in that part of town. The best part was that the owners were willing to let him fix up a few things in exchange for a longer lease. Jake had signed it immediately.

Nerves fluttered in his belly as he opened his front door, flicked on the lights that illuminated the entire space, and kicked off his shoes. "Can I get you a drink? Something to eat?" Jake wiped his hands down his pants and groaned when Cassidy grasped both his wrists, curling her hands around his.

"How about we put some music on?" she asked with a soft smile, encouraging him to relax. "Dim the lights a little too." He nodded and handed her his phone.

"It'll automatically pair to the speakers. Pick whatever you like." Jake motioned to the lamps sitting beside his bed. "Phoenix, could you turn one on, please, and I'll get these lights?" They each did their thing, and Cassidy sat down on the end of his bed. She brushed her hands over the soft covers. She'd been there before. The first time he'd seen her naked, her hair spread like a halo around her, and a satisfied smile on her face was like a wet dream—every man's pinup fantasy. Her skin was like silk, and he'd lost himself caressing her breasts, belly, and thighs. He couldn't wait to do it again, this time with Phoenix.

She crossed her legs and slipped the pointed-toe stiletto off her foot. Jake had no idea how she could wear them all day. Or even for five minutes. She dropped the shoe at her feet, and the thud seemed to jolt Phoenix out of his reverie. He fell to his knees and eased the second shoe off her foot, placing both to one side as he propped her feet in his lap. Sitting there cross-legged on the hard floor while he rubbed Cassidy's arches was more than Jake could take. He didn't want to miss out on a single part of this moment. Crawling onto the bed behind Cassidy, he pressed up against her back, his knees bracketing her hips. He eased the pins out of her hair and passed them to Phoenix. Her blonde mane fell into a long ponytail, the silky strands brushing his fingers as he removed the tie and massaged her scalp until she moaned.

Jake brushed her hair over one shoulder and kissed a line down her throat over the other. Massaging the tense knots in her shoulders, he met Phoenix's gaze. The other man darted his tongue out, the pink muscle wetting his bottom lip. How could Jake be jealous of Phoenix's own lip? God damn, he wanted that tongue on him. On Cassie. Phoenix moved his hands up to her calves, continuing his ministrations. Cassidy hummed and murmured quietly, "I could get used to being spoilt like this. It would be even better though—" She shifted like she was uncomfortable. "—if I could get this damn skirt off."

Jake huffed out a laugh and pressed a kiss to her shoulder, trailing his fingers down her back to the zipper. He eased it down and whispered, "Lift your arms up, Cass." Untucking the sexy camisole she wore, the material silky against his fingers, he inched it up over her ribs. As much as Jake wanted to see her porcelain skin revealed, he watched Phoenix. The man was riveted, his gaze roaming over their woman as Jake undressed her and tossed the silky material to the side, letting it flutter to the floor. Phoenix pressed his hand against his visible erection, and Jake splayed his fingers over Cassidy's ribs. He expected to meet skin, but instead, there was more satiny material. He looked over her shoulder to see her breasts cupped exquisitely by a white satin corset-looking thing that ended at the bottom of her ribs. A strip of pale skin peeked above the waistline of her skirt, and Jake was desperate to know whether the underwear she wore matched her bra. It didn't matter either way; it was all going to end up on the floor in a few moments.

He nudged her, and Cassidy turned her head. "Stand up for me." She did, but Phoenix didn't shift back, the move leaving Cassidy pressed almost against the man seated on the floor. Phoenix took over, gently easing her skirt down her legs and tossing it aside. Jake had his answer, and what he saw was a work of art.

Cassidy wore the tiniest underwear he'd ever seen. Two straps wound around her hips, meeting in the middle where a circle no bigger than a pea joined the pieces to a third strap that plunged between her perfect cheeks. He wanted to know what the front looked like, but if the back was anything to go by, it would be divine.

Dropping his gaze, he watched as Phoenix splayed his hands over her creamy thighs, framing the band of lace that wrapped around them, holding up the sheer tights hugging her legs. He slowly rolled the lace down, kissing a slow path along her thigh as he stripped her. Jake couldn't resist the temptation to do the same, and he scrambled off the bed, falling to his knees almost opposite the other man. The bite of the hard flooring under his joints barely registered as Jake pressed his lips to Cassidy's hamstring, slowly dragging his tongue up her leg to the curve of her arse. His fingers brushed against Phoenix's, and he hummed, knowing that this time they were all exactly where they were meant to be.

Cassidy's fingers curled into his hair, tugging his bun free and letting his hair fall loose. Just like he'd done to her, Cassidy ran her fingers through it, and he hummed, loving her sensual touch. He watched as she reached for Phoenix, slipping her fingers into his hair too. The man moaned and looked up at her, adoration on his face. No words were spoken, but Cassidy seemed to know exactly what was in his head. She flipped the covers off the bed then sat down, letting them pull away each of the tights before she scooted further up the mattress, lying like temptation personified in the middle.

Jake didn't need to be told twice, but Cassidy's words stopped him in his tracks. "Kiss each other. It gets me hot when you two make out." He smiled and turned to Phoenix, watching as the other man's nostrils flared with barely re-strained desire. Jake flicked open the top button on Phoe-nix's shirt, running his fingertips down the divot between his pecs as he moved to the next one. He watched Phoenix's pulse fluttering like a hummingbird in his throat, and he leaned in to kiss him there.

One button after another, he undid the shirt until the front panels hung open, his golden skin and smattering of chest hair revealed. Jake moaned, desperate to taste him. He licked his lips and pushed the shirt over Phoenix's shoul-ders, revealing a happy surprise. He pressed a kiss to his pec. Chest hair tickled his chin, and he moved there to kiss that before shifting lower and licking the barbell pierced through his nipple. Capturing it in his teeth, he tugged gen-tly, and Phoenix bucked his hips forward, moaning loudly. Cassidy's husky laugh encouraged him to do it again, but this time, he rubbed Phoenix's rigid shaft through his jeans and tested the weight of his balls in his palm.

Jake tugged his jeans open and shoved them over his hips. Phoenix wore tight black boxers that moulded to each ridge and valley of his lithe body, and Jake's knees almost gave way. His man kicked off his jeans and cupped Jake's nape, pulling him closer. Phoenix crushed their mouths to-gether in a ravenous kiss that left Jake breathless as Phoenix plundered his mouth. All that golden skin under his palms burned deliciously as Jake explored his lover. The curve of his shoulder muscles and bulge of his biceps, and the ripple of muscle in his back as Phoenix shifted, embracing Jake tighter, were addictive. The valley that ran down his spine and the twin dips at the small of his back were sexy as fuck.

He slid his palms lower, grasping each firm cheek in his hands. Phoenix's low growl turned him on so badly that it ripped a moan from Jake's throat. He pulled Phoenix's hips against his, needing more friction, and ground down on the man.

He could do it all night. Kiss and lick Phoenix until he'd come so many times his limbs were jelly, and he was so sated he couldn't lift even his lips. But there was the woman who'd made it all possible with them, and he'd never forget her or leave her wanting. Jake pulled back, resting his forehead against Phoenix's. "Get on the bed, Phoenix. Show Cassie how much you want her too."

"I want you there as well." Phoenix's words unclenched something deep within Jake. He'd always been on the outside. Detached from everyone around him—care of his father's ruthless brand of parenting. Cassie was changing him. She showed him every time they spoke, every time they touched, what it was like to be wanted. And now, with Phoenix saying the same thing, it was as if he'd looked inside Jake's soul, giving him the one thing he desperately needed, but had never dared ask for.

Phoenix curled his hand around Jake's tie and tugged it gently, pulling him out of his head. "But you're wearing far too many clothes." He ripped his socks off, and giving Jake the best view of his tight little arse, he crawled up the bed, pausing only to uncross Cassidy's ankles and spread her thighs. He settled between them and bent to kiss her. But they didn't stay like that for long. Phoenix shifted so he was on his side, his leg pinning one of Cassidy's down.

Jake stripped out of his clothes, throwing his tie carelessly on the floor as he fumbled open each of the buttons on his shirt. One piece came off after another until all he had on were navy blue briefs. He kneeled on the bed, lifting Cassidy's foot to his lips. He kissed the tip of her big toe and kneaded her arch with his fingers until she moaned. Kissing his way to her ankle, then her calf, he licked the back of her knee, then up those sexy legs. Phoenix was stroking her pussy through the satin of her white panties, and Jake licked between them, tasting both of them on his tongue. Cassidy was wet, the material soaked through. He licked again, tasting her essence, and moaned, his cock throbbing with need.

When Phoenix pulled her panties to the side, shifting at the same time, Jake looked up to see him licking her nipple and sucking the pebbled peak into his mouth. Cassidy was watching Jake with a blissed-out expression. Eyes glassy, her lips parted on an inhale. He wanted to feel her legs tighten around his shoulders as she rode out her first orgasm of the night.

He curled his lip, the smirk the only warning that he— no, they—were going to rock her world. Jake reached out, slipping his hand into Phoenix's underwear, and grasped the rock-hard shaft trapped there. Phoenix grunted and pumped his hips into Jake's grip. With his other hand, he stroked Cassidy's entrance, wetting two fingers with her juices until he could slowly work them inside her. Silk-covered steel and the tight grip of Cassidy's warmth as he slid his fingers in and out were sensory overload, but Jake needed more. He touched his tongue to her clit and swirled the nub before sucking the bundle of nerves between his lips. Cassidy arched off the bed, crying out from the sensation as he and Phoenix took her higher. They worked together, completely in sync without the need for words. But when Phoenix spoke, he shot to the edge.

"How much do you want Jake inside you? Hmm? Do you go bare? Has he felt your pussy gripping him with nothing between you?"

Letting go of the other man's shaft, Jake squeezed the base of his own cock to stop himself from going off like a firework.

"Yes," she cried on a breathy moan. "Want you inside me."

"Not yet, beautiful," Jake murmured against her clit before nipping her with his lips. "First you come. Then it's Phoenix's turn to be inside you. I want those pretty lips of yours wrapped around my cock." When she whimpered, Jake knew he'd give her what she wanted. He doubled down, fingering her deeper and stroking her G-spot on every pass while eating her out like a man starved.

The choked cry was the only warning he had before her pussy strangled his fingers with a vice-like grip before it released and tightened again. Over and over until she was limp and sweating, he pressed his fingers in and licked her.

Only when she tried to pull away did he let up, giving her a reprieve.

"Where are your supplies, Jake?" Phoenix asked. He smiled, desire and happiness swirling around inside him. It was the first time he'd called him Jake rather than Jacob, and he liked his name on his lover's lips.

"Top drawer." He motioned beside the bed and watched Phoenix stretch out, reaching for the rubbers.

"I'm on birth control," Cassidy explained as Phoenix brought the packet to his lips. "Jake and I have both been tested." She left the words unsaid, but the invitation was clear. Their first hook-up might have been reckless, but Cassidy wasn't a loose cannon. She wouldn't offer to go without a condom unless she intended this to be much more than a one-night stand.

Phoenix hesitated, his gaze bouncing between them. "I haven't been tested. Not in a while anyway. I've never gone raw before, but..." He shook his head.

"It's okay." She smiled. "Whatever you're comfortable with. I'm pretty sure I saw a few chocolate ones in there. I quite like the taste of them, and if you want to see our results anytime, just ask."

"Thank you." He leaned down and kissed her, and Jake eased his boxers down over those lean hips. "It's not that I don't trust you—"

"There's no need to explain—"

"I want to. With you would be amazing. But Mum fell pregnant with me when she was super young, and they weren't ready for me. My parents struggled for so many years before they could finally pull themselves up out of a mountain of debt. I need to do my bit to keep you safe, not just from anything I might have picked up, but from my swimmers too. Condom is an added layer of protection."

Cassidy smiled, love hearts in her eyes, and she tugged Phoenix down. Jake sat there, stunned. Completely flabbergasted. He loved how Phoenix respected Cassie. How he cared for her, even at his expense. What man turned down going raw when their woman had assured him a condom wasn't necessary? He certainly hadn't been strong enough—he hadn't even bothered with the assurance. Phoenix was something else. Both the kind of man Jake wanted to be like, and one he wanted to be with. He was never a condescending arse, and when he'd been upset, he hadn't lashed out aggressively. He'd talked and listened to their explanation. Everything he did, his words, and every move he made was like another lasso capturing Jake, drawing him in and tying them together. And Jake was falling hard.

Phoenix shifted until he was between her legs, their mouths never separating. Jake plucked the foil packet still clutched in Phoenix's hand and reached between the other man's legs. Pulling Phoenix's cock down, he rolled on the rubber and kissed a line up his leg over his arse, the same way he'd done to Cassidy. They were the polar opposite— flawless porcelain curves against soft dark hairs and wiry muscles—but together, they were perfection. He reached down again, and when Phoenix shifted, thrusting back to grind his cock against Cassidy's clit, he guided him into her tight heat. Both of them moaned, and Cassidy lifted her hips, letting him push in deeper.

"Jake, get your arse up here," Phoenix growled, rocking with deep, hard thrusts into their woman. Jake didn't hesitate, shifting to kneel beside Cassidy's shoulder. He worked his cock. He wanted to come on them, paint both of them with his seed and mark them as his. Cassidy tilted her head, opening her mouth so he could feed her his cock. The invitation was too tempting. Seeing those red lips close around his steely flesh sent him spiralling to the edge of sanity. But when Phoenix grasped his sac and used it to tug him closer until his cock slipped from Cassidy's mouth with a pop, he saw stars. Phoenix swallowed him, his tongue caressing him as he looked up into Jake's eyes and sank his lips right to the root of Jake's cock. He kept going, breathing through his nose until he pressed it into the springy curls at the base of his dick and the muscles of Phoenix's throat tightened around his cockhead as he swallowed.

"Oh, fuck," Jake breathed, his voice wobbling as the tingle at the base of his spine started. "Too good. I'm gonna blow."

Phoenix released him and used the saliva coating his cock as lube to jack him while Cassidy licked his sac. Jake fell to the side, his face even with their hips, and reached between their bodies to play with Cassidy's clit. If he was coming like a freight train, so would they. He worked her until she was screaming her completion and Phoenix was grunting with each thrust.

"Fuck, so tight," his lover uttered before slamming home again and letting out a string of curses.

Jake was so close, and the two of them working him would catapult him over the edge within moments, but he couldn't get the vision of them wearing his cum out of his mind's eye. Jake was up on his knees again and pointing his cock at their chests as he frantically jacked off. A grunt left his lips as Cassidy's hand snaked up and played with his star, her long painted nails too sharp to do anything more than rub the spot, while Phoenix kneaded his balls. They were all breathing hard, but Jake's breath caught in his lungs on a silent scream as he shot all over the two of them.

He fell sideways, and Cassidy shifted so he could pillow his head on her leg. Phoenix disposed of the condom, and Jake heard cupboards opening and closing. He liked the sound of that. Phoenix making himself at home in his place was right.

When Jake's limbs were finally working again, and he could string a sentence together, he flipped around and drew the sheets over them. Cassidy curled into him and asked, "Can I keep him?"

Jake nodded. "I hope so."

Phoenix hovered at the door to the bathroom, watching them, but not coming any closer. That wouldn't do. Jake tugged the sheet down and patted the space behind Cassidy. With a shy smile, Phoenix crossed the room and climbed in. Propping himself on his elbow, he wrapped his arm around Cassidy's waist and started, "I don't have to stay—"

"We want you to." Cassidy twisted so she was looking up at him and cupped his face with her hand, her thumb running along his cheek. "Both of us want you here." Jake affirmed her comment, leaning over Cassidy to press his lips to Phoenix's.

"I want to be here too." He looked down and bit his lip, his cheeks a rosy pink as he played with a lock of Cassidy's hair. "Is it weird that I feel like I've known you forever, but we're still practically strangers?"

"I don't know about strangers. We know a couple of secrets about you," Cassidy teased.

"Yeah?"

"We know when you're drunk, you're a brat who doesn't like wearing clothes," she continued playfully, and Phoenix groaned, resting his head on her shoulder and rolling it from side to side. Cassidy's giggle was melodic, and Jake couldn't help but grin at the other man's embarrassment.

"Will I ever live that down? Better yet, will you recreate what happened after I passed out like a bloody amateur?"

Jake laughed and ran his fingers through Phoenix's hair, leaning in to kiss his forehead. "Any time."

He looked up, first at Cassidy, then Jake, pinning him with a look filled with gratitude and humility. Jake swallowed, warmth blooming in his chest when Phoenix spoke quietly, saying, "Thanks for putting me to bed that night. You cared for me, and you didn't have to."

"I like to think that if you came across one of us in the state you were in, you'd do the same—"

Wide-eyed, Phoenix nodded. "I would have. If I saw someone I knew drunk off their face, I'd definitely want to see them home safe." He pursed his lips, a mix of frustration and disappointment with himself flashing in his eyes. "The fact that I can't remember half the night tells me how messy I was. You probably thought I was some stupid kid needing to be tucked in."

Memories crowded Jake's brain—Phoenix playful and flirty, touching himself, and that smouldering kiss... there was no way Jake thought Phoenix was a kid, and definitely not a stupid one. He looked down to Cassie, who was still leaning into Phoenix, but staring up at him, both of them seemingly waiting for him to speak.

Jake trailed his eyes along the man's broad shoulders, to the piercings in his nipples, and down to his waist. He couldn't see anything below the sheet, but he'd touched and tasted enough to have memorized the details. "Yeah, Phoenix, I'm not thinking you're anything like a kid." His voice was gravelly. Jake cleared his throat and tried to redirect his thoughts into safer terrain. What was he thinking about before? Oh, yeah. Being put to bed.

Huh.

He cocked his head, his brow furrowed, remembering back to his childhood. He didn't think much about the days before he'd moved out of home, but now that he was... "How old are kids when their parents stopped tucking them in?"

"Mine had to make sure I actually went to sleep, so I was like fourteen when they stopped coming in and turning out the light," Phoenix explained. "I'd read all night otherwise. Why's that?"

"I don't ever remember being put to bed or tucked in. Mum probably, but I don't remember. I was young when she and my father split, and he never did it. So... yeah."

Cassidy opened her mouth as if she wanted to say something, but nothing came out. When she closed then opened it again, Jake raised his eyebrows in question. "What?"

"Your dad never tucked you in at night? How old were you when they divorced?"

Jake really didn't want to get into it with them. Not now. Not ever, ideally. "He's not that kind of person. He was... hands off." He lifted his tone, forcing a levity into it that he never felt when talking about his father. "Anyway, doesn't matter. What about you? What weird things did you do as kids?"

"I ate dogfood," Phoenix admitted with a cringe. "The dry biscuits only, but I used to sneak into the pantry and share them with our border collie. Mum would catch me hiding in there and shoo us out."

Cassidy scrunched up her nose and added, "Ew!"

"I was like three. Gimme a break." Phoenix laughed and pointed to Jake. "He wanted weird. What about you, Little Miss Pernickety?"

"I was perfectly normal. Nothing crazy to report here." Cassidy's smirk had Jake curious. It was one of those I-have-a-secret-but-I'm-not-telling kinds of smiles, but he wanted to know, and he was willing to play dirty to find out. He grasped her ribs and Cassidy squirmed. Instead of tickling her though, he leaned down and captured her nipple, licking and nibbling until Cassidy grunted and thread her fingers into his hair, holding him there.

"You gonna tell us?" Phoenix teased. "Or do I need to start on the other?"

"Go ahead," she hummed, lifting her arm, and rolling more onto her back. Jake sucked a little harder and released her with a pop, then backed away, putting enough distance between them that the arm still gripping him was outstretched. It earned him a shove from Cassidy and a grumbled "Teasing bastard." When Jake didn't move back, she huffed and added, "I was like Phoenix, reading every moment I could, but I loved any competition." With Jake's laugh, she shoved him again and pouted. "I was a bingo nerd, okay? I used to hang with my nan all the time. We'd go to bingo twice a week from when I could count, and when we weren't there, I was in her garden trying to get my plants to outgrow hers." The affection in Cassidy's tone was wistful. Her lips turned down and Jake shifted closer, needing to comfort her. Phoenix did the same, hugging her to them. She added, "She died a couple of years ago. I miss gardening with her. Bingo was fun too. I liked the competition."

"Do you competitively crochet too?" Phoenix teased, dropping kisses on her shoulder up her throat.

"Shut up."

"Cross-stitch?" Jake laughed at her scowl, and she shot him a single finger salute.

"Be careful or you'll wake up to me stitching your mouths shut and certain other pieces of anatomy closed too," she threatened. But if her narrowed eyes and pursed lips were meant to scare Jake, it failed. He swallowed his snort of laughter and nodded, playfully saluting her.

"Point taken," Phoenix said with a grin. "We're suitably scared."

"You should be." Cassidy glared at them, her eyes still narrowed. "I tell a mean ghost story too. You'll be terrified."

"Of how bad it'll be." Jake rolled his eyes, baiting her again.

They talked until the dawn's rays began to colour the sky, their laughter ringing through the small apartment and a few deeper moments too where Jake was glad they could comfort each other. As the sun broke through the still-open blinds, Cassidy closed her eyes, visibly wrung out from another orgasm after taking both of them together. She snuggled into Phoenix who was still pressed against her back, and he had a peaceful, indulgent smile tilting his lips upward. Jake didn't want to miss a moment, but the thought of getting a few hours' sleep curled around his lovers was too tempting.

His decision was made when the sun shifted, reflecting off the window in the building opposite. It streamed in and shone straight onto Phoenix's face. He grimaced, scrunching his eyes closed tighter to block out the light. Jake shifted Cassidy toward him and Phoenix shuffled forward, but within moments, they were all in the sun again. Jake stumbled out of bed, closed the blinds, and returned. "Hop in behind me?" Phoenix asked, his voice barely a mumble.

Silently, he lifted the covers and crawled into Phoenix's side, Jake the big spoon. He kissed his shoulder and his throat before nuzzling into Phoenix's hair. "G'night," he whispered, and Phoenix hummed, sounding like he was already asleep.

* * * * *

Jake woke up hard as a board. The hot body in front of him was grinding against his cock, making it slip between firm cheeks and prod a hole that he really wanted to be inside of. He grasped Phoenix's hip, steadying him as he thrust forward, and the other man gasped, "Oh, thank fuck. I thought you'd never wake up."

Jake blinked open his eyes, wincing at the light streaming in from behind the closed blinds. "Sit tight for one second," he ordered, kicking off the covers and hitching Phoenix's knee forward. Without shifting from his spot behind the man, he reached between his lover's legs and gave the man's cock a firm squeeze

Jake heard the toilet flush, and the running water in the bathroom announced Cassidy was already up. She opened the door a moment later and paused, resting her shoulder on the doorframe. "Mmm, lovely view to wake up to."

Jake smiled at her over his shoulder and flicked open the lid of the lube bottle, squeezing a generous amount onto his fingers. He needed inside this beautiful man, stat. He wasted no time, sliding slippery fingers down Phoenix's cleft and circling the tight pucker there. He pushed back against his digit, and Jake knew this wasn't a time for teasing. One finger, then two, he twisted and stretched the muscle, readying Phoenix for the intrusion. Jake moaned. The tight clench and heat enveloping his fingers were making his cock jealous. He couldn't wait to sink inside him.

Phoenix's breathing sped up, and he arched his back, silently begging Jake for more. He added a third finger and marvelled at how wide his man was being stretched. But even Jake's patience was about to snap.

Tearing open the foil wrapper, he slid the rubber down his length and applied a generous coating of lube, slicking up both his cock, and the hole he was about to slide into. Pulling Phoenix's hips back, the other man bent his leg, opening himself up and giving Jake unfettered access. He rubbed his cockhead against Phoenix's pucker, lubing him up more, and slowly pushed. Phoenix went rigid, his sphincter tightening impossibly around Jake's cock, forcing him out. "Breathe, babe." Jake stroked his flank and reached around to play with his balls until Phoenix blew out a breath and he eased forward again. Slowly he pressed in, the head of his cock pushing past the resistance. He stilled, letting Phoenix get used to him.

"Move," Phoenix begged a moment later. "I need you." Jake shifted forward, thrusting in short, easy movements until he was fully seated. The intensity of the moment was rocking his world. Phoenix surrounding him, knowing

Cassidy was watching… it shot him to the edge far too quickly. He squeezed his eyes closed, clenched his jaw, and counted back from one hundred. But his hips had another idea, the twitching in his cock driving him forward until he was grinding against Phoenix, pressing in even deeper. His man shouted, his hand immediately clamping around the base of his dick.

Propping himself on one elbow to gain some leverage, Jake slid out until just his cockhead remained buried and thrust forward again, his hips slapping against Phoenix's as he bottomed out. His eyes met Cassidy's over Phoenix's shoulder, and he watched her reach down to play with her pussy, sinking two digits deep in perfect synchronicity with his thrusts. "Fuck," Phoenix uttered, his hand moving in long pulls over his erection. Cassidy had pulled up a chair and propped her legs on the bed. She widened her stance, spreading her legs further until both Jake and Phoenix had a clear view of her pussy glistening with her juices. As if being buried in the hottest man alive wasn't enough, Cassidy gave him a visual that he'd never forget.

He smoothed his hand over the rounded globe of Phoenix's butt and sucked in a breath when his channel tightened around him. Fuck. He was in heaven. Cassidy and Phoenix together were perfection. The fact that he got to play with them? Mind blowing.

How was this even his life?

Cassidy licked her lips, and Jake knew he could make it even better for her. He pulled out of Phoenix, and the other man whimpered. But Jake tapped his hip and added, "On your knees. I want deeper in you." Phoenix scrambled to move into place, facing Cassidy and giving her one hell of a view of the man's cock pointing up at his navel, thick and hard, while his balls hung tight and full. Jake couldn't resist the sight. He leaned forward and licked a stripe up that beautiful cock, Phoenix's pre-cum bursting onto his tongue. Salty and tangy, he wanted to lick the man from top to toe to get another taste. But that was for another time. His cock demanded that it be buried again, chasing nirvana.

This time, Phoenix accepted him easily, and Jake's thrusts picked up pace, but it still wasn't enough. He knelt back, pulling Phoenix onto his lap, spreading the man's legs as wide as Cassidy's, and holding onto him. Phoenix leaned back, wrapping an arm around his shoulders, pressing their bodies closer. Sweat-slick skin slid against his own, and the smell of sex in the air drove Jake wild.

He couldn't get enough.

Phoenix turned his face, searching for Jake's lips, and they met in a messy kiss. It was all tongues and teeth as Jake closed his fingers around Phoenix's throat, holding him in place. With Phoenix now holding onto him, Jake used his free hand to jack his man. Surging into the tightest channel he'd ever been in and watching Cassidy get off on the visual of the man splayed out in front of her impaled on Jake's dick, shot putted him to the edge—

Cassidy screamed, scrambling off the chair. Shock and fear, not ecstasy, painted her face. She slid to a crouch at the same time as a voice boomed across the space, shouting, "What the fuck do you think you're doing?" Jake froze, but his hips twitched involuntarily, still chasing the high he was on the precipice of only a second earlier. The most primitive part of his brain—the one for mating and fighting—screeched to a standstill before winding up, ready to explode.

That voice.

He knew it. He'd know it anywhere.

It still haunted him. It still controlled him.

And Jake would always hate him.

His father.

Jake shoved at Phoenix, tipping the man off his lap, and spun around, his arms out and using his body as a shield between his lovers and the snarling man who was still holding a key in his hand. One that Jake hadn't given him.

"What the hell? Get out," Jake screeched, his voice a couple of octaves higher than its usual pitch.

"Don't you tell me what to do, boy." The sneer on his father's face was full of derision. Pure hatred. His latest wife pursed her lips like there was a bad smell in the air, and she looked down her nose at Jake like he was dog shit on the bottom of her shoe. Silently she shifted her stare to Cassidy and Phoenix and sniffed derisively. He hadn't seen Cassidy put on Phoenix's shirt, but she stepped up beside him before shouldering her way past his father's latest wife to move over to the real powerhouse—his father. Cassidy was shouting something at him, the man narrowing his eyes at her before he spat, "Sit there and shut the fuck up."

Jacob launched himself off the bed, getting in front of a still-yelling Cassidy. Straightening to his full height, he narrowed his eyes and stared his father down. Jake was as naked as the day he was born, aside from the condom hanging off his now limp cock, but he didn't care. He was too far gone to give a shit about what his father thought anymore. He ground his teeth together, standing chest to chest with the man, ready to come to blows if that's what it took. His voice was low, barely loud enough to carry over the ruckus his partners were making, but the lethal wrath was unmistakable. "I. Said. Get. Out."

"You're done," his father gloated, the sneer terrifying Jake.

A movement in the corner of his eye caught his attention, and Jake shifted his gaze. The mountain of a man who loved to intimidate and coerce—Maxwell Denyer's attack dog slash driver—stepped over the threshold of the still-open doorway. With a nod from his father, he bared his teeth in a low growl. He shoved Jake back, almost knocking Cassidy off her feet. Jake reached for her, steadying her, but when the man grabbed Phoenix, Jake lunged for him. He threw his weight against the beast. But he didn't budge. Jake was no match for him. Like a fly trying to push over a mountain, Jake's impact didn't even slow him down. With his giant mitt already wrapped around Phoenix's bicep, he tossed Jake off like a rag doll.

It sent him sprawling, his arms cartwheeling backward uselessly.

He was on a collision course for the floor.

Jake reached out, trying to stop his fall, and Cassidy shouted, shoving his father out of the way.

It was like a slow-motion movie, one where the hero was falling, watching everything around him happen at warp speed. Cassidy was racing to him, her arms outstretched to try and catch him, while Phoenix struggled against a man that was twice his size, shouting the whole time. But it was no use. Phoenix was no match for him—the jeans around his knees didn't help either—when he was using his brute strength to force Phoenix out the door.

His hand hit the soft pile of the plush rug laid out on the floor. At least it would break—

Searing pain struck him, fire travelling up the back of his head and down his spine.

Jake's world went black.

NINE

Cassidy

"**J**ake!" Cassidy screamed as he fell, his head bouncing off the coffee table with a sickening crack. "Shit!" Falling to her knees, she grasped his head, steadying his neck as he groaned.

"Help me, you idiot," she screeched at the woman who looked like she'd sucked on a lemon. "Call an ambulance." Turning to the older man who, by his looks, could only be one person—Jake's father—she snarled, "Where is he taking Phoenix? You fucking hurt him—"

His hand curled into her hair, and he yanked backward, making her back arch until she had to let go of Jake. She screamed, lightning bolts of pain ricocheting through her scalp, and she clawed at his hands. Her fingernails bent backward with the force she was applying. He snarled in her face, spittle landing on her cheek. "And you'll do what, little girl? I'll ruin you before you even lift a finger. Your job, your apartment? They'll be gone by the end of the day. You're done, slut. Just like that faggot is." He spat at Jake, a glob of sputum landing on the carpet by his arm.

Cassidy dry retched, but she forced down the urge to do it again and gathered all her courage. She sucked in a breath and dug her nails deeper, wishing she could see whether she was drawing blood. Knowing the points in her nails could do exactly that gave her a grim sense of satisfaction, and she hissed, "You don't scare me." He wrenched her hair harder, and pain tore through her head and neck as he bent her at an unnatural angle. Tears sprang to her eyes, and Cassidy tried to blink them away. She hated herself in that moment. The show of weakness would only give him more ammunition.

He laughed, the sound as cold as an Antarctic gale, his blue eyes flashing like ice. Jacob's were the same colour, but they were always warm, always sparkling with laughter. "That's a mistake you'll only make once." He shoved at her, dropping her to the floor on top of Jake, jostling his semi-conscious form.

When Jake whimpered, Cassidy launched into action. She scrambled off him, dashing away from the man who'd thrown their morning into chaos. Where had Jake dropped his jacket? He'd held her phone when they'd gone to dinner with his clients the night before. God, it felt like an eternity ago. *There, on the chair.* She dashed over and searched the pockets, her fingers closing over the rectangular device as the door swung open again and the monster who'd dragged Phoenix out reappeared.

"All done, boss," he grunted.

"Good." His father tossed a disgusted look over his shoulder at his son and strode to Cassidy, using his height to intimidate her. It worked, but Cassidy refused to let it show. She stood her ground, staring at him with her eyes narrowed. His glare turned into a sneer, the baring of his teeth as feral as the man himself. He may have been wearing Armani, but there was nothing civilized about him. "If you're thinking of calling the police, think again. I'm untouchable in this town." He eyed her like she was a juicy steak, and Cassidy had the urge to take a shower and scrub her body with a wire brush.

"We'll see." She turned and walked away, moving to crouch next to Jake and call an ambulance. The door closed behind her with a resounding snick, and Cassidy lost her composure. Kneeling there on the floor, the blue-grey rug under her, she curled into Jake's chest and wept. Her hands shook and her vision blurred, but she pushed through and punched in triple zero.

Before she could press Dial, she heard Jake whisper hoarsely, "Cass, babe."

"Jake? Oh shit, you scared me. Hold on, I'm calling an ambulance and the police."

"No." He struggled to sit up, so Cassidy shifted, dropping her phone and propping a hand under his elbow to help him upright. He touched the back of his head tenderly and winced at the lump she could already see had formed. He would have one hell of a headache. At least he wasn't bleeding too.

She slid around to sit behind him so he could lean on her and picked up her phone again. "I'm okay. I don't need an ambulance, and no police." He eased the phone from her fingers and dimmed the screen, placing it face down on the floor. "It's pointless. My father will just call in a favour and make the complaint disappear. Worse still, he'll twist it around, and you or I will end up being questioned."

"What?" Her voice was shrill, shock raising its volume far too loud for a man who'd been out of it only a moment earlier. "That's ridiculous? This isn't the wild west. It's bloody Sydney. That's got to be illegal." She reached for the phone again, but Jake put his hand on hers, stilling her movements. He entwined their fingers, and she wrapped an arm around him, grateful that he didn't appear to be hurt too badly. "They have Phoenix, Jake. What if they hurt him?"

"Fuck." He rubbed his forehead with his free hand. "I don't think he'd do that… but I don't know. I don't trust them."

"We need to call the police then and get him back," Cassidy urged.

"My father operates in a grey area filled with shadows and secret handshakes." He shifted, sliding down a little so he could rest his head on Cassidy's shoulder and sighed. But it wasn't one of contentment. It was weighted. Heavy. "He's a lawyer, but he doesn't do normal legal work. He fixes problems for people in powerful positions, but he has a high price. Instead of getting paid in billable hours like a normal lawyer, he stockpiles favours. He does something for you, and he expects a favour in return in the future. Sometimes it's legal, and other times not so much. But when he calls it in, he expects you to comply, or he makes public whatever dirt he holds." He huffed out a laugh that held no humour. "He's been responsible for anything from the end of marriages and the ousting of politicians at every level of government, right through to people serving life in prison or avoiding it. He has eyes everywhere too."

"He threatened both of us, and his goon took Phoenix. We need to go to the police, Jake. Call someone. Anyone. We can't just do nothing." Cassidy shifted, trying to dial again, but before she could, Jake's phone rang from across the room.

He sighed and stood up, walking slightly unsteadily to the chair his jacket was slung over. It stopped ringing before he picked it up, but when he looked at the screen, he closed his eyes and shook his head. Blowing out a breath, Jake pressed a few buttons, bringing the phone to his ear. "Charles, hi," he answered after a moment. He nodded. Nodded again and said, "Yeah. I'll come in and clean out my office." A pause. He shook his head and pursed his lips. "Fine." He lowered his phone and grasped the bridge of his nose with his thumb and forefinger. "That was my boss, my father's best mate. I don't have a job anymore. Apparently, he just accepted my letter of resignation to finish immediately."

"What? You didn't send him anything."

Jake sighed. "This is what my father does. I wasn't even supposed to be working with Charles. I was accepted into the residential division, but my father pushed for me to be in commercial. He had more control that way. Now he's telling me he's pissed."

"Fuck that," Cassidy muttered and called the police. The man might have thought he was untouchable, but Cassidy was not going to back down.

* * * * *

They'd been out all morning, combing the streets around Jacob's apartment, searching every inch of the nearby park. They'd shouted themselves hoarse. But nothing. There was no sign of Phoenix. The police had come and gone too, telling them to wait for a call, and Cassidy and Jacob had gone straight out again, this time driving around. But all they did was cover the same ground they'd covered on foot. Cassidy was shaking, panic clawing at her throat. Was he hurt? Had the man working for Jacob's father just pushed him onto the street? Put him in a rideshare or a cab and sent him home? Or had he done something far more sinister?

Cassidy's mind was running in circles, and she was fighting against imagining every worse-case scenario. She couldn't fathom it. Refused to believe that something worse than Phoenix going home had happened.

But as the hours ticked by, it was becoming harder.

When Cassidy's phone buzzed, she jumped for it, fumbling as she lifted the device. She frowned. The name that appeared wasn't someone she'd expected to hear from. Frank Walker was one of her smaller clients, but he was also a favourite. Summoning all her professionalism, she answered, amazed that her voice was steady. "Frank, good to hear from you. How can I help?"

"Cassidy, sorry to call you on a Sunday, but this can't wait until tomorrow. We've been reconsidering our representation, and as of Monday, we'll be transferring our properties away from CIR to another agency."

His words were like a slap to the face, shocking in their intensity. "Oh, um," she stammered. The niggle of concern that Jake's father wielded more influence than she had given him credit for grew, and her concern for Phoenix ratcheted up. Surely this was a coincidence, though. "Okay. May I ask why?"

"I'd actually prefer not to say." She looked at Jake, wide-eyed, and he scooted closer, wrapping an arm around her shoulders. Through the phone she heard the rustling of papers in the background. "I need to go, but Cassidy?"

"Yes?"

"Thank you. It's been a pleasure working with you." She opened her mouth to ask why they were leaving if it had been such a pleasure. What had she done? But the line was already dead.

"You okay?" Jake asked, his brow furrowed and lips turned down in a frown.

"That was one of my clients. They're pulling their properties from me," Cassidy explained, hating the vulnerability in her voice. The uncertainty and confusion too. The fear that his father was responsible. If he could persuade a client with whom she had a great relationship to move their work, what else could he do? What else had he already done?

Jake ran his fingers through her hair and tugged her close, wrapping Cassidy in his embrace. She rested in his arms but couldn't relax like she wanted to. Klaxons wailed in the back of her mind, telling her to get as far away from Maxwell Denyer as she could.

Moments later, Jake's phone rang. It was the police, but not the officer he'd expected. Jake put the phone on speaker. "Sorry, what was your name again?" he asked.

"Mr Denyer. I'm Senior Sergeant Campbell. I have taken over the investigation from Constable Moynihan." Cassidy flicked her gaze to Jake. He'd paled, his jaw clenching hard.

With a small shake of his head and a huff of breath, he said, "I have Cassidy here with me, Sir. You're on speaker."

"Hello, Miss Phillips. I have some news for you both in relation to Mr Phoenix Black. We contacted Mr Black within the last hour. He assured us that he was unharmed as you had reported. We spoke about your allegations against Mr Denyer Snr, and he provided us with his explanation. Your stories do not match, Mr Denyer and Miss Phillips. The allegations you made against Mr Denyer Snr are serious, and yet, it seems that the most damning evidence is against the two of you."

"What?" Cassidy demanded. "What evidence?"

"Mr Black has declined to press charges against you—"

"What the hell are you talking about?" Cassidy threw her hands up in the air and stood, unable to contain the sudden burst of anger surging through her. "We were assaulted, just like him. How is there evidence against us?

What is the evidence? We deserve to know." Her voice rose until it was shrill in pitch as she yelled at the police officer.

Jake gave her a sad smile and pressed a button on the phone before saying in a resigned voice, "This is what my father does." The police officer kept speaking, but it was white noise in Cassidy's ears. Everything turned fuzzy around the edges, and she couldn't concentrate on his words. She couldn't fathom how their story had become so twisted unless there were people lying.

Of course there were.

Cassidy had told the constable the truth. She'd aired their dirty laundry and told her everything that happened from the moment she'd woken up to calling them. She'd seen the judgement in her eyes. But Cassidy had naively thought she could rely on the officer to help them. Admitting they didn't know Phoenix's last name was humiliating, but there was a good enough reason for that. The officer assured them it wouldn't be hard to find out if they knew where he worked. That had been all Cassidy cared about. They didn't have his number, didn't have any way of contacting him except at work—and he wasn't there.

Jake had backed her up, confirming everything. Surely the police believed them. They were the victims, after all, and they were there to protect the victims. Weren't they?

But Cassidy was coming to understand just how powerful his father's influence was. There were four other people in the room. Clearly three of them had lied, but what about Phoenix? What had that awful man done to him to change his story and make Jake and her the villains?

Cassidy looked at the man still sitting on the couch, and her heart clenched tight in her chest. She liked him. He was sexy and fun, and his smart mouth had broken down all her walls. She hadn't been looking for someone special to come into her life. In fact, she'd sworn off relationships because of the drama that undoubtedly followed and its impact on her career. But he'd crashed in, and no matter how much she tried to resist him, it was no use. She could tell herself that she despised him, but Jake would be his charming, annoying self and Cassidy caved. Except that it wasn't just that she'd given in to his charms. She'd discovered that he could be her perfect match. Cassidy wielded being poly as a weapon—it threatened most guys knowing that Cassidy wanted multiple relationships—but Jake hadn't flinched. He'd accepted her immediately and then encouraged her to explore a triad relationship with him.

Then they met Phoenix.

She wanted it to work. She really had, but what was she getting herself into? Phoenix was already backing away with his arms up in surrender. Was she going to stick around and let Jake's father detonate her carefully crafted life plan? Meeting Jake's father once had been enough. How much chaos would he create if she dated Jake long term? Or if they broke up? He'd already wreaked havoc once, and Cassidy had too much to lose. She'd worked too hard to get where she was only to have the police think she was a criminal and her favourite client take his business elsewhere.

She moved over to the windows and stared unseeingly out of them. She had to put a stop to whatever was growing between them. Self-preservation was key at this point. She heard the clunk of something dropping against the timber coffee table, and a moment later, Jake's bare shoulder brushed against hers.

"I should go," she murmured. "I think we should take a break. Let things settle down a bit." Her stomach churned, nausea sweeping over her. Cassidy didn't want this, but she had to do it.

"What are you saying, Cassidy? Be straight with me."

She turned to him, and the look of devastation in his eyes nearly bought her to her knees. "I like you, I really do, but…" She sucked in a breath and gathered up the courage to lay it on him. "I won't let myself become collateral damage to your father's twisted games." Before she could chicken out or rethink what she needed to say, Cassidy confessed her fears. "I have a professional reputation to uphold, clients I don't want to lose, and a career that I've spent a hell of a lot of time building up. I didn't want a relationship because of the impact it would have on my work. When I found you, I thought things might be different, but it's so much worse than I expected." Cassidy saw the impact her words had with the draining of colour from Jake's face. He looked like she felt—as if she'd gutted him, cutting his heart straight out of his chest. He closed his eyes, and the sunlight streaming in through the window caught on the tear wetting his eyelash, refracting the light like there were a million tiny diamonds forming.

She knew that the next words out of her mouth would be the end of their relationship—there was no coming back for them, but Cassidy had to think about what she needed, and her highest priority was getting away from the toxic father of the man she could have fallen in love with. "I never believed for a moment that dating you would have this kind of impact. The police think we hurt Phoenix. People go to jail for things like this, and…." She shook her head, unable to continue. Tears sprung to her eyes, and she covered her mouth as a sob tore free.

Jake nodded and reached for her, pulling her into his embrace. When he wrapped his arms around her, Cassidy burrowed deeper into his hug. She didn't want to walk away, but what else was she supposed to do? "Yeah," he murmured, his voice quiet, but even though it was barely a whisper, she could hear the pain infused in that single syllable.

She eased away and gathered her jacket and shoes, slipping into the stilettos and collecting her phone. "Guess I'll see you round." He nodded, and Cassidy forced herself to walk out the door, closing it softly behind her.

* * * * *

Cassidy sat on her lounge room floor, cross-legged and eating the pizza that had been delivered. Her laptop was propped on her coffee table, paperwork spread out on either side of her. She was trying to catch up on the research she'd been neglecting for a few weeks.

Her phone vibrated, and Cassidy flinched, laughing self-consciously at her ridiculousness. She saw her boss's name flash up on the screen, and an anvil dropped in her stomach, the weight of fear pressing down on her. Not once had he ever called her on a Sunday afternoon. Why now? It couldn't be a coincidence. "Hello, Michael, to what do I owe the pleasure?"

"Cassidy," he started, his voice careful, like he was choosing his words. "I've had three telephone calls this afternoon from clients of yours."

"Oh, God. No," she gasped.

He continued on as if she hadn't said a word. "They were all seeking to terminate their agency contracts with us. When I pressed for information, they weren't forthcoming other than to say that they cannot work with you or anyone on your team. I tried to assure them that we can simply transfer their properties to a different agent, but all have now sent through written notices of termination."

"I can explain—"

"Don't bother. Whatever the reason, it's irrelevant. Your actions have cost the agency hundreds of thousands of dollars in lost clientele. Some of these organizations have worked with us for a decade."

Cassidy sat stunned, her mouth opening and closing as she tried to form a response. But what could she say? That it wasn't her fault? That every one of those clients was being blackmailed by a man who collected secrets and called on favours when it suited him? The police hadn't believed her, and they had no reason to doubt the veracity of her

claims. Why would her boss, when he had already wit-
nessed the fallout of her stupidity in getting involved with
the wrong man? "I can help win them back. We can get new
clients—"

"No, sorry, Cassidy, but you've left me with no choice
here. HR has advised me that I am within rights to terminate
your employment, effective immediately. We will have your
personal belongings from your office packed up and delivered to you. HR also requested that I remind you of the non-
compete clause in your contract."

Fire burned in her belly. That bastard had just destroyed
years of work, and why? Because she was sleeping with his
son? Because she condoned Jake's sexuality? Or because
she had stood up to him? Cassidy was surprised by the level
tone in her voice. "I'm being fired? Without allowing me to
explain my side of the story?"

"Whatever your explanation is, it doesn't change the reality that the agency has lost a not insignificant proportion
of its long-term clients in the space of a single day, all of
whom have noted you as the reason. Cassidy, I understand
having a bad day, or a week, or even a shitty month, but
being a professional requires you to put aside your own
problems and put the clients first."

"This has nothing to do with me PMSing or whatever it
is you think was going on, and you know it. You'll be hearing
from my lawyer." She pressed her finger on the End button
and ground her teeth together, rage and impotency flowing
through her veins like lava. She threw her phone across the
room, and it bounced with a sickening crack off her TV, the

screen shattering in a spiderweb pattern as her phone thudded to the floor. She stood and dragged her fingers through her hair, tugging on the ends until the sting penetrated the all-consuming need to punch something. No, she didn't need to punch something. She needed to punch someone.

Maxwell Fucking Denyer.

Cassidy paced, seething as the full weight of what had happened pressed down on her shoulders. She could only afford the rent on the apartment she was leasing if she had a job. Same with the payments for the furniture she'd bought. Her car too. She had enough saved for a few weeks at the most. Even if she had a rock-solid case against CIR for unfair dismissal, it would take months to be resolved and cost a fortune that she didn't have.

The walls were closing in, and she was kicking herself for every one of the stupid choices she'd made. She had to get out of there. She needed air. She needed... to go home. Cassidy grabbed her phone and keys and was out the door to her apartment before she could rethink things. She looked like a mess—leggings, socks, and a ratty old T-shirt with her hair pulled up in a messy bun on top of her head—but she didn't care. Neither would her parents.

Cassidy was on the motorway heading west out of the city within minutes of exiting the building's underground car park. Sunday evening traffic was non-existent, and the trip to her childhood home went quickly.

* * * * *

Her parents had gone to bed, but Cassidy couldn't sleep. She lay in her bedroom, staring at the ceiling fan as it spun in lazy circles in the shadowy light. Her posters of the boy bands she loved were long gone—her parents turning the room into a guest bedroom when she'd moved out. Even though the room was completely different now, it was still home.

Cassidy's phone sat beside her, mocking her. Logically, she knew her boss wouldn't take her back, but she still found herself hoping. Any hope she had, though, was outweighed with guilt and fear. She'd walked away from Jacob to save herself, but who did he have to turn to? His father? He hadn't spoken to his mother since he was a child, and he didn't have any siblings. Could he confide in his friends? Was there anyone in his corner? Or had she left him alone? The world didn't revolve around her—she wasn't that egotistical to think she'd become the centre of his universe— but they'd developed something special between them. A connection. Something deeper than a fuck and run. He'd crawled under her skin without Cassidy even realizing it. It hadn't taken long, but Cassidy had become hopelessly addicted to him. Was she that for him?

The distance she'd enforced was torturous, but there was no going back. It was over. The knowledge eviscerated her. She ached, an emptiness yawning inside her chest like a gaping wound. But it wasn't just that she wouldn't see him again. Knowing that Jacob could be alone, that he might be sitting around his apartment without anyone there to hold his hand or console him like her family had done for her, broke Cassidy. She wanted to be that person for him. But it was impossible. She'd been the one to end it, not him, and she knew he'd respect her decision too. He wouldn't call her. Neither would Phoenix. But it didn't diminish the desire to speak with them. She didn't have Phoenix's number and never would—given his comments to the police—but Jake's was burning a hole in her pocket. Tempting her to dial him. Getting in contact with him though would only lead Jake on and hurt her. But she couldn't walk away either, not until she knew he was okay.

"Bugger it," she murmured, calling him before she could second guess herself.

Jake picked up on the second ring. "Cass, hey, it's good to hear from you." His voice was warm, if not a bit hesitant, and she couldn't help the smile that tilted her lips. She was happy for the first time since she'd left. But the knowledge of what she had to tell him would crush that. She wanted to hold on and bask in the sensation just for another moment.

She blew out a breath. "Can we talk?"

"Yeah. Yeah, of course," he murmured.

"I'm leaving Sydney for a bit. I'm taking some time and going up to the Gold Coast."

The line was quiet for a moment, then he cleared his throat. "Yeah? When are you going?" His voice was higher than normal, as if he was forcing a bubbly answer.

She sighed. "Tomorrow morning at eleven."

Silence again. "I'm glad you were able to get the time off."

A bitter laugh escaped her lips. "Yeah, I don't have to worry about that. My boss told me not to bother coming back. I apparently lost the agency four clients in one day."

"Fuck. My father—"

"Pretty much what I guessed. Anyway, yeah..."

"Cass, can we work through this? Is there any way to save what we have?"

This time she was quiet. Confusion reigned supreme. She wanted—did she ever—but she was scared too. Of hurting him as much as herself. A couple of months earlier she'd hated him. She'd wanted to inflict physical pain on him. But things had changed. Knowing she was responsible for the rawness in his voice, the vulnerability interlaced with pain decimated her. What should she do? Self-preservation was a powerful instinct, but Cassidy was protective of Jacob too. She was fighting the desire to give him everything he needed, to be a safe spot for him to land, with her own fears. She'd been reticent about a relationship, because ultimately it would mean sacrificing her career, but even though she wished she had her job back, the thought taking up the most room in her head was what Jacob needed. And that terrified her the most. Her heart screamed at her to be brave, but her head demanded she run. That she protect herself. But speaking the words out loud was like swallowing glass, slicing her open from inside out. "I'm sorry, Jake. I can't. I've lost everything—"

"You could still have me," he whispered. His words wrapped around her like a blanket, but Cassidy fought to free herself. To shield herself. He was an incredible man, but his father was someone she never wanted to cross paths with again.

It was time to sever the tie. Permanently.

Squeezing her eyes closed and summoning all her strength, she ground out, "I don't want you." The lie was bitter on her tongue. "Goodbye, Jake."

TEN

Jacob

A mix of white-hot fury at his father and panic at the knowledge he had to let Cassidy go stole over Jake. Hearing her say she didn't want him and was leaving gutted him. It was as if she'd taken an axe to his chest and carved out his heart before stomping on it. He knew she wasn't trying to be cold—he'd seen that defence mechanism being used before where his father was concerned. She was trying to protect herself.

His father had done this to him. To them. Cassidy and Phoenix were caught up in the fallout. They didn't deserve any of the mess that had landed in their laps or to be humiliated in the way they had been, and Jake would be damned if he didn't try to fix it.

A plan formed in his mind.

Eleven a.m. Surely there weren't too many flights for the Gold Coast leaving then. Jake looked them up. Four flights, two with the same airline, one three times the price of the others and another with the discount carrier. He made a note of the details, looking up the terminals to see how far apart they were. Three of them were close, but the fourth was too far away to run between. If Cassidy had picked that flight, Jake would miss her. But the others? He could talk to her one more time.

Jake paced, wondering whether what he was about to do was insanity or genius. Stalker-like or romantic. He didn't want Cassidy to think the former, but he couldn't just let her leave. Once she left—once the agency got around to cancelling her mobile phone—he would have no way of contacting her again.

He sucked in a breath and wiped his palms on his shorts. His mind was made up.

* * * * *

Jake pushed through the door to Grounds and scanned his surroundings, looking for the man who'd been con-stantly on his mind for what felt like months. The café was busy, people lining up at the counter and others waiting for their coffee to be called out. Most of the tables were full, too, unsurprising for early on a Monday morning.

He lined up, waiting for his turn, and as the queue moved forward, Jake kept his gaze tracking around the room. The one person he wanted to see was either out back, on break, or not there at all. He hoped it wasn't the latter but was steeling himself for the disappointment. Jake looked at his watch, calculating how much time he had left, and put on his most charming smile for the older woman serving. "What can I get you, hon?"

"An espresso, please, and is Phoenix here?" he asked.

"No, sorry, he isn't." She shook her head, pushing the white square device closer to him so he could scan his card. "What's your name?"

"Can I leave a message for him?" Jake asked.

"He's no longer working here." The matter-of-fact answer had the impact of a wrecking ball crashing into the side of Jake's world. His entire foundation shifted, falling away and leaving him in that horrible state of flux where he knew he was about to fall, crash landing in a painful heap, but the rapid descent hadn't begun yet. He swallowed and opened his mouth, devastation stealing his words. She lifted her gaze to him, her pursed lips softening when she saw what must have been painted on his face. If his expression was anything like the utter devastation wreaked by the tornado that had ripped through his insides with the news she'd just delivered, there would be no hiding his distress.

"Since when?" he whispered.

"This morning." She motioned to the side where people were waiting. "Your name, sir?"

"Oh, um, Jake." He stepped to the side, but before the next person in line could speak, he leaned over the counter and added, "Do you have a number for him?"

The lady raised her brow at him and replied, "You know I can't give you that even if I wanted to." She held up her hands in a stopping motion. "And before you ask, no, I can't pass on a message."

Jake nodded once, his mind fighting the knowledge that he had no way of contacting Phoenix. No way of finding him.

But wait. He did. "Never mind the coffee," he called out, dashing out of the café. His heart raced, pounding out a staccato rhythm as he looked up and down the street. Phoenix lived in the student accommodation only a few blocks away.

He sprinted for the apartment building, his shoes slapping the pavement as he dodged between the morning commuters on their way to work. He uttered, "Sorry," and "Excuse me," as he muscled past people.

The building loomed up ahead, and Jake pumped his legs harder, pushing himself until his chest was tight and oxygen was sawing in and out of his lungs, burning them with every inhale and exhale. He slammed through the door and hit the button for the elevator, pressing it over and over, muttering, "Come on, open."

As the doors obeyed, he stepped in and cursed. He'd forgotten needing the security fob to get upstairs. Could he get up the stairs? Unlikely, but it was worth a shot. He stepped out of the lift and went to the stairwell. The door was locked. "Bloody hell."

"You looking for something, buddy?" a woman behind him, carrying a moving box, asked.

"A friend." That word didn't seem enough to describe the connection he'd experienced with Cassidy and Phoenix. It was only a few moments in time—barely a drop in the ocean in the grand scheme of life—but they'd had something special. "He lives here, but I don't have his number. I was going up to his floor to see if he was in."

"What level?"

"Fifteen."

"There's no one left up there. I've just come from level fifteen. Everyone's already moved out."

Jake growled and slammed his fist against the wall behind him. "Fuck. Why's everyone leaving?"

"End of semester and the rent's due tomorrow so we're all moving out today."

"Do you know the other people on level fifteen? I'm looking for Phoenix." He sounded desperate even to his own ears, but the woman froze, her gaze hardening.

She flicked her gaze to the door before standing up straighter and pulling her shoulders back. "Do I know him? No, I don't."

Jake studied her eyes for any flinch, but she didn't crack under the weight of his gaze. He was certain she was lying, but she had one hell of a poker face. He sank back against the door and scuffed his shoe against the linoleum floor. He could picture the sands of time slipping through his fingers; Phoenix going with them. He didn't want the man to become a memory—the one that got away—but what choice did he have? If this woman really did know him, she wasn't saying. But maybe he could tell her what he needed to say. Maybe if the universe was favouring him, she'd pass it on.

The doors opened behind him, but he ignored the interruption.

"He's… hell, I don't even know how to explain how in-credible he is. I really like him—so does Cass—and I needed to apologize for everything that happened. My father is an arsehole, and Phoenix copped the worst of it. I needed to make sure he was okay. See it with my own eyes, you know? But yeah—"

"Yeah, sucks that you can't tell him. But look, unless you're a resident here, you shouldn't be in the building so…" She left the rest unsaid, but there was no mistaking her intentions. He wanted to wait. Everything in him called to him to find Phoenix. To sit in front of the building for a week, a month, if he had to. To walk the city and knock on every door until he found their man.

But he couldn't.

Now he was in a race against time. One that meant he was going to lose one of them. Two people who, in the shortest period of time, had become the most important to him, and now he had to give one of them up.

No, he couldn't think like that. Wouldn't.

He would get them both. He had to. Jake wouldn't give up. Not on them. Not on himself.

Time wasn't on his side. He was being forced to choose who to chase first. But that's all it was. Not a permanent choice, just one that determined the order in which he would get them back.

He needed to move. Needed to act. Jake glanced at his watch again. *Shit.*

Until he could get back to Phoenix, he needed to rely on hope. He needed the woman before him, especially if, as he suspected—or hoped on a wing and a prayer—that she knew Phoenix to help him. "Look, I know you said you don't know him, but in case you run into him, can you give him this?" He slipped a card out of his wallet and handed it to her. "I'm not working there anymore, but I can always be reached on my mobile. Day or night. I want to speak with him. Really want to speak with him."

When she nodded, he spun on his heel, stopping dead in his tracks. He knew the man before him. But from where? He'd seen him around before.

It took a second, but then it hit him. He'd been with Phoenix the night before last. They'd walked to the club together.

Trav.

"I'll tell him," the man—Trav—said. He reached out for the business card Phoenix had left with the woman and held it up. "I can't guarantee he'll call. He's pretty pissed, but I'll give him this."

"Thank you," Jake breathed. "You have no idea how much this means."

* * * * *

The airport was busy. People streamed along the walkways hauling luggage behind them. He dashed through the massive concourse, dodging between people as he ran, not slowing his pace until he reached the line for security.

He was late and there was a long queue.

He needed to get to each of the three gates and hope that he saw her. Jake prayed that she hadn't chosen the fourth, or he'd have no chance.

Watching the clock and tapping his foot anxiously, he inched forward as security scanned each and every person and their hand luggage. He flipped his phone over and over in his palm, wishing he'd been able to contact Cassidy. She'd either blocked his number or had her phone turned off. He was doing this low tech. Relying on timing and sheer luck to point him in the right direction. Jake had never been a big believer in fate, but there was no doubting the universe had aligned to give him a taste of what he truly wanted. He couldn't, no wouldn't, believe that the glimpse was just to torment him. To tease him only for it to be snatched away.

On paper, Jake wasn't the best kind of person—he despised the only family he had, he was a failure in his career, and had never really amounted to much of anything—but he had to believe that there were reasons for that too. His father's meddling, the control he exerted over every aspect of his life had bled into Jake's too. His father had treated him as a pawn from the moment he'd been born. Used to further his father's agenda. He'd enjoyed watching Jake fail to achieve the impossible standards he'd set, making his life hell for doing so.

Jake's pansexuality was just another of those things he'd failed at. He could just imagine the lecture his father would have given him had he voluntarily come out to the man. Perhaps, if he'd done that rather than getting busted right in the middle of loving on the most beautiful man he'd ever seen, Jake would have stood a chance.

He huffed out a laugh, but the bitterness it left in his mouth was telling. There was no way his father would have accepted him. That was why he'd kept it a secret—some misplaced desire to maintain the last remaining tie with the only family he had—but Jake understood now. He'd seen the way his father had spat vile hatred at him like he was an abomination rather than his own son. He'd hurt Jake, and the people who were coming to mean more to him than Jake could ever have fathomed. Now it was time for Jake to step up and reclaim his life.

He knew what he wanted and what he had to do.

Jake smiled, grim determination settling within him. He would get them back, and he would escape his father's clutches once and for all.

Finally passing through security, Jake sprinted through the wide walkways to the gates he needed. Announcements played overhead, airline staff calling passengers to their flights. Destinations awaited. Holidays, business meetings, last-ditch attempts at having the woman he was falling in love with hear him one more time.

He skidded to a stop at the first gate and scanned the crowd of people. There, among a group of businesspeople, was a blonde head of hair swept up into a high bun. He couldn't see the woman properly. Jake stepped closer, jockeying for a better view. She turned, and he held his breath.

It wasn't her.

"Damn it," he muttered under his breath, looking around again. The gate was packed, but no one else stood out. He gritted his teeth and hoped beyond any sort of reasonable measure that he hadn't missed Cassidy on his perusal. Glancing around one last time, he ran to the next gate.

The boarding call was announced. There. It was her. Unmistakeably, the woman of his dreams.

"Cassidy!" His voice boomed over the hum of the crowd, and she froze mid-stride. She turned slowly as she swept the crowd of people, looking for him. But Jake was already moving, his legs carrying him toward her. She found him, and as her gaze locked on his, the look she shot him had his steps faltering. Heat and longing mixed with a healthy dose of anger.

"You," she breathed as he snapped out of the spell she'd cast over him.

"Yes, me," he murmured, reaching for her hand. "Cass, I'm sorry. There are no words to describe what he did to you. To us. I know I'm responsible for everything he did and for all the damage he caused. I don't deserve forgiveness, but I'm going to ask for it anyway." Cassidy started to shake her head, but Jake reached out, cupping her face and running his thumb over the smooth skin on her cheek, stilling her movement. "I want this. Us. Both of you, and I'm willing to fight for it—"

"How? How can you fight him? Your father's a monster. With a few telephone calls, he's managed to completely screw up both your career and mine. What chance do we have against that?"

"A much better one if we stick together." He sucked in a breath, resisting the urge to wipe his palms down his jeans. "Let me come with you. I already have a ticket. We can go away together and talk. See if we can save what we have."

Cassidy's lip twitched as if she was fighting a smile. With surprise colouring her tone, she said, "You're nervous, but you didn't let go of me."

Jake huffed out a laugh. "You have no idea how nervous I am. I'm running on adrenaline and I'm about to pass out. I'm that crazy."

"You didn't wipe your palms." Cassidy squeezed his hand and brought her other to his waist, slipping under the duffel he was carrying to pull him closer. "You were never the problem, Jake. But your dad—"

"I'm falling in love with you," he whispered. She stopped talking the moment his words registered, her mouth hanging open as her eyes widened. He watched her as her gaze left his, scanning his face as if she was seeing him for the first time, before their eyes locked once more. Still, she didn't talk. But there was a kind of wonder playing on her lips and in her eyes. A spark that he hadn't seen since the night before when they'd been together.

He waited, forcing himself to let Cassidy react in her own time. Holding his breath, Jake watched, fighting to keep his face neutral. His heart stuttered to a stop, halting its frenetic beats when Cassidy closed her eyes and looked away.

"I was determined to walk away from you. My head was telling me to never want to see you again. But like I said, the problem was never you. Your dad is awful. Officially the worst person I have ever met. Someone needs to stop him, but I can't risk any more. I have nothing left. I told you last night that I didn't want you." Her voice was quiet but firm, and Jake's gut sank. There was no doubting her words. She gazed up at him, and the truth shining in her eyes stole his breath. "It was a lie. I'm falling for you too, Jake—"

He reacted in a fraction of a second, instinct taking over well before his brain had a chance to catch up. Eliminating the distance between them, he stole her next words, letting them die on her tongue as he silenced her protest with a kiss. He pressed his lips to hers. The touch was sweet—completely chaste—but it rocked his world. This was his last moment to persuade her. His final chance at having half of what he wanted. His brain frantically tried to formulate counter-arguments to the ones that were no doubt bubbling on Cassidy's tongue, but it had short-circuited with the brush of those strawberry-tasting lips against his. Jake wasn't sure whether he was riding cloud nine or struggling under the weight of a giant boulder about to crush him.

Cassidy's tongue slipped out and touched his lip, and he opened for her. Sound faded, his world reducing to the two of them wrapped around each other as he showed her just how much she meant to him. Cassidy pulled him closer, clutching him tighter, and Jake stilled. Against her lips, he whispered, "You're not pushing me away?"

"No." Their gazes locked and the certainty in them squashed Jake's doubts. Happiness bloomed in his chest, wanting to burst free like a geyser. This was the Cassidy he'd first met. The one filled with fire. With determination. "I want this, Jake. I want you and Phoenix. Your dad scares the shit out of me, and I'm probably crazy for not running away, but I can't do it. I've spent the whole morning trying to figure out how to ask you to either stop me from going or to come with me. I had to turn my damn phone off to stop looking at it every two minutes."

Jake laughed, the fizz of happiness bubbling out of him. "I thought you'd blocked me. I've never been happier to be wrong." He nuzzled her cheek with his stubbled one and sighed. "What do you want me to do, Cass? Do I stay here and wait for Phoenix, or do I come with you? Tell me what you need me to do."

She bit down on her lip. "I want you with me. Let's go away for a few days, regroup, and then come back for him. We know his shifts at Grounds and where he lives. We go there and bring him back to us."

"It's not gonna be that easy. He finished up at Grounds. His boss told me this morning that he's no longer working there, and I went by his apartment. He's moved out, but I saw his friend—the one he was with the other night. He said he'd give him my number. We've got no other way of contacting him though. Phoenix is gone from the only two places we know."

Cassidy's shoulders slumped, and she shook her head, her expression crumbling. "I don't want to give him up."

"Neither do I. But it's not over yet. Have faith. He'll call. I can feel it." Jake pulled her close again and held her tight. An announcement over the PA system broke into their bubble. "Shit, that's the last call for my flight. It's your decision. Together or apart? Here or the Gold Coast?"

She smiled and nodded. "Together on the Gold Coast for a few days. We'll work out a way to find him and get our lives back in order, then come back for him."

Jake grinned and nodded, pulling back so he could catch his flight. He didn't want to give her a kiss goodbye. There was nothing final about this hour's separation. What they were doing and where they were going was all ahead of them. "See you in an hour."

He let go of her hand and stepped backward, smiling at her. Joy, pure and as strong as the sun's rays, filled him and he was sure it reflected in his wide grin. She was beautiful, standing there with a matching smile on her face and her hands stuffed in her pockets. Even dressed casually, she looked a million dollars in jeans, a knitted singlet, and matching cream heels. It took everything in him not to eliminate the distance between them again. She opened her mouth as if to say something, and her smile turned shy. "See you in an hour. Don't leave me waiting."

Hearing those words had the weight lifting off his shoulders. He was floating, riding a high that had, only twenty-four hours earlier, crashed and burned. They weren't complete—they had a way to go to get there again—but they would do it. He knew they would. He raised his hand and placed it over his heart before holding it out to Cassidy. He might as well hand his heart over to her. She already held it anyway. "I wouldn't dream of it."

ELEVEN

Phoenix

The weekend was a complete and utter clusterfuck. Getting thrown onto the street barefoot and with his jeans barely buttoned up was humiliating. The threat he received from the ape of a man who'd shoved him out the door, glared at him, pointed down the street, and growled, "Leave, and don't come back," terrified him. It wasn't so much the words or even the actions, but rather the look in those dead eyes. Eyes so cold and unflinching, devoid of any emotion that a shiver had run down his spine and made the hairs on the back of his neck stand up.

Phoenix didn't even remember what happened next, except that he found himself crashing through his front door hours later after having run half the city, trying to lose the feel of those eyes watching him.

He hadn't noticed the pain in his shoulder until he'd lifted his suitcase to shove some clothes in it. Fire shot through his arm, and Phoenix clutched it, shouting out in agony. It hit him then. Everything he'd been through. Every second of the rollercoaster of emotions he'd experienced in twenty-four hours crashed into him. The physical ache coalescing with the emotional destruction wrought upon him levelled Phoenix.

Then his friends had barged through his door, teasing him until they'd seen the tears tracking down his cheeks and the bruise forming around his arm. Rachael and Stevo's expressions had changed when he finished explaining how he got his injuries. They looked at him with wide eyes and stony silence. He couldn't tell whether they were disgusted, surprised, or holding in a laugh. Was the whole thing his fault? Had he brought this on himself? Was it because he'd chased the two people who'd captured his attention from the moment he'd met them? Some cosmic karma biting him in the arse? But then Rachael had spoken, and the hatred spilling from her mouth made him flinch. Until he realized she wasn't talking about him. Within minutes, she'd ordered Trav to get a rideshare to the hospital and plotted out the bones of a civil suit.

Phoenix was drained. It was as if all his energy had been sucked out of his bones, leaving him a husk. He had nothing left to argue, so he followed along, letting his friend lead the way and trying to avoid the others' wary gazes. They hadn't said much since they'd found him, and it made him antsy. What were they thinking?

When the ordeal at the hospital was over, he'd begged Rachael to go home. Drugged up on pain pills and his shoulder strapped with his arm in a sling, he wanted to curl up and hide under his covers. But Rachael insisted the police needed to be involved.

That's when he'd received the phone call from a Senior Sergeant Campbell. He'd excused himself from his friends, ducking into the bathroom in the emergency ward to talk privately. Except he didn't do much talking. The officer explained how he'd been asked to do a welfare check on him because of a concerned citizen making a complaint against Jake and Cassidy. Phoenix tried to explain his side of the story—how he'd been with them, and they'd been happy until they were interrupted. But every time he spoke, every time he tried to get the words out, the officer cut him off. He accepted one-worded answers, and that was it. Anything more and the answers repeated back were totally different to the ones Phoenix had given. His words were being twisted against him, and Phoenix knew when to shut up. The whole conversation had him wary. Anxiety spiked, his heart rate quickening and breathing shallowed out. Even locked in the bathroom, he couldn't help looking over his shoulder. He had to get away. Had to cut ties with anything that would bring the two men and woman who'd walked in on them out of his life.

That was a week earlier. Moving out of the apartment wasn't fun, especially with the torn muscle in his shoulder rendering him mostly useless. Thank goodness for his friends. If it wasn't for them, he'd still be trying to lug his bags out. Resigning from Grounds was bittersweet—he was only leaving a week early, but he knew he'd left his boss in the lurch. She'd understood when he explained his arm was in a sling, and he was on painkillers strong enough to level a horse.

Now, a new chapter was beginning, and Phoenix was excited. It was his first day on the job, and he was sequestered with a group of about fifteen people, most of whom were around his age, in the grand lobby of the office tower getting his security tags. The person from HR at the firm had checked his photo ID, and he was grinning happily at the security guard taking his photo for his access pass.

"There you go," the woman said a few moments later, handing him a card that looked much like a credit card, the silver chip included.

"Thanks." He stepped away, rejoining the group of new hires who were sipping on coffee and eating pastries as they waited to be escorted up to the firm's conference room for their first day of induction.

Half an hour later, they were ready, and Phoenix was anxious to get started. He couldn't wait to dive into whatever cases the litigation department was looking after. Big or small, he didn't care. It had been a dream of his to be in court ever since he could remember. It was his parents' doing. They'd always done their best, but hand me down uniforms and last year's textbooks were the norm for him. Both his parents worked hard, endless hours every day just to make ends meet, and Phoenix had quickly learned to help where he could. His mum had begged him to study hard so he could get into university and be anything he wanted. He'd taken it to heart. High school legal studies had given him a taste of law. Rereading *To Kill A Mockingbird* after studying American colonial history and realizing the similarities with the indigenous Australian experience had cemented it. He wanted to make a difference. To help the disenfranchised and be able to stand up in court and fight for the people who needed it. The firm's extensive pro bono policy—the work done for the benefit of the community at no charge—had inspired Phoenix to apply. Now, he was itching to get started.

"Welcome to Stark Williams Lawyers. My name is Maisie Wilkins, and I am the human resources director." She acknowledged the indigenous elders, past and present, and got started, instructing them to open the induction pack and reviewing the plan for their first two days at the firm. Much of it was learning the basics of the computer systems and hearing about the specializations of each of the divisions within the firm, how the national and international offices worked together and meeting each of the executive partners. Once they were placed in their divisions the next day, they would meet with their supervising partners and have a chance to get started.

"Right, so now that you're settled in, I'd like to introduce our first guest. Mr Denyer is one of the executive partners here at the firm and has a long and prestigious list of clients. Please welcome him."

Phoenix clapped along with the other new hires and swivelled in his chair to get a glimpse of the salt-and-pepper-haired man walking in. His heart stopped, lodging in his throat. Right there, dressed in a navy-blue three-piece suit with a crisp white shirt and charcoal paisley tie, was the man who had ordered his ousting from the apartment. Different eyes haunted him—cold dead ones—but he knew who the real powerhouse in that relationship was. Mr Denyer hadn't laid a hand on him, but he'd turned Phoenix's special night into a nightmare, one that he kept reliving every time he tried to sleep.

Shrewd blue eyes scanned the faces at the table until they came to a halt at Phoenix's. He swallowed, waiting for a reaction. But other than Mr Denyer's eyes narrowing fractionally, there was none. Phoenix slowly released the breath he hadn't even realized he was holding as the other man's eyes slid away from him.

Mr Denyer looked to Ms Wilkins, and she stepped forward, tilting her head close so that he could whisper in her ear. With her back to the boardroom's other occupants, she didn't see the cold glint in Denyer's eyes when they locked on Phoenix's. A shiver ran down his spine, and he tapped the pen against his hand in a rapid beat. Clenching his teeth, Phoenix held the other man's gaze, refusing to back down. His hands may have been shaking and sweat trickling down his spine at the stare, but Phoenix wouldn't show him any weakness. Not after he'd already seen him naked and impaled on another man's cock—his son's.

Ms Wilkins nodded and stepped away, walking out the door.

"Good morning, and congratulations. Stark Williams is a leading multi-national law firm. We are the best because we employ the best of the best. Some of you will thrive here. All of you will be challenged—"

The door opened, and the same lady who'd taken his identification slipped in. "Mr Denyer, my apologies for interrupting." He turned to her, giving her a gracious smile before locking eyes with Phoenix. His blood ran cold. That look—the smug satisfaction Denyer flashed him was all too familiar. It was the same look he'd given Cassidy when he'd told her to sit down and shut up before Phoenix had been hauled out of the room. "I need to borrow one of our new recruits. Mr Black, can you please come with me?"

The frenetic tapping of his hand stilled, his body reacting while his mind screeched to a halt, processing the words that she'd just spoken. He swallowed, his mouth as dry as the Sahara, and nodded. Placing the pen in the supple leather portfolio, he closed it and moved to pick it up. "Leave it there," she instructed with a professional smile that did nothing to ease his nerves. He picked up the phone he had facing down on the table and slipped it into his pocket as he stood.

"Excuse me," Phoenix murmured as he pushed the chair out, buttoned his jacket, and studiously ignored the other eyes on him. The door closed behind him, and he looked back to the woman who'd collected him. "Is everything okay?" he asked.

"Please, step in here." She motioned to a smaller meeting room, with a round table and four of the leather high backed chairs in the main boardroom. Seated at the table was Ms Wilkins, and standing in the corner, looking down at Phoenix with a cruel glint in his eyes and a smirk on his lips, was the bastard who'd dragged him out of the apartment and thrown him to the ground, not caring in the slightest that he was still half-naked.

"Mr Black—"

"What's going on? I don't think I should miss Mr Denyer's presentation—" He couldn't believe the words coming out of his mouth. Not miss Mr Denyer's presentation? He wanted as far away from the man as possible, not to work for his firm. Not to bill clients for time where a share of those profits went to a man who'd humiliated and hurt him. Not one whose voice he could still hear as he disrespected both Jake and Cassidy, not to mention himself. He wanted to help people, not work for a firm whose executive partners and their minions behaved like they were above the law.

"Mr Black," Ms Wilkins started again. "We regret to inform you that the department you were slated to work in has reconsidered its resourcing requirements for the next year and no longer require a graduate to join them." She held out her hand, motioning for the security pass hung on a rainbow lanyard around his neck.

Phoenix stood and slipped the card out of its clear plastic sleeve. "I'm not an idiot, Ms Wilkins. I know exactly why my employment is being terminated. Do your other LGBTQIA staff know how homophobic Denyer is?"

"Excuse me?"

"He was there." Phoenix pointed to the man glaring at him. "Ask him what set Denyer off." He dropped the card on the table and walked out of the office, head held high. He didn't get far on his own though, before Denyer's hired muscle grasped his elbow roughly and escorted him out, down the lift and out the front doors.

The morning sun hit his face, and a breeze straight off the harbour blew around him. Phoenix squared his shoulders and took his first step of... unemployment.

Fuck.

TWELVE

Jake

The location of Cassidy's family's holiday home was amazing. No wonder she had fond memories of holidaying there. Right on the water, there was a sun-drenched jetty with two deck chairs sitting at its end. The back garden wasn't much more than a sloping lawn, but Cassidy had shown him the box filled with old lawn games they used to play and the hammock that hung from hooks perched halfway up two thick palms. Come nightfall, he had every intention of curling up with Cassidy in it.

The house was exactly as he'd expected a holiday home to be. Straight out of the seventies, complete with a green-and mission-brown kitchen and timber panelling with the ugliest patterned carpet he'd ever seen. But the original retro styling was cool in its own right, giving the house a vibe so detached from Sydney's modern hustle and bustle that it forced them to slow things down.

When they'd first arrived, the air was stale, and a layer of dust had settled over everything. They'd turned the green refrigerator on, wiped everything down, and opened the house up to let it air. It had kept him busy, his focus off his phone, but he hadn't let it out of his sight. The second day was worse. They'd spent it following the shade, shifting the deck chairs around the yard as they stared out at the water watching the boats and jet skis pass them by. Jake lost count of how many times he'd lit the screen of his phone up, checking over and over again for a missed call or text.

But one never came.

The third day he was even more restless. But it was more than Phoenix on his mind now. Hiding on the Gold Coast—and that's what they were doing—wasn't going to get them anywhere.

They'd undoubtedly needed time to adjust. Getting his head around the fact that he barely recognized his life anymore was a trip. Jake had never been so overwhelmed before. His entire universe had shifted, undergoing a radical transformation. One day he'd been working, trying to win over a man he was insanely attracted to. The woman he was falling for was helping; she wanted their man just as much. But then things changed, and although the woman of his dreams was still standing next to him, he'd lost the boy. He had no idea how to get him back. Add to that the fact that he was unemployed and about to be homeless, and Jake needed time to find his feet again.

His first priority needed to be getting back on some kind of track. There was no chance in hell he'd move back in with his father—especially after what he'd done. When he'd moved out, Jake promised himself he'd never step foot in the mausoleum he'd grown up in again, but to rent some-where, even a room, he needed to have a steady income.

The time he'd spent waiting for Phoenix to call hadn't been spent idle, though. Jake had done some soul searching and knew he was at a fork in the road. He could either choose the well-travelled path, or he could make some changes and forge his own way. Commercial real estate was never his passion. He'd been thrown into it and had put up with the tediousness because he didn't really have a choice. With his father and Charles looking over his shoulder, he'd been stuck there. His father's declaration that he was done was the closest thing to being disowned that Jake could hope for. There was still a conversation that needed to be had—his father needed to hear some home truths—but for once, Jake didn't feel the weight of his father's interference on him. He knew he was on his own, and the thought was freeing. Like a portal filled with a monster had finally been closed.

Was he brave enough to walk his own path now? To strike out into residential like he'd always wanted? If he played his cards right, he could get in with one of the smaller agencies, build up some experience and then start his own business. He could be his own boss one day.

Jake smiled. Yeah, his career was suddenly looking very different to what it had been only a week ago. But it was exciting too. He could now see a path that had been cov-ered in brambles and overgrowth open up in front of him. It would undoubtedly be a bumpy ride, but the grass really did seem greener on this side.

Cassidy was affected by all this too. She'd been quiet. He could see that she was processing and needed time and space to come up with a Plan B for her life. Her landlord, while sympathetic, couldn't assure her that her lease would be renewed if she fell behind in the rent. Unless she could find another job quick smart, Cassidy would be moving in with her parents and commuting to whatever job she landed. Add in the non-compete clause and it restricted the areas in which she could work. Jake hated that he was the cause of all her problems—thanks to his father—but walking away wouldn't help her. He needed to make it right.

"What do you think of this?" Jake asked, spinning his laptop around to show her. They'd tweaked Cassidy's CV earlier in the day, and he was now working on his own. Cassidy was onto her job search, finding positions she could apply for, but most of the ones she found represented a significant backward step. She wasn't willing to travel that route yet, and Jake didn't blame her.

"I like it." She hesitated, and Jake looked over to her, noticing that she was no longer on the job search websites but on social media.

"Missing anything?" he asked, unsure of whether he really wanted to know her answer. It tore at his heart that she could be yearning for Sydney already.

She looked at him with a furrowed brow, confusion creating a line down her forehead. She opened her mouth before closing it again then gave a small shake of her head. "Huh?"

He pointed to the screen. "Your friends."

She pursed her lips and shook her head, sadness radiating from her. "I know you said Phoenix would call, but I don't think he's going to. I started looking for him, and I might have found his account, but it's private, so I can't see anything. His photo isn't the clearest, and I can't zoom in on it to be sure it's even him. I need his approval to follow so I can send a message." She sighed, her eyes dull, devoid of the spark that made her larger than life. "I just feel useless, you know? Like here we are on holiday, and we don't even know how he's doing."

Oh, Cassidy. He resisted the temptation to take her into his arms—they hadn't done more than smile shyly at each other since their declarations in the airport—and he didn't want to push his luck. Jake nodded, resting his elbows on his knees and lacing his fingers together to stop himself from reaching for her. "Maybe we should head home?"

"Yeah, maybe."

Jake stared at the way the ripples on the water sparkled in the sunlight. "Do you want that? We can book tickets now if you like."

She shrugged. "I don't know. I'm kind of scared to go home. Your dad…" She shook her head. "Why did you give him a key to your apartment?"

Jake huffed, anger pulsing through him at the sheer number of fraudulent dealings his father was involved in. Cassidy was right—someone needed to shut him down. "I didn't. The agent said that apparently I contacted them and asked for another set to be cut so I could give them to my father, and that he was collecting them directly. He walked in, showed his ID, and walked out with the keys."

Cassidy looked at him wide-eyed, her mouth popping open. "You're kidding?"

He shook his head and blew out a breath. "No, but nothing surprises me any more." He paused, not wanting to talk about his father. He wanted to get back to what was important to him—to them—Phoenix. "I telephoned Grounds earlier." He held his breath, waiting for Cassidy's reaction. Her gaze snapped to his, and she leaned forward, mirroring his pose. "Figured I'd try one last time to get Phoenix's number."

"What happened?"

"I spoke to one of the baristas and then the manager again. I asked to pass on a message or for them to give me his number, but they wouldn't. I practically begged them. They hung up on me."

Her shoulders dropped, and she held her head low. "When I was a kid, Mum and Dad used to have these thick telephone directories they kept near the phone. Everyone we knew was listed. Anytime they wanted to look someone up, they'd just flip it open and call them. Now, there's no hope of finding someone's number. People don't even have landlines any more."

Jake smiled. "I remember that too. My aunt had a magazine rack that my uncle made, especially for them." He picked up the bottle of water sitting on the concrete by his feet and took a swig. "We've called the university, Grounds, and the building he used to live in. None of them will give us anything. Not surprising given privacy laws. We know his name but don't have any contact details, and he's got my number but hasn't called it. Where does that leave us?"

Cassidy turned to him, her lips pressed in a tight line and her brow furrowed. "Absolutely nowhere. It leaves us no closer to speaking with him." She scrubbed her forehead with her hands, letting out a frustrated groan before tucking her hair behind her ear. Jake itched to run his fingers through those thick blonde waves. "The only thing we haven't done is ask for his number from the police, but as if they'll give it to us."

"Yeah, let's not go there." He could just imagine how disastrously wrong that conversation could go, especially after the Senior Sergeant had accused them of hurting Phoenix.

* * * * *

The sun was setting over the mountains, the air cooling as the shadows lengthened and darkness descended. They'd gone for a walk along the foreshore, ending it at the famous fish and chip shop near the swimming hole and kids' playground. Families surrounded them, and Jake watched with a wistfulness that had never struck so hard. It wasn't a desire for kids of his own—he didn't want to be responsible for screwing up a kid's life like his father had done to him. It was for his own upbringing. The broken relationship he had with his mum and the utterly toxic one with his father. One that he needed to do something about to be free from.

Pelicans flew in, landing and gliding smoothly along the water. They gathered in front of the doors, waiting to be fed. Their squawks and the excited, happy chatter of the kids around Jake brought him peace. It helped him pluck up the courage to make the call. He needed to cut the final ties with his father, but telling his only family he wanted nothing to do with him any more was proving more difficult than he'd anticipated.

Fear wasn't making his gut churn, and his heart beat harder. The nervous energy coursing through him was from knowing he was about to leave his father with no one. Sure, he had his latest wife, but they never lasted long. The women his father latched onto soon lost their sheen, and his father would toss away his latest toy in favour of a new shiny object soon enough. It happened every time. His heart hurt for his only family, but when Jake thought about what Maxwell Denyer had done to him just in the last week, he stiffened his spine. The nerves turned to determination. His father had made his bed, and now it was time to lie in it. He couldn't forgive him for hurting Cassidy and Phoenix. No matter how much his father thought him a failure, his lovers didn't deserve the shitstorm that had rained down upon them because of the man.

Jake wiped his palms on his shorts and brought up his father's number on his phone. Two, then three rings later, and stony silence met his ears, and Jake looked to see whether his father had ended the call or picked it up. "Hello?"

"Jacob," his father answered, his words clipped and his tone cold. There was no emotion in his tone, no affection or happiness, and the earlier guilt at pushing his father away evaporated.

Jake closed his eyes and mentally hugged the little boy who'd grown up scared of his father's shadow. His only wish as a child was that he could make his dad proud. Earn his love. It was a wish that would never be fulfilled and one he'd given up on. He straightened his spine, steadied his breathing, and wiped his sweaty palm on his shorts. "Father, we need to talk."

"I don't have time at the moment. You'll need to book an appointment—"

"Make time," he snapped, standing up and pacing. The man he'd become, the one who'd lost nearly everything curtesy of his father, was finally ready to stand up for the little boy he'd once been. "This is important."

His father sighed as if he was being put upon. "Very well."

It was now or never. His chance to break free of the chains his father had bound him in. "I've had enough of this toxic thing we have going on. It's time you forget that I ever existed. Your interference has ruined—"

"You did that," the other man spat, his voice a growl filled with accusation. "You were the one whose career was hanging on by a thread—"

"You think I'm worried about my job?" Jake asked incredulously. It was the least of his concerns.

"And this is why you'll never make anything of yourself, Jacob. You'll never see anything like my success—"

He huffed out a laugh, but it held no humour. "You know, I'm absolutely fine with that. I don't want to be anything like you, Father. I want my friends and lovers to be with me because they love me. I don't collect information on people to use it against them. I don't buy them or threaten them. You have nothing and no one in your life who you haven't manipulated and used to further your own agenda. You're selfish and hateful, and one day you'll piss off the wrong person. Karma will come and collect payment, and I can't wait to see you realize you're alone and have nothing and no one there for you. You are the epitome of everything wrong with society, and I want nothing to do with you—"

"Are you finished?" he asked.

"Not even close, but I will say this. Write me off as dead, Father, and I'll do the same for you. If you see me in the street, don't bother looking twice."

"If that's how you want it, fine." The cold, calm voice filtering through the line was detached. There was no show of emotion at all, and not for the first time Jake wondered if his father was even capable of feeling anything.

He bit down on his tongue, resisting the urge to apologize so he could slink back into the shadows and hide. He knew he was pushing his father, tormenting him into snapping, and when he did, Jake had always been worse off. But it was time to make his final stand and push for what he needed, or he would never be free.

He hadn't expected his father's reaction, though. Giving up that easily wasn't in his father's blood. A chill ran down Jake's spine. Even now, when Jake was nearly a thousand kilometres away with a third of the country separating them, his father terrorised him. How far did those tentacles of his influence reach? Jake closed his eyes, taking strength from the calm surrounding him. The cool breeze and the sound of water lapping at the shore, children playing, and people laughing. "Yes, that's what I want."

"Very well." His father paused, and Jake's shoulders slumped in relief. "But here are my rules." His ears pricked up like a dog's, and the hairs stood up on the back of his neck. Danger, danger repeated itself on a loop in his head, because there it was, his father's impossible demands. "Leave Sydney and stay gone. Don't come back. Don't even step foot in the city. If you do, I'll end you—"

"Is that a threat, Father? Are you actually telling me—"

"There's that mind of yours wandering up into the clouds again imagining the most ridiculous notions." The flippant response was nothing Jake hadn't seen before, except the patronising comments were usually reserved for the women who tried to argue a point with his father. His go-to was accusing them of being overly emotional or irrational. But Jake wasn't deterred.

"Well, set it out for me, then. You say you'll end me. What exactly does that mean?"

"Don't back talk me, boy."

Jake laughed, the sound just like his father's condescending tone, and something inside him snapped. Rage boiled through his blood, his vision tinged with a red haze as all the pent-up emotion of being bullied for decades rose to the surface, cascading over in an unstoppable torrent like the churning waters of Niagara Falls. "Or you'll do what, Father?" His voice was unrecognizable. Arrogance oozed from him, mirroring his father's callous disregard for Jake. "You know what, don't answer that. You want me out of Sydney, fine. Consider me gone." His voice was louder than he intended, booming out over the happy families, until he reined in his anger. Seething, he slammed his finger on the button ending the call, and resisted the urge to hurl it into the blue lapping waters of the Broadwater. Crushing the phone in his hand—he would be surprised if it still worked—he forced himself to breathe. He dropped it on the table and balled his fists, leaning over as he tried to calm his breathing. White-hot fury bled through his vision. His father had dealt his final blow, going for the jugular.

"Jake?" Cassidy asked quietly, sliding a hand up his back to cup his nape. He turned to her when she tugged him into her arms, and she held him, rocking him back and forth as his anger dissipated, and he was left with a hollowness—a void as deep as a black hole—in his chest. Shuddering breaths wracked him as the reality of what he'd just agreed to began to sink in.

"I told him—"

"I heard." She pulled back and cupped his face. "Are you okay?"

"I... I don't know." He shook his head and his shoulders slumped.

"Cassie?" an unfamiliar voice called, and Cassidy pressed a quick kiss to the corner of his mouth before she turned and motioned to the man. "Give me a second."

Jake watched as she turned and walked away. It wouldn't be the last time she did it either, except that when it happened next, she would likely never return.

Dinner was quiet, Cassidy seemingly lost in thought and Jake replaying the conversation on repeat in his head. He pushed the chips around the greaseproof paper lining of the unwrapped package, leaving his fish untouched. Nausea crawled up his throat, telling Jake he hadn't dreamed the conversation with his father. Any hope that it was just a nightmare he'd wake up from was shattered when a seagull landed on the metal seat next to him and squawked. He jumped, fright shocking his heart into a few pounding beats. He'd just agreed to leave Sydney, to walk away from everything he knew all because of his father.

He'd be leaving her.

And Phoenix.

What had he done?

In a fit of rage, he'd gone and ruined everything, and now he was going to pay the price for his stupidity. His heart was about to be broken; losing Cassidy was now almost a certainty.

"I'm sorry," he whispered.

"Don't, Jake." She held up her hand and shook her head. "Just give me a minute, all right?"

He nodded, the cracks in his chest deepening.

* * * * *

Cassidy

She couldn't believe what she'd heard. That man was... insane. Telling Jake that he'd end him? Who said those kinds of things? She was so proud of him for standing up to his father, but at the same time, he'd just changed the course of his life. If he contacted his father again to say the deal was off, what would the consequences be? On the one hand, Cassidy wanted to ask what he could really do? But with what she'd seen so far, the answer seemed like a lot.

Flopping back on her bed, she brought her parents' number up in her phone and dialled. "Hello?"

"Hi, Mum." Cassidy paused. "Can you talk? I need some advice."

There was a shuffling on the other end and the sound of a door closing before there was quiet. "Sure, honey. What's going on?"

"Well, you know how I was at your place and said that I had a bad break-up, and things were crazy, and I needed to get away because work had gone to hell in a handbasket too?"

"Yes," her mum said, stretching the vowel out.

"There's more." Cassidy winced when her mum groaned. "I was trying to make a poly relationship work. We hit it off, and Jake, the man I'd been sort of seeing, Phoenix, our guy, and I were in bed together. Jake's dad walked in on us, and he... well, he wasn't happy. I don't know who the heck he is, but one minute we were together, and the next, Jake and I had both lost our jobs. We don't know if Phoenix wants to see us again. We haven't heard from him."

"Okay." Her mum blew out a breath, and there was a shuffling on the phone again. Cassidy could just imagine her rubbing her forehead to knead out the headache she was no doubt giving her mother. Cassidy had come out as poly to her family years earlier. Her parents were incredibly supportive, never blinking an eye at her desire for a non-traditional relationship. Her mum understood, having romanced two partners at the same time before meeting Cassie's dad. She'd never doubted her dad's support either. She could remember his words like it was yesterday too. "Regardless of whether he experienced love the same, the world was a beautiful place because of its differences, not the things that made it the same. If people experienced love differently, then who was he to question it. It was simply another thing to love."

She may have come out, but she'd never actually introduced her parents to a partner, never mind two. Cassidy hadn't found anyone she wanted to take home to meet them. Would they still support her if it was in the open for the world to see?

"Hi, baby girl," her dad said. "Your mum just waved me over. What's going on?"

Cassidy closed her eyes and repeated herself. She was met with silence on the other end. Before she chickened out, she added, "Jake met me at the airport and asked to come with me to the Goldie. He's here with me. We're in kind of a weird spot, though, tiptoeing around each other. He rang his dad tonight to tell him that he was done speaking with him. I only caught the tail end of the conversation, but Jake's dad said he needed to leave Sydney. He was pretty angry and agreed."

"So what are you thinking?"

"What do I do? Do I tell him he's insane, that his dad is a psycho and come home, get a new job somewhere outside of the city and pretend things never went south? Or do I do something crazy?"

"Cassie—"

"Do you love him?" her dad asked, interrupting her mum.

"I could," she whispered. "I'm kind of already most of the way there."

Her dad chuckled. "What in the world does that mean?"

Cassidy huffed out a laugh. "When I broke it off with him, it hurt. I had to turn my phone off so I wouldn't call and ask him to come with me. Then he showed up and everything felt right again." She smiled, thinking back to their meeting in the airport and the last time she'd kissed him. She wanted that again, but she didn't know how to get back there. "I don't want to be without him, but…"

"But you don't want to leave your home," her mum finished, her voice filled with understanding. "You know the saying 'home is where your heart is'? It's right. If he's the man you want to give your heart to, does it matter where you're living? As long as you're together, that's all that should matter. Moving could be the beginning of something wonderful; a new adventure for you to pave your own way."

"But what about you?"

"We'll still be here. You can come and visit whenever you want, and we'll do the same," Dad reassured her. He'd always known exactly what to say, and this time was no exception. "Be brave, Cassie. You know you want to."

THIRTEEN

Phoenix

THREE YEARS LATER

P hoenix tightened his charcoal tie over the pale pink shirt he wore, centring the strip of silk down his chest and smoothing it until it ran perfectly into the vest a couple of shades lighter than his tie. He shrugged into his jacket and picked up his briefcase before calling out, "Andi, I'll be back in a few hours after this conference."

"Not a problem, Mr Black," she said with a smile. "I'll hold your calls until then. Do you have lunch organized?"

"No, I don't." He shook his head and recalled the drink bottle sitting on his desk. If he didn't remember to have any water, he'd end up with a monster headache. The same one he'd had the last three days in a row. It could have been the stress, though. This case was the first really big one he'd been a part of. He was still fairly junior in his career, but he'd worked tirelessly since being hired just over two years earlier. His boss was the kind of supervisor he could only have dreamed of, even if he could never really be himself in front of him. On Phoenix's first day at the firm, his boss had encouraged Phoenix to learn as much as he could, then focus on one of their practice areas. He wanted him to spread his wings and fly. The firm was a small one—two partners and five lawyers—all of whom worked in property law. It didn't give him much choice, but he was grateful for any opportunity after working in a bar for nearly a year after his morning-only stint at Stark Williams.

Since then, however, Phoenix had discovered he was good at fine details. He could pour over documents and identify loopholes, or in this case, where the developer had taken shortcuts. Their clients owned a building that was failing, the floors tipping, walls cracking, and roof leaking, all within three years of it being built. He didn't feel ready to run the settlement conference on his own, but there was no getting out of it. His boss was in a delivery room with his wife. Phoenix was the only other lawyer who had any real knowledge of the case and what the owners were trying to achieve. The stress of such a high-profile case was taking its toll, and Phoenix reached for the drink bottle, taking a swig before realizing just how parched he was.

"I'll have something here for you when you get back," Andi said, interrupting his thoughts.

He smiled at her. "Thank you." He'd barely eaten anything in days, but like a mother hen, she'd been at him to stay healthy. It wasn't just the stress of the case riding him. He'd had too much on his mind. His flatmate, Rachael's younger brother Pete, had moved out, taking his search for Byron's fabled gold into the outback. Phoenix knew it was coming. But walking into Pete's room to see it stripped of the posters and maps he had tacked to the walls had knocked the wind out of him. Then to hear that he'd fallen for the station owner? Phoenix's stomach had rebelled, and he'd puked his guts up. He'd secretly been lusting after Pete ever since the man had moved in. A little shorter than him, lithe with slim muscles, freckles, and a shock of red hair, the younger man wasn't traditionally handsome in that blond god and goddess way of his first loves, but he was cute and smart. But he hadn't wanted to risk his friendship with Rachael—the only one of their group of university friends who'd continued speaking with him when he'd needed to bail on their expensive apartment. Phoenix had ended up in a two-bedroom dump he'd shared with two other people; it was all he could afford on a waiter's wages. Even her husband, Steve, barely looked at him anymore.

Pete had gotten under his skin though, and not seeing his smiling face every day had cut Phoenix far deeper than he'd expected. Had he fallen in love with him? He didn't really know. But when Pete had walked out, he'd missed the persistent, dedicated, and focussed man more than anyone since he'd stolen a taste of what life could have been like with lovers like Jake and Cassidy.

Thinking that had pulled him into the past and Felicity, the woman he'd been sleeping with, hadn't appreciated it.

He'd been moping. Losing his friend had ripped the Band-Aid off the loss he'd suffered years earlier. She'd been pushing for more commitment, and he'd been drowning. He was right where he'd been on the day he was shoved onto the street still half-naked, the feel of Jake buried in him still a sweet ache in his arse. Felicity had been there, lying naked in his bed, waiting for him to strip off and slake their lust when all he could think about were the three people he'd lost. He'd hesitated too long, and when she asked him what was wrong, he'd confessed everything. She'd pulled her clothes on and walked straight out of his apartment, and Phoenix watched her go, far less affected by her departure than he should have been.

He pushed through the double doors of the meeting room in the mediator's offices. The conference was starting. The case had been a welcome distraction. Of his one hundred and fifteen owner clients, three were with him. They entered together and he held his head up, feigned confidence he didn't quite feel, and stepped into the meeting room. Bruce, the mediator, was already seated at one end of the table. The developers' legal team sat opposite, and another man stood facing away from him, gazing out of the windows to the street, two levels below. There was a familiarity with him that had Phoenix on edge, but he needed to focus.

He held out his hand to the woman in the middle, flanked by the two more junior men. "Phoenix Black, Telford Lawyers, and this is Mary Sciberras, Donald Lee, and

Kristine Varga, owners within the building." She shook his hand and introduced herself as Katarina Rossi.

"And this is our lawyer, Maxwell Denyer." Phoenix froze, a flash of heat rushing through his veins followed immediately by a dousing of ice-like fire. His breath caught, and he turned startled eyes to the man who had now spun on his heels and was stalking toward the table with a smirk on his face.

"Mr Black. We meet again. What a pleasant surprise."

"Ah, yeah." Phoenix shook off the panic that had enveloped him that morning and straightened his spine, calling on every ounce of confidence he could muster. "Well, let's get started, shall we? I'm sure we're all anxious to progress this matter."

An hour later and he was happy with two concessions the developer had made. All his clients would have their rent paid for at least another month while independent engineers inspected the property. They'd also agreed on the process for buy-backs of the units that were most heavily affected. With each minute that passed, and each agreement ticked off, Phoenix settled in. He could do this. He knew the case inside out. He knew what his clients wanted to achieve, and they were on their way to getting it. Now they were covering the administrative matters, the seemingly trivial things that actually made some of the biggest differences to the way these cases progressed.

"No, that's unacceptable," Denyer said as he sat back in his chair and crossed his ankle over his knee. The way he sat was a show of dominance, but Phoenix wouldn't let himself dwell on the memories that assailed him every time he looked in the man's direction. The hatred in his eyes as he had his goon drag Phoenix kicking and screaming from his lovers' arms, and the smug smile of a man who'd decapitated Phoenix's career before it started. No, he needed to stay in the here and now. Focussing on his clients' needs was the best way.

"It's standard practice, Mr Denyer," the mediator reminded him.

With a professional smile in place, his opponent said, "Regardless of standard practice or otherwise, there are no statute or court rules governing the procedure. Therefore, it is open for interpretation. I will not agree to exposing my client to additional expense simply to facilitate an expeditious resolution to a matter which raises complex legal questions."

"Facilitating an expeditious resolution will, in the end, save your clients significant expense," Phoenix reminded him.

"Ah, but you're making a fatal assumption here, boy. You're assuming that your clients will win, and I can tell you that won't be the case. I'll enjoy nailing your arse to the wall—"

"That's enough," Bruce cut in. "Mr Denyer, remember that you're speaking to a colleague here. He may be younger than you, but just like you, he's an officer of the court, and you will show him respect."

The glare that he shot Bruce should have given Phoenix a sense of satisfaction, but Denyer's comment had the impact of a bulldozer. His words had crashed through the foundation of shaky confidence Phoenix had hastily built in the face of his opposition, leaving him a sweaty, freaked-out mess. He adjusted his tie and pulled his shirt away from his throat as he tried to gulp in a breath of air. But his lungs had seized. The room closed in on him as his heart rate accelerated and his mouth filled with cottonwool. Phoenix closed his eyes, and he was right there, back in Jake's apartment. Back in Jake's arms. Falling in love with the man all over again. He watched Cassidy watch them as she sat opposite, smiling like the picture he made with her boyfriend was the most beautiful thing she'd seen. The loss of them had hit him hard. Then, the theft of his dream job and the loss of his friends and his hope had tripled the impact. Phoenix had been alone, indebted to his eyeballs—he still was—and on the verge of homelessness for months.

The memories hit him again, over and over like a boxer pummelling his opponent. The fear and anger, the powerlessness of being unable to fight off Denyer's goon and being thrown out like garbage rather than being shown an ounce of decency, bubbled up and swamped him, drowning Phoenix.

"I…" he gasped, yanking at his shirt and tie until the top button was undone. "I need to go."

Voices sounded behind him, but the buzzing in his ears drowned them out. He needed air. He needed to get away from him. Phoenix stumbled to the stairs, bumping his shoulder along the walls like a drunkard, but it was the only thing holding him up. His legs had turned to jelly, and he couldn't breathe. Gasping for breath, his vision swam, and Phoenix tripped, falling onto his hands and knees on the landing.

Just a little more.

He crawled forward, somehow still holding his brief-case. He reached for the doorknob. Pulled it down.

He fell against the heavy door. It swung open.

The rushing noise of the city hit him full force. Horns and the rumble of cars, bikes and trucks, and the rattle of jack-hammers. Sirens. People talking and heels clicking on con-crete pathways. The crinkle of wrappers and tinkle of ice. Phoenix gasped and filled his lungs with air. He coughed and gasped again, the crushing hold on him finally loosening as he pulled himself up onto a raised garden bed that doubled as a seating area and rested his elbows on his knees.

He closed his eyes, and Jake's vivid blue ones morphed to green. Were they Cassidy's he was picturing or Pete's? He was messed up. Pining over lost lovers and a friend who clearly didn't feel the same. But he needed that friend right now. He needed the comfort that his former flatmate pro-vided. The unwavering friendship was born of years of fa-miliarity.

Phoenix fished his phone out of his jacket pocket and, with shaking hands, brought up Pete's number. He dialled, not even knowing if he had reception a few hours south-west of Longreach in the middle of the desert. Luck was ap-parently now on his side, and the crackle of a sketchy line sounded before Pete's voice came over the phone, "G'day, Phoenix. How are things in the big smoke?"

"Pete," he choked. "I…" A sob got caught in his throat, and Phoenix sucked in a shuddery breath.

"Talk to me, Phoenix. What's going on?" Pete's voice had morphed from laid-back and happy to serious and all business in the blink of an eye. The concern in his voice choked him up even more. "It's okay, I'm here. Take your time."

"Everything's gone to shit," he cried, wiping the tears that were now falling without pause. "I can't breathe."

"I need you to close your eyes, Phoenix, and focus on my voice." He did. After a few minutes of Pete leading him through a slow breathing exercise and reassuring him over and over that he was okay, the weight crushing his chest lessened enough that he could talk. He wasn't sure whether the nutshell summary of the clusterfuck his life had just become made sense, but Pete had heard enough to know he was teetering. "You sound like you need a break, my friend."

"I can't get away."

"Your mental health is more important than everything, Phoenix. If you can't function, you can't look after your clients. You know I'm right. Call in sick, run a bath and soak for a while." There was a shuffling on the phone like a hand was being placed over it and a muffled conversation in the background.

"G'day, Phoenix, I'm Scottie," a deep voice floated over the airwaves to him, and a pang of jealousy hit him. This was the man his friend had fallen for. "Pete's throwin' some clothes into his bag, but he won't be there until tomorrow. You think you'll be okay until then?"

"I need to get out of here," he mumbled, looking around at the unfamiliar faces. He wanted to go home. He wanted to curl up in his bed and sleep, but it'd been weeks since he'd had an unbroken night's rest. His dreams were filled with jumbled memories and long since completed exams that he didn't feel prepared for morphing into courtroom failures. He couldn't slow his mind down, even now when he felt completely detached from his own body, like a prisoner in someone else's skin.

"Okay, we can help. Get yourself to the airport. We'll get you on a plane into Longreach, and we'll be there to pick you up."

Phoenix shook his head, his heart rate tripling and his breath coming faster. "No planes. I can't breathe. No planes."

"It's okay," Pete said into the phone. His voice was low. Calming. "No planes. Can you drive? Are you up to driving? Windows down, long open roads, and no traffic. You can see the sky from horizon to horizon."

"Yeah, I can do that," he mumbled, relief swamping him.

"I'll send you directions, okay?"

"Yeah." He nodded, sucking in a breath a little easier this time.

"Phoenix, I need you to listen carefully," Scottie said. "You can't make it here in one go. It's nearly a twenty-hour drive. We'll send you a route that'll take ya through Dubbo. There's a small town a couple of hours past there. We can meet you there. We'll book into the tourist park on the river and stop there for the night. Then we can do the rest tomorra, okay? We'll all be here late arvo."

No, he didn't want that. He didn't want to inconvenience them. It was a hell of a drive. "I'll be okay on my own. You don't need to drive out." He paused, his chest loosening as he thought about the wide-open spaces Pete had sent him photos of. "Town past Dubbo tonight. Your place tomorrow. I can do that."

* * * * *

Phoenix pulled up at the homestead. It was like something out of a movie. An oasis in the desert. Red dirt surrounded him from horizon to horizon, broken only by the spindly blue-grey vegetation. The sky was the bluest of blues he'd ever seen. As if a filter had been applied to a photograph. It was unreal.

The familiar face jogging down the steps and around to his car was a welcome sight. Phoenix stumbled out of the front seat, almost falling flat as Pete caught him and wrapped him in a strong embrace. His hair was almost the same colour as the desert dirt, and Phoenix couldn't help but smile. "Thank God you're here," Pete breathed. "I've been worried sick."

"I'm okay," he choked out.

"Bullshit. You're anything but okay." Pete pointed to the smaller building set a way away from the sprawling two-storey house. "You're staying in the guesthouse. It'll give you some privacy, but you're expected for meals in the main house."

"I can't impose—"

"There isn't any takeaway you can run out and grab out here. Trust me, you'll need to eat, and Ma and Nan will be offended if you miss their cooking. They're the coolest. They'll help you. We all will."

Phoenix tripped, the weight of the mess he'd made of his life making him stumble. Pete was there for him, propping him up and half dragging him into the little house.

He stepped over the threshold and looked around. Polished timber floors, white walls, and antiques that looked like they'd been handed down over generations were everywhere. "You need to freshen up, then get some sleep. Come on." Pete led him by the hand into the bathroom with its old-fashioned shower pointing down into the clawfoot tub. He turned the water on, warming it, and getting a fresh towel out while Phoenix stood there, unable to move. Exhaustion warred with numbness. It had set in after the panic had subsided, and the hangover it left him with was hard to push through.

Pete turned to him and unbuttoned his shirt, making quick work of stripping him out of the material. "Let's get you down to your underwear, okay?" Pete fell to his knees and unlaced his shoes, and for the first time, Phoenix noticed how dusty they were. Pete tapped his leg, and Phoenix braced himself on his friend's shoulder, lifting his foot so Pete could take off his shoes and socks. He looked down at his friend and realized that the love he'd experienced for his friend was exactly that—friendship. He'd never been in love with him. It was a relief to finally understand. To know for sure. It buoyed him and gave Phoenix the strength to take over.

"It's okay. I've got the rest."

Pete looked up at him and grinned. "Good. I was hoping you wouldn't make me take off your pants." Pete turned and switched off the taps, pulling the shower curtain back. "All the toiletries you need are there. I'll be in the other room, so if you need anything, call out."

Pete left and closed the door behind him with a soft snick. "Thank you," Phoenix breathed, not loud enough that his friend would hear, but to Pete nevertheless. He sank down into the steaming water and laid his head back, resting on the porcelain. He looked down at himself. He'd lost weight, the lithe muscles he used to sport wasting away. His pecs were flat now rather than rounded, the bars in his nipples looking ridiculous. Stress had hollowed out his face, too, dark circles forming under his eyes and his cheekbones protruding. His hip bones were like peaks, and his legs long and lanky. He barely recognized the man he was looking at. It scared him.

Phoenix's eyes closed, and sleep crept up on him. The knock at the door startled him. "You okay, mate. Haven't fallen asleep, have you?"

He huffed out a laugh. "I'm good." Phoenix scrubbed himself before emptying out the water and drying off.

Wrapped in the rust-coloured terry-towelling robe, he wandered out to find Pete turning down the bed.

"In," he ordered. "You need to sleep."

"Can you stay for a bit?"

"Of course." He walked around the other side of the bed and sat down as Phoenix climbed in, robe and all, and covered himself up. Looking at his friend, he smiled.

"You look good. Happy."

"I am. Scottie's…" Colour suffused Pete's face, and he laughed. "He's pretty damn amazing." He paused and patted Phoenix's hand. "Real talk?" When Phoenix nodded, he added, "You look like shit. You're a husk of the man I left only a few months ago. What the hell happened?"

"Work." He shrugged, not really knowing how to explain the destructive cycle he'd gotten into. "You left, and then Felicity left too. I'm not… upset about either one of you. I'm happy for you, and it was the right thing for her. I didn't love her. I was wasting her time."

"What brought on the anxiety attack at work?" He'd known this question was coming. Pete wanted more details than he'd been able to give the day before on the phone. He supposed it was now or never. But Pete also deserved to know the full story, not just the edited snippets he'd told others. So that's what he did—came clean to his friend about everything.

It wasn't easy. His emotions were far too close to the surface to be able to bury them. Even thinking about Jake and Cassidy had the tears pooling in his eyes, his breath coming quicker as he thought about that fateful morning.

Pete's hand on his was a steady comfort, and Phoenix flipped his hand over, threading their fingers together to keep him tethered. Memories assailed him, buffeting him with the force of a category five cyclone. The walls closed in on him, squeezing his lungs and blacking out his vision as he spoke about the fallout from losing his first legal job after a couple of hours.

Stark Williams Lawyers had been a dream, one that Maxwell Denyer had shit all over. But he'd survived. Scraped knees and a little battered and bruised, he'd pulled through and was starting to make a name for himself. But then he was back. Tightening the noose around Phoenix's neck until he was about to snap. He wasn't cut out for it. He wasn't strong enough or ruthless enough. He wasn't even stable enough.

Pete pulled him into his arms and let him cry. His T-shirt was soaked, but he never stopped rocking him. Whispering calming platitudes to Phoenix to let it out and that he'd be strong again one day. That it was okay to be overwhelmed. To need help. To have a broken heart.

When his eyelids got heavier and the tears dried up, Pete helped him lie down. Exhaustion settled over him like a blanket, and he pulled the sheet higher, cocooning himself. The hollowness inside him was cleansed somehow, like he'd purged the weight he'd been carrying for years.

The screech of a galah had him blinking open his eyes. He was alone, the covers on the other side of the bed rumpled where Pete had lain earlier that afternoon. The light was fading, and Phoenix sat up, more rested than he'd been in months.

He reached for his wallet. Pete had placed it on the bedside table. He flipped it open, the black leather supple in his hands from years of use. He reached in behind the couple of business cards he had stored there and pulled out the one he'd never been brave enough to call. It was creased now, the blue abstract depictions of the high-rise buildings faded. The word City Scape appeared underneath in block lettering, the address along the bottom two lines of the card. On the other side, a name, number, and email address had teased Phoenix. Trav had told him years ago that Jake was no longer with the agency, but he was still on his mobile. Phoenix had never summoned the courage to call him.

He'd also never grieved for them. Years had passed, and Phoenix had buried the pain, unable to face it for fear of breaking. He didn't let himself think of them much any more either, the wound still as raw as it had been the day he'd been tossed on his arse. Did he regret it? Yeah, he did. But at the same time, he didn't. How could he? For those few weeks leading up to it, and their one night together, his life had been perfect, a future that was like a dream laid out before him. Two people to love, the job of his dreams, hope lighting up his future.

Then it had all come crashing down, and he'd been broken. Something inside of him had cracked, and he'd never been able to put it back together.

Maybe now he could work on that. Build himself up again until he was whole once more.

FOURTEEN

Phoenix

The bonfire they sat around was mesmerizing. The colours flickered as the logs turned from the faded greys and browns of weathered timber to glowing red, then black as the fire burned through them. Peace surrounded him, the sounds of nature such a radical change from the hustle and bustle of the city. He could have been on a different planet to the one he'd come from; the outback and Sydney were worlds apart. He still couldn't believe the dirt and the skies were real. Everything was so big too; it was almost unfathomable. Pearce Station was thousands of square kilometres—horizon to horizon and beyond.

By night, their world changed again. It was as if he was staring at a carpet of diamonds. The moon and stars, brighter than he'd ever seen them before, winked at him in a sky that was otherwise pitch black. No clouds swirled overhead, and the clear night allowed him to see the trail of smoke floating in the air above like a beacon to their bonfire.

He breathed in the cool night air and marvelled at the lack of the lingering scent of exhaust fumes. It was fresh and clean, a balm to his soul. He could see the appeal of a place like this. Freedom and enough space to stretch your legs. But unlike Pete, who'd taken to the station like a duck to water, he couldn't see himself being so isolated. At least if he was around people, he could fake it. Out here, it would be a lonely, hard life for a single person. He could only imagine how Scottie would have felt thinking he was the only gay man in the world, guarding his secret with his life.

Phoenix had only been at Pearce Station for three days, and yet he'd been welcomed from the first moment he'd driven through the gates. The hotchpotch of people—three generations of women and the lone man of the family together with their workers and now Pete too, were clearly family by choice as well as blood. They were an interesting bunch. Scottie and Pete were so obviously in love, and thankfully no one batted an eyelid about it. His friend deserved that—a man to love him unceasingly and a family who didn't feel the need to criticize everything about Pete, like Rachael, Stevo, and his parents had done. The way the ruggedly handsome station owner looked at his lover had Phoenix swooning.

It was something he craved. Something he'd shied away from for years, but with Scottie and Pete showing him what it meant to be loved, he knew one day he wanted that again. But first up, he needed to own his sexuality. He'd chosen to go to Sydney because it was home to Mardi Gras. He'd wanted to come out, live life as a proud bisexual man, but things hadn't gone to plan. First there was the beating he'd narrowly escaped, then he'd been too scared to tell his friends. Trav knew because they'd shared a bedroom. But Rachael and Steve were clueless, finding out when he'd come home injured. Then he'd landed the job at Telford Lawyers and he'd realized just how religious the partners were. His bosses were great people, but he didn't want to risk them finding out and having a problem with it. He'd never told Pete either, not seeing the point when he was focussing on his career. He'd been single for much of the last few years, and the flings he'd had were rarely anyone he had a repeat with. When Felicity had suggested a friends-with-benes arrangement, he'd thought it would be perfect. For as long as it went on, he wouldn't have to risk his bosses finding out about his sexuality, and him ending up unemployed again—he wasn't about to give anyone else an excuse to fire him.

Except that by walking out, he had, hadn't he?

Phoenix rubbed his forehead and sighed.

"You wanna talk about it?" Phoenix startled at the question. Craig had shifted over so they now sat next to each other, and as he swung his gaze around the fire, Phoenix noticed for the first time that they were alone. "They all went their own ways while you were thinking," he said by way of explanation. "Dunno if I'm the right person to talk to, but I'm listening if you want to try me."

Phoenix nodded and gave him a small smile. He appreciated the hospitality and their attempt to include him even though he was a basket case. "What's the deal with you,

Ally, and the tall bloke? Sam? She seems to be close to both of you." Phoenix closed his mouth and blew out a breath. See? Basket case. He would never normally ask a question like that, but the way they looked at each other told him there was something more to the image they portrayed to the world.

"Yeah, Sam. We're together, in our own way." There was more to their story, and when Craig explained it, Phoenix couldn't help but think how lucky he was. "What about you? You seeing anyone?"

"Nah, I did have a friends-with-benes type arrangement, but there was a certain redhead that I couldn't stop thinking about." Phoenix motioned to the house where Pete had gone to check in on Scottie and Ally. "When all the shit went down with work, he was the only person I wanted to talk to." He shook his head, disbelieving that he could have thought for a moment that he and Pete were supposed to be together. If he hadn't had the courage to come out to him in the years they'd lived together, how could he possibly have been the one? When he considered what it must have taken for Scottie to have opened himself up, Phoenix knew that he and Pete were only ever meant to be friends. "He talked me off a ledge I wasn't sure I could come back from. Then when he invited me here, I felt like I could breathe again. Being back in the country was exactly what I needed."

"Where are you from?"

"Bit west of the Gold Coast. The 'rents own a small farm. They used to be pretty self-sufficient, but now that they're older, they rent the barn space out for weddings and parties, that kind of thing." The truth was that his parents weren't old. His mum was barely seventeen when she'd had him. His dad dropped out of high school to get a job and support them, and the only place they could afford to rent was out in the country. His dad commuted to whatever building site he was labouring on every day, and his mum picked up as many odd jobs as she could where she didn't have to pay for childcare. Then, one of the local farmers had passed, and the family property was subdivided. A parcel came up for sale, and his parents had bought it, wanting more space and the ability to be self-sufficient. They'd worked non-stop, paying off their loans until they were financially stable enough that they were no longer living week to week. Phoenix had moved out the moment he could, wanting to take the burden of looking after him away from his parents. He'd used the excuse that he hated it there, but it was a lie. "I moved to Sydney to go to uni."

"What did you study?"

"Law. I wanted to be a judge by the time I was forty and hang out on Oxford Street in my spare time." Phoenix's laugh held no humour, and he couldn't help the grimace. "As if I'd have spare time. Anyway, I had a position with one of the best firms in the country, learning the ropes in court with plans to do an internship with a top QC—a barrister. It all went to shit when the partner of the firm busted me in bed with his son while his son's girlfriend watched us."

Craig sputtered out a shocked cough. "What? How?"

"They arrived unannounced for Sunday brunch." Phoenix shot him a smirk, but the pain squeezed his throat tight until he was blinking back tears, and he fought to keep the wobble out of his voice. "I worked hard for that position, but it wasn't supposed to happen that way. That one night was worth it, though. I'll never forget them." The calm, collected tone of his words surprised him. He was a mess, had been for far longer than he wanted to admit, but everything he'd said was true. He couldn't regret being with Jake and Cassidy—not when he'd experienced perfection, if only for a minute—even though his life had been turned upside down afterward.

Craig looked like he was working up the courage to ask a question. Phoenix waited him out, happy to stare at the fire. Thankfully he asked about growing up on the Gold Coast before he asked another question about Sydney. "Are you looking forward to going back?"

"I don't know if I can. Go back there, I mean." He paused, not really knowing how to explain what fighting the heart-stopping panic, fear, and instinct to run took out of him. In the end, he went with being frank. "Every time I think about getting on that train or even going back to my apartment, I have a bloody anxiety attack. I was nearly hyperventilating trying to figure out how to get my job back."

"Why do you need it back?"

His question shocked Phoenix, and he raised an eyebrow at the seemingly clueless man. "Do you have any idea how expensive Sydney is? You can't just keep an apartment there and not work your arse off."

Craig furrowed his brows, this time looking at Phoenix like he'd missed the most basic of points. "So, give it up. Move somewhere else. Go home. Stay in Longreach. Whatever. Why do you need to live in Sydney if you're not happy?"

"Because…" He paused and looked at the other man, the cogs in his brain turning over. Was the answer to run away? Just throw his hands up in the air and say fuck it? It didn't seem like the right thing to do, but damn, it was tempting.

Could he find something else? Do something else that would never nearly break him again? Could he get a nine-to-five job, something that didn't have a lot of overtime? He wanted to blame Denyer. He wanted to put all his problems on the man's shoulders to wear like a karmic blanket, but Phoenix couldn't. He'd been the one to lose his friends. He hadn't fought for them, hurt when they'd been bitter about his need to move out. Then he'd buried himself in work, sacrificing himself in the misguided belief that he could catch his career up. And for what? So he could spread his mental state so thin that he was at breaking point. That one cruel word, one barb from an opponent, had him crashing and burning. But what choice did he have? He was a lawyer. It was what he'd trained to do. A university degree and years of work just to get where he was. He'd be crazy to change careers now, especially when he was on the cusp of stepping his career up. That thought alone was enough to send his pulse skyrocketing and his chest tightening, but he managed to choke out, "It's expected. It's what I am."

"Okay," Craig conceded, accepting his answer just like that.

Their conversation meandered, winding back to coming out and what it had been like for Phoenix as a teenager. He hadn't expected to find so many LGBTQIA people at the station, but it was refreshing to know that both gay and bi men had found a soft place to land well outside of the rainbow flags hanging on Oxford Street. But mid-conversation, Craig went quiet. He looked like he'd seen a ghost, the colour in his face draining and his lips turning down. Thoughtfulness morphed into horror, and he reared back as if his own thoughts had reached out and slapped him.

He took off. Sprinted away in the direction of the cabins.

Phoenix wasn't sure what to do with the fire now that he was alone out there. Did he let it burn out? Did he throw a bucket of water over it? Could he even leave it to go and ask at the main house? His questions were answered when Pete and Scottie wandered out hand in hand, coming to sit next to him. "Sorry 'bout that. Had some paperwork I needed to wrap up."

"All good. I was talking to Craig. He's a nice guy." They exchanged looks, the silence loud in the still of the night. "What? What am I missing?"

"He wasn't an arsehole?"

"No." Phoenix shook his head, wondering why Scottie would ask that. "We were talking about Sydney and work, and then what it was like growing up bi. Coming out, when we realized, that sort of thing."

"Bi? Coming out?" Pete asked. "What?" There was an edge of panic in his voice, and Phoenix swallowed. He thought back over their conversation. Craig had asked him questions, and he'd answered them. The conversation had been one way; Craig hadn't shared any of his experiences. Had he made a terrible mistake in assuming he was bi?

"But Craig, Sam, and Ally are together. He's bi, isn't he? I thought—" Phoenix furrowed his brow. He was sure Craig had told him they were together. Or had he imagined the whole exchange? He supposed that it was more than possible for each of the men to be with Ally but not be together. If Craig had been disgusted by Pete and Scottie's relationship, then it was probably likely, not just possible.

But it just didn't seem right.

"Ah—" Pete started but then looked to Scottie. The other man reached out and squeezed Phoenix's shoulder.

"You have nothing to worry about."

Phoenix intrinsically trusted Scottie. He knew he was good people if Pete trusted him. But this time, Scottie sounded like he was trying to convince himself. Why would he have something to worry about?

"Have I screwed up badly? I just assumed," Phoenix said, shaking his head and trying to make sense of what he'd seen and heard from Craig with the wary way Pete and Scottie were talking about him.

"Craig was a bit of a homophobic arse when Scottie came out. He packed his gear and left," Pete explained. Phoenix nodded. That's what Craig had said.

"Yeah, but then he came home, right?"

"Yeah. But they've always just been friends."

Craig had said they were new. Had their relationship only started since he'd arrived back at the station? Maybe his relationship with Ally, but even that didn't sound right. The three of them were too in tune. Too aware of one another. They interacted so naturally. It was as if the three of them anticipated one another's moves, like they'd been together for a millennium. Or had they just been orbiting one another, never touching?

He just hoped that he hadn't put his foot in it. That he hadn't inadvertently crossed some line that made Craig lose his shit and leave again. How offended would he be if Phoenix had made a wrong assumption? He wanted to say that they were all adults, and it would just get brushed over, but Phoenix had seen how fragile some men's masculinity was.

Pete looked to Scottie, an unspoken concern marring the V in his brows. "Do you need to say something?"

"Yeah. I'll go have a chat with them." Scottie smiled tentatively. Phoenix supposed he was trying to reassure him, but Scottie's smile looked more like a grimace. He strode in the same direction that Craig had taken off in, leaving him and Pete alone.

"Craig said that they were together," Phoenix explained, begging him to understand he hadn't meant to say the wrong thing.

"He did?"

"Yeah. He said that it was new, and they were still working things out."

246 • ANN GRECH

Pete huffed out a breath and shook his head. "Bloody hell, I don't envy Ally. Figuring out a relationship where there was no chance of the two blokes touching each other—no matter how innocent—would be like navigating a minefield. Craig's... Yeah." He shook his head again.

Pete couldn't see it. Phoenix huffed out a laugh, surprised that his normally observant friend was so blind. Were they seeing the same two people? Craig looked at Sam like he'd hung the moon, not like he'd blow up if they accidentally touched. Maybe only Phoenix could see it—maybe the longing was something that only he could see because he'd experienced the same feeling for years. Burying the desire for the one thing—or in his and Craig's cases, the two people—they wanted left an ache inside. But Phoenix could see the longing between the three of them as clear as day. It ran as deep as the oceans and was as expansive as the universe. "Craig's the blond one, right?" he asked, making sure he hadn't accidentally mistaken him for Sam, the man Pete had described as much more sensitive. "In that case, I think he might surprise you one day."

The look Pete shot at him—like he'd grown two heads—had Phoenix barking out a laugh while Pete grumbled, "Doubt it."

* * * * *

A day later and every muscle ached. The younger crew—Scottie, Pete, Ally, Craig, Sam, Den, and himself—

were building a watering hole of some sort, aimed at looking after the native wildlife rather than the cattle. Scottie wanted to rehabilitate the land, and the drought that the station, and most of Australia, was caught up in was brutal. Phoenix had seen images of cracks in the ground but had never really associated it with anything other than mud drying out after the rains. Deep cracks were always something that happened on the ice caps when a chunk fell off. Seeing the deep angry scars marring the land in far too many places was shocking. He took so much for granted living in the city. The water restrictions imposed on them in Sydney meant no washing their cars except on grass, rather than native animals dying of thirst.

The eye-opening experience was exactly what Phoenix had needed. Despite every muscle in his body aching, he was enjoying himself. Finding himself again.

He could think. Breathe. Shake off the pressure of work and the fallout that he was going to have to face by running away.

Even though he was halfway around the country and felt untouchable this far away from the city, his thoughts had constantly ping-ponged back to the dismal reality waiting for him. Naturally, his boss had been notified of his actions in the mediation. He was expecting the call, but Phoenix still didn't know how upset he was. He couldn't bring himself to check his messages. When the call came through, his boss's name flashing on the screen, Phoenix's hands had begun to shake, and his breathing sawed in and out of his lungs so fast that he'd become lightheaded. Dizziness descended, and with the white spots in his vision, panic had surged through his veins. He was paralysed. Unable to answer the phone.

He was still sitting there trying to calm himself down fifteen minutes later when Nan had knocked on his door to let him know coffee and scones were being served up at the house if he wanted to join them. She'd sat with him, holding his hands while he freaked himself out about what the message would be when the text came through.

Nan had checked it for him, reading the message and responding on his behalf when Phoenix couldn't stop his hands shaking long enough to type it out. Then, in the way Phoenix was learning was so typically her, she ordered him up and out before he could rethink himself. Within minutes, he was surrounded by family, a plate full of scones, jam, and cream in front of him. They were all gathered there, eating and laughing at Jono's retelling of how Scottie had terrorised his sister with stories of crocs inhabiting the billabong. They were too far southwest for them, the desert too dry for the water-dependent reptiles, but to a child, that fact had been lost in the panic. Ally eventually got her payback, though, when she'd spotted a perentie sunning itself on the rocks nearby, and she'd startled it, forcing it into the water where Scottie had been swimming. He'd caught the tail end of it slipping into the water and had moved like Roadrunner to get out of the water before he could get eaten.

Ally had high-fived Ma while Sam and Craig eyed each other over Ally's head, Phoenix noticing that flash of longing they shot each other. But this time, Phoenix could see the difference, the heat, that flashed between them.

That's when Scottie had cleared his throat and redirected the conversation to their plans for that day. Thankfully, they'd finished the physical work and were relaxing around the fire, toasting marshmallows. Phoenix passed one to Sam, who asked, "How long do you think you'll stay?"

Phoenix looked up at the night sky, a million stars lighting up the blanket of darkness floating above them. He'd never get sick of seeing it, but he wouldn't get to see it for much longer. His time at the station was limited. "Got a message from my supervising partner demanding that I be back before the end of the week." He poked the fire with the stick he'd just toasted a marshmallow on and watched it catch fire, burning slowly.

"As in the day after tomorrow?"

Phoenix nodded, sadness enveloping him. He needed more time. He wasn't ready to go back yet. He wasn't strong enough. Like panes of glass balanced precariously on top of each other, he was wobbling. Teetering on the edge. One gust of wind and he knew he'd topple over. The resulting crash, he feared, would be catastrophic. But what choice did he have? He sighed. None and fuck all. "I'll be leaving when we get back. If I get a move on tomorrow, I'll be back in Sydney early enough to stop in at the office before my boss heads off for the day."

It was as if Ally reached into his soul and plucked the one shred of hope he'd been subconsciously clutching onto. She cleared her throat and spoke quietly, saying, "You know, you could always walk away. Make an alternative future for yourself. Maybe you left because you needed to see your truth reflected back at you before you could see your path."

Phoenix shook his head. "Yeah, don't know about that alternative path option for me. This is the only real way for me to get to the top." But the words tasted bitter on his tongue. A future that he no longer recognized as one he wanted—or could even have without sacrificing so much of himself that he feared he'd have nothing left—stared back at him. Did he really want that anymore? Was it his destiny? Had it ever been if all he'd done since graduating was fight to keep his face above water? The questions swirled in his mind in an unending loop.

He guessed he'd never know if he didn't go back and try.

* * * * *

"In one kilometre, turn right onto Quilpie Thargomindah Road," his navigation app announced. Road was a stretch of the imagination. It was a dirt track, as red as the fire he'd sat around the night before, that cut through the desolate landscape. Somehow, it was full of life. The land was dying of thirst, old-growth trees slowly fading, and animals dying where they fell. And yet, despite all the odds, nature rallied. It fought. Kangaroos bounded along the side of the road, and he'd seen emus dart in and out of the fences, crossing the road and dashing away. Eagles circled high above, riding the thermal breezes as they searched for prey. He hadn't seen a single vehicle in hours, though, and that was a good thing. His hands shook and his breathing was choppy. Phoenix didn't trust himself to manoeuvre his BMW in traffic. He hated this version of himself. He hated the uncertainty that clouded his thoughts and the weakness that had taken root deep within.

But he was an adult, and adults faced up to the messes they'd made.

"In one hundred metres, turn right onto Quilpie Thargomindah Road." He could see the sign up ahead. The T-intersection he was coming up on. Quilpie was straight ahead and hours beyond that, the ocean. Brisbane and the Gold Coast. His parents. To the right was the road to Sydney. His apartment, his job. Everything he was working for. Behind him was the comfort of a family he had just met and never wanted to forget.

He slowed down, his finger hovering over the indicator.

His heart rate spiked, his hands shaking harder. Phoenix's vision dotted. He braked, stopping his car in the middle of the deserted road as his breath squeezed his lungs. The instinct to breathe was strong, but the crushing weight on his chest stalled his ability to inhale. The road before him swam in his vision, and light-headedness threatened.

"Breathe," he ordered himself, forcing down the urge to vomit. He closed his eyes and sucked in a breath, and in that moment, he knew.

His decision was made, for better or worse.

FIFTEEN

Jacob

"Cassie," Jake called, walking through the house they called home. He was proud of their efforts in the three short years they'd lived on the Gold Coast. The restored Queenslander was evidence of the hard work they'd put in building and growing their business. Phillips Real Estate had been open almost as long as they'd made the impulsive decision to move to the Gold Coast. They had initially operated from Cassie's family holiday home, then when the business had a regular clientele, he and Cassie had moved to the shack they'd purchased, slowly renovating every inch of it. The location was a dream—a couple of blocks away from the rolling ocean waves along Main Beach—one they'd never dreamed of being able to achieve in Sydney.

But it was a reality. Their reality.

Jake placed the success of their business solely on Cassie's shoulders. She was a natural entrepreneur and an expert at research. When he'd agreed with his father not to return to Sydney, he'd feared Cassie would up and leave.

Instead, she had demanded silence, gone to bed early, and come back out the next morning with a determined set to her lips.

She'd spent the whole night researching, looking at which "it" agencies there were to work for. It led down a rabbit hole, and within a couple of days, she'd identified a gaping void in the market. With the help of a friend of hers in banking, she had the bones of a business plan to achieve a dream she had hatched because of him. They'd used their last dollars to transfer their licences to Queensland, register a business name, and buy ramen noodles to eat. Jake had a couple of early successes, first getting listings, then selling the homes to interstate contacts within a few days. They hadn't gotten paid those commissions until the keys changed hands four weeks later, so they'd maxed out their credit cards, sold everything they could to stop haemor-rhaging money on debts, and eaten more ramen. It had taken a few months of hard work and financial stress, but once the word got out, they'd gotten ahead in leaps and bounds.

In less than twelve months, they'd saved a large enough deposit for their house, and with no need for a storefront office, were still able to happily operate their business from home.

Jake paused at the front door looking over the garden oasis to his beautiful girlfriend. Despite it being winter, she was on her knees wearing only a bikini, white linen shirt, straw hat, and gardening gloves. Cassie's hands were buried in the dirt, shifting it around and lovingly cradling a worm that she moved out of the way of her trowel. The woman before him was completely different to the uptight, angry one he'd met at his university alumni event. Now, Cassie was laid-back and quick to laugh. She was happiest dedicating her time to a few loyal clients rather than fighting her competition to become the biggest and best. It didn't matter to her anymore. Climbing the corporate ladder meant one thing—less free time for her. As the joint owner of her business, she knew she was already at the top. Working more also meant that she had to put on a suit more often, and Cassie was happiest dressed down in casual gear.

"Yeah, babe. I'm out front." She stood and dropped the gloves she'd been wearing, flashing Jake a smile as he padded down the steps. Eyeing the tanned strip of flesh that peeked between the open lapels of her shirt, Jake licked his lips and held up the phone.

"I know." He smiled as she let her shirt fall from her shoulders before she pressed herself against him. Jake leaned in and kissed her in a slow melding of their lips, his tongue sneaking out to tease hers. She wrapped her arms around his shoulders and hitched a leg around Jake's hip. He plucked the strings on her bikini top, tossing the triangular panels away to reveal her pert breasts. Still holding the phone with her client waiting on hold, he nibbled his way down to her nipples and sucked on the pebbled tips until she rolled her hips against him, seeking friction. "Your muffins are cooling on the rack, and I have Kevin on the phone," he breathed against her chest as he lapped at her skin, still salty from their morning swim.

"Mhmm," she moaned as he fell to his knees and eased the tiny white bottoms down her legs.

"Answer the phone, Cass," he teased as he nipped her hip. Licking across to her pussy, he spread her lips open and tasted the sensitive nub before sucking it between his lips. Cassidy ground against his face as she plucked the phone from his hand and answered the call.

"Hello, Kevin, Cassidy here. How can I help?" Her voice was surprisingly even as Jake slid two fingers into her channel and curled them, finding her G-spot. She hissed quietly before sliding her fingers into his hair. Rocking her hips, Cassie rode his digits as she chased her release. He loved her like this. Completely debauched and taking her pleasure. On display for the world to see, even if the only eyes who could peer in on their oasis belonged to the birds, she was still that confident, driven woman he fell in love with. But now she concentrated on the things that brought her the most reward, and orgasms morning, noon, and night was one of her favourites.

"Mhmm, yes. Not a problem," she gasped as Jake hooked her leg over his shoulder and ate at her like a man starved. Her juices coated his fingers, and he resisted the temptation to suck on them, capturing the rich flavour of her essences as he pulled them free from her depths. Her fingers tightened in his hair, his scalp screaming in a clear message. But Jake wanted to take her higher, and it had been far too long since they'd had another man in their bed to slake her lusty needs.

He brushed his middle finger over her star, and she pushed back, silently begging him to do it, the tight muscle quivering in anticipation. She'd loved being taken like that—he and Phoenix inside her at the same time had taken her higher than he'd ever managed since. But it had been years since then. Their imaginations and a collection of toys were the only additions they'd brought into their bedroom since him.

Before the memories could bury his libido, Jake doubled the attention he was giving to Cassie. He refused to think about that fateful time, not while the woman of his dreams—the one he loved with his whole heart—was in his arms.

"Okay, I'll call them, propose it, and let you know." She dropped the phone, the case clattering on the concrete path, and she moaned. "Jake." She cried out when he penetrated both her openings together. She rocked her hips, pushing back against his fingers, then thrusting forward so he could press his tongue against her clit again.

Her orgasm rocketed through her when he eased a second finger past her sphincter and sucked hard on her clit. He flicked the bundle of nerves with his tongue, and that was it. Her pussy clamped tight around the thumb he had lodged there, and she shouted his name, the contractions in her core going on and on.

When she settled, he withdrew his fingers, his mouth trailing a path up her body as he stood. Cassie gripped his face between her hands and pressed their lips together, no doubt tasting her essence on his lips. He clenched his hands, digging his fingertips into the soft flesh of her arse, trying not to come in his pants like a teenager. With Cassie rubbing her naked body all over him like a playful kitten, his dick was happy for her to go to town, but it became increasingly difficult to stave off his orgasm. She was more like a sex kitten than a playful one.

Cassie stepped backward, a sexy swing in her hips as she tiptoed along the curve of the path she knew by heart. He followed—like he would always do, without reservation. She reclined back against the timber railing on the stairs leading to the apartment they'd built above their garage, arching her back and presenting her breasts to him. Jake's moan turned into a growl of desire when she trailed her fingers down his bare chest. Following his happy trail, she circled the button of his cargo shorts, sliding her pointed nail along the waistband. He squeezed his eyes closed, hissing as she teased him. His cock throbbed, pre-cum soaking his briefs. Her husky laugh was a puff of breath against his cheek as she palmed his straining erection.

Jake gasped. "Damn," he moaned, opening his heavy lids to gaze at her. Naked as the day she was born, her skin glowed a golden brown. It was all the hours she spent outdoors now, working in their garden, swimming at the beach and naked in their pool. Jake could get off staring at her fully clothed, but naked, she was something else. Now, her eyes had a sated glow, her cheeks and lips flushed pink. Her breasts rose with each inhale as she caught her breath, and she rubbed her thighs together like she hadn't yet had enough. He wouldn't need much more than her teasing touch to set him off like a firework.

"You know you want to," she challenged, biting down on her still glistening bottom lip. She reached up, grasping the thick timbers of the railing, and bent her knee just enough to invite him to take what he so desperately wanted. Jake gripped his shaft through the layers of material, his nostrils flaring as he took her in. She had him wild with lust. Completely out of control.

He popped the button on his shorts. Dragged the zip down. Kicked them off. Wearing only black briefs, Jake stroked himself through the material, eyeing his prize—the woman who never failed to send him into the stratosphere. When Cassie rubbed her legs together again, Jake lost all pretence that this would be a slow seduction. Tugging the front of his briefs down to free his cock, his rock-hard length slapped against his belly, and his balls drew up, pressed snugly against his body with the material of his underwear. He stroked himself, pricks of sensation following his path along his cock. Engorged and leaking, Jake eyed the length of Cassie's slim arms, upturned breasts, narrow waist, and long legs. He imagined hooking them over his elbows and slamming into her, his cockhead plunging deep into her core.

His cock flexed, pleading with him to satisfy the urge.

"Mmm, you liked whatever you just thought of," Cassie murmured, her voice husky as she swiped at the tip of his cock with her fingertip. She snagged the pearl of pre-cum that had beaded there and sucked on her finger. She hummed and gripped the railing again, resting her foot on one of the steps near her waist. She was completely open to him, the visual short-circuiting his brain. His restraint snapped.

Jake stepped forward and hooked his arm under her raised leg. She was as light as a feather, and he hoisted her up until she hooked her other leg over his elbow. Open in every way to him, she was the sexiest thing he'd ever seen.

He shifted, bringing the tip of his cock to her opening and thrust gently forward, rubbing her until she squirmed. He teased them both. But the joke was on him.

Cassidy arched back, catching his cock on his next pass, and Jake's resistance crumbled. He couldn't stand the wait. Knowing how her heat wrapped around him, clutching him tightly as he tunnelled into her depths, almost made him cross-eyed with need. He impaled her in one swift plunge. She moaned, and he cried out when his hips pressed flush against hers, a full-body shudder travelling through him.

Sensation overload.

He withdrew to the mushroom head of his cock and slammed forward again. The sounds their bodies made slapping together were the bass. Cassie's pants and his grunts added in was a symphony. Hot as hell to listen to. It was a feast for the senses.

Overwhelming.

All-consuming.

He thrust again. The tingle at the base of his spine had started already. His balls were drawn up tight. On edge, he leaned in, his chest hair abrading her pebbled nipples.

Cassie moaned, arched into him, and pressed her body as close as she could. He slowed his thrusts, grinding against her clit more than pumping into her.

"Fuck," she cried. "Kiss me."

He slammed his mouth against hers, their kiss filled with a sultry heat like a summer thunderstorm. Cassie's internal walls fluttered around his cock, and she pulled away, tipping her head back as she whined. She was close again, and he needed to hold out until she came. It was good motivation, and Jake clasped her butt in his hands, squeezing the fleshy globes as he pulled her down onto his cock over and over. Her breasts bounced with the motion.

When she arched into him, trying to press harder onto him, he bent to suckle on her nipple. He scraped his teeth gently along the beaded flesh, and Cassie shouted. Jake pressed in deep, his orgasm roaring through him like a runaway train. His dick throbbed, pulses of his seed unloading into her.

Jake came back into his body slowly. He slumped against her, his head swimming with the endorphins racing through his body, while Cassie held both their weight up.

"Well, that was a lovely surprise," she teased when he lowered her legs back down to the path.

"Mhmm," he agreed. "I want to take you out tonight. Spoil you." He kissed a line up her throat, tickling her with his stubble. He wanted to celebrate their anniversary with a night of dancing in her arms and making love until the early hours.

"Why, Mr Phillips, I'd love that." Jake grinned at her use of his name—the one he'd legally adopted two years ago to the day. They weren't married, but he'd wanted to take Cassie's name from the moment he'd met her family. They'd accepted him with open arms, and he'd cried like a baby.

"Good." He brought their lips together for a smiley kiss and smoothed his hands over the rounded globes of her arse as she tangled her hands in his hair.

* * * * *

Their Saturday night was spent outdoors in their next-door neighbour's yard—a housewarming party for Robyn, Mike, and Ezio, and Mike's kids. Robyn had lived in the apartment above their garage for a short time, and she and Cassie had become fast friends. Cassie was warm and funny, but it took her a long time to open up to people. With Robyn, it had been instantaneous.

Having them move in next door had been good for Cassie, and for that, Jake would always be grateful.

When the previous owners had contacted him to help them sell their house, he'd known it was perfect for Robyn and her two partners. Mike had expressed to him a few times how much he'd love to raise his kids in a place like theirs. It was only a matter of time before Robyn and Ezio had talked him into it.

The guys were as madly in love with each other as they were with Robyn. He could see how much they adored each other. Their path had been rocky, but through it, their bond had grown stronger, and Jake was thrilled that his and Cassie's friends were happy.

He sat on a lounger celebrating the completion of his friends' outdoor renovations. But instead of being happy for Mike, Robyn, and Ezio's new life together, he was filled with envy. Cassie was in his arms, and he was forever grateful they'd been able to work it out, but Jake couldn't help wishing he and Cassie could have had the same—another man to love. The longing was so intense that the ache had lodged itself under his skin. In his bones. There was a desperation to deliver on the promises he'd made to Cassie but also to feel the touch of the man he'd yearned for.

Phoenix.

Even after all these years, his name still conjured a warmth that settled in his heart. At the same time, though, the sharp twist of a knife in his chest stole his breath.

Jake concentrated on the flames dancing in the iron firepit until the stabbing pain subsided to a dull ache. He hated the envy. He was happy for his friends—he really was—but he couldn't help wanting the same.

It wasn't just Robyn, Mike, and Ezio who'd found one another either. Their other friends—people who had become dear to Jake and Cassie too, were visiting as well. Connor, Katy, and Levi were just as obviously made for one another. Their inside jokes, the smiles reserved for one another, and the way they gravitated together, always touching, made Jake want to scream. It was as if they missed one another even when they were standing in the same room.

He hadn't seen Phoenix for years and knew there had to be a point where he let go, but it was hard. And the likeness between Connor and Phoenix was enough that Jake's heart ached watching how Levi got to dote over both his lovers.

Cassie must have sensed his struggles. She turned to him, her eyes roaming over his face. Jake tried to smile, tried to reassure her, but he couldn't. His shoulders fell, and Cassie cupped his face, kissing him softly. "I need some air," he whispered.

"Want some company?"

He shook his head and took the empty bottle she was holding. "I'll get you another." Jake motioned to the coolers filled to the brim with drinks.

She waved off his offer. "I've run out. I only bought a couple over with me. The others weren't cold," she said by way of explanation. "I'll duck home later and get the six-pack I put in the fridge before we left."

"I'll do it."

Jake stood, and when Mike's gaze met his, he pointed next door. "Grabbing some more drinks for Cassie. I'll be back."

"I'll come with you." He sprang up and clapped his hand on Jake's shoulder before he had the chance to object. Flashing a small smile his way, Jake led Mike out the front gate. "So," he started before huffing out a laugh. "I'm just gonna come straight out and ask you something, yeah?"

"Of course." Jake nodded, turning to Mike more fully as he pushed open the gate to his yard. Had he been wallowing so much that he'd missed something the matter? "Is everything okay?"

Mike smiled, one genuinely filled with happiness. "Yeah, it's good. We're better than good." He licked his lips, and his smile faded before he looked back toward his home. Jake got the distinct impression that he'd rather be anywhere except there with him. "You and Cassie seem a little off. Is everything okay with you two?"

Jake froze then sagged, his shoulders slumping as the wind was taken out of his sails. God, was he that obvious? He had been off, but he thought he'd been doing a half-decent job of hiding it. Clearly not. "Cassie and I are good. I'm just going through a rough patch, but I'll be right." Mike raised a brow at him as if to ask whether that was all the information Jake was giving him. Jake groaned and added, "It's hard seeing how happy everyone is."

"You're not happy? Is it like depression unhappy?" Mike sat on the front step, resting his elbows on his spread knees, looking at him with furrowed brows, the concern in his eyes clear. Jake appreciated his willingness to talk, especially when he thought it could have been depression. But he would rather do almost anything than talk about why he was down. Maybe that had been his problem. He and Cassie had both dealt with what happened in their own way. While they spoke about Phoenix, the premature way their relationship crashed and burned and the way his hope had died after that were things they tended to steer clear of. Maybe getting it all out would help. Jake sighed, sinking down next to him.

"It's not depression." Jake blew out a breath. "I don't even know how to describe it. Jealousy maybe? I'm envious as hell." Mike tilted his head, inviting him to keep talking. "Cassie and I are happy. We're solid. But our relationship looks different now than what we expected it would when we first got together."

"Cryptic much?" Mike smiled and nudged him with his shoulder. "You can tell me. I won't say anything, not even to Rob and Ez."

"I'm pan and Cassie's poly. Well, I suppose I'm poly too." If the news surprised Mike, he didn't show it. "When we lived in Sydney, we met a guy—Phoenix—and we both fell for him. It was quick. Intense too. We clicked so well." Jake smiled sadly. "But then some stuff happened—none of which was any of our fault—and it didn't work out. Cassie and I moved up here because of the other things that went down, and we lost contact. I've had trouble moving on. I still love him."

Jake sucked in a breath, shocked to his core that the words had slipped out. He'd never said it—had not even acknowledged it given the futility—and now there he was laying it on Mike. He'd never even told Cassie, not that the news would come as a surprise to her.

But now the words were out in the open, hovering there in front of him, it was... wow. Oddly freeing, like he could finally own it. He didn't know whether he would ever really be ready to move on, but he'd been stuck idling in neutral for years now. Going nowhere. It was time he fulfilled his promise to Cassie.

"And seeing all of us loved up in trios makes you wish you'd worked out," Mike concluded. When Jake nodded, he added, "It's not too late to find someone else or find him again."

"Yeah," he agreed. "Cassie has probably been ready for years, but I—"

"Wait." He held up his hand. "You haven't spoken with her about this?"

"Generically, sure. Every now and then we've mentioned bringing in another person, but not in any depth. We've never planned anything since Phoenix. Looking for someone just kind of got shelved when we crashed and burned. Cassie hasn't ever asked to try again. She knows me well enough to understand that I wasn't ready."

"Do you think you're ready now? Or might be one day?"

"One day, I think so. Maybe we just need to get out there. Something casual with no strings attached." Jake nodded, trying to convince himself that he wouldn't back out if they ever actually got to that point.

Mike regarded him for a moment, and his lip twitched. "Yeah. Dude, one step at a time. Maybe just have an honest conversation with your girl."

Jake knocked his shoulder into Mike's. "Thanks, man. It was good to talk about it."

"Anytime."

Jake stood and motioned to the door. "Let me get the cider and we'll head back. Get you back to your party."

Cassie welcomed him with a smile that grew when he kissed her grinning lips before sliding in behind her again. "You seem happier."

"Mike and I had a chat. It helped." Cassie leaned into him, and Jake wrapped his arms around her, keeping her close.

When the conversation diverted to how the woman with pink hair, Adelaide, knew Katy, Connor, and Levi, there was mention of a butt plug. Jake groaned and turned his face against Cassie's shoulder to hide his laugh. But from his position, he had eyes directly on Connor. The man not only snagged but held his attention.

He couldn't look away, no matter how much he should.

It was as if he was intruding on an intensely private moment between Connor, Levi, and Katy. With eyes locked on Katy's, Levi sank his teeth into Connor's shoulder—just a playful bite—and Katy watched her other man as his eyes rolled back, and he arched into Levi.

It was times like this when what he'd lost stood out so starkly to him that the ache in his chest overwhelmed him. The wound that his father had inflicted on them multiplied infinitely by Phoenix turning away. It tore at his soul. Shredded him into a million pieces. Cassie had wanted Phoenix just as much as he did. He knew it was why neither one of them had pushed to open their hearts to another person again. He could usually stifle the agony, shove it back into the box he had carved out for Phoenix, but this time he couldn't. His emotions were too raw. Too close to overflowing already.

Yet, he still couldn't look away.

As Levi turned Connor's face and kissed him while Connor reached for Katy, drawing her in close, Jake fisted his hands in Cassie's white linen shirt.

Gritted his teeth.

Turned away.

The pain in his chest was a physical manifestation of his heartbreak, stealing his breath until Jake was sure the spots in his vision were a warning he was about to pass out.

"Mate, you got an issue with this?" Will, the burly cruise ship captain whose pretty boyfriend was wrapped around him, asked. Even though Jake's eyes were locked on the trio, he knew immediately who Will was talking to.

"He doesn't," Cassie answered quickly, more than grateful she understood exactly what he was struggling with. Jake slowly uncurled his fingers and straightened the loose linen before him. He met Mike's eyes, and his friend gave him an encouraging nod. Mike was right. He needed to open up about his feelings.

"I don't have a problem. I'm one of you—I'm pan—but it's been a while since I've been with a man. Last time didn't end well. It ruined everything—"

"No, it didn't," Cassie interjected, spinning to sit sideways on the lounger. Waving her hand in the direction of their house, then their friends, she added, "Look at everything we have because of it."

"But we don't have him, do we?" Jacob's words were quiet, but the silence following them was deafening. Cassie shook her head and cupped his face, leaning her forehead against his cheek.

"I wish we did too, but Jake, we have to accept that he made a decision. I hate seeing you hurting; I want you happy."

Jake nodded and wrapped his arms tight around his girlfriend. "I want the same for you."

"I am happy," she reassured him. "And I love you. That's more than enough. You're more than enough."

"I love you too." He nuzzled her cheek, slipping his hands into her hair and dropping a kiss on the corner of her mouth. He pulled back and smiled, but he knew it would look strained. "Might just have to get back into it, though, if you guys are anything to go by. Anyone know a good swingers' club?"

Adelaide cleared her throat. "Actually, I do." She reached into the purse by her feet and slipped Cassie a dark business card. Jacob looked over her shoulder, but she passed it to him. The Exchange, Members Only Club was embossed in silver serif lettering. He flipped it over to see an address in Surfers Paradise. Jake slipped it into his shirt pocket and nodded his thanks. "I'll put your names down as my guests. We can exchange numbers and I'll give you the tour. We can have a chat about relationship pressures when you're jumping into a poly relationship too."

"Thank you," Cassie murmured and squeezed his hand. A weight lifted off his shoulders, knowing he was doing this for Cassie. Phoenix would always hold a piece of his heart, but no matter what Cassie said, he wanted to give her this.

Perhaps letting someone else in—even just for the night—was what they needed to move past him.

"So... how good was the State of Origin?" Jake asked, grinning at New South Wales' win. There was a round of collective moans and a few choice words.

* * * * *

Their rideshare pulled up in front of a three-storey building along the main street in Surfers Paradise. The large windows and high hedge intersected by an ornate black gate made it look more like a home for an A-lister than a club. But understated was probably a good thing where the clientele was going inside to get naked. At least, that's how Jake assumed it would work. He really didn't have much of a clue.

He stepped up to the curb and held out his hand for Cassie to hold as she slid out of the low car. Wearing a long-sleeved black dress with a plunging back that made Jake want to peel her out of it, she was gorgeous. Her hair was loose in long curls, and her make-up was artfully applied to look like she had none on at all. His girlfriend was a wet dream, one that Jake could never get enough of. Giving Cassie what she'd always wanted made him happy. Hopefully, he'd be able to go through with it.

He was determined to at least see whether it was an option. Cassie had needed a little persuasion, and he could still see she was nervous. Giving him a small smile, she smoothed her dress down and blew out a breath. He waited, making sure that she wasn't going to call the whole thing off. But when she eyed the building with more than a cursory glance, he knew she was intrigued. "Shall we?" he asked.

"Yeah." Cassie nodded, then laughed. "I've got butter-flies."

He grinned. "Me too. But no pressure. We'll check it out and see whether it's somewhere we want to visit again."

The smile she shone his way was more genuine this time. "Come on, let's find Adelaide."

The gate was unlocked, and as they pushed through, Jake spotted her immediately, drinking a cocktail at one of the mosaic-topped tables with ornate iron chairs. She was hard to miss with pink hair laying in waves around her shoulders.

Passing through the gate was like stepping straight into an Italian piazza. Terracotta tiles lined the ground, and wide pots were placed in each of the four corners with tall palms in them. A tall fountain was nestled among the vines creeping up the fence, and a handful of people mingled there. Jake adjusted his collar and motioned for Cassie to walk ahead of him to Adelaide.

"Hi, guys. Welcome," she said warmly. "Would you like a drink before we begin the tour? There's another bar inside if you'd prefer."

"Let's take a look around," Cassie said, squeezing Jake's hand.

"Excellent. First stop is right here. This is the piazza. It's strictly a place to chill out and enjoy the sun or the night air. We're open twenty-four-seven from Thursday noon to Monday at 9:00 a.m. There are also some other nights throughout the year where special events are held."

"*We're* open? Do you work here, or are you a member?"

"I'm a sex coach here so I supervise sessions, guide participants, and see some on a regular basis to do classes with. I also do a few demonstrations of products I sell—toys and that sort of thing." He was sure she was underselling herself. Her job sounded different from anything he'd ever heard of before, and he could only imagine the highs and lows a career like that could have.

She led them up the stairs to the front entrance, through another ornate iron gate, which swung open silently and through a heavy timber door. Once inside, they passed into a foyer area where a woman dressed in all black, topped with a black-and-gold vest, sat behind a desk. She smiled when she saw them. "Evening, welcome to The Exchange. You must be Cassie and Jake. I'm Brooke."

"We are." Cassie shook her hand, and Brooke held out a tablet to her. She did the same with Jake. Brooke explained the privacy requirements, access to the private website where membership documents would be available, and took copies of their photo ID.

When they'd finished, Adelaide instructed, "Right, come on through." She pushed against a panel in the wall that Jake would never have guessed was a door. To their left was a grand staircase that curved up a level. Above it was a second matching staircase leading to the third floor. His earlier impression about the club looking like a mansion wasn't far off—it was grand and incredibly classy. "There are four main areas in the building—one to each floor. Ground level is a bar and sitting area. This is where all the demonstrations and parties are held. We'll come back here, so I'll show you this level after we've seen the other areas. Below us is the basement pool, sauna, and steam rooms. One level above us is the colosseum—our amphitheatre for public play—the role playrooms and group area, and the level above that are our private rooms. Each of those is more like a hotel room with complete privacy." They followed Adelaide down a level to the pool deck and through a glass gate that acted as a safety fence.

The pool was decorated like a Roman bath with a line of arches separating the pool area from the loungers placed alongside. Vines grew along the walls, and as they walked passed the loungers and moved to the refreshment stand, Jake could see panels of opaque glass above them—the pool would have natural lighting during the day. Ahead of them, a group of people gathered around a lounger, watching and cheering as moans echoed off the walls. Adelaide stopped walking at the cart, but what Jake thought was a simple bottled water stand turned out to be so much more. "We provide condoms and lube throughout the building in stations like this. We ask that you dispose of them in the rubbish bins provided." She opened the cupboard door and pointed to the sterile bin. In the other side, towels were rolled up and stacked neatly. "The towels are for your use too, but again, please place the soiled ones in the hampers."

A shout rent the air, and Jake turned, curious at the show being played out only a few metres away. "Feel free to check it out," Adelaide encouraged. Cassie wandered over there, and Jake followed, standing behind her as they looked between heads to see a man on his back, cum over his belly with his legs held apart by a man buried inside him, and another kneeling to the side with his cock deep in the man's throat. A few of the audience members had their cocks in hand and were jacking themselves in time to the wet slurping sucks and thrusting of hips. A woman was bent at the waist while a man pumped into her from behind. The crowd here was mostly men, but they'd seen a few women upstairs.

Jake licked his lips, and Cassie pressed her rear end against the erection he had no hope of hiding now. "Is this your scene?" he whispered.

"Honestly?" When he nodded, she winced. "I don't know if I'd have sex here, but watching would be good, I guess."

"Okay."

They left the basement soon after and toured the other floors. Adelaide's description was spot on. The third floor was simply a corridor with doors spaced regularly off each side. She showed them how to locate an available room, explained cleaning procedures and reserving rooms during the busy times. The spaces themselves were opulent, California king beds with white linens and a mountain of pillows. Leather chaise lounges, dark timber side tables, gleaming polished timber floors, and flowing white curtains finished the look in the bedrooms, and the bathrooms were stone and glass. Gorgeous, all of it. Some of his higher-end clients could have done with consulting their decorator.

"Let's take a seat," Adelaide invited, moving over and sitting cross-legged on one of the chaise lounges. She waited until he and Cassie sat down on the other one before she started speaking. "You mentioned at Robyn, Mike, and Ezio's party that you were looking to join a swingers' club. Have you had an open relationship in the past?"

"No, never open." Cassie explained how the two of them got together and then met Phoenix.

Adelaide nodded. "And after you went your own ways, you haven't been with anyone else?"

"No." Jake shook his head. "I wasn't ready, and Cassie didn't push me."

"How long ago was that?" She smiled, threading her fingers together on her lap.

"A few years ago." Jake looked to Cassie and slid his hand into hers. "Three."

"That's a long time for the two of you to be exclusive. Was the decision to open up your relationship again one that you've spoken about for a long time?"

"Initially, yes. But not as much recently. It seems like we've been in a holding pattern for a while."

"And what triggered you to act now?" She paused, then added, "Are you ready now when you haven't been in the past?"

"I'm not sure this is for us." Cassie went to stand, but Jake tugged her hand.

"Adelaide has a point. Maybe we need to talk more about it."

Cassie blew out a breath and sank back down onto the seat. "Seeing the people downstairs was hot, but… I don't know if that's really me." She tucked her hair behind her ear and looked around the room. "This is more my style, but I can't imagine ever being without Jake. So, for me, adding someone else is a possibility, but I won't swap partners for the night."

"The good thing is that this club is whatever you make it. If you want to come here and hang out at the bar and never use the other facilities, never do anything apart from having a drink, that's completely up to you. We have many members who simply enjoy the inclusivity and lack of judge-ment that comes in a space like this. It doesn't matter how you identify, or if you want to participate in more, you'll be accepted here." Adelaide reached out and patted Cassie's hand. "My concern is that you seem to be jumping into this in somewhat of a knee-jerk reaction." Jake looked down, picking at an invisible thread on his pants. She was right. "Feel free to tell me I'm wrong here, but, Jake, your reaction to Levi teasing Connor wasn't one of arousal or even that wanting to explore that side of you again. It looked like pain."

He cleared his throat. "It was. It killed me watching them, knowing they have what I wanted to give to Cassie. I know she loves me as much as I love her, and we're happy together, but I gave her a promise."

"Jake—" Adelaide coaxed.

"Don't do this as some misplaced duty to me to fulfil a promise we made years ago. I love you, but I won't let you destroy what we've built. I've told you that you're enough. Believe me, Jake. That's what I need from you now. Not sex with some stranger." Cassie's words were determined. Frustration flashed in her eyes, and Jake smiled. Relief squeezed his throat, his words getting caught. Unshed tears stung his eyes and he nodded, his shoulders dropping. Jake huffed out a laugh, overwhelmed with the emotions swamping him.

"I believe you," he whispered, his voice breaking on the last word.

Adelaide stood and smiled down at them. "Take all the time you need. I'll wait for you down at the bar. When you're ready, we can talk more about what you want."

The door clicked closed, and Jake pulled Cassie into his lap, burying his face in her shoulder. "I'm sorry. I've screwed everything up."

"No, you haven't." Cassie ran her fingers through his hair, her touch soothing the broken pieces within him. "But you need to let go of this obsession you have with fulfilling a promise you made before we even really knew each other. I'm poly and I'll always be poly. Being in a monoga-mous relationship doesn't change that, just like you're pan and will always be pan despite being in a hetero relation-ship." Cassie hooked her finger under his chin and lifted his face to hers. "If we find someone tomorrow, or in ten years and we fall in love with them, then great. But let's not push ourselves to do something we might regret just to prove a label we already know is true."

"You don't want to join?"

"No. I don't want to ruin what we have." She cupped his face and tucked a stray lock of hair behind his ear. "Do you?"

Jake shook his head. "Not really. I want to want to, if that makes sense, and I love being able to give you what you need or want. So, if this is it, I'll be here in a heartbeat. But can I see myself down on the pool deck? Or in any of those role playrooms coming onto someone to get my dick sucked? Or get someone else off? No, I don't think so. Not when I haven't even thought of another person apart from you and Phoenix like that in years."

"Oh, Jake." Cassie pressed her lips to his in a sweet kiss. It was comfort and love, and he sank into her embrace.

"Why am I broken, Cass? Why couldn't I move on when he could do it so easily?"

She shook her head. "If you're broken, then so am I. I've never wanted anyone else since the two of you either."

"Let's get out of here." Cassie nodded, and Jake stood, holding his hand out to her. They left the room hand in hand, the weight on Jake's chest lighter. He knew they were making the right decision.

"We'll go tell Adelaide our decision before we go. Maybe we can grab a drink at the bar too."

"Sounds good."

Cassidy squeezed his hand, and they stepped into the lift together. When it opened on the ground floor, the hum of conversation greeted them. There were a lot more people mingling now, drinking and flirting. Even though everyone was there with one aim, no one seemed to be in a rush to get up or downstairs. They seemed content to enjoy the buzz in the room.

Once again, they spotted Adelaide quickly. Dressed in dark clothes, her pink hair made her stand out, despite sitting alone at a table in the corner. Moving over to join her, Jake asked, "Can I get you a drink?"

"A Sprite would be great, thank you."

"Usual, babe?" Cassie nodded and smiled as she slid onto the chair opposite their host.

Jake walked to the bar and scanned the shelves for the gin Cassie was partial to. His eyes landed on a shock of coal-coloured hair, and Jake raked his gaze down the man's body. He wore the same uniform as the other staff, his clothes fitting him like a glove. The brocade vest highlighted his broad shoulders and tapered to a slim waist, framing a perfect arse, hugged by a set of dress pants that were tailored to perfection. Jake swallowed, adjusting himself as he closed the distance between the high-topped tables and the bar. Damn, the closer he got, the finer the man was.

His hair was short but looked like it was growing out from a closely cropped cut. The strip of skin between his hair and shirt was bronze, and as he shifted, reaching up to take down a bottle of Jack, Jake got a glimpse of stubbled cheeks.

The man turned.

Jake's steps stuttered to a stop.

He opened his mouth to speak. Nothing came.

Rushing sounded in his ears.

He sucked in a breath, suddenly lightheaded.

On wobbly knees, he stumbled forward, reaching for the bar.

Their eyes met. Recognition, then shock flittered across the familiar face.

Jake watched in slow motion as the bottle of Absolut slipped out of his hand. It fell, the corner hitting the floor first.

It shattered, the sound ringing out.

"Phoenix, what the hell?" a man boomed. There was anger in his tone and Phoenix flinched.

A form moved into Jake's peripheral vision, but he couldn't look away from Phoenix. The man he'd dreamed of endlessly stuttered, "Ah. Um."

"It's you," Jake breathed, finally finding his words, before the man who'd spoken before cursed again. Without a word, Phoenix turned and strode away.

Jake blinked. A different man stood across from him. This one wore a scowl, his receding auburn hair so different from Phoenix's. He was older too—mid-fifties at a guess. Had Jake just imagined the whole exchange? Was Phoenix really there? "What'll you have?"

"The bottle." Jake motioned to the floor and handed over his card.

"You don't—"

"It was my fault."

The man swiped his card without another word before handing it back to him.

SIXTEEN

Cassie

J ake stumbled back to the table, his face ghost white and his hands empty apart from his credit card. He slid onto the chair next to hers and opened his mouth as if to say something before closing it again and scrubbing his hands over his face.

"Jake?" she asked, worry sitting like an anvil in her belly.

He turned to her, his eyes wide and glassy. Reaching out, he fingered one of her curls, his hand trembling. Cassie grasped it between hers, steadying him. He was her rock. Always steady, always ready with an encouraging word. To see him speechless and rocked to his core—especially after their conversation—was something she hadn't seen for years. Not since Jake had jettisoned his father from his life.

"I…" He shook his head and laughed, a shocked sound jumping from his throat. "Phoenix…"

Cassidy furrowed her brow. Confusion reigned. What was Jake talking about? She knew he was trying to put her needs first, despite not wanting to be with anyone else. The tour had solidified her decision too. It had shown her what she thought she wanted a few years earlier. But the more she saw, the more she realized that the club wasn't for her—well, except the cosy rooms on the top level. She loved that other people could find what they wanted there, but it wasn't for Cassie. And the idea of sharing Jake? No, just no. There was only one other person she was interested in doing that with.

"He's our new bartender. Did something happen?" Adelaide asked.

The words slammed into her. Like the crack of a gun at point-blank range.

It had to be a coincidence.

Someone with the same name.

Cassidy swivelled her gaze to the other woman and opened her mouth before turning back to Jake. Her movements were slow, like she'd fallen out of sync with the rest of the world.

"It's him." Wonder lit up Jake's eyes, disbelief lacing his words and a smile that he couldn't contain curling his lips.

Wide-eyed, Cassie dropped Jake's hand and dashed to the bar. The heels she wore clicked on the dark timber floors. Eyes turned in her direction, but she didn't care. Phoenix was there. He was really there.

But then she stopped. Her feet skidded to a halt.

He hadn't called. He hadn't reached out. He'd rejected them. He didn't want them. Why would he want them now? She stood there, warring with herself. Did she go to him now? Or did she walk away like he'd done to them?

Popping up from behind the bar, carrying a dustpan and brush, she saw his hair first. Jet-black, messy locks that looked like he'd run his hands through them. His skin was paler than she remembered, the bronze not as pronounced. But they'd all changed—she was almost a different person to the high-strung corporate shark she'd once been.

With her heart pounding in her ears, she watched as he emptied the glass fragments in the bin and reached for a mop. His movements were methodical, precise but also fluid. He washed his hands after he'd finished and reached for the black towel he had slung over the bar. He moved like he was familiar with the place, but he was only new. Why was he there in the first place? He'd been studying at university.

He looked up. Their gazes clashed.

He leaned against the bar like he was unsteady on his feet and sucked in a breath. Tears pooled in her eyes, and Cassie brought a hand up to her mouth.

Then he moved.

Strode to the end of the bar and lifted the keep before he ran to her, his steps slowing as he came closer.

He stopped just shy, their bodies only a foot apart. He reached out, then dropped his hand. He waited for Cassie. Waited for her to choose him.

But he hadn't chosen them.

Her tears fell, and strong hands closed around her biceps, the familiar touch comforting. Cassie turned to her man and wrapped her arms around him. Seeing the man they'd wanted for so long, who they'd waited for, right there in front of them was overwhelming. Jake enveloped her in his embrace, his familiar touch comforting. Hard muscle met her fingertips, but he cradled her with infinite gentleness.

"I have to get back there, but I'll be on break in an hour. Can we talk?"

"You've had my number for years. You could have talked to us anytime." The hurt in Jake's voice eviscerated her, and Cassie squeezed her arms tighter around his waist. "But yes, we're over there." Jake must have motioned to the table they'd been sitting at, his arm leaving her back for a moment before he cradled her again.

"I don't deserve the chance, but I'm grateful for it. Cassidy?" Phoenix called, and she pulled back far enough that she could see him. "I'm sorry for hurting you." His gaze bounced between them, landing on Jake's. "I always regretted not calling."

She couldn't name the emotions coursing through her. She was a jumbled mess. Confusion, hope, and a wariness that she hadn't experienced in a long time warred for attention. Could she trust him? She wanted to. All she'd ever wanted was the three of them. Hope reared its head, lifting itself above the quagmire of emotions still fighting in the shadows, and Cassie latched onto it.

Phoenix paused before crossing through the keep. He looked over his shoulder and lifted his lips in a small smile. His expression was filled with regret in the almost sad curl of his lips and hope in the sparkle of his eyes.

Oh yeah, hope was winning.

"We're joining up, aren't we?" Cassie asked, already knowing Jake's answer. His eyes flashed a stormy blue, need boiling in them.

"For him." Jake clenched his jaw and nodded once.

Cassidy smiled, relief coursing through her. They were on the same page. Her tears started again, and she nodded. Laughter bubbled up her throat. "Good, that's what I want too."

Jake took her hand and threaded their fingers together, bringing her knuckles to his lips. "We have a lot to talk to Phoenix about. He hurt both of us, but maybe it was a fair turn of play after what my father did to him. Either way, I can't walk away this time without fighting for him."

* * * * *

Cassie looked up as Phoenix stopped at their table carrying a tray with another round of the drinks Adelaide had ordered. After two trips to the bar resulting in no drinks, she'd taken matters into her own hands. Phoenix lowered the tray, and Adelaide said, "The Sprite is mine, but I might take it to my office to drink." She stood and smiled down at Cassie and Jake. "I'll have Brooke text the password to you. Just sign the forms and email them back. We'll get your membership organized from there."

"Thank you," Jake replied, squeezing Cassie's hand. He hadn't let go of her since they'd spoken to Phoenix, and Cassie clung to him. She needed the grounding, or she would get blown away like one of those tumbleweeds in the desert. Her entire world had shifted in the last couple of hours. It wasn't the club; they would have already left if that had been the only thing they'd seen tonight. But seeing Phoenix—the man who was their unfinished business... the one who'd gotten away? It had flipped her upside down.

Phoenix placed the rest of the drinks on the table, Cassie's gin and soda with a squeeze of lime, Jake's whiskey, and two shot glasses of clear liquid. She motioned to the empty chair, and Phoenix slid in. He took one of the shot glasses in hand and tipped it back, swallowing it down and wincing with the burn.

"So, you're joining?" he asked just as Jake said, "How long have you been working here?"

"Yes," Cassidy answered, but didn't elaborate, not wanting to get side-tracked with the whys of their membership. They'd been upfront with Adelaide, telling her exactly what they'd first decided and what brought about the change of heart. She'd smiled, seemingly pleased that they'd taken the time to talk it out.

"I've been here a few weeks. Haven't even officially left Sydney yet, but I can't bring myself to go back and pack my stuff. What about you? Are you visiting the Coast, or do you live here?"

"We live here. Moved up a week after we last saw you." Jake's words hung in the air, and Phoenix downed his second shot before nodding slowly.

There was a pause, the weight of the silence between them heavy. "I'm sorry I never called."

"I wasn't sure your friend passed on my number. I hoped he did, but the rejection seemed easier to deal with, knowing he might not have."

Phoenix nodded, and Cassie swallowed, dread filling her. She knew some things would hurt—none of them had any closure with the way things had ended—but Cassie dreaded Phoenix's words. He had the power to eviscerate them. But shy of telling Phoenix to walk away—which would hurt just as much—she had no power to protect Jake from him.

"He did, but then my life kind of imploded and the time didn't seem right. To be honest, I was looking over my shoulder for months, and I needed a bit of distance. I picked up your card so many times, but the more time passed, the harder it was to call."

"Why were you looking over your shoulder?" Jake asked, his tone guarded.

"The guy that interrupted us that morning?" Cassie saw Jake's spine stiffen and the grip he had on her hand tightened. She braced herself, sending up a prayer to the gods that whatever he was about to say wouldn't shatter the foundation of strength Jake had built up over the years away from the toxic influence of his father. "Turns out he was my new boss."

"Fuck," Jake hissed, recoiling like he'd been slapped.

Cassie shifted closer, trying to shield him from the pain, as if by wrapping herself around him, she could use her body to deflect the self-inflicted blows that Jake would launch at himself. The guilt he carried over his father's actions was unfair, but no matter how many times she tried to reassure him that his father's actions weren't his own, Jake disagreed. Cassie wrapped her arm around his back, needing to comfort her man. But it was no use. He shook his head and downed the glass of whiskey in one gulp.

"I didn't put two and two together until about a week later. He's your dad, isn't he?" When Jake nodded, Phoenix's shoulders slumped.

"He ruined all our lives that day. We both lost our jobs, and without mine I couldn't afford the lease on my apartment—"

"They can't do that without cause, and even then, they need to give you appropriate notice and an opportunity to correct your performance. The circumstances in which the legislation permits employment to be terminated without notice would hardly apply here," Phoenix interrupted, his jaw set and his eyes fiery. "Never mind the breach of anti-discrimination laws."

Jake huffed out a laugh that held no humour. "You met my father. You saw the influence he and his firm wielded, and probably still does. Do you think a little thing like employment laws or anti-discrimination legislation would stop him?" Phoenix shook his head, his mouth in an O. Jake added, "I'm sorry he hurt you," and Phoenix seemed to fold in on himself even more.

"I'm sorry too."

"Were you a lawyer? Why are you working in a bar?" Cassie asked, puzzled.

Phoenix rested his forearms on the table and sighed. "Yeah, I am. Was." He shook his head and shrugged. "I don't even know anymore. After I got kicked to the curb from Stark Williams, I went back to Grounds and asked them for my job back. But given my boss knew I was leaving, she'd already hired a full-time barista. They didn't need me anymore. She felt sorry for me and put me in contact with a friend who owned a bar. I worked there for nearly twelve months before I got a job at another law firm. Then I worked there for two years. I was the first into the office and last one to leave every day." He pursed his lips. "I was getting there, building up my knowledge and setting myself up for tougher assignments. We had a case, a big one, and I thought they were my ticket to stepping up my career. Then my boss's wife went into labour early. We were scheduled to have a mediation that day, but instead of cancelling it, my boss told me to go in his stead. I still can't believe he thought I was ready." Phoenix huffed, and a look of disgust crossed his face. "Turns out I wasn't. But I tried. I was there, ready to do it, and then I got introduced to the defendant's lawyer. Your dad—"

"I haven't spoken to him in years," Jake murmured, barely loud enough for Phoenix to hear over the chatter in the bar, but he stilled, tilting his head to the side thoughtfully. "Not since he hurt us. He's not my father any more."

Phoenix nodded and reached out for Jake's hand, clasping it on the tabletop. That small move of comfort brought back memories of the time Phoenix had opened up to them. Jake had reached for him, silently lending his support to help Phoenix through his retelling. This time though, she couldn't tell whether he was giving or seeking comfort. Regardless, Cassie loved seeing it there; she just hoped for Jake that the rest of Phoenix's story wouldn't break him.

"Denyer was their lawyer. He's a mean son of a bitch, and I snapped. Full-blown anxiety attack. I had to get out of there. I ran away, straight to the bloody outback if you can believe it. I stayed with my old flatmate, his boyfriend, and their extended family for a few days to get my head on straight. My boss called me back to Sydney, and I left the station. I shouldn't have even tried to go. I wasn't ready. When I got to the turnoff, the same thing happened. I was right back in that mediation again."

He ran his hands through his hair and rubbed his eyes. Exhaustion radiated off him. A bone-deep weariness that was much more than working late or missing a few nights sleep. He looked defeated. Beaten down. Cassie longed to reach for him but couldn't bring herself to. Not yet.

"I was paralysed. I couldn't take the turn." His voice hitched, and the invisible wall that was stopping Cassie crumbled. She didn't hesitate, slipping her hand into his, trying to reassure him like she was doing to Jake. The three of them were joined now, each of them connected.

The warmth of Phoenix's hand in hers spoke of strength and vitality, but the two men before her were both broken in their own way. She was the strong one; they needed her, and this time she would fight for both of them. Cassie squeezed Phoenix's hand, and he closed his eyes before slowly exhaling.

"I couldn't go. I ended up back home at Mum and Dad's farm in Tamborine an incoherent mess. I got a job here a week ago. My boss at the bar—he and I became friends when I was working for him—told me to call these guys and give his name as a reference. And here we all are." He smiled, but it didn't reach his eyes, and he withdrew his hands from theirs, twisting them on his lap. He was visibly retreating into himself.

"Are you okay now? With your anxiety attacks?" she asked gently.

"I… sort of? I need to go back to my apartment and clear my things out. That's screwing with my head, but working here is good." He looked around the bar, then down to his watch. "I need to get back to it."

Jake nodded, and Phoenix stood, but Cassie wasn't letting him walk away. Not now, not after she knew what he'd been through all alone. Jake had wanted to fight for him, but Cassie knew him. The guilt over his father ruining Phoenix's career twice would be crushing him. She was strong enough to stand in Jake's stead. "Phoenix." He paused in the middle of pushing his chair in. "Come out on a date with us. We came here to the club looking for something. At first, we didn't think we were in the right place. But we are—we found you."

"I don't—"

"Think about it, and this time call me." She fished a card out of her purse and handed it to him, pressing it into his palm and curling his fingers around it. "Even if you decide it's a no, call. You have friends here—more than just us.

There are people who will care about you and can understand what you've been through both with work and in life.
You just haven't met them all yet."

Phoenix looked down at his hand and nodded once.
"Okay."

"When are you working next?" Jake asked.

"Tomorrow until midnight."

"We'll be here."

Phoenix nodded again and motioned to the bar but
paused and dropped his fist onto the chair. "I still have it,
you know. Your card. I figured you would have changed
your number by now. I was too chickenshit to call."

Before either one of them could say anything, Phoenix
headed off. Cassie held out her hand to her boyfriend.
"Let's go home." When he nodded, she led him out hand in
hand.

The night air blew around them, a cold breeze straight
off the Pacific, and with it, the weight that had resided on
Cassie's shoulders for years lifted. Joy bubbled through her
veins. Pure, unadulterated happiness. She meant what
she'd said to Phoenix—they'd gone there hoping to find
something. They'd been attempting to plug the gaping cre-
vasse that Phoenix being torn out of their lives had caused,
albeit in the wrong way.

When Adelaide had made Cassie see what Jake was doing, she knew it was the wrong way to go about it. She'd
been ready to walk away. To turn her back and never see
the club again, but they'd stopped to tell Adelaide their decision. What a sliding door moment it was. Never in her

wildest dreams did she think they'd find him there. Now that they had, though? A lot of water had passed under that bridge. A lot of pain and misery had befallen them since their last encounter. Some healing was needed, as well as reconnecting and learning the new them. For all three of them. Jake and Cassie may be a couple, but they needed to get to know the part of each other that they'd only explored once with Phoenix. Jake's pansexuality and Cassie's poly-amory were almost as unfamiliar to each other as the two of them were to Phoenix. But she was prepared for it. Ready to put in the hard yards to get the results. She wasn't sure whether that was friendship or more, but one thing was certain—The Exchange was about to become a favourite haunt for them.

They were quiet on the trip home and while they went through their routine getting ready for bed. She padded to the bed and slid in, curling into Jake's side. "Think we'll get a second chance?" he murmured.

"Yes."

"Just like that?"

"Yep. Because even if we only end up friends, he's in our life where he belongs. I hate that he's been through so much. We had each other for support. I just hope he had someone there for him too." Cassie ran her hand down Jake's chest to his waist and tucked herself in closer. "That first year when we were starting over, everything was fall-ing apart for him, and I hate imagining he was going through that alone."

"Yeah, me too."

They didn't talk much after that, and if Cassie's thoughts were anything to go by, Jake's mind was in a spin too.

* * * * *

"What'll it be, Mr Phillips? We don't serve double-shot almond cappuccinos with every sweetening known to man here." Phoenix managed to keep a straight face as he wiped the bar down and rested his hands on the sparkling top as Cassie slipped onto the stool.

Jake's reaction was priceless. He froze halfway onto the seat, opened his mouth and closed it again, then wiped his hands down his pants. It was a move Cassie hadn't seen him do for years. Not since he'd escaped from his father's clutches. She loved the man he'd turned into—each small success built him up, giving him some much-needed self-assuredness. His confidence grew, and he worked hard to prove to himself that he could handle things. Jake still left all the big business decisions to Cassie, but she knew it was more out of respect for her than any lack of ability on his part.

She cracked a smile and bit down on her lip to stifle her laugh, but Phoenix's raised eyebrow set her off, giggles peeling out of her as Jake looked like a deer in headlights at the man, and Phoenix asked, "Same as last night?"

Jake shook his head, his face flaming red, and squeaked, "No." He cleared his throat, squared his shoulders, and added, "I'm driving tonight. Just a Pepsi, thanks."

Phoenix smirked, winked at Jake, and turned to her. "Cassidy?"

"It's Cassie now, and yeah, I'll have the same. A gin and soda with lime." She smiled, and he nodded, collecting two glasses.

"The card you gave me last night has both your names on it," he prompted, filling the glass with the on-tap Pepsi and looking up at her from under thick lashes for a moment. She could fall into those hazel eyes, getting lost in them like she did with Jake's azure ones.

"We own Phillips Real Estate," Jake explained, then paused when Phoenix flicked his gaze to Jake and opened his mouth as if to ask a question. He lifted the glass to the bar top and passed it to Jake.

Phoenix bruised some lime in the bottom of a glass, reached for the bottle of Hendricks, and measured out a shot before asking, "When did you get married?" He kept his gaze on what he was doing—filling the glass almost to the rim with soda.

"We're not married," Cassie explained. "Not for lack of asking, though." Phoenix furrowed his brow, and his eyes widened as he handed over the glass. Cassie laughed. "I proposed, but he said no." She rolled her eyes and shook her head, motioning with her thumb over her shoulder to Jake. She didn't miss Jake's smirk, the familiar tease one she liked to remind him of.

"What?" Phoenix asked, his gaze bouncing between the two of them and settling on Jake. "Are you nuts?"

Jake shook his head and wrapped his arm around her shoulders, pulling Cassie in for a kiss to her temple. She loved being there in his arms and looked up at her boyfriend with what she knew was love in her eyes. "I said no because marriage would have meant it was just the two of us. That didn't suit Cassie—she's always wanted a committed relationship with more than one person. Over the years, I've realized that it didn't fit me either."

"I..." Phoenix shook his head in disbelief. "You're still nuts, man."

"I suggested an alternative, which I think fits us better." Jake smiled down at her, and she nodded. It absolutely did fit them better in every way. Their commitment was personal to them. It didn't need to be made legal for it to count.

"What's that?"

"You saw it on our card."

Phoenix held up his finger, asking us to wait a minute while he served another customer.

"He's interested in finding out more about us. That's a good sign, isn't it?" Jake asked quietly.

Cassie nodded and looked toward the man they were hoping would choose them. Phoenix's eyes flicked toward them, and his lip turned up in a half smile before shifting back to his customer. "I think so." She closed her lips around the straw and sucked, the drink refreshing on her tongue. She hummed, and Phoenix paused in the middle of making a drink, his reflected gaze locked on hers in the mirror. She bit down on her lip, feeling like the cat that got the cream as Phoenix moved to serve another customer, all the while looking at them.

When he finally came back to them twenty minutes later, he refilled Jake's glass and made up another drink for Cassie, moving slower than he had with the other customers. He was lingering there, wanting to spend time with them. "If you aren't married, why do you have the same name?" Phoenix asked, obviously understanding the reference when Jake had mentioned their business card.

"I changed my name to Phillips," Jake answered before looking at her. The love in his gaze, the absolute adoration, took her breath away, even after the years they'd been together. "We promised we'd always love and respect each other and do our best to make each other happy." Their vows were uttered on a picnic blanket down by the beach on a night where the full moon shone silvery in the sky. There hadn't been another person in sight for miles. The ocean and the stars their only witnesses. The physical evidence of their commitment was in their home and business—both were a labour of love they'd nurtured together every step of the way. But their love was in the everyday things too. The way that Jake never complained about picking up her wet towel off the floor. It was in the way Cassie worked her hardest to make their home warm and welcoming, a far cry from the sterile environment he'd grown up in.

Phoenix nodded, seemingly contemplating his answer. "Can I ask why?"

"My family name was a reminder of a person I'd come to despise. I wanted to leave him behind." On the face of it,

Phoenix would probably think Jake was referring to his father. And he wasn't wrong. But Jake's sense of self-worth had been so beaten down, was so incredibly low, that he'd hated himself too. Severing ties with his father was the first step. Moving away was the second. Disowning his father's name gave him the push to also leave behind the lifetime of verbal abuse. It helped him break free. The combination was like winning the trifecta for Jake. It was the final hurdle for him to look at himself in the mirror and know he truly was a different person. Jake liked the person he saw now. Cassie could see it in the way his smile reached his eyes and the way he held his head high. "I wanted to become part of something that had love at its centre, and for me, that was Cassie and her family. I asked her parents for permission, and then we filled out the paperwork."

Phoenix smiled, but it was sad. Was it because he pitied him, or because he wanted to be a part of something like that himself? Cassie could only guess, but he was called away again, leaving them alone once more.

"I haven't seen you around here before," a man said from behind them. He was standing with a woman who rested her hand on Cassie's stool and leaned in.

"And we'd remember you both," she mock whispered in Cassie's ear, flashing her ample cleavage at Jake.

"They're not interested," a harsh voice announced, and Cassie turned to look at Phoenix. He was breathing hard, his gaze as sharp as a dagger as he leaned over the bar. The woman stepped back immediately, but the man wasn't so deterred.

"What makes you think that? We've only just joined them."

"Because they're mine." He narrowed his eyes at the man, his nostrils flaring like a bull getting ready to charge. "And I don't share."

The man's lip turned up in a sneer, spoiling for a fight, but the woman wrapped her arm around his and smiled apologetically at them. "Sorry, we didn't know. Come on, Shane, let's go."

"You need to go out back and cool down. Ten-minute break." The same man that had been there the night before sidled up to Phoenix and leaned against the bar. "And I don't care how well they suck your dick, pull that shit with my customers again and you're out."

Phoenix turned and stalked away, leaving Cassie bereft. Jake's hand tightened on hers, and she squeezed back. A moment later, he pressed his hand against his chest and pulled out his phone. He showed her the screen—a text from a new number.

Sorry. I was an arse. I know you came here looking for something, but it's not them.

Cassie was her own woman. She prided herself on being independent and confident, but that possessive alpha in Phoenix rearing its head was like a drug to her. Jake was like that too—try to come between them and he flipped from his calm, laid-back self into a bear. And Cassie loved it. Jake smiled, that giddy grin she loved to see, added the number to his contacts and typed out a response, showing Cassie before he hit the paper plane sending the message.

Could it be you? We'd like it to be. It was spot on. That's exactly what Cassie wanted. Was their meeting serendipitous, or fate? Cassie didn't care either way, but Jake had been right the night before. They were going to fight for what they wanted, and Phoenix was it. She had to pace herself. Not get carried away with the possibilities. It was hard, and she was still wary, but the seed of hope had firmly implanted itself in her brain.

A moment later he responded. *IDK. I want to say yes, but it's been a long time. We're different people, and I'm a mess. I don't want my shit to affect you.*

Jake ran his fingers through his hair and groaned, and Cassie's heart broke for both of them. They had so much in common. The desire to protect others from things that weren't their doing or fault was ingrained in both Jake and Phoenix, and Cassie wished she could take some of that burden from them. *You still finishing at midnight? Maybe we can talk?*

Phoenix's response made him laugh, and when he showed her his phone, Cassie grinned, remembering the conversation like it was yesterday. *My dad's picking me up. Car's in the shop, so I'm schlepping it with the old man. Next he'll be tucking me in.* A second message flashed up on the screen only a moment later, and Cassidy snorted out a laugh at the rambling. *That sounded... wrong. He's not gonna put me to bed. Not like that. Actually, not at all. Scrap the last part of that message.*

Jake smiled indulgently. He'd been like that around Phoenix once upon a time too. It wasn't lost on her how the tables had turned; Jake was a different person to the one she'd met a few years earlier. He'd shaken off that self-doubt, and she knew they could help Phoenix do the same. They would. She was determined. *Call him and cancel. We'll drive you home.*

Okay.

That one-word reply was everything. He was opening himself up again, trusting them to look after him. Cassie's heart soared and the weight on her shoulders lifted. They were by no means in the clear—not that she even knew what that meant in these circumstances—but that bubbly excited hope fizzed in her veins like champagne, and Cassie counted down the moments until they could talk again.

The remainder of Phoenix's shift crawled, especially because the older man—his boss—directed Phoenix to serve the customers on the other end of the bar while he minded the section Cassie and Jake sat in. Cassie bit back her pout and had to coach herself not to stare daggers at the man. Considering Phoenix was still on trial, she didn't want to rock the boat. The last thing she wanted was for him to lose his job because she'd been acting like a spoilt brat stomping her foot that the sexy bartender wasn't serving them. On the surface, Jake handled things better, but Cassie knew he was on edge, and like shaking the bottle ready to pop the cork, it ramped up her excitement. Jake was staking his claim without words, not taking his eyes off their man the entire time.

When Phoenix's interminable shift was finally over, and he slipped out from behind the pass to stand next to them,

Jake lost his cool. He pulled Cassie against him and pressed his steely erection between her cheeks, groaning in her ear. Her clit throbbed and her breath lodged in her throat. Phoenix's nostrils flared and Cassidy reached for him, tugging him closer. He moved, standing in their personal space. He was close enough that Cassie could feel the heat radiating from his body. She could reach out and palm the bulge he was sporting, watching Cassie squirm against Jake's grinding hips and seeing her no-doubt glassy, half-lidded expression.

Phoenix inhaled sharply and Jake hissed, "Fuck." He pressed harder against her, and ground out, "Want to bend you over right here so we can take turns making you come apart."

Oh fuck. She wanted that. To be between them, right there and then. But she also wanted more than that, and she needed to be strong.

* * * * *

Cassie peered out the front windscreen as Jake pulled into the farm Phoenix had pointed out. A white clapboard house that was well-loved sat at the end of the gravel drive, and Cassie could just imagine Phoenix as a kid riding around the area on his push bike. Darkness surrounded them except for the lone porch light illuminating a small staircase and a happy red front door. Even if there was traffic travelling along the country road that late, the house was hidden from view by a curve in the driveway and plenty of trees.

A dog's barking broke the silence, and Phoenix hopped out, hushing him. It couldn't be the same one Phoenix had had as a boy, but being there and seeing what he saw as a child retold in the memory he'd shared years earlier tightened the connection that had gone slack with the passage of time and distance between them.

"So, this is where you grew up?" Jake asked as he followed him out of the car, Cassie tentatively walking around the back to join them.

Phoenix turned back to them after patting the black-and-white dog and sending him back to bed. "Yeah. Far cry from Sydney."

"Sydney wasn't right for us either. What matters is whether you're happy here," Cassie assured him. "We all have paths to follow. Sometimes you end up in a different place to where you imagined you'd be, but the twists and turns in your path are what make life interesting."

"The path has a pretty good view right now." He smiled tentatively and Cassie bit her lip, hope surging in her. She hoped more than anything that she wasn't reading more into the tentative steps forward they'd made. "But what I'm feeling scares me half to death."

Jake reached out, linking their fingers together and tugging him against them. "What's the scariest part?"

"You heard me at work. 'They're mine.' No you aren't. You can do whatever and whoever the hell you want." His words tumbled out, a fast rant as he shared his insecurities. "You joined the club so that you could sleep with other people, and a day later I'm laying claim to you? How can I go from not knowing who I am any more, to knowing exactly what I want in the space of a few weeks?" He stopped talking, his eyes wide. It was as if he was shocked by the admission. He knew what he wanted? He wanted them? Cassie was floored. Only a moment ago she'd been schooling herself into not overreacting, not projecting her hopes and desires onto his reactions. She hadn't stopped thinking about Phoenix for years, and it was hard to avoid the trap of jumping in headfirst when she saw him again thinking that they could pick right back up where they'd left off.

But hearing those words was a siren call.

"You don't have to make a decision now, Phoenix," Cassie assured him, going against her innermost desires. Curbing her hope and stopping that bubbly champagne-like excitement from exploding out of her was tough. If it was up to her, they'd turn around and head straight back to their place and stay there until they'd gotten naked and sated so many times none of them wanted to leave again, but this was more than sex. Phoenix had been struggling with his mental health and she wanted—no needed—to support him. To help him heal. "We didn't come tonight to force you to choose us. We came because we just found you again, and we were being selfish. If you need us to stay away, we'll do that." Jake's gaze flashed to hers. His eyes were wide and his mouth open in an O with shock. She slipped her hand into Jake's and squeezed before leaning in to kiss Phoenix on the cheek.

He turned his face, bringing his hand up to cup her cheek and hold her in place while he brushed his lips against hers. Cassie's eyes drifted closed at the gentle touch, the reverence with which he kissed her, stealing her breath. "I should tell you to go," he murmured between brushes of their lips, his tongue stealing out to tease hers as he kept his touch gentle. Cassie's heart flip-flopped, see-sawing between looping and swooping like a kaleidoscope of butterflies and clenching tight at his words. The ball of tension in her gut tightened when he pulled his lips away and he turned to face Jake. Their gazes locked, and they shifted closer together, the gap between them lessening as Jake pressed against him. This time, Cassie's heart stuttered, hope stringing tight like an archer readying to loose an arrow. She didn't breathe, didn't dare move in case she broke the spell the two men were under.

They hovered there, breathing each other's air as their lips were a hair's breadth apart. Jake lifted his hand to Phoenix's face, cradling it like he was a precious gift, and Phoenix murmured, "But I can't seem to stay away." Phoenix's words snapped Jake's apparent last thread of control, and Cassie could have sobbed with relief. She surged forward, hugging him tight as Jake slammed his mouth against Phoenix's, licking and sucking, nipping and caressing him as he let the years of heartache bleed away. Cassie blinked back tears of pure happiness and kissed Phoenix's neck, unable to pull away from his smooth skin and the rich scent filling her senses. Jake clawed at Phoenix's shirt and vest, reaching for the warm skin he'd no doubt find underneath.

Phoenix moaned and tilted his head back, shuddering at Jake's touch. Cassie closed her hand over Jake's, and he sucked in a breath, the trembling calming instantly. He choked out a strained laugh and smoothed his fingers down Phoenix's front before slipping his hand around the other man's waist and bringing their bodies into perfect alignment. "Sorry, got carried away," Jake apologized, and Cassie slipped out from between them, letting them kiss. Phoenix only broke away to join his lips with hers once more.

Jake's breath caught when Phoenix brushed his hand against the one she had pressed to the small of Jake's back. He moved down, squeezing Jake's arse. His hips rocked forward, and Phoenix moaned, a choked sound coming from the back of his throat. Jake slid his hand lower, teasing the spot just above the waist of Phoenix's pants.

"Touch me," Phoenix begged into the quiet of the night before Cassie captured his lips again.

She swallowed his moan as Jake dropped to his knees, and the clink of a belt buckle sounded in the quiet night. Cassie speared her fingers into Jake's long hair and held him close, experiencing him loving on Phoenix from another angle. She kissed their man, and Phoenix's fingers brushed hers in Jake's hair, completing the circle.

Phoenix hissed, and Cassie pulled back to watch what Jake was doing. He was on his knees in the gravel, seemingly uncaring of the sharp points, as he reverently held

Phoenix's steely length in his hands and ran his tongue from base to tip. Without breaking eye contact with Phoenix, he hummed and licked at his slit before closing his lips around the head. Phoenix shuddered and thrust gently into Jake's mouth, slaking his lust with the man who Cassie loved with all her heart. With a hand in Cassie's hair, Phoenix turned her face and took her lips in a blistering kiss. Pants and moans, grunts and breathy sighs and the three of them re-connected right there in the still of the cold night up in the mountains.

"Come for him, Phoenix. Let Jake taste you," Cassie whispered, nibbling a line down his throat. She wanted that too, wanted to taste and touch him, and Cassie had to re-mind herself that they had time. They had to give Phoenix time too. But tonight, they all needed this. She needed to get as close to this man as she could. Being wrapped in his arms and doing something as intimate as kissing him was everything. Jake's possessive side, the one desperate to show Phoenix what he could have, was determined to make his knees buckle and scramble his brain so that Phoenix would want to keep coming back. But Cassie knew it was more than that too. She knew that Jake intrinsically wanted to show Phoenix how much he cared. He wanted to make him feel better than he ever had before, to look after him and tend to his needs. And if the way Phoenix was holding onto them both, grasping tight without hesitation, was an indicator of how he felt, Cassie knew he needed their touch. He needed reassurance that he was here in the present, and not buried in painful memories that had almost destroyed him in the past.

Phoenix's hips jerked, his breath catching, and a gravelly moan sounded from his throat. Cassie captured his lips again and slid her hand down to his balls, cupping them and teasing the wrinkled skin while Jake worked his cock with his hand and that talented mouth. Cassie had never thought this moment would ever be possible again, and she committed it to memory. Phoenix right there in her arms, riding the edge, while Jake took him there. Jake's moan rumbled up from below, and Phoenix shouted, Cassidy swallowing his cries as his body tensed like a coiled spring. Shudders wracked his body, and he cried out again, thrusting forward and burying himself in Jake's throat.

When Phoenix pulled back, gasping for breath, Cassie stared at him. Damn, he was beautiful. She wished the moment could have lasted forever, because seeing him like that—open and vulnerable, yet euphoric too—was something that Cassie wanted to do forever.

Tearing her eyes away from Phoenix, she looked down at her man. With glistening lips and glassy eyes, bliss radiated from him. He was incandescent with happiness and that warmed Cassie more than anything. She loved the man more than she could fathom and seeing him happy was the best gift of all. Part of that ecstasy was likely the glow from his orgasm, his fingers still wrapped around his spent cock. His knees would no doubt be feeling it the next day, but Cassie didn't help him up just yet. Instead, she bent to taste Phoenix on Jake's lips. The burst of something sweet and salty was addictive, and she wanted more, diving deeper into Jake's mouth, licking at their combined essence.

"Taste him too," Jake murmured.

Cassie didn't hesitate, swiping her tongue across the pearl of glistening cum that had beaded at Phoenix's slit. Combined with Jake or alone, it didn't matter. Both were flavours she couldn't get enough of, and when she closed her lips around the mushroom-shaped head of his now-flaccid cock and swirled her tongue around Phoenix's slit, his shaft bucked against her. She caught another taste of the heady nectar and hummed.

Phoenix groaned out a laugh. "You two are trying to kill me."

"It's not a bad way to go, though, is it?" Jake asked, reaching out to Phoenix to help him stand. Cassie cuddled into Phoenix's shoulder and steadied Jake as he stood, her own heels wobbling on the uneven surface of the gravel drive. Phoenix looked away and opened his mouth as if to say something, then stopped. Jake's face fell. "But you're still unsure about us." His voice was flat, a dejected tone to it. Disappointment radiated off her boyfriend, and Cassie reached for him, wanting to soothe the hurt. She knew how much he wanted Phoenix to join them, but even after what had unexpectedly happened a moment ago, they needed to give him time. Time to choose them. They couldn't make the decision for him.

Jake forced a small smile and leaned in to brush a lingering kiss on his cheek. "You should go inside. It's late and you worked hard tonight."

Phoenix gripped his shirt, keeping him close. He nuzzled Jake's cheek as if he couldn't pull away. "Will I see you again?" Phoenix asked, his forehead pressed to Jake's shoulder.

"We meant what we said before—you've got friends in us, and in our friends. We're here for you whenever you need us," Cassie said, intentionally leaving off the part she really wanted to say.

He licked his lips and breathed Jake's aftershave in— Cassie had done the same many times—adding, "And if I'm ever ready for more?"

Jake didn't hesitate in his answer. "Then we'll be here for that too."

SEVENTEEN

Phoenix

*H*ave you eaten tonight? He smiled at the text from Cassie that had come in about twenty minutes earlier. He was sitting in the break room, trying to summon the energy to get up, but he was exhausted. It was his first day back working the six till midnight shift after doing double shifts three nights in a row. Working nights was fine—he often worked until nearly midnight after a full day in the office anyway. But his body was trained to sleep during the early hours of the morning, and those few doubles had knocked him sideways.

No, but I have a can of soup and Vegemite toast with my name on it.

Give me five minutes... Okay. But five minutes for what precisely? Apparently, he didn't have long to wait.

"Phoenix, there's a woman here trying to give me a container of food for you. You better get out here," Kellie said after sticking her head into the kitchen. A grin split his lips, and he pulled himself out of the chair. Cassie and Jake had kept their words, waiting for him to contact them to take the next step together. But it didn't mean he hadn't seen them or spoken to them. Jake had driven him home when his car was stuck in the shop for a second night after the part failed to arrive. They'd also set up a three-way chat, talking about absolutely everything and nothing all at once. Now that he was back at work for the weekend, they'd taken turns delivering meals to him. They were sweet gestures, making it clear that they were thinking about Phoenix but never pressuring him.

He pushed through the door to enter the bar area and leaned his hip against the pass. "Hi, beautiful." He smiled at Cassie, looking cute and casual in a pair of jeans, thigh-high boots, and a sheer white button-down shirt that revealed a lacy bra Phoenix wanted to peel off with his teeth. The sizzling attraction between them hadn't lessened any in the time they'd been apart. Phoenix had to fight every urge to say to hell with it and take them both to bed. Both Jake and Cassie had grown more attractive in the years that had passed.

"Hey, sexy." She held up an insulated bag. "Scalloped potato, roast lamb, and mint gravy." He lifted the bar pass and stepped forward, taking the bag from her and depositing it on the countertop before slipping his arms around her waist.

"I probably shouldn't be fraternizing with the members." He leaned down and kissed her, brushing his lips over hers in a barely-there kiss. "Ask me how much I care."

Cassie palmed his chest, brushing her thumbs over his pierced nipples and sending sparks of awareness through him. But she shook her head. "Find out whether it's a problem. If it is, we'll give up our membership." He kissed her again then, slipping his tongue between her lips and tasting her sweet mouth.

Reality crashed over him. Was he leading her on? Them? He hadn't given Jake and Cassie an answer yet. It was unfair of him to kiss her like he had some right to do so. He pulled back and rested his forehead against Cassie's. "I'm sorry. I shouldn't—"

"It's okay. I'm the one who shouldn't be pressuring you." She smiled gently at him and cupped his cheek. "Go and eat dinner. The sooner you finish your break, the sooner you can get home to sleep. You look exhausted."

He nodded, a yawn forcing its way out of him. His words were muffled by the hand he held over his mouth. "I am. This weekend has been brutal."

Cassie's brow furrowed, and she ran her thumb down his cheek, still holding him tight. "Tell me if this is out of line, but we have an apartment over our garage. It's not tenanted at the moment, but it is furnished. Jake and I spoke, and we want you to use it if you need to. If you don't want to drive all the way home tonight—especially being so tired—we only live five minutes away—"

He appreciated the offer. More than she could ever know. He'd had to pull over twice over the last two days to wet his face and wake himself up before attempting the treacherous climb over the mountain. But he had to be careful with his money. He was already eating into his savings while he still had his apartment in Sydney. He needed to get down there and move out before he completely emptied his bank account. "How much rent do you normally ask for?"

She shook her head gently. "For you, nothing. We can't find a tenant we're happy with, so it's just sitting empty. You can use it whenever you want. When we find someone, we'll let you know."

He nodded, a weight lifting off his shoulders. He rested their foreheads together, his eyes sliding closed in relief. "Thank you. Maybe just for tonight. I don't know if I can make it home without falling asleep at the wheel."

"We'll pick you up then." She leaned in to kiss him, brushing her lips against his before she stepped back. With his eyes still closed, Phoenix held onto the ghost of her touch for as long as he could. "Go." She laughed. "Eat something. You're dead on your feet."

He smiled, his heart flip-flopping in his chest. Watching her walk backwards while not breaking her gaze was sexy, but so like Cassie too—fun and flirty. She tilted her head, motioning to the door he'd come from, and Phoenix grinned, stepping behind the pass and closing it.

He popped his dinner in the microwave to warm when he heard movement in the kitchen behind him. "Nearly ready for the demonstration?" he asked Adelaide. She was standing there, looking effortlessly beautiful in a little black jacket and blouse with pink pants and heels. The latter two matched her hair precisely. The whole look was banging, but it was the shoes he loved best. He had a thing for those pencil-thin stilettos. "You look great tonight," he added.

She smiled at him, but it didn't reach her eyes. Phoenix narrowed his and asked, "You okay?"

"Yeah." She nodded but quickly looked down, concentrating on peeling the label off the glass bottle of soda she held. "Just a little nervous about this demonstration. It's a big deal, and I'm second-guessing the wisdom of it. My... ah... volunteers have a lot to lose if things go pear-shaped."

"What are you doing with them? I didn't think this place was a BDSM club." The shock in his voice had Adelaide huffing out a laugh. It was exactly what he'd hoped would happen.

"No, it's not that kind of scene." She furrowed her brow, concern lacing the frown on her lips. "One of the guys who will be on stage is a bit of a celebrity and the other works with kids. If either was recognized or word got out—"

"Then the club would rely on its confidentiality agreements and sue the pants off whoever is responsible." Adelaide looked at him wide-eyed, and Phoenix was glad this was something he could genuinely help her with. If his legal background had taught him anything, it was that the law— the whole system—was a tool for businesspeople to deploy. As long as they could pay for the best representation, the people who knew the ins and outs of every requirement, they could make it work for them. "It's not foolproof—nothing ever is—but the clients here are used to seeing celebrities. They're familiar with the *Fight Club* rules around this place, and the club's got plenty of legal avenues to prevent anything getting out or getting it taken down if it does get out."

"What about rumours?"

"Slander and libel—defamation laws. Again, not always ideal. But if your guys—"

"My volunteers."

Phoenix raised his hands apologetically and continued. "Sorry, your volunteers. If they've decided that it's okay to get up on stage, shouldn't that be enough?"

"They've never done anything like this. I'm just worried. Protective of them, you know?"

"Yeah." The microwave beeped, and he took the food out. Adelaide breathed deep, a blissful expression on her face.

"That smells so good. Mum's recipe?"

He smiled, his cheeks hurting from how wide he was grinning. "No, a friend's." He realized she knew who, and he added, "Cassie's."

"What's the story with you three? Did you know them in Sydney?" She sat down at the table and crossed her legs, waiting for him to speak.

"I did. It's been a few years since I saw them. We... ah... got together back then and... um... it didn't work. Not because of any of us, though. Just intervening circumstances. We lost contact. They were the ones who got away for me." He smiled again, thinking about how they'd found their way back to each other, his cheeks heating as he did. He couldn't believe he was having this kind of conversation with a co-worker—he never would have dared tell anyone he'd ever worked with before anything like this—but it felt right. He'd clicked with Adelaide. She was a good listener and had made it clear that he could always talk to her. He was glad they could speak too. He hadn't realized how much he'd needed to until he was opening up to her. Phoenix couldn't bring himself to confide to Pete yet, and his parents would flip their shit. They'd tell him to stay away without even listening to him. But what did he have to lose now, except a chance to be happy? Jake's dad couldn't do any more damage; Phoenix was the one who detonated his career this time.

Adelaide's smile was secretive. "I'm happy for you, and I'm glad they feel the same." He laughed, happiness bubbling inside of him. But then it occurred to him, he hadn't told Jake and Cassie that he wanted to try again. Why? What was holding him back?

Phoenix sighed and shook his head, the disappointment in himself shocking him. "We're not together."

Her eyes widened and brows lifted momentarily until she schooled her features. She was clearly surprised. "You don't sound happy about that. Are they holding back?"

"No. It's me. I asked for time and they're giving it to me." He sighed. It made sense when he'd said the words. He'd wanted to settle in on the Gold Coast before jumping into what he knew would be a whirlwind relationship. "I've had a rough time these last few months—burnout and anxiety—and I wanted to make sure I was making the right decision, you know? They've been great. They told me that I have friends here and they've made it clear that they'll still be there if that's all I can give them."

"You were a lawyer." When he nodded, sliding into the chair so he could eat, she continued. "Cassie, Jake, and I have some mutual friends. One is a doctor who walked away from his career on a cruise ship, partly because of burnout and partly because he fell for a passenger, which is totally against the rules. The other is a lawyer who worked in Perth. They both ended up here on the Coast. Robyn was with Mike—the passenger Ezio fell for—for a few months when Ezio came back into the picture. They're a triad now. Robyn, the lawyer, would understand your job issues, for sure. She had an awful case, and she came close to having a breakdown because of it. Ezio would understand your concerns about getting involved with a couple, too, just like our other friend Connor would. Con is former army. He joined because he'd fallen for his best friend's girl and had to get away from them. When he was honourably dis-charged a few years later, he realized it wasn't just Katy he wanted, but Levi too. The three of them have been going strong for probably a year now. Ménage relationships aren't as rare as you might think, and our friends are pretty au fait with them."

Phoenix held the fork suspended in mid-air. He opened his mouth and closed it again. "Um, okay. They weren't kid-ding?"

"No." She smiled at him. "But them saying you have friends here clearly isn't the only reason you're holding back."

"I'm wondering if my reasons are stupid, to be honest." He shrugged, trying to downplay his fear, then changed his mind. He needed to talk this out. "I think it's just the amount of upheaval I've had lately; it scared me. I didn't want to commit to them before I've had a chance to work on me first."

"That seems like a pretty good reason to me." She smiled and patted his forearm. "Just don't let fear hold you back. When you find your person or people, fight for them."

"You sound like you're speaking from experience."

Her smile said it all, even though her words were contradictory. "I don't know what you're talking about."

"Sure you don't." He grinned, and Adelaide laughed, her cheeks glowing pink. "Well, even though you aren't telling me who your lucky person is, I'm happy for you."

"They're pretty great."

"*They* would be to deserve you."

Adelaide smirked, picking up his emphasis on they. Not that it gave him anything to work with. "They" had enough variations that her partner could be any gender or even plural. He kind of liked that—he knew Cassie and Jake had a few friends in poly relationships, but he liked to think of Adelaide as his friend too. If she was in a poly relationship as well, maybe he'd be accepted as easily into their friend group as she and her partners had been.

She looked down at the classic watch on her wrist, tapped her fingers on the table and plastered a smile on her face. "Looks like I'm up."

"Break a leg," Phoenix said around a mouthful of food. "And, hey, if you ever want to introduce your they to me, I'd love to meet them." Her smile this time was genuine.

EIGHTEEN

Phoenix

F ifteen minutes left on his shift, and Phoenix was struggling to stay upright. It was a bad look that the bartender was yawning every minute or so, but the fatigue attacking him was brutal. His body was screaming "enough," and yet his mind raced, the conversation with Adelaide playing on a loop.

His cock was hard enough to hammer nails with too.

Adelaide's on-stage demonstration had ended with a bang. Two spectacular orgasms to end the night. The men could have been racing car drivers hosing the crowd down with those oversized, shaken up champagne bottles. Or fire hydrants. The whole experience had been eye-opening. Phoenix had no idea what being a sex coach would involve, but he hadn't expected that. He'd thought it would be a table set up with a few packages like you see on weekend craft markets. Instead, she'd walked the audience through the couple's toy choices. Then once Liam and Kingston got started, she adjusted King's hold and positioning to help Liam sink into a space that Phoenix had never imagined was possible. He was trussed up in stirrups, his arms holding onto the cushion by his head, and King had catered to every one of Liam's needs with Adelaide's gentle instruction. Using the different toys, he created a scene with Liam that had Phoenix riding the edge of an orgasm.

Adelaide showed a different side of herself too—or maybe an extension of what he'd already experienced. She was a caregiver, genuinely wanting to help people. She gave King feedback and checked in on Liam with every step of the couple's session together, helping them get the best out of their experience. Largely hands-off, apart from brushing Liam's hair off his face, she respected their boundaries. But at the same time, she shared something intensely intimate with them too. Their chemistry was off the charts, and Phoenix was glued to the show. Were they her clients? Was it like that with everyone she coached? There was no hint at her nervousness—their performance was seamless—and when things got serious, both men had ended up quivering messes covered in cum. Phoenix almost felt sorry for the ruined clothing King still wore; his vest and pants were destined for the rubbish. But damn, the visual of one man completely naked except for a mask covering half his face, while the other had just unzipped, was hot as hell.

He lifted the bar pass, moving out of the way as Adelaide led her two volunteers through the door into the privacy of the staff area. They would be able to shower and change back there, eat something, and decompress for as long as they needed without interruption. He followed them into the back room, carrying a tray with a Sprite and three bottles of water. "Can I get you anything else?" he asked as Adelaide adjusted the collar of the fluffy white robe Liam wore. Not breaking his gaze, Adelaide didn't answer immediately. It was almost as if they were having a silent conversation.

"A couple of Pepsi Max would be great."

"My blood sugar is dropping a little," King said. He was leaning against the table, his hand held out in front of him, visibly shaking. "My lips are tingling too."

Liam moved into action, taking his lover by the elbow and easing him over to the couch. "Sit down. We'll get you sorted."

Phoenix's adrenaline spiked. The man was awfully pale and shaky, and he knew it didn't bode well for a diabetic, if that's what he was. He showed King the Sprite. Was that what he needed? Liam reached for it and asked him for a couple more. Phoenix didn't hesitate, ducking out of the room and collecting a few more bottles, before heading back there. Kingston had sweat beading on his forehead, and Liam was unbuttoning his vest. Adelaide took the drinks, and he asked, "Can I get you anything else?"

"I've got it, Phoenix. Thanks," Adelaide responded, ushering him out the door and closing it behind him, effectively cutting off any discussion. It was time to wrap up his shift anyway. His replacement had already arrived and was looking after the bar, so it just left Phoenix to clock out and collect his things.

Still shrugging into his jacket, he lifted the pass and found Jake waiting for him. Phoenix could have kicked himself for saying he wanted to wait to get this man naked. His blond hair, still tied in a bun, and charcoal suit pants and vest with a crisp white shirt were like catnip to Phoenix. King had been dressed similarly—minus the shirt—but he didn't compare to Jake. Damn, he wanted to peel the man out of his clothes and lick every inch of the beautiful couple.

Phoenix couldn't help but want to get closer to him.

"You doing okay?" Jake asked, smoothing down the lapels on Phoenix's jacket.

He nodded and closed his eyes, the exhaustion he'd been carrying catching up with him once more. "Tired," he mumbled, rubbing his gritty eyes.

"Let's get you home."

Home. He liked the sound of that. He hadn't really had a place he'd called home for years. Not since he'd been forced to leave the house he'd shared with Trav, Rachael, and Stevo. After that, he'd bounced around trying to find his feet. His job at the law firm had meant he could get a place of his own, but it'd still been like a share house. Living with Pete was solid and consistent—a safe place for him—but their mismatched furniture, motivational posters, and satellite maps strung up everywhere were hardly homely.

Jake rested his hand on the small of Phoenix's back as they walked to the exit. Phoenix was floating on cloud nine with the possessive move. He wanted to burrow into that warmth and rub Jake's scent all over himself. Phoenix blinked, shocking himself with the direction of his thoughts.

It wasn't a cold night by comparison to Sydney, but he'd been hot under the collar for a while, and the disappearance of Jake's hand as he passed him his car keys left Phoenix shivering. He slid into the passenger seat and waited for Jake to start the car before he adjusted the heat.

"Warm enough?" Jake asked.

"Yeah." Phoenix yawned and snuggled into the seat.

They didn't talk again on the way to Jake and Cassie's house, but it wasn't an uncomfortable silence. Jake held his hand and let Phoenix drift in and out of sleep as the street-lights passed overhead. True to her word, their house was only minutes away from the club. Phoenix sighed happily. He was grateful he didn't have to make the hour-long drive to his parents' place.

"I'll show you the apartment so you can get some sleep." Cassie opened his door before Jake was even out of the car, and he walked up the stairs with them. The apartment was airy, even though it wasn't overly big. Large windows with sheer curtains covering them let the moonlight in, and a single light in the bathroom cast far enough across the space that he could see the all-white kitchen and a doorway to another room. "Lounge room and kitchen. Bathroom through that door and bedroom in here," Jake said, leading him through. A queen-sized bed and two bedside tables filled most of the space, leaving a narrow walkway around it. Excluding the second bedroom he had, the little apartment was almost the same size as his place in Sydney, but twice as stylish.

Cassie came to stand behind him and slipped off his jacket with Jake's help. She reached around him and unbuttoned his vest while Jake dropped to his haunches and unlaced his shoes. Phoenix kicked them away, and Jake peeled off his black socks, tossing them in the pile with the rest of his clothes. Phoenix undid the buttons at his cuffs and hummed as Cassie tugged his shirt off.

Jake's eyes locked on the barbells in his nipples, and Phoenix's cock pulsed, his hole clenching. Jake moved to his belt buckle, tugging it free, before he unzipped Phoenix's pants, ignoring the semi he was now sporting. Jake's warm hands cupped Phoenix's face, and his eyes fluttered open, looking at Jake's iridescent blues. "Goodnight," he whispered, reaching up to kiss his forehead. Cassie wrapped her arms around his waist and pressed her forehead to his back. In that moment, he wanted everything. Not just sex. Everything.

"Will you stay?" Phoenix whispered.

"I have a conference call with New York in thirty minutes," Cassie murmured. "And you need sleep. We'll talk in the morning, yes?"

He nodded, disappointment eating at him. "I can stay," Jake said before pressing his lips to Phoenix's. It was a chaste kiss. One that was barely there, but it sure packed a punch. His knees went weak, and he floated on air. Then Cassie was there, brushing a whisper-soft kiss over his lips too, and Phoenix couldn't help his goofy smile.

Jake tossed his jacket on the floor and toed off his shoes as Phoenix climbed into bed. He rolled onto his side to face Jake when he climbed in and closed his eyes to wait. He heard whispers of Jake and Cassie's conversation and, after a moment, the close of a door. Jake's strong arms wrapped around him, and Phoenix sank into his warmth.

* * * * *

The birds chirping and the crashing of waves were the first things that registered. The second was warm sunshine on his face. Phoenix reached out, but the bed beside him was empty. And cold. He woke up alone most mornings, rarely spending the entire night with anyone he slept with, but despite it happening countless times before, this time he'd wanted a different outcome.

He sat up, resting his feet on the floor, and looked around the unfamiliar room. His shoes were neatly placed near the door, but he didn't remember putting them there. Cassie and Jake had helped him undress, but where were his clothes?

Then he heard it. The unmistakable click of a keyboard in the next room. Phoenix stumbled into the bathroom, hoping they didn't notice him walking out of the bedroom. He needed to wake up more before facing them. A splash of water on his face woke him enough to function, and he stumbled out into the lounge room. The sight that met him stole his breath. There at the table was Cassie, typing away on her laptop, her fingers a blur. Jake sat on the couch look-ing comfy in a pair of grey sweats and a black long-sleeved Henley that fit like a second skin, his socked feet up on the small coffee table. Tablet and stylus in hand, he drew on the screen and nodded in time with a beat only he could hear through the headphones he had on.

"Hey, you," Cassie said and stood up, moving over to him. She looked adorable in a pair of jeans and a white cable-knit jumper, her hair in a messy bun atop her head. He smiled, not really knowing whether he could reach for her as she came to stand across from him.

"Mornin'," he rasped, his voice still scratchy from sleep. Phoenix rubbed his chest, noticing for the first time the chill in the air as he stood there in just his underwear.

Their movements must have gotten Jake's attention, because a moment later, he was wrapping his arms around Cassie's shoulder as he came to stand behind her. "How did you sleep?"

"Yeah, well. Thanks. What time is it?"

"Nearly noon." Cassie hesitated, and Jake squeezed her shoulders as if encouraging her to go on. "We were going to stop and have some lunch if you'd like to join us?" The question was formal and awkward, and if Phoenix wasn't looking right at Jake, he would have missed the wince that flashed across his face.

"I don't have to stay if you don't want me to. If I'm in your way, or whatever… I can—"

"We want you to stay," Cassie said at the same time as Jake replied, "No, stay."

He smiled, his cheeks heating, the flush staining his skin all the way down to his chest.

"That answers that question," Jake uttered, pointing to his face and chest before dropping his hand to adjust himself. It made Phoenix flush harder, remembering what it was like to have Jake inside him. His arse clenched, and a shiver wracked his body, this time not from the cold. "Okay. Um, do you maybe know where my clothes are? I don't remember where I put them last night, and I can't find them."

Cassie smiled, stepping forward and hooking an arm through his. Phoenix's eyes travelled down Jake's body, landing on the hand he still had pressed against his dick, and he couldn't help but lick his lips at the sight. Jake groaned. Cassie laughed and said, "Come with me."

Call him rash, stupid, or whatever, but Phoenix's mind was made up. He wanted Jake and Cassie—whatever they were prepared to give him, he'd take it. He paused, not knowing how to communicate what he wanted with them. Not without an hour's worth of conversation, but his brain wasn't up for that, not after the weekend he'd had.

Phoenix hooked his thumbs under the waistband of his boxer briefs and slid them down, letting them hit the floor before he stepped out of them leaving them on the floor as he headed into the bedroom. Giving Jake a glimpse of his butt probably wasn't the best way to tell him he wanted a relationship, but it would get Jake to follow him.

"Teasing bastard," Jake muttered as Cassie gave him the same lingering look over his exposed body, his cock hard and at the ready. Knowing these two people were as attracted to him as he was them was one hell of a turn on.

Cassie bit her lip, and Phoenix couldn't help but step forward and tug at her chin, capturing her lips with his. He nipped her bottom lip, and she ran her hands down his body, flicking her thumbs over the barbells in his nipples. He shuddered, pulling her close as he swiped into her mouth with his tongue. God, this woman... she captivated him and drove him wild.

She opened to him, the sweet taste of strawberries on her lips, and Phoenix walked her back a step. Her legs hit the mattress, and Phoenix moved to push her down and crawl on top of her. But she sat before he could move, pressing her lips to his hip and licking her way down the V framing the thatch of trimmed hair at the base of his cock. Jake's strong body moved behind him, those hands on his hip and his rigid cock nestling in the valley of his arse. Phoenix rubbed himself all over them, wanting to get closer to both Jake and Cassie.

Needing to.

"My turn to taste," Cassie murmured as she captured his crown between her lips and licked the precum beading at his slit. She hummed, and if it weren't for Jake's hands holding him steady, as the other man rubbed his covered dick against his arse, Phoenix would have punched his hips forward.

He wanted this. More than anything. But he needed something else first.

"Stop," he breathed, immediately hating himself as he said the words. Cassie pulled away within a split second, and Jake stepped back, the cold draught he created making Phoenix shiver again. "I want... I need..." He took a breath and blew it out, shaking his head. It wasn't just what he wanted or needed. This was about them too. Phoenix gathered the courage to speak, hoping he could make sense of what they'd helped him realize. "I don't want sex." When Cassie's eyes widened, and he could feel the blast of arctic cold suddenly radiating off Jake, he rushed to clarify himself. "At least, that's not all I want. I want to give you both more than that. I..."

Jake stepped up behind him and wrapped his arms around Phoenix's waist, resting his chin on his shoulder. "You can tell us," he encouraged.

Phoenix leaned his head back and reached for Cassie, cupping her face. "I'd really like to try that dating suggestion you had. You know, the one where I can hold your hands and kiss you in front of people. You deserve more than just someone who wants to fuck and run."

Cassie nuzzled her face against his hip and whispered, "We want that too." Jake turned Phoenix's face, taking his lips in a searing kiss. If the chaste one the night before had made his knees weak, this one floored him. Both sets of hands were everywhere, their lips ghosting over every inch of his skin. But Phoenix's touch was limited. He couldn't reach more than Cassie's hair, and his grip on Jake's butt was hampered by the clothes between them.

"Get naked. Please. I need to touch you too." He gasped as Cassie licked the length of his throbbing cock from base to tip. She pulled back and slowly stripped off her sweater, tossing it aside to reveal a sexy satin camisole. The rich champagne colour highlighted the golden tones of her tanned skin. He couldn't wait to see where the tan lines were so he could lick them. Cassie popped the button on her jeans and arched up, slipping them over her hips. Jake reached forward helping ease the denim down her legs, and brushed his lips up along Phoenix's hamstring to his arse. He cried out, his hand closing around his cock as he stroked himself.

It was a feast for the senses—Cassie in front of him, her arms above her head and blonde hair spread out on the bed underneath her with one knee up, only giving him a hint of the tiny triangle of satin covering her pussy. The thin strap of her underwear followed the curve of her hip to her waist and highlighted the long length of her legs. He wanted to spread them and dive in, but he wanted to kiss her lips just as much.

Behind him, Jake licked and bit his butt, getting closer with each move to his clenching hole. He needed to be joined with them. To take Jake into his body and to bury himself inside Cassie until they couldn't tell where one of them ended and the other began. He wanted to merge with them. To capture a piece of their love just for himself. He wanted to finally be able to love them.

His love had lived in the shadows for years, being buried under mountains of hurt and fear. But now, he was ready. He wouldn't make the same mistake again. He wouldn't walk away or let anyone else control him. It was their time to shine. Their time to win—their very own threepeat.

Propping a knee up on the bed, he bent and reached for Cassie's legs, opening them so he could crawl between her knees. He licked a slow path up the inside of her leg, her smooth skin like silk against his tongue. He pressed his nose against her mound and inhaled, smelling the scent of her arousal. Shifting the sexy-as-fuck excuse for panties, he licked a stripe up her pussy, his tongue gathering the juices that coated them. Her flavour burst onto his tongue, and he moaned. It turned into a cry when Jake, without warning, buried his face between Phoenix's cheeks and licked his hole. Phoenix licked, sucked, and nibbled at Cassie's clit, his fingers sinking into her tight heat as she rode his face, and Jake did the same to him.

"More," he begged when the teasing licks weren't enough. He needed the stretch and burn. He needed friction and to experience the strength of Jake's thrusts as he punched his hips forward and bottomed out in Phoenix's channel.

Cassie's breathless moans turned into pants, and her movements stuttered, becoming jerky as Phoenix relentlessly tagged her G-spot and her clit. "Pinch her nipples," Jake mumbled, never lifting his lips from Phoenix's balls as his thumb stroked over his star. "Give her an orgasm, and I'll give you my fingers."

Phoenix could get behind that promise. Reaching up with one hand, he slid it under her camisole and batted Cassie's own fingers away. "Mine," he uttered, pinching her nipple before curling his fingers and renewing his attention on her sensitive channel and bundle of nerves. Two then three strokes and a bit more pressure on her nipple, and Cassie arched up, crying out as her pussy clamped down with a vice-like grip on the fingers he had buried within her.

The pulsing on his digits made his dick jealous. He wanted in there. Buried to the hilt.

"Mmm, good job, babe," Jake encouraged, shifting his mouth away from his sac. Phoenix cried out at the loss, then moaned when Jake spat on his hole and slid his thumb slowly in. Phoenix couldn't help pressing back into him, taking his finger deep. He rocked his hips, riding the intrusion as he silently begged for more.

"Jake, hurry up," Cassie demanded, her fingers snaking down and rubbing her clit. Seeing her fingers tipped with pink nails—painted to match the pale shade on her toes—slide against her soft folds ramped up his need.

Jake pulled out of him and Phoenix mewled. A chuckle hit his ears. "Both knees up on the bed, babe. Spread yourself open for me." A condom landed next to him, and Phoenix closed his eyes, grateful for Jake's forethought. Cassie tapped his arm and wiggled her arse on the bed.

"Come up here, Phoenix. Put that condom on and get inside me." Gripping the foil packet in his teeth, he tore it open and slid it on his aching dick. He would be lucky to last at this rate, but he'd beat that mother down if it meant being buried in Cassie for even a moment longer.

Cassie ripped off her camisole and invited him into the valley between her legs, her calves squeezing his hips. But that wouldn't do. Phoenix spread his legs, opening himself up to Jake, and Cassie's legs widened too, resting on his spread thighs. He leaned down and kissed her, their tongues tangling as he made love to her mouth.

Phoenix hissed with the shock of the cold lube landing on his heated hole. Jake's chuckle had him looking over his shoulder. The sight behind him was riveting. Jake, naked and hard, was one to behold. A six-pack and tanned skin on display, he was biting his tongue, the tip peeking out between his lips, as he stared at Phoenix's arse.

When Phoenix clenched his hole, the other man's reaction was immediate. He gripped the base of his dick, squeezing hard. Jake's eyes rolled back in his head, and he breathed out slowly.

"Jake," Phoenix rasped. "Lube me up and get inside me, stretching be damned. Just go slow, yeah?"

Jake's eyes popped open, meeting Phoenix's gaze before he focussed back on his hole. This time Phoenix was ready for him, pressing two fingers against his own opening as he gritted his teeth against the pinch.

The other man moaned, but like Phoenix had done to Cassie, Jake batted his hand away and growled, "Mine."

More lube landed on his arse, and Jake squeezed a generous amount onto his hand and coated his latex-covered cock. He nudged Phoenix forward, and then turned his attention back to the beautiful woman in his arms. "Get inside Cassie, love," Jake ordered.

Cassie's eyes flashed, a smile tilting her lips. "You have no idea how long I've dreamed of this happening again," she whispered.

"I never stopped," Phoenix admitted. "I pretended I didn't want you, ignored the pull I felt for far too long.

Punished myself by staying away. But I'm done fighting. This is what I want. You and Jake."

"Make love to me, Phoenix."

He grasped the base of his cock and rubbed the tip through the folds of her wet pussy, using her natural lubricant to ease the way inside. She was tight and wet, her channel gripping him with a delicious drag. Wrapped in her arms, her naked body pressing against his as he thrust forward ever so slowly until he bottomed out inside her, Phoenix was nearly complete. He only needed one more thing—Jake.

The man behind him wasn't wasting any time, his dick notching against Phoenix's hole every time he thrust forward, fucking the valley between his cheeks.

"Jake," he begged, need overwhelming him.

The pressure increased, slow and easy, Jake petting his flank like the most precious of pets. Almost instinctively, Jake pulled back, easing out of him as the stretch became too much. It was slow going, Jake repeating the move as he inched forward ever so slowly, a little more each time until the stretch of Phoenix's ring no longer burned. The pop of Jake's cockhead pushing past the tight muscle had them both groaning and Cassie crying out.

"Oh my god, your cock just got even thicker," she gasped.

Phoenix pulled out of her tight heat, pushing his hips back against Jake until the other man was buried deep. He fucked himself on Jake's cock, riding the thick shaft as he impaled himself over and over, and on the forward thrust, pushed into Cassie. Jake moaned, and Phoenix arched back, reaching for his man. He needed to be closer, every part of them to be touching.

Jake pushed forward, pressing against Phoenix until he was sandwiched tight between the gorgeous couple he wanted to call his own.

Their moves were slow and deep, grinding against one another rather than skin-slapping fucking, and Phoenix had never felt so desired. Their hands never left his skin. Their lips caressed every inch they could reach. And Phoenix did the same, touching and tasting his lovers until Cassie's legs tightened against his hips. He reached down, stroking her clit, and this time, the vice-like grip of her pussy strangled his dick.

Pulses like waves in the ocean engulfed him as Cassie cried out, and Phoenix's movements stuttered. Jake took over then, thrusting harder into him, filling and stretching him tight. He pushed him deeper into Cassie with every thrust. The tingling at the base of his spine began, and he hit the point of no return. As much as Phoenix hated knowing it was about to end, his body reached for the peak, readying to freefall over the precipice.

Jake curled his hands under Phoenix's arms, holding their bodies tight together. His heaving breaths sounded in his ear as he licked away the sweat trailing down Phoenix's face and throat. Their bodies slid together, Cassie still cradling Phoenix's cock as Jake thrust into him. Sweat beaded on his brow and burned his eyes. He needed to blink, but he fought the urge. He didn't want to miss a moment of this.

He didn't want to open them, even after a millisecond, and find that this was a dream.

Cassie cupped his face and brought her lips to his. "Let go, my love. Be with us. Stay with us."

Behind him, Jake murmured, "Your ours now, love. We're keeping you."

The thoughts circled around in Phoenix's head, whipping up a storm until he was carried away, and just like Dorothy, he landed in a soft space, his orgasm rushing through his body as his lovers held him tight.

Phoenix sobbed, utterly overwhelmed and overcome.

Gentle hands on him and soft kisses brought him back to himself, and he realized Jake was shifting him, taking off the condom and pulling him into his arms. Tears tracked down Phoenix's cheeks, and he held Cassie tightly. He couldn't let her go.

He'd wasted years. Walked away from not one, but the two loves of his life. He'd hurt them and hurt himself too. "I'm sorry," he gasped.

"What for, my love?" Cassie asked, running her fingers through his hair.

"I hurt you. I ran, and I ruined everything. We could have been together this whole time, and I ruined it."

"No, baby. Shhh." Jake held him tighter. "You haven't ruined anything, and we're together now."

"What if I fuck up again?"

"We'll still be right here," Cassie said against his lips, kissing him gently. "We all screw up from time to time, but you won't lose us."

"That's what love is. Being there for each other through good times and bad. And Phoenix, I love you."

Phoenix blinked open his eyes and turned to Jake, who propped himself up on his elbow, hovering over Phoenix. "You do?"

"I do. I have almost since the moment I first saw you. You were so… proficient. So competent. The place was a whirlwind, and yet around you was this aura of calm. Then I got to know you a bit and learned how hard-working you are and how driven. That's my weakness." He paused and looked at Cassie, his eyes full of love. Then he turned back to Phoenix, and he saw it. He saw the love in Jake's eyes, the tears starting to pool there. Jake laughed and wiped at his eyes. "You're making me cry now." He leaned in and pressed their lips together. "I love you, Phoenix, just as much as I love Cassie, and no matter how much you think you've screwed up, my love is stronger than that."

"Mine is too," Cassie said. "I love you too, Phoenix. You belong with us. I'm so blessed to have found the love of a man as amazing as Jake, but the two of us aren't complete without you. There was a piece of us missing, and now that you're with us, we're whole again."

Phoenix brought their joined hands to his lips, kissing both their knuckles. "I've been hiding for so long, skating along without letting anyone in. I couldn't even admit who I was—one of my best mates, the flatmate I lived with for years, didn't even know I was bi. I hated myself, and I think it's because I felt like I'd thrown the best part of me away. It was you. Both of you." He sucked in a breath, his tears threatening to fall again, and finally said, "I love you both, too."

The weight Phoenix had been carrying for years lifted. Dissipated into the afternoon sunshine like fog scattering on the morning breeze. The pieces of himself that had been shattered were mended. Bonded together stronger than ever before. Lying there in Jake and Cassie's arms, he was whole again. Loved and cherished.

He was home.

NINETEEN

Cassie

Cassie stood at the gate. The flight from Sydney had landed a few minutes ago, and the passengers were disembarking. She watched as they walked across the tarmac, looking for her guys. *Her guys.* That made her smile. The month since Phoenix had chosen them had been both crazy good and interesting. Phoenix stayed in their apartment whenever he was working, driving home to his parents' place on Monday morning. He liked helping them out on the farm, and his being there during the week to help set up areas ready for weekend events was something he enjoyed doing.

He was happy, smiling more and more often as the days went by, and that lifted both Jake and her too. They were walking on air half the time, and the rest, pining for their man.

Phoenix had told them that his parents had noticed the change in him too. The goofy smiles and teasing telephone conversations every time he'd spoken to either her or Jake had clued them into Phoenix being in a relationship. His mum, bless her, hadn't wanted to pry but reassured Phoenix that they'd love whoever he brought home—man or woman. It had been the opening he'd needed to break the news, and he'd taken full advantage, asking her to set two extra places for dinner that night. If she was shocked, she hadn't shown it.

They were cautious, however, recognizing their names as soon as Phoenix introduced them. The silence around the room when Phoenix confirmed they were the same Jacob and Cassidy he'd known in Sydney was tense. His parents had a silent conversation, their expressions guarded, and Cassie had held her breath. The last thing she wanted was for any kind of confrontation, but the longer they didn't speak, the harder her heart beat and the pit in her stomach grew.

The only question Phoenix's dad asked was "What about Jake's father?" There was no censure from him being with two people, no derision about his son's bisexuality. The only thing they were worried about was Phoenix getting hurt again by the man who'd humiliated him and thrown his career off course. For that, Cassie was grateful. The depth of their caring nature showed through in their support and acceptance once Jake explained that he no longer had a relationship of any kind with his father. Knowing Phoenix had them in his court as well as Jake and herself made Cassie happy.

By the end of their visit to the mountain, Cassie had a new pumpkin scone recipe to try, and Jake had launched his

drone and taken enough footage to record new promo-
tional videos for their website.

Buoyed by their reaction, Cassie had called her parents
the next time the three of them were together and broken
the news. They'd been ecstatic, flying up the next weekend
to meet Phoenix. Her mum had hugged him tight and said,
"Welcome to the family." Then she'd dragged him into the
kitchen and tried to feed him—the best acceptance he
could have asked for.

Jake's loping stride was unmistakable as he stepped off
the airstairs onto the tarmac. Phoenix was right behind him,
and Jake reached for their man, taking his hand as they
walked along the pedestrian zones to meet her at the gate.
She couldn't wait to see them again. They'd been gone
nearly a week—the longest five days of her life—while they
packed Phoenix's apartment up. It was time, though, and
there had been no way he was doing it alone. Not after the
anxiety attack he'd had the night before they left. He was
almost catatonic, and Cassie had never been more terrified
in her life.

She jostled her way to the front of the crowd and held
out her arms as they walked through. Phoenix grinned as
soon as he saw her and, without letting go of Jake, swept
her into his arm and kissed her. Cassie's heart fluttered and
her belly swooped. The butterflies flapped their colourful
wings as he teased her with a swipe of his tongue on her
lower lip. But when he kept their kiss chaste enough that
they wouldn't get ejected for public indecency, Cassie
swooned. She cupped his cheeks, running her thumbs

across the stubble there. He had dark circles under his eyes and the crease between his brows was more pronounced. But his smile was genuine. It calmed the worry, the constant low-key panic of not knowing if he was okay.

"I've missed you."

"I missed you too. We both did."

She kissed Jake then, slipping her arms around his waist, and he whispered, "He's doing better, especially today," before kissing her throat.

"Let's go home." She grasped Phoenix's hand, and together they walked out into the morning late-winter sun.

* * * * *

The bed shifted, and Cassie blinked her eyes open. Phoenix sat facing away from her, the screen of his phone lighting up the room. He stood and tiptoed naked out into the hall. He'd been at work that night, but she'd been too tired to wait up for him. Jake had worked, letting their man in after his shift before they both crashed when Phoenix arrived home.

Phoenix spoke in hushed tones before he climbed into bed a moment later.

"Hey," she whispered as he slipped back under the covers. Cassie reached for him, his feet already cold after being out of bed for a few minutes. "What has you awake?"

"Been thinking." He kissed her forehead. "About maybe renting the apartment from you and living in it full time.

Mum and Dad don't really need me living at their place to help them, and I'd like to be closer to you."

Cassie smiled, barely resisting the urge to let out a gleeful cheer. Jake slipped his arm around her waist, and she asked in a whisper, "Who did you call?"

"The removalists. I left a message to ask them if a change of address was possible."

"Move your things in here," Jake mumbled, sounding half asleep. "Live with us."

Cassie couldn't argue with her boyfriend's reasoning, even if he had just woken up. "You heard him. If you're ready, we'd love for you to move in."

"I…" Phoenix grinned, the shy smile she'd seen lighting up his features more often these last few weeks making an appearance. "I'd love to." Cassie shifted, and Jake let her go, propping himself up on his elbow and rubbing his eyes. She grinned at him and straddled Phoenix's waist, kissing him with smiling lips as he laughed happily. Jake was there too, wrapping his arms around them and tackling them until he could capture Phoenix's lips with his own.

"Call them back, love," Jake ordered. "Give them our address."

"Yeah?" When Jake nodded and Cassie smiled, passing him the phone, Phoenix made the call, breathlessly repeating the address as Cassie and Jake slid under the covers and kissed their way down his body.

As the sun rose, a few hours and a couple of orgasms later, Cassie sat back against the padded headboard with Phoenix's head resting on her thigh. He was still on his stomach, his legs spread, and hole still slicked with lube. Jake had rolled off him and tied off the condom, tossing it in the general direction of their bathroom. "One down, one to go."

"Hmm, what's that?" Phoenix asked.

"We got you to move in, now I have to persuade you to ditch the protection." He nuzzled Phoenix's ear and trailed his fingers down his spine to his crack. Cassie watched as he gently circled his fingers over Phoenix's well-used hole. Her pussy clenched as he tilted his hips up, silently begging for more. She knew the feeling. Jake had a talent for making sex mind-blowing.

"I'll get tested tomorrow if you put your fingers in me." He gasped as Jake obliged, kissing a trail down his back and adding a second, then third finger. Their eyes met over Phoenix's body, and Cassie licked her lips as she watched Jake grasp his cock and stroke it back to hard.

Phoenix cried out when Jake pulled his fingers free, then moaned when he guided his cock into the valley between Phoenix's cheeks, pressing them together and thrusting forward in one long slow stroke. Phoenix arched up, lifting his arse higher, silently begging Jake to breach his hole. Jake flipped them, rolling onto his back and taking Phoenix with him. Her two men lay sprawled on the bed, Jake on the bottom, and Phoenix writhing on top of him, still trying to fill his hole. When Jake gripped his hips, Phoenix groaned, "Oh fuck, yeah. Want you inside me again."

Cassie hummed, pulling open the drawer next to her and reaching for two more rubbers and the lube. She started with Jake, suiting him up and coating his sheathed cock liberally with slip. Tugging Phoenix's ankles up by his hips, Jake tilted his butt to just the right angle so he could thrust forward and enter him in one long, agonizingly slow stroke.

Phoenix went rigid. "Fuck," he breathed, panting. His eyes slipped closed and a moan rumbled from his chest. Jake held still, letting him adjust, but Phoenix cried out, shifting atop of their man.

They were beautiful together. Cassie would never get sick of watching them come together. The way Phoenix opened his body for Jake, letting him take them higher every time they made love was spectacular. Whether it was hard and fast or slow and easy, they moved in perfect synchronicity, creating a flawless picture of ecstasy. But Phoenix needed Jake, and he was holding out on him.

Jake had already been inside him once that night and the time before had Cassie taking both of them inside her. But it didn't matter that they'd already taken the edge off with two rounds. Phoenix's cock was like steel, its mushroom head almost purple. Pre-cum leaked from his slit, and his balls were drawn up tight. He was done adjusting to the intrusion. Now he needed Jake to move.

Kneeling between their legs, Cassie had the perfect view and even better access. She closed her slicked-up hand around Phoenix's shaft and moaned when he punched his hips forward, fucking her fist. When she trailed her fingertips down over his balls down to his hole, stretched tight around the base of Jake's shaft, both her men moaned.

Scraping her nails gently over Jake's balls, she watched as he thrust up, slamming his cock into their lover. Phoenix shouted, arching into Jake and scrambling for purchase on the headboard to brace himself. She loved seeing him like that—out of control—while Jake cared for him.

"Cassie," Phoenix moaned. "I need you."

Cassie brought the second condom to her teeth, tearing it open and rolling it down Phoenix's engorged cock. Jake slowed his movements as Cassie stood, straddling both men and braced herself on the headboard too. Phoenix gripped his cock, angling it up for Cassie to mount, and she lowered herself slowly onto him. She was wet—it was impossible not to get off watching them—but Jake's cum inside her helped too. She couldn't wait until she could take Phoenix's cock free from the damn barrier between them too. While she loved him for insisting on protection, it was time to ditch it.

She needed to feel their power between her legs and tested the reaction when she raised up and slid back down Phoenix's shaft until she was fully impaled on him. His cock throbbed inside her tight channel, and she moaned. The lusty grunt that left his lips when Jake slammed up was illicit, and Cassie couldn't get enough. Jake thrust deep, driving Phoenix into her to the hilt. Cassie moaned with each move, her back arching as she crept her fingers down and rubbed her clit. Full to the brim with Phoenix's thick cock buried in her, Cassie's channel throbbed. Jake set up a steady rhythm. His hard strokes reverberated through Phoenix and into her. Her breasts bounced with the force, and Phoenix's eyes zeroed in on them. Leaving her clit, she pinched her nipples. Sensation shot down, centring in her clit. Like a tongue stroking it, her nerve endings lit her up every time she pinched her nipples. The grunts and moans, the feel of Jake fucking them and Phoenix's eyes on her was all Cassie needed.

The quickening in her pussy started, and Phoenix cried out, "Fuck," in a wobbly voice.

She came hard, her pussy clamping down and waves of ecstasy rolling through her, sweeping her away into an out-of-body experience. Senses heightened, every pulse of Phoenix's cock into the catch of the condom rippled through her. When Phoenix's orgasm was renewed by Jake's final thrust, his groan telling Cassie just how hard he'd come, it dragged her own on and on. Cassie floated in bliss.

* * * * *

A FEW DAYS LATER

The sun had set and the party—more of a mid-week get-together of their nearest and dearest friends—was in full swing. She and Jake had wanted to celebrate Phoenix moving in with them, and popping a bottle of champagne with friends had seemed like a great idea.

Cassie offered the platter of bite-sized delights she'd baked to Ford, Connor's cousin, and his partner Reef. She'd only just met them but knew they'd keep in contact after they went back to New Zealand after their weekend trip.

"So, was Con serious when he said you worked northern and southern winters?"

"We do. We love it."

Cassie shook her head, amazed, and laughed. "I couldn't imagine anything worse."

"What's not to love? Skiing—"

"Snowboarding." Reef interrupted with a grin.

Ford rolled his eyes, and Cassie laughed again. "Fireplaces and nights spent curled up with each other. Hot tubs after days on the mountain…"

"Frozen hands and feet, shovelling snow, layers and layers of clothes. No thanks." Cassie shuddered. "Even Sydney is too cold for me now."

"Our place in New Zealand doesn't often get snow. It's mostly just cold, but as long as you're dressed properly, you're fine. When we're in Italy, we stay in the staff housing. All the hard jobs are done by the resort maintenance staff. It's just like a long working holiday."

"How long have you been doing it for?"

"It's my third year," Reef answered. "But I was a pro-snowboarder before, and Ford's a mountain rescue paramedic, so between the two of us, we've been chasing winters forever." When Reef snuggled into Ford's embrace, Cassie couldn't help but smile. They were smitten with each other.

"Enjoy the sunshine while you're here."

She moved over to Phoenix and Adelaide, talking quietly together. They'd developed a special friendship, and she loved that for him. He'd been lonely in Sydney, and although his closest friend was a day's drive away, Phoenix now had people surrounding him who cared deeply about him.

Now that she thought about it, a road trip could be good for them. They'd contemplated a holiday together, but moving Phoenix up had been a priority. Now that they were together, perhaps they could head to Pearce Station before it got too hot out west. Phoenix could catch up with Pete, and they'd all be able to spend some uninterrupted time together making more memories. Cassie smiled, about to suggest it to Phoenix when Adelaide said, "I'm really glad you didn't let fear win. Letting your heart decide was definitely the right way to go." Cassie's heart filled to brimming, and she kissed Phoenix's cheek as Jake joined them, wrapping an arm around her waist.

"It was." He paused. "Can I ask a personal question?"

"Sure."

"The demonstrations you do with your volunteers… how does your partner handle that? Do they get jealous?"

"They're usually pretty different to the one you saw."

"Oh, okay." Phoenix seemed like he wanted to add something, and Adelaide smirked.

"Hopefully you'll get to ask them. They're on their way."

Phoenix's smile lit his face. "I'm glad. I'm dying to know who they are with you being so secretive about them all the time." Cassie didn't know what he was talking about, but Adelaide obviously did.

Her eyes widened before she blinked innocently. "I don't know what you're talking about."

"Sure you don't." He grinned, rolling his eyes.

"Yeah, I think we're ready to tell our closest friends. It'll be nice to be able to go some places together and act like it too." Adelaide smiled wistfully. "We've had enough of hiding, but it's been necessary. It still is." She lifted her glass and added, "Anyway, I need a refill," effectively heading Phoenix off at the pass before she ducked over to the kitchen sink filled with ice and bottles of wine.

Cassie left Jake and Phoenix together as she took the platter to Connor, Levi, and Katy. The two men were cuddled up together, and Katy sat across their knees. She and Levi were giggling conspicuously on the couch while Connor looked pained. Robyn, Mike, and Ezio sat opposite them on the other sofa with Nick, and Emma perched on the armrest of the chair deep in conversation.

"Beautiful place you have here," Levi said, wiping a tear from his eye as she stopped by them.

"Thanks?"

"No, seriously. It's great. We were laughing about something entirely different." Connor flushed red and adjusted his perch on the couch. He was leaning over, his weight all on one side of his butt. He looked uncomfortable, shifting and sucking in a breath. Katy snorted with laughter again.

"You okay, Con?"

He cleared his throat and shook his head. "I'm fine," he squeaked and shifted Katy's leg higher on his lap. His eyes were dilated, and he was breathing in shallow breaths, his cheeks flushed pink.

"If you're not feeling well—"

"Oh, he's fine," Levi drawled, snaking his hand around Connor's waist. Connor sucked in a breath and stood abruptly, almost dumping Katy off his lap.

"Excuse me," Con breathed before he rushed out of the room.

"Go. Stop teasing him, you shit," Katy breathed, elbowing Levi, and stood. Turning to Cassie, she asked quietly enough that only she could hear, "Do you have somewhere where they can have a few minutes privacy?"

"Ah, yeah. Our office?"

Katy leaned in, lowering her voice further. "Adelaide gave Levi the toy he'd ordered for Con when she picked us up. They might need somewhere with a lock on the door."

Cassie looked at her wide-eyed and laughed. *Oh. Oh, lucky bugger.* "Check out the apartment above the garage. The keys are by the front door."

Levi dashed off, and Katy took a savoury pastry off the platter and gave Cassie a devious grin. "Let them work it out of their systems." Cassie blinked, and Katy added, "He caused the problem. Now he can fix it—not that it'll take longer than a minute or two." She shrugged like it was no big deal and sat back down on the couch, sitting like a queen in the middle seat. "Then I'll get the benefits of holding out for round two later."

Cassie snorted out a laugh and shook her head, searching out her guys. She couldn't help her smile. Phoenix was talking to Reef, his eyes locked on Jake and lips turned up in a shy smile. Phoenix's face flushed, and he looked away, only to clash gazes with her. He laughed and bit down on his lip, and she focussed her attention on Katy again when she spoke. "He looks happy. You all do."

"We are. We love having him with us again."

Robyn slipped her arm around Cassie's waist and squeezed her. "Cassie's in love," she teased. "Where'd your guys go?" she asked Katy.

"They're checking out the apartment. Levi's interested in exploring some real estate options," Katy responded with a straight face, and Cassie unsuccessfully stifled her snort of laughter.

Robyn nodded, completely clueless as to what was really transpiring. "Good idea. The market's insane, and Cassie's definitely the one to help you out if you're looking at renovating, and Jake was brilliant when we bought our place." She motioned to where Jake had been standing, and Cassie followed her gaze. She watched as he pulled Phoenix into his arms and started slow dancing to the soft music playing in the background.

"He is pretty wonderful." Cassie smiled like a lovesick fool. "They both are."

"That they are," Robyn responded, squeezing her waist again. Cassie looked at her and grinned. Of all the friends Cassie had, Robyn was her favourite. She was the kindest, wisest woman she knew, and both she and her guys deserved every piece of happiness they could steal.

Both Robyn and Ezio had been a godsend for Phoenix too. They'd talked to him for hours, Robyn reassuring him that walking away from a career that took more than it gave wasn't a failure. It was strength. Ezio and Mike had been friendly ears, listening to Phoenix's concerns about joining her and Jake's relationship and talking it out with him. "You should be over there with them, not serving us food," Robyn scolded, taking the platter out of Cassie's hand and shooing her away. Cassie took the hint with a laugh.

Her guys spotted her coming and opened their embrace, slotting her between them, Jake pressed to her back, and Phoenix moved in front of her. With both men's arms wrapped around her and Cassie hugging Phoenix, they moved slowly together.

"This is wonderful. But—" Cassie's gut fell. Wasn't he enjoying himself? She opened her mouth to ask Phoenix why, but he pressed a finger to her lips with a smile and added, "But now that I'm here with you, I want more." He grasped her hand and brought it to his lips. "I've finally found a place to call home—with you. You've become my best friends, and I love you more than life itself. Even though it's quick, it also hasn't been."

Cassie nodded. He was their home too. The piece that made them all complete.

"I fell for both of you years ago, and I never stopped loving you." He leaned in and brushed a kiss over Jake's lips. "When you ordered that ridiculous coffee, I didn't know

356 • ANN GRECH

whether to roll my eyes or kiss you until you changed your mind." Jake smiled and nuzzled his cheek.

"My brain had switched off that day. Seeing you there—"

"Believe me, I know." He brushed his lips against Jake's again and turned his attention to Cassie. "You, you're a flirt. Made me so jealous when you asked me to meet the guy who wanted to date you. I didn't know whether to go all caveman and carry you out over my shoulder or ask to watch. It was so damn confusing when I realized I wanted both of you. Then it hit me that just getting laid would never be enough, and I had no idea what to do. I never imagined for a second I could have you both." He bent and kissed her slowly, his tongue sneaking out to taste her strawberry lip gloss. "We might not have seen each other for years, but I never stopped loving you."

"I love you too," Cassie whispered, reaching out to stroke his cheek with her thumb and kissing him again.

"Me too. Both of you," Jake murmured. "I'll always love you."

"I'll always cherish both of you. Care for you and be there to celebrate your successes. I'll hold your hand when you're sad and lift you up when you need it. I'll stand in front of you to protect you and love you until the day I leave this world. Then, I'll wait for you so we can spend an eternity loving each other."

Cassie blinked, the tears forming on her eyelashes spilling over.

"Don't cry, baby," Phoenix murmured, kissing her tears away. His eyes softened when he turned to Jake, and he lifted his hand to their guy's cheek. The sniffle from behind her clued Cassie into Jake's failure to keep the tears at bay too.

"I'll care for you and respect you for the rest of my life. Loving you is easy—"

Cassie knew the words Jake was reciting. She'd made the very same promise to him that night on the beach. Jake paused and looked at her, and Cassie nodded, her heart overflowing with love. The tears slipping free were happy ones. Grateful ones for bringing them back together and letting them have this moment and every one to come. A future of joy and wonder. A future where she could love the two men who'd given her the world.

She joined in, reciting the same vows she'd made to the man who'd stood by her, proving the strength of their love. She'd memorized the words years earlier, but they'd never held more meaning than right then—when they were finally complete.

"Loving you is the easiest thing in the world. I'll strive to be a better person for you. When times are hard, I'll do my best to make you smile. I'll care for you when you're ill and comfort you when you're sad. I'll have your back when you need me and be your biggest cheerleader. Then when we're old and grey, I'll love you like I do today."

Phoenix crushed them in a hug, and Cassie breathed him in, his spicy cologne rich and heady. Something she couldn't get enough of. She'd been wary when he'd come back into their lives. Scared that he would hurt Jake, and Cassie wouldn't be able to protect him from heartbreak. Hope had reared its head, too, peeking above the dark clouds that had surrounded them.

She and Jake had built a life together, a good one. They were happy. In love and content together. But nothing compared to their life now. Phoenix healed them just with his presence. Glued the broken pieces within each of them back together. He completed them. Cassie knew they did the same for him. She'd seen the changes in him too, the weight lifting off his shoulders as he let go of the stress he'd carried for years. As he forgave himself for feeling like he'd failed. As he learned to love the man he was today and all the days to come in the same way that Cassie and Jake loved him.

Whispered utterings of love were shared between the three of them, and Cassie held on tight, never wanting to let her men go, but when Phoenix spoke, she pulled back and looked at him, her eyes wide.

"Jake shares your name. Can I do that one day too?" he asked.

"Yes," Cassie and Jake answered in unison, laughter bubbling up from deep within, like a well overflowing. "A hundred times yes," she exclaimed.

Clapping sounded from around them, and Cassie remembered their friends. She looked around the room, seeing the people who had accepted them into their lives. She hadn't been lonely since moving to the Gold Coast, not with Jake by her side, but having people who had become like family to them, she realized just how lucky she and Jake were. Having Phoenix come back into their lives made them blessed.

"I'm so glad fate finally got its arse into gear," Jake added with a kiss to her throat.

Cassie laughed and reached for Phoenix, hugging him tighter. His smile softened, and Phoenix pressed his lips to Cassie's as Jake kissed his way up Phoenix's throat and pressed his lips to theirs in a messy three-way kiss.

They stayed like that; Jake pressed to her back, swaying slowly as Phoenix walked around them, trailing his hand up Cassie's arm and over Jake's shoulder before he slid his hands down to her waist.

Cassie spun, this time placing Jake in the middle, and smiled as he leaned his head back on Phoenix's shoulder and closed his eyes. Sliding a hand into Phoenix's hair, he turned his face and kissed their man. Cassie cuddled into his shoulder and closed her eyes too, forever grateful for the two men she called hers.

No matter what their future held, Cassie knew one thing for certain. They would always be together and in love. Fate had taken its time, but they got there, but it was all the more reason for Cassie to cherish every moment of loving the man who'd stolen her client, then her heart, and the one who completed her.

And love them, she would.

And they lived happily ever after

Want to read Craig, Sam and Ally's story? Return to Pearce Station in Three of Us. https://books2read.com/u/m0wnD0

Two cowboys walk onto a ranch. The girl falls for both. But they're in love with each other, and she's stuck in the friend zone. Sounds like a bad joke, right?

Welcome to my life...

But I think I was wrong; my two cowboys are just friends.

It's been the three of us since the day we met. I've settled for friendship for over a decade, but I want more.

I've fantasized about getting between them, but they don't think I'm *that* type of girl.

It's about time these boys wake up and realize they're in love with me.

And each other too.

Hold my beer while I sort this mess out.

Three of Us is a standalone book in the Pearce Station universe. You'll meet new friends who become family and fall in love with Ally, Sam, and Craig.

Available on Amazon:
https://books2read.com/u/3y7M8e

About Ann Grech

By day Ann Grech lives in the corporate world and can be found sitting behind a desk typing away at reports and papers or lecturing to a room full of students. She graduated with a PhD in 2016 and is now an over-qualified nerd. Glasses, briefcase, high heels and a pencil skirt, she's got the librarian look nailed too. If only they knew! She swears like a sailor, so that's got to be a hint. The other one was "the look" from her tattoo artist when she told him that she wanted her kids initials "B" and "J" tattooed on her foot. It took a second to register that it might be a bad idea.

She's never entirely fit in and loves escaping into a book—whether it's reading or writing one. But she's found her tribe now and loves her MM book world family. She dislikes cooking, but loves eating, can't figure out technology, but is addicted to it, and her guilty pleasure is Byron Bay Cookies. Oh and shoes. And lingerie. And maybe handbags too. Well, if we're being honest, we'd probably have to add her library too given the state of her credit card every month (what can she say, she's a bookworm at heart)!

In 2019 she was an Award-Winning Finalist in the Fiction: LGBTQ category of the 2019 Best Book Awards sponsored by American Book Fest for her story In Safe Arms.

She also publishes her raunchier short stories under her pen name, Olive Hiscock.

Ann loves chatting to people online, so if you'd like to keep up with what she's got going on:

Join her newsletter (you'll get two free books!):
https://landing.mailerlite.com/webforms/landing/d8m4r2
Follow her on TikTok:
https://www.tiktok.com/@anngrechauthor
Like her on Facebook:
https://www.facebook.com/pages/Ann-Grech/458420227655212
Join her reader group:
https://www.facebook.com/groups/1871698189780535/
Follow her on Twitter and Instagram: @anngrechauthor
Follow her on Goodreads:
https://www.goodreads.com/author/show/7536397.Ann_Grech
Follow her on BookBub:
https://www.bookbub.com/authors/ann-grech
Follow her on Amazon:
https://www.amazon.com/~/e/B00IJPO3EM
Visit her website for her current booklist:
http://www.anngrech.com/

She'd love to hear from you directly, too. Please feel free to e-mail her at ann@anngrech.com or check out her website for updates.

Ann Grech's Books

RULE OF THREE

*Gift Unwrapped (MMF) part of the Holiday Kisses
Anthology*
Three Hearts (MMF) (Also available in audio)
Yes, Captain (MM)
Triple Beat (MMF)
Threepeat (MMF)
Third Time's A Charm — coming 2022
Triple Threat — coming 2023

PEARCE STATION DUET

Outback Treasure I (MM)
Outback Treasure II (MM)

SPINOFF FROM PEARCE STATION

Three of Us (MMF)

UNEXPECTED

Whiteout (MM)
White Noise (MM)
Whitewash (MM)

MY TRUTH

All He Needs (MMM)
In Safe Arms (MM)

STANDALONES

Home For Christmas (MM)
The Gift (FMMM - free for newsletter subscribers)
Take Two (MM – free for newsletter subscribers)

M/F TITLES

One night in Daytona
Ink'd

www.ingramcontent.com/pod-product-compliance
Lightning Source LLC
Chambersburg PA
CBHW020256120726
47904CB00001B/219